ELIZABETH'S WAR:

Missouri, 1863

To Judy,
Thanks so
much!

Dene

D.L. Rogers

THE WHITE OAKS SERIES by D.L. Rogers

Tomorrow's Promise is the first book of the series released in 2008
Brothers by Blood is the second book of the series released 2008
Ghost Dancers is the third book of the series released 2007
Caleb is a continuation of the series released 2010
Amy is a continuation of the series released June 2011
Maggie is a continuation of the series released June 2012
Beginnings concludes the series released June 2013

The Journey released in 2009
Echoes in the Dark released in 2009

Elizabeth's War: Missouri 1863 released in 2014

Cover design by Glen Dixon

DLRogersBooks
www.dlrogersbooks.com

Dedication

Although this book is a work of fiction, Elizabeth McFerrin, a resident of the Austin, Missouri area before and during the Civil War, was my inspiration. This book is dedicated to her, her family and the thousands of other displaced men, women and children who were forced to leave their homes after the issuance of General Order No. 11. Names have been changed to protect descendants of both Union and Confederate participants in this story who may still live in the area.

Cover Information

From 1935 to 1939, Dorothea Lange's work brought the plight of the poor and forgotten – particularly sharecroppers, displaced farm families, and migrant workers – to public attention. Her poignant images became icons of the era. Lange's best-known picture is titled "Migrant Mother." The woman in the photo is Florence Owens Thompson *(Wikipedia)*—the woman on the cover of ELIZABETH'S WAR: Missouri 1863.

Before I began my journey with ELIZABETH'S WAR, I had no idea who Dorothea Lange or Florence Owens Thompson was. The only thing I saw in the photo proposed for the cover of ELIZABETH'S WAR was a mother in great pain, as *my* Elizabeth would have been, that grabbed my heart. Not until after the release of ELIZABETH'S WAR did I learn about Dorothea Lange and her photos. I considered changing the cover, but decided *my* Elizabeth was best served by what I already had. It was a conversation starter, too, for those who knew the photo.

Although ELIZABETH'S cover is a famous photo (taken from the realm of public domain), please receive it in the way it was intended, to grab your heart and make you FEEL the pain *my* ELIZABETH felt during General Order No. 11.

D.L. Rogers

This Book is Also Dedicated In Loving Memory To:

Sandra Carroll, co-worker and dear friend who left us too soon. Sandra loved *The White Oaks Series* and was impatient for each new book to arrive. She was an inspiration to many to be a better Christian while among us, and is now one of God's angels guiding us from above. God Bless you, Sandra, you are sorely missed.

I Would Also Like to Thank:

Tom Rafiner - ELIZABETH'S WAR would not have become reality if not for Tom's book *CAUGHT BETWEEN THREE FIRES, Cass County, Mo., Chaos, & Order No. 11 1860-1865* and my introduction to the "real" Elizabeth.

Carolyn Bartels, publisher, mentor, and friend, who continues to light my way with her advice, experience and guidance.

Claudia McHale, my editor, for keeping my grammar and all things related correct.

As always, my husband for being my "sounding board" with interruption after interruption during his down time for my "what ifs," "how would they have done this," and "how do I's...?" I might not be totally lost in the writing realm without him, but I'd be wandering more often, trying to find my way home. Thank you, Dave, for your understanding and helpfulness. I love you greatly.

Sadness and cruelty gripped the land with a stern hand and a hardened heart. Blackened spires of brick and stone reach toward the sky like gnarled fingers begging for mercy—or seeking death. Once symbols of warmth and security, they stand silent against the darkening horizon, the homes that once embraced them now cold, black ash— visual proof destruction is the only winner in the war that rages upon the land to leave behind scorched, burnt earth.

They called it General Order No. 11. *She* called it a license to burn, steal and murder. Her name was Elizabeth, a widow and mother of five young children who survived General Order No. 11 only because she was too stubborn to quit. The struggle wore her to the marrow of her bones, but despite the odds, she and her children survived to tell the story.

This is her story. Elizabeth's story. One of many waiting to be told.

THE PLAYERS
(At the Time General Order No. 11 is issued)

THE MIERS	THE BARROWS
Elizabeth	Rebecca
James	Thomas
Steven – 16	Helen – 14
Nora – 15	Clara – 13
Vera – 10	Edna – 12
Sally – 5	Joshua – 11
Joseph – 4	Francis – 10
	Richard – 8
	Benjamin – 6
	Andrew – 5
	Little Robert – 9 mos.

ANNIE & HER GIRLS

Annie
Carl (deceased husband)
Eleanor - 8
Caroline - 6

GENERAL ORDER NO. 11

**Headquarters District of the Border,
Kansas City, Missouri, August 25, 1863**

First. All persons living in Cass, Jackson and Bates counties, Missouri, and in that part of Vernon including in this district, except those living within one mile of the limits of Independence, Hickman's Mills, Pleasant Hill and Harrisonville, and except those in that part of Kaw township, Jackson county, north of Brush Creek and west of the Big Blue, embracing Kansas City and Westport, are hereby ordered to remove from their present places of residence within fifteen days from the days from the date hereof.

Those who, within that time, establish their loyalty to the satisfaction of the commanding officer of the military station nearest their present places of residence, will receive from him certificates stating the fact of their loyalty, and the names of the witnesses by whom it can be shown. All who receive such certificate will be permitted to remove to any military station in this district, or to any part of the State of Kansas, except the counties on the eastern borders of the State. All others shall remove out of this district. Officers commanding companies and detachments serving in the counties named, will see that this paragraph is promptly obeyed.

Second. All grain and hay in the field, or under shelter, in the district from which the inhabitants are required to remove within reach of military stations, after the 9th day of September next, will be taken to such stations and turned over to the proper officer there, and report of the amount so turned over made to district headquarters, specifying the names of all loyal owners and the amount of such produce taken from them. All grain and hay found in such district after the 9th day of September next, not convenient to such stations, will be destroyed.

Third. The provisions of General Order No. 10, from these headquarters, will at once be vigorously executed by officers commanding in the parts of the district, and at the stations not subject to the operations of paragraph First of this Order – and especially in the towns of Independence, Westport and Kansas City.

Fourth. Paragraph 3, General Order No. 10, is revoked as to all who have borne arms against the government in the district since August 20, 1863.

By order of Brigadier General Ewing

PART I
RAIDERS, RADICALS
AND
REVENGE

CASS AND SURROUNDING COUNTIES

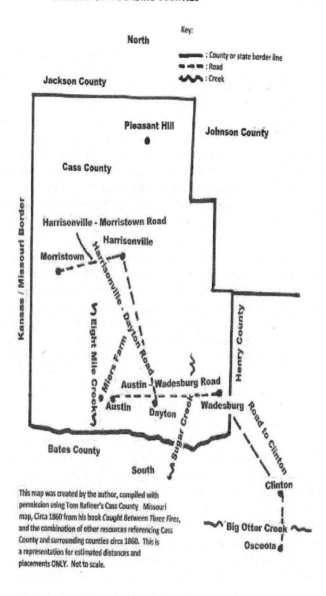

This map was created by the author, compiled with permission using Tom Rafiner's Cass County Missouri map, Circa 1860 from his book *Caught Between Three Fires*, and the combination of other resources referencing Cass County and surrounding counties circa 1860. This is a representation for estimated distances and placements ONLY. Not to scale.

Chapter One
(Late April 1861)

Elizabeth Miers stopped her mending, pushed her hair out of her eyes with the back of her hand, and set the basket on the floor between her feet. She sagged against the straight, cane-backed chair and closed her eyes. The delicious aromas of cornbread and roasting chicken drifted from the house to the shaded porch and her stomach growled. She sighed, opened her eyes and gazed out across the 60 acre farm she and her husband, James, owned a mile and a half northeast of Austin, Missouri. The small town was growing when they'd settled to raise a family, a few crops, and a little livestock, but was now a thriving merchant town—and hotbed of politics. Politics Elizabeth hated.

For over five years they'd lived in the shadow of terrible violence, where men on both sides of the Missouri/Kansas border were set upon, even murdered for their politics, many times in front of loved ones begging for their lives to be spared. Day after day their home was bolted against the night, their guns loaded and ready. They awaited the sound of horses thundering toward the house, signaling the arrival of raiders come to take what was theirs—or burn it to the ground—as many had already suffered.

Cass County, which included Austin, Dayton, a few miles south, and the much larger Harrisonville, fifteen miles north, increased every day in political hatreds and was split almost equally between union and southern supporters. Families were divided on whether Kansas should come into the Union as a slave state or free. Brothers sided against brothers, fathers against sons, and in Austin and Dayton, neighbors stood against neighbors in indignant righteousness of their beliefs. According to many, The Almighty was on their side—regardless of which side it was. All Elizabeth knew was that she hated everything about what was happening and wanted only to be left alone to live their lives without fear of reprisals for what they did – or didn't – believe. *Wasn't that what this nation was founded on?* she mused. *The right to believe what you wanted?*

The country was tearing itself in half. The slave states

teetered on the brink of secession in order to govern themselves, while the north promised to abolish slavery and preserve the Union—at all costs. Tempers were high everywhere. No one escaped it. For the past few months whenever James and Elizabeth went into Austin for supplies the store was abuzz with nothing but talk of the South's threat to secede or the recounting of neighbors raided by Kansans, their stock stolen, barns burned, and even murder. Elizabeth had taken to making James go into town without her, unable to listen to folks who had been her friends, pitted one against the other with such vehemence. Neighbors who only seven or eight years ago had helped each other build their farms, homes and barns. Each time James left it was with a pistol in his belt in case mischief called in the short distance between home and Austin.

She and James held no slaves. When they married they couldn't afford such an extravagance. Although an accepted practice in Missouri, Elizabeth didn't believe in it. James saw no wrong with the institution, but to adhere to her wishes, they spent what savings they had on cattle, horses and seed instead. They were young and healthy and, with only 60 acres, could work the land themselves. They never aspired to more property than they had. There was enough to house and feed them and their emerging family, which began with Steven, now almost sixteen and born two years after their marriage. Nora followed two years later, Vera five years after that, then Sally, now three, and Joseph, two.

"Mama, how long before you're finished?" Nora snapped her mother back to the present when she stepped onto the porch, hands splayed on her hips. "The chicken and cornbread are almost done."

Elizabeth glanced up at her oldest daughter, at thirteen almost a woman. Barely over five feet Nora was slender with black hair and bright green eyes. High cheekbones, usually flooded with color from her uncontrollable shyness, marked her as her mother's child, also with high, strong cheekbones and black hair, now liberally shot with gray. Generous lips gave Nora a pouting air, but it was her timidness people saw, not flirtation or manipulation like most girls her age displayed.

Nora cocked her head at her mother's lengthy perusal and Elizabeth smiled sadly. Fear gnawed at her spine like some dreaded disease, fear for her children and what was coming. "I was just thinking about how grown up you are, Nora."

Her daughter blushed and smiled, but said nothing. The prettier of the two daughters, Nora hid her beauty behind her shyness. She spent the majority of her time with her mother and younger siblings, helping any way she could. When they ventured into town, she was aloof with the boys her age, never speaking with or approaching them. Elizabeth wondered if her daughter would break through her bashfulness to meet a boy she might someday marry, but that day was a long way off, *she hoped. Nora was much too young to think about such things!*

"Mama?"

"Oh, I'm sorry, Nora." Elizabeth looked down at the basket on the floor. "I got distracted. I'll be done in a few minutes."

"You're always distracted these days, Mama. What's the matter with you?"

Unwilling to burden her daughter with her fears, Elizabeth said, "Just wondering where your father and Steven are. They should have been back by now." She'd sent James and Steven to town for supplies—and to find out what was going on in the county.

"Oh, Mama. You worry overmuch. They'll be home when they get here. In the meantime, will you please finish, supper will be ready and we'll still be waiting!" The exasperation in her voice made Elizabeth smile. Nora was thirteen going on twenty and most responsible, a trait she would need in the coming years, Elizabeth feared.

Nora whirled toward the house, her skirt swirling around her ankles. "I'll be back in ten minutes, Mama," she called over her shoulder before disappearing through the door. Elizabeth chuckled under her breath. *When had Nora become the mother and she the child?*

The rumble of hooves coming toward the house drew Elizabeth's attention. She stood up, stepped to the edge of the porch, and shaded her eyes to see who was coming. Recognizing Solomon, James' white gelding and Blaze, Steven's black, she relaxed.

Her ease didn't last long. Something was wrong, she could tell by how they pushed the horses and the way her husband rode Solomon.

She waited on the porch until they slowed down in front of her. James jerked Solomon to a halt, jumped from the animal's back and handed the reins up to Steven. "Take 'em to the barn. Rub 'em down and water 'em, but not too much, we don't need 'em to go down with the colic after that hard run," he added. "And give them some grain when you're done."

Steven looked ready to bust with excitement, but James' stern look made him do as he was told. The boy clucked Blaze toward the barn with Solomon trailing behind, both horses still blowing.

"What's wrong?" Elizabeth asked the moment her husband turned around.

He stomped up the steps, his face tight, shaking his head. "I don't even know where to start." He wiped sweat from his brow, although the April day was cool.

Whatever he was about to say didn't bode well. "Start at the beginning. What's going on?"

James plopped into the chair Elizabeth had just vacated. He swallowed and pursed his lips, "They've done it, Liz."

Elizabeth sat down on another chair to her husband's left, took his hand and gazed at the man she'd loved for so many years. Nearly six foot tall, lean and dark-skinned from hours in the sun plowing and preparing the soil for crops, he had a strength about him that was much more than his tight arms and chest. It came from deep down in his soul that Elizabeth saw every time she looked into his dark brown eyes or his smiling face. She pushed a strand of sandy hair off his brow. "Tell me," she whispered.

"They did it. The confederates fired on Fort Sumter in Charleston Harbor, South Carolina. They shelled it for two days before the Union commander, Anderson, surrendered. The war is on, Liz, and we're right in the middle of it."

"How can we be in the middle of it here when they're fighting in South Carolina?"

"It may have finally exploded at Fort Sumter, but we've been fighting our own war here for years. Kansans will take their revenge on Missourians now, and it won't matter which ones." His voice was so low and laced with fear, chills raced up Elizabeth's spine.

Elizabeth felt like the roof had fallen down on her. She was trying to catch her breath when Steven came running from the barn. He took the steps two at a time and stopped in front of her, his brown eyes, so like his father's, blazing.

"Did you hear?" he shouted. "Did you hear they blew that damned Yankee fort right out of the water?"

"Watch your language, young man," James chastised before Elizabeth had a chance.

"Sorry, sir, but it's about time. About time something finally happened."

"You don't know what you're talking about, son." James' voice was stern.

"I do, too!" Steven shouted. He was tall and lanky, very much like James when he was young, Elizabeth mused, ready to bust out of his boy's body and become a man. "It's all anybody talks about whenever I'm in town."

"You don't know what you're talking about right now!" James shouted, causing Steven to snap his mouth shut. James took a moment to tamp down his temper before he continued. "Sumter was not blown out of the water. Forts Moultrie and Johnson fired on it for two days before Major Anderson finally surrendered. The fort is still intact—according to all reports. It's been surrendered by the Union garrison, but it still stands."

Elizabeth watched the play of her son's face as he tried to keep his temper after being chastised, and proven incorrect, by his father. It had always been that way, even when he was little. His father having to prove what was right to a son who constantly questioned and defied him with a strong will so similar to his own.

Steven stood immobile collecting his thoughts before he said, "Even if that's true, it doesn't matter. We're at war." He shoved a strand of the same sandy-colored hair as his father's off his forehead, and Elizabeth marveled again at the similarities between father and son, both in physical build and facial features. Both had square chins and high foreheads, hawkish noses, sharp cheeks and dark eyes. Eyes that grew even darker when angry, as Steven's were now.

James' head drooped and he nodded. "Yes, Son. We're at war."

"So now we can fight, Pa."

"Fight who, son? Reverend Newton from right here in Austin, who is an outspoken Unionist—even though he holds slaves? What about Reverend Dolan? Or perhaps young Joseph Fricke, our neighbor who's also spoken in favor of the Union cause? Or how about Mr. Robbins or Mr. Bartlet? Do we just grab up a shotgun and shoot them down because they believe in preserving the Union, regardless some of them even hold slaves?"

Color rose up Steven's neck and into his face until he shouted, "All right! I understand what you're saying. But what about the damned...sorry, the Kansas raiders that have been crossing the border and stealing from Missourians for years? Taking what they want easy as you please and running back home. Now we can stop them. We've been lucky, Pa, but how long will that last? Especially now that we're at war and, to them, we're the enemy? They have an excuse to take what they want from us now." Steven stood defiant, waiting.

"Of course we're worried about raiders attacking this place. Why do you think we keep our weapons ready all the time? But that doesn't mean we *want* to run headlong into war. You have no idea what can happen...."

"I do so! I'm not a little boy, Pa. I'm almost sixteen. I know what going to war means. If it means fighting for the right to protect ourselves and *keep* our right to decide what we want in *our own state* without a bunch of blue bellies telling us what to do, then I'm all for it!"

"Even if that means fighting for the continuation of slavery?" James challenged.

Steven's lips tightened and his nostrils flared.

"Yes sir—for now—but not forever. Slavery is an outdated institution. Most slave holders know that, but nobody can figure out how to get out of it without destroying the South's economy. If they'd give us time we *could* figure it out but," his voice rose, "those damn...those Yankees won't give us the time. They want it stopped right now and they don't care how they do it!"

Elizabeth was proud of her son. He had given a great deal of thought to what was going on in the nation, had obviously listened to the different points-of-view he'd heard in town, and absorbed it all.

The boy, now a man from what Elizabeth saw in front of her, stood rigid, his hands in fists at his side. His head was cocked, ready and waiting for his father to challenge him again.

"So if we fight a war that will continue slavery, you will fight for that continuation?"

Steven swallowed. "I'd fight for my home—and Missoura."

Nora stepped through the door. "What's everybody shouting about? What about Missoura?"

Elizabeth felt like the world was tilting around her. She pulled her hand out of James', laid it across her chest, and slouched against the chair. "When did the world go crazy?" she asked nobody. "What *does* this mean, James?"

Elizabeth's heart clenched as Vera stepped out beside her older sister and brother. "What's going on?"

Elizabeth closed her eyes. "Tell them."

James sighed. "Fort Sumter in South Carolina has been fired upon."

Nora's eyes went wide. "What does *that* mean, Papa?"

"It means the country is at war."

Vera's huge amber eyes looked blankly at her father then turned to her sister, her mother and brother, then back to her father, but she said nothing. From her demeanor, Elizabeth knew Vera wasn't certain about what she was being told, but knew it wasn't good.

"War? But what does that mean for *us*, Papa?" Nora whined.

Her husband shook his head and Elizabeth knew he had no real answer for his daughter. "Only time will tell us. Most folks know I have secessionist views—even though we don't hold slaves. Regardless, I believe each state has the right to decide for themselves what they want, without the jacklegs in Washington City telling them what to do. I believe, too," he looked directly at his son, "that slavery is cruel and outmoded and must be stopped, but like you already informed me, the South needs time to figure out *how* to end it without destroying its economy—time the Yankees won't give us."

James shook his head in bewilderment. "The hot heads on both sides are shouting their cause is just and right, but nobody wants to listen to the other. In Harrisonville today, two men I've never seen before came to blows. They wound up shooting it out in the street. One man was killed and the other will probably die in the next day or two if he hasn't died already. It was very ugly and helped a lot of people decide which side they're on. Those who refused to declare were bullied, told they had to make a choice, that there was no more riding the fence. It's one side or the other and they'd better make up their minds quick—or someone would make it for them."

Elizabeth reacted as though she'd been hit. "And how did you declare?"

James shook his head and sighed. "I tried to stay out of it. Tried to keep a cool head, but everybody was screaming, shouting at their neighbors like they were strangers—or enemies." He ran his fingers through his hair. "I declared for secession." He looked up at his son. "For all the same reasons Steven has so aptly pointed out. We need time for the system to be dismantled. It can't happen overnight. Although I never disagreed with it, I wouldn't fight *for* its continuance, and I could never fire against my home state. Never."

Tears welled in Elizabeth's eyes and her chest tightened like a vice was being turned around it.

"That's not all," James continued. "There's a meeting scheduled at the courthouse in Harrisonville on April 26th. Cass County will vote whether to secede or stay with the Union. Right now the county is split almost evenly, but what if that changes? If the balance shifts to one side or the other, if we're not on the side with the majority, then what?" He shook his head again and frowned.

Staring at her husband and son, fear cut through Elizabeth like a knife. The sunny April day was now dark and dismal, and Elizabeth despaired if their lives would ever be the same again. In her husband and son she saw the future of the country. Fathers would fight sons. Brothers would fight brothers. Families would be shattered. The only thing she wasn't sure about—was how long it would take.

Chapter Two
(Mid-June, 1861)

Elizabeth's heart pounded like a horse shoer's hammer. She'd never known fear like she felt right now, awakened in their beds by riders pounding up the lane, men shouting and firing guns into the bright, moonlit night.

Elizabeth was out of bed seconds after her husband.

James turned hard eyes to her. "Hurry, I'll rouse Steven, if he isn't already awake. Get the children."

Elizabeth was so scared she could only nod. Her hands shook so much she couldn't find the opening of her day dress to slide over her head, wasting precious moments. *Please, please, please, Dear Lord, protect my family this night*, she prayed over and over in her head.

Dressed but barefoot, she hurried to gather the children. Nora, Vera, and Sally were sitting up in the bed they shared in the large room at the back of the house, the covers balled in fists at their necks, eyes wild with fright. Little Joseph was still sound asleep in his fold down cot attached to the wall.

"What's happening, Mama?" Nora cried.

"Make it stop, Mama, make it stop!" Vera shouted.

"Shhh, girls. We must all go to the front room. Hurry now, hurry."

Clutching their long nightshirts the girls jumped out of bed. Nora hauled Sally into her arms and Elizabeth awkwardly lifted a still slumbering Joseph over her shoulder.

"What's going on?" Vera asked again, voice quavering, following behind her mother and sister.

Elizabeth ignored her daughter's question and herded everyone to the other room.

James and Steven were already positioned at the two windows, the shutters open wide enough to slide out a rifle barrel. Elizabeth put Joseph on his feet, the little boy whining and swaying. Elizabeth pointed. "Vera, Nora, sit down on the floor between the wall and cabinet with the children. Quickly now."

"They've finally come, haven't they, Mama?" Nora

shuffled the two little ones toward where her mother had directed. Her words were said matter-of-factly, like she'd been waiting for this night for a long time.

"Yes, they've come. I want you both to keep your brother and sister quiet on your laps and do *not* move until I or your Papa tells you it's all right. Do you understand?"

Neither girl spoke, but each nodded, their eyes as wide as the full moon outside. Needing no further encouragement, they squeezed into the corner with Joseph and Sally on their laps, their arms wrapped tight around the sleepy, whining smaller children who understood none of what was happening.

Unsatisfied a stray bullet wouldn't find one of her children, Elizabeth cleared the heavy oak table in the middle of the floor with one stroke of her arm, shattering two glass candle holders, a plate of fruit, and a glass left there after supper. "Help me move this," she ordered her son who hurried from the window to help. In moments the table lay on its side in front of the cowering children.

Four windows in the house needed defending. Two were in the front room, one to the right of the door and one on the left wall, the third was in James and Elizabeth's bedroom on the right side of the house, and the fourth in the loft, where Steven slept.

"Go," was all James said to his son before the boy scurried up the ladder carrying an older-model Spencer rifle and a six-shot Colt revolver, one of two pieces James had purchased recently in preparation for such an attack. "Liz." He handed her a small squirrel rifle, a Colt, and pointed her to their bedroom. "I'll take the brunt of it here."

Elizabeth hurried to the bedroom, laid the Colt on the table under the window, opened the shutter enough to slide the rifle barrel out, and waited. She didn't wait long before three men emerged into the moonlit yard from behind the house on her right headed toward the barn. They disappeared inside and re-emerged a few moments later leading Solomon, Blaze and Poppyseed, Elizabeth's palomino mare.

"You, inside!" someone yelled from the front of the house. The children shrieked in the other room and Elizabeth almost dropped the rifle.

"What do you want from us? We've got no quarrel with you. There are children in here!" James yelled from the window.

"You know what we want," came the reply.

What did *they want?* Elizabeth's skin bubbled up with fear. *Had they come to take her husband and son away because they believed in the southern cause? Were they here to burn their house down and leave them homeless?* Her mind was whirling, waiting for James' response when a rifle exploded from the front of the house. She didn't know where it had come from and thought she'd choke on her heart. Poppyseed, the greenest of the three horses being led from the barn reared. The man leading her tried to hang onto the rope, but the mare was having none of it. She pawed the air until the rope jerked through the man's hands. He shrieked and the horse raced away, the rope flying wildly behind her. Feeding on Poppyseed's fear Solomon and Blaze reared and jerked away from the men leading them, thundering off into the darkness after Poppyseed. Regardless of the graveness of the situation, Elizabeth smiled and said a silent prayer they might escape this night with their lives *and* their horses.

Her attention was drawn from the men, blowing on their rope-burned hands, when someone out front shouted, "Whoever's up in that loft better make sure if you shoot again you don't miss!"

"I didn't miss the first time! I hit exactly what I intended. Next time it'll be right in the middle of your gut!" Steven shouted from the loft.

Running footsteps drew Elizabeth's attention and she turned in time to see the three men who'd been leading the horses disappear around front. Her pounding heart roared like a train in her head, but she forced herself to stay steady, watching for any mischief at the rear of the house or near the barn. With each shouted threat from out front, her children whimpered and cried. She wanted to run to them and comfort them, but she stayed put, aware if she left it would leave them all vulnerable.

Her husband's voice drew her attention. "My son means what he says. And he's not the only one inside this house that can shoot. I can hit the eye out of a squirrel at 60 paces without trying, so it won't be difficult for me to hit any one of you!"

Bile rose in Elizabeth's throat when she spotted three men creeping from the front of the house along the left wall toward her. One man carried a torch. She waited until they were only a few feet away before she said, "I suggest you stop right there, drop the torch and put your hands up."

The man carrying the torch didn't hesitate. He dropped the torch and jerked his hands in the air. The other two did the same. When they looked up Elizabeth couldn't believe her eyes. Two were neighbors, the Harrison boys!

Shaking off her surprise and allowing anger to replace it, she said in a deep, even tone that brooked no argument, "You boys better think hard about what you mean to do. I'm not usually a violent person. I try to be a good, Christian woman. But when you attack me or mine, my children in particular, there's a side of me you boys don't want to see—and won't live to tell about if you don't git outta here." She paused a moment to let her words sink in before she added, "I'll give you ten seconds to make up your minds whether to do as I say or defy me, but if you doubt my words, I promise I'll blow a hole right through you."

"You ain't got but one shot in that squirrel gun, Miz Miers," the unknown man challenged of the single-shot .32 caliber rifle she had pointed at them.

Elizabeth chuckled so deep it sounded evil even to her. "You haven't seen what I've got next to me. And I'll let you in on a little secret. I've shot many a varmint in my lifetime with this rifle I'm pointing at you boys, and to me right now you're worse than any one of those slimy creatures. You threaten my family any further, you'll find out exactly what I can, and will, do when I shoot each one of you just like one of those critters I've pulled this trigger on many times before. So make up your minds. You gonna skedaddle? Or am I gonna show you exactly what me and this rifle, and whatever else I've got next to me, can do? One, two...."

"We believe you, Miz Miers. We'll go," Roger, the older Harrison brother shouted.

"Good. Throw those guns in the dirt, kick them away, tuck your tails between your legs and run back out front with those other cowards who are threatening my family! I don't *really* want to shoot anybody tonight, especially not neighbors, but if I'm provoked further I will not hesitate!"

Slowly, using only two fingers, Roger pulled his weapon, threw it down and kicked it away. Elija, the younger brother, heaved his rifle away and waited, but the third man hesitated.

"Walker, don't be a fool. Do what she says," Elija said.

Elizabeth thought she was going to be sick and her hands started to shake, but she couldn't let them see it. She *could not* back down. Everything she loved was at stake. "Throw it down, now!" she shouted at Walker. The brothers jumped and raised their hands higher in the air.

Walker put his hand on his pistol, but Elizabeth sensed he had no intention of throwing it away. The weapon glinted in the moonlight as he drew on her and, without a moment's hesitation, she pulled the trigger. The rifle exploded, shattering Walker's arm below the elbow. He screamed and fell to his knees.

"You shot me!" He rocked back and forth, holding his elbow with his other hand. Blood ran down his arm, through his fingers and dripped on the ground.

"She told you she would you dumb peckerwood. Elija looked up at Elizabeth. "We're going now, all right?"

"Take him with you. And don't come back!"

The Harrison boys grabbed Walker and dragged him out front, his blood leaving a dark trail in the dirt behind him. Absently, Elizabeth wondered if he'd die before someone stopped the bleeding, but she pushed the thought from her mind. He'd brought it on himself and she would shoot him again if need be.

Elizabeth had no idea how many men were outside her home, but there had to be at least a dozen or so. Anger began to gnaw at her belly like bad food then started to boil like a witch's cauldron the more she thought on what these men were doing. *They had no right! How dare they attack her home! There were children here! Innocent children! They hadn't done anything to anybody! They just wanted to be left alone!* Anger overrode all rational thought and exploded like an uncapped volcano. She dropped the spent rifle on the bed, grabbed the pistol and headed for the front room.

James was yelling out the window, but she had no idea what he was saying. She stomped to the front door.

"What are you doing!" James screamed from beside her, but she ignored him.

She threw open the door and stepped outside. "You men!" she challenged, standing straight as a post, her legs braced. Elizabeth held the cocked pistol at the ready, moving it back and forth between the men on horseback.

She saw and heard rifles lifted and cocked through the thundering in her head. She was crazed with anger, and until that anger was spent, these men would either listen to her—or shoot her. But not before she was heard!

"If you men want to shoot someone so badly, here I am! Will you shoot a woman? Or is there still a shred of moral, Christian decency in you? If you intend to shoot us all, perhaps I should save you the trouble and bring my babies out here right now so you can dispense with them first!" The children shrieked in the background, spurring her anger even higher. She was charged like lightning and would have her say. "Cowards! Coming in the middle of the night to threaten my family! Every one of you is a coward!"

She aimed her pistol at the lead rider. "Hello, Mr. Bartlet. It's a fine, moonlit night for a raid, don't you think? And Mr. Warren? Did you get your crops planted? Oh, perhaps not. I see you've found other things to keep you busy." She stood defiant, stared down every man, and said hello to each one she knew.

"You came here threatening my home and my children. I won't hold with that, and I'll shoot the first man who makes a move toward my house. You may shoot me down, but I'll take one or two of you with me before the ammunition in this gun is spent!" She swung the gun at Mr. Bartlet. "You'll be the first one I shoot, Mr. Bartlet. Count on it. Ask that man over there, whose arm is dripping blood, if I'll shoot you if I say so, and if I don't hit what I aim for?" She waved the pistol at Walker, woozy on his feet, watching her with blazing, hate-filled eyes, his arm wrapped in someone's kerchief, but still dripping blood. She thought her heart would explode, but she couldn't stop now. She'd gone too far. Anger and indignation rode her back like a serpent.

James stepped out beside his wife, his rifle raised and ready, his pistol tucked in easy access at his belt. "I guarantee you men, she means what she says. She's as good a shot as most men." He paused and smiled. "But I'm better, and whoever she misses, I'll be sure to take with me before I'm done." He swung the rifle toward another of their neighbors and the man shifted uneasily in his saddle.

"And whoever they miss, I won't!" came Steven's voice from the upper window. "And I've got a good view of every one of y'all from up here, so you can bet I'll take a few down before any of y'all even get close to the house!"

"So, gentlemen, unless you intend to shoot me, my husband *and* my children," Elizabeth raised a hand to encompass the house, "the children screaming and crying in that house behind me, I suggest you git on outta here and leave us to our own business!"

The men sat in stunned silence. Seemingly unnerved by her bravado, knowing they'd lost the upper hand and unwilling to die to test her and her family's mettle, those farthest away turned their horses and melted into the night.

Minutes later when the last rider passed beyond the front gates, Elizabeth grabbed James' arm, cried out, and slid to the floor in a faint.

Chapter Three
(June 27, 1861)

James slammed into the house. Elizabeth jumped, knocking the bowl of flour from the cabinet counter where she was kneading dough. Flour billowed into the air then settled on the floor at her feet. Sally and Joseph, drawing at the table, shrieked and started to cry, still traumatized from the raid. Vera and Nora ran in from their room, their faces etched with fear.

Elizabeth looked up, ready to chastise her husband for his rude entry, but the words never made it to her lips when she saw his face. "What is it?"

"You aren't going to believe what's going on at the church in Austin." He shook his head in disbelief.

She took a deep breath. After all that had gone on in the past few weeks, she'd believe anything. "What?"

"They're recruiting."

"Who's recruiting?"

"Our very own Reverend Dolan—now *Major* Dolan of the *Union* army—is recruiting four units for the newly formed Cass County Home Guard. I'm sure you remember our neighbors Mr. Bartlet and Mr. Warren, the ones who visited us the other night?"

"Yes," she answered, leery.

"They're forming their own units."

Elizabeth was unable to speak she was so stunned, so she waited for her husband to continue.

James chewed his lower lip. "They're mustering three units right here in Austin and one in Crescent Hill. Over a hundred men are at the church right now waiting to join up. A lot of men are there from Dayton, too. Aside from Reverend Dolan, Mr. Bartlet and Mr. Warren, the two Dunham boys are down there, Mr. Barnard and so many others I can't even repeat all their names. It seems at least half the male residents of Austin and Dayton are there." He snorted again and slapped his hat against his leg. "Things are going to get bad, Liz, really bad. I can feel it."

Elizabeth ignored the flour and the floor. "I thought Cass

County voted to support the Confederacy at the meeting in Harrisonville in April?"

"They did."

"So why is there recruiting for the Union going on in Austin?" She shook her head. "I don't understand."

"At that meeting in Harrisonville one man spoke out for the Union. Reverend Newton. He was chased out and has been in hiding ever since, recruiting for the north whenever and wherever he can."

Elizabeth swallowed what felt like an apple in her throat. *What did all this mean? Did it mean Cass County was swaying toward the Union? Were they, in essence, living in enemy territory, since James openly and vehemently declared for the south after the raid on their home?*

"What about the Missouri State Guard? Why aren't they stopping it?"

"From what I heard, General Rains and the State Guard were camped in Austin last week, keeping the Yankee recruiting to a minimum." He shook his head and curled his lips in distaste. "I heard they burned and looted a lot of Union homes on their way here. But..." He sucked in a breath.

"But what?"

"He and his troops fled to Bates County a couple days ago when they heard Major Sturgis and his Yankee troops were headed here from the west and General Lyon was converging from the east." James ran his fingers through his hair. "Now that Sturgis is here and Rains is gone, the Union recruiters aren't afraid of reprisals."

"Mama? What does all that mean?" Nora asked, reminding Elizabeth her children were all in the room, listening.

"You all go back to your room. Everything is fine, just fine."

"It doesn't sound fine," Nora grumbled before ushering her siblings away. "It doesn't sound like anything is going to be fine ever again," she tossed over her shoulder before the door shut behind her.

Elizabeth wanted to weep at the desperation in her daughter's voice. If the war came to their doorstep, Nora, her sisters and brother might well suffer more privation, fear and, very possibly even death, than they had already suffered. She was as certain of that as she was that the sun would rise tomorrow.

James had been pacing so long Elizabeth thought he would wear a groove right in the floor of the front room.

"James, please."

He jerked to an abrupt halt and glared at his wife. "Please what, Liz? Please stop worrying about what's going to happen? Forget there's a war on? Stop worrying about our crops and livestock that need tending, but aren't being taken care of because I'm afraid of being shot right here on my own property? Stop worrying about you and the children? Please tell me exactly what you want of me, Liz?"

Elizabeth was taken aback by her husband's harsh tone. Especially since she wasn't sure *what* she was asking herself. They were both on edge after James recounted dozens of stories he'd heard in Austin this morning about the ever-growing hostilities.

"This country is at war, and our home is smack in the middle of enemy territory, Liz! Major Dolan's Home Guards have set up camp right outside Austin. Dolan and a hundred and fifty of his men were in Kansas City earlier this week receiving 500 guns for his battalion. Five hundred guns, Liz!" James' head shook in weariness and uncertainty. "And Jim Lane has warned that in a very short time the forces in Western Missouri will be able to take care of secession *without* regular troops. Lane thinks because the Home Guards are more familiar with the leaders of secession and know the necessity of putting an end to their power, their work in routing them out will be quicker and more effective than the regular army." James ran his fingers through his graying hair, his eyes haunted, and Elizabeth saw his fear like a living thing in front of her.

"Is my name on their list, Liz, as one of the 'leaders of secession'? Am I being watched, even though I've done nothing except defend my home against my neighbors?" He ran his fingers through his hair again.

"Has one of our neighbors, whom I might have openly disagreed with on the issues at some time, *put* my name on that list? If so, how do I refute it? How do I keep us safe from the Home Guard when they're right in our backyard? Or the Jayhawkers—Jennison's Kansas ruffians—if they decide to come a-calling?"

Elizabeth had no answer. She stepped beside him, laid her hand on his arm and was about to say as much when he continued as though she weren't there.

"Does that mean they plan to kill anybody they believe is leading or a part of the rebellion? Will the law be forgotten and men gunned down like dogs, dependent upon who is wielding the weapon? Possibly me or Steven, if we're caught unawares, or we're somewhere someone thinks we shouldn't be?"

Elizabeth swallowed hard and laid her head on his shoulder. "I don't have any answers, but I promise you we will not run away. This is *our* home and has been for too many years for us to walk away without a fight. I'll be right beside you if it comes to it."

He kissed her cheek, wet with tears. She feared for the lives of her family, each one of them, but most especially her husband and son. They were men, and men were gunned down with no provocation these days, regardless whether they were grown, still a boy, or which side they professed to be on.

These were sad, dark days, days that would grow darker before light would shine again, Elizabeth was certain of it.

Chapter Four
(July 1861)

"I'm tellin' ya, Pa," Steven said around a mouthful of food. "People in these parts will remember Jo Shelby and his rangers a long time after this war is over. If it weren't for them, why, Siegel's Germans might have taken Carthage instead of our Governor Jackson. Or would have, at the least, delayed long enough for that Union General Lyon and his troops to reach Siegel and render aid."

James nodded and pointed his fork at his son. "Shelby and his men may well have saved the Confederacy at Carthage, but I still think it was our superior numbers that took the day. Had Lyon and his troops arrived, it may have easily turned the other way." He cocked his head askance. "We took Carthage, but at the loss of two hundred men. Was it worth it?" James asked his son.

"I believe so, Pa. We've shown those Yankees we're a force to be reckoned with, that even when they're in pursuit, we'll somehow turn the tables, become the pursuers, and turn it to our advantage. We've drawn the first blood, won the first victory in this war, and given those Yankees pause."

James smiled at his son, proud of the man he was becoming. A staunch confederate since before the raid on their home, Steven kept his head and looked at all the facts before rendering judgment. All he said was true. After being chased out of Jefferson City by Union Brigadier General Nathaniel Lyon and his troops, and pursued by Colonel Franz Siegel and his Germans, displaced Governor Claiborne Jackson and his 4,000 loyal confederate followers had turned the tables on the hunters outside Carthage. On July 4, upon learning that Siegel was camped ten miles north of Carthage, Missouri, Jackson opened artillery fire from a ridge above Siegel's camp. Siegel's forces had retreated into Carthage to later escape Jackson's pursuit under cover of darkness, James had learned from a soldier returning from Carthage he'd met in Austin last week.

"All I know, Pa, is that we won at Carthage and proved to those da...those Yankees that we won't run like they thought we would when this war started. We've proved we're going to stand and fight for our land and our homes." His face suddenly reddened like it did when he was a little boy hiding something.

"Is something else on your mind, son?"

Steven worried at his lower lip, then straightened in his chair and blurted, "I'm joining up."

"What?" James looked toward the back bedroom where Elizabeth was tucking the younger children into bed. Lowering his voice he said, "When did you decide this—and without my permission?"

Steven cleared his throat and took a deep breath. "I decided the night our neighbors came a-calling, but wanted to wait until the time was right. I can fight, Pa," he hurried on before his father could interrupt. "I'm sixteen now, old enough. They'll take me. I can shoot as good or better than most any man. I've made up my mind, Pa. I leave in the morning."

James felt like he'd been gut-punched. His head was spinning and he felt weak. "I forbid it."

Steven's eyes pinched and darkened with anger, but in an even tone he said, "Pa, you can forbid it all you want, but unless you tie me to my bed or stand guard over me every hour of every day, I'm going. I've thought it through and I'm tired of talking about fighting. It's time for me to be *part* of the fight for our independence from the north."

"Soldiering is a rough life, son, even if you don't see battle, which I pray to God if you follow through with this, you won't."

"I'm going, Pa."

"What about your mother?"

Steven reddened again. "Ma knows."

"What!"

"I made her promise not to tell you. We were talking one day about the raid and what's going on in the country and it just came out. I didn't mean to tell her and not you, but I wanted to tell you in my own way, when I was ready and the time was right. Don't be angry with her. She doesn't want me to go any more than you do, but she understands *why* I have to go."

"Well, hell! I understand *why* you want to go, too. It doesn't make it easier to accept that you *will* go, regardless of whether I forbid it or not."

"Besides," Steven said with a grin. "At least I'm going to fight for the right side—unlike these other jacklegs around here signing up with the Federals."

James shook his head and frowned. "Right side, wrong side. Which one *is* the right or wrong side in this fight, Steven? We both believe in the same God, both live in the same country, and both have the same fundamental beliefs in what this country stands for. So how can one side be *more* right than the other?" he asked.

It was Steven's turn to shake his head. "I don't know, Pa. All I know is that I have to fight for what I believe and for the safety of my family. And I believe in our state and our right to govern ourselves without the federal government telling us what to do. I know part of this war is about slavery. We both agree it should go away, but we know it can't happen overnight, either, without destroying the south. Hell, sorry, heck, half the men in the Home Guard hold slaves, but yet they're still fighting *for* the Union. So how can this war be about getting rid of slavery if they're fighting for the Union yet keep slaves?" He shrugged his shoulders. "All I know is that I could never fight against my home state, and that's why I have to go, Pa. I'm going one way or another, but I'd rather go with your blessing."

James closed his eyes and drew a deep breath. His son, his boy, his child was now a man, a man who would head off to war in the morning. The house suddenly felt like it was tilting on its foundation as he tried to reason it out in his head. Steven's hand on his shoulder pulled him back. He laid his own hand over his son's. Tears filled his eyes and he squeezed. "You have my blessing, son. I pray this war is as short-lived as everyone thinks it'll be." He turned and looked Steven square in the eyes. "And I pray to God you come back when it's over."

Several weeks had passed since the June Union recruiting push in Austin and, as James predicted, things got worse with every new day. The Home Guard and, worse yet, the unsanctioned Jennison's Jayhawkers, roamed the countryside unmolested, looting and burning those citizens who remotely favored the southern points-of-view. Even Constitutional Unionists, those who held slaves but believed in the sanctity in the Constitution, the Union and its preservation, were set upon. Homes were destroyed, livestock stolen, crops burned, and women and children left destitute and homeless.

Of an evening, if a family had the misfortune of being visited by the Home Guard or Jayhawkers, improperly answered questions led to many a man being dragged from his home and hung or shot in front of his wife and children while they begged for his life.

Elizabeth crawled on the bed and ran her hand over the cold, empty spot. James should have been waiting here for her to join him, a smile on his face to tell her what he had in mind once the lamps were blown out, but her husband wasn't here. Tears filled her eyes and she stretched out, her heart breaking. James had been gone for two days. She had no idea where he was hiding, had refused to tell her where he was going before he left, so she couldn't accidentally give him away if visited again by raiders. Her stretched emotions got the better of her and she grabbed a pillow, pressing it over her face to keep the children from hearing the sobs erupting from her throat. Holding the pillow in place with one hand, she pounded the bed with the other, crying in muted silence until her tears and energy were spent. Shoving the pillow away she sucked in air to regain her breath and composure. Once again calm, she stood up and pulled off her day dress, wishing the hands moving over her body were her husband's instead of her own. But they weren't James' hands and with another sob, she despaired if she would ever see him again. Gone only two days, it felt more like two years.

"Damn this war!" She shoved her fist in her mouth and bit down to stifle another outburst. She didn't want to wake the children. They were having a hard enough time dealing with their father and brother being gone. They didn't need their mother to fall into a state of sadness over their situation. She was doing the best she could without Steven and James. That was all she could do. With an angry swipe she brushed away the tears and slid back into bed, wrapped the pillow in her arms and pulled it close to her chest, a pitiful replacement for a husband in hiding.

***

Caught in a frightening dream, Elizabeth tried to scream, but her voice wouldn't work. Horses pounded up the lane, their big eyes and white teeth glowing in the moonlight and heading straight for her. The riders, all in black, their eyes glowing and teeth gleaming, grinned maliciously when Elizabeth met them on the porch. They raised their weapons and Elizabeth shouted for them to go away, reminding them this was her home and she would not give it up for anyone.

The thundering crash of the front door shattering brought her bolt upright in the bed. The shrieks of her children brought her to the realization it was no dream!

Without taking the time to snatch her robe from the end of the bed, she ran into the front room and came to a skidding halt in front of five men, her nightshirt swirling around her ankles with her abrupt stop.

"Mama?" Vera screeched from the doorway of their room. Elizabeth thought she was going to be sick, fear her children would be harmed gnawing at her like a rabid dog. It was at that moment she realized she hadn't forgotten only her robe, but the pistol from the table beside the bed and her stomach flipped. She was half dressed and unarmed!

"Nora!" she called to her oldest daughter. "You children go into my room and stay there until I tell you otherwise." Nora stood frozen in the doorway, eyes glued to the men leering at her. "Now!" Elizabeth screeched like an old washer woman to make her daughter move.

Nora hurried back into the room to reappear moments later with Vera and a whimpering Sally and Joseph. Nora herded everyone into her parents' bedroom where they huddled together in the middle of the bed, eyes wide and full of tears.

Her children where she wanted them, Elizabeth raised her chin. "What do you men want?" She hoped she showed more bravado than she felt. "Only the children and I are here."

"Strike a light!" a man close to her yelled. Lanterns flared, illuminating the front room in menacing bright light. The men in front of her had meanness in their eyes as they stared at her body outlined in the loose-fitting night dress. She clutched the neck tight against their stares, helpless to do anything else.

Straightening her back she said, "I asked you men once and

I'll ask again. What do you want? It's only me and my children here."

"Where are your men, *Mrs.* Miers?" A man stepped out from behind the others and Elizabeth recognized Walker, the man she'd shot the night of the first raid. Coming closer, she noticed the arm she'd shot was twisted unnaturally, the fingers gnarled and useless-looking. *She'd done that.* Looking up from his worthless appendage she raised her chin and stared into his blazing eyes, so much as telling him she'd do it again if necessary.

"My husband and son are not here."

A man Elizabeth recognized as an Austin resident pushed his way forward and spit tobacco juice on the floor. "The boy is off fightin' for the Rebs."

Elizabeth opened her mouth to protest, but decided it was more prudent if she didn't.

"He lit outta here a few weeks ago," the man continued after wiping his mouth with the back of his sleeve. "But her man is still around, leastways far as I know."

"Well," another man drawled. "Let's just find out. And if he is here..." The man let the sentence hang and warning tore up Elizabeth's back like a whip. Every nerve in her body snapped.

"He's not here I tell you."

"So you say." Walker stepped closer. "Well, Miz Miers, we don't believe the wife of a traitor."

Elizabeth wanted to rail at him that her husband was no traitor, but again decided prudence was best in this situation and held her tongue.

"Where is he?" Walker screamed, spittle flying from his mouth and landing on her cheek when she didn't answer quickly enough. She blanched and thought she'd throw up, but forced down the bile. She couldn't show weakness.

"Believe what you believe. He's not here." She wiped her face with her fingers and raised her chin again.

"Probably heard us coming, skedaddled out the back, and is hiding in the corn field. No matter, we'll look for ourselves," Walker said with a sneer.

Elizabeth felt faint. How was she going to protect her

home and children from these ruffians? She pulled her back up straight as a post and shouted, "Do *not* take one more step into my home you...you vermin!"

Walker slapped her across the face. She went to her knees holding her bloodied lip.

Nora ran from her parents' bedroom and grabbed her mother around the shoulders. Her eyes snapped with hatred as she glared at Walker, standing spread-leg in front of her mother. "You leave her alone!" Nora shrieked.

"Go back in the bedroom. I'm all right," Elizabeth told her daughter once she regained her senses. She kissed Nora on the forehead with a wince and Elizabeth pushed her toward the bedroom as she gained her feet. "Please, Nora, I'm all right. Go back with your brother and sisters." She smiled, wishing she could ease her daughter's fear, knowing it was impossible.

"That was to remind you of your place, woman," Walker snarled in Elizabeth's face after Nora returned to the bedroom. "We're here to find that rebel husband of yours and you won't keep us from it."

"If you intend to...search," she said instead of destroy, "my home, then at least let me go to my children. Please. They're scared," she said with a catch in her throat.

"Go on, git in with your brood, but stay out of our way." The man who had spoken earlier pushed her and Walker aside and headed toward the back of the house. "They'll need you soon."

The veiled threat almost made Elizabeth's knees buckle. Instead she ran to the bedroom as furniture, plates, pots, pans, and anything else not nailed down shattered with resounding crashes.

She meant to slam the door when she got inside the bedroom, but Walker was right behind her. His eyes fell on Nora, sitting in the middle of the bed, Joseph on her lap.

Elizabeth had that feeling again. Reason was flying out the window with the threat to her children. She took a deep, calming breath. It was now or never. While Walker leered at Nora, Elizabeth inched her way to the night table and grabbed the pistol. She whirled on Walker, whose eyes got so wide when he saw the gun she thought they'd pop out of his head.

"Mr. Walker, you recall who did that to you?" She waved the gun at his mangled arm. "And you better know I'll do it again, if needs be. Now step away from my children."

"Miz Miers, there are four other men in your house and more outside..."

"And there are six shots in this pistol!" she hissed at him in a low voice. "And after I kill you with one of them, I'll have five left in this gun and *six* more in yours." Furniture and glass shattered in the other rooms. Without taking her eyes off Walker, she told the children, "Make lots of noise, scream and yell to cover what's going on in here."

The children did as told and she waved her pistol at Walker again. "I do not intend for you men to leave my home in ashes and my children homeless. Now back on outta here."

Walker hesitated and Elizabeth shook her head. "Didn't you learn your lesson the first time, *boy*?" she exaggerated. "I *will* shoot you if you don't do what I say. Now back up."

He hesitated again and Elizabeth steeled herself to the fact she might well have to shoot this young cuss. The children were making all kinds of racket behind her, drowning out their words.

Instead of doing what she told him, Walker lunged. She pulled the trigger. The sound of the exploding gun ricocheted through the house and everything went quiet in an instant.

Walker staggered toward Elizabeth, blood flowing from the hole in his stomach. He grabbed at her for support, but she stepped back and let him fall as two men, one of them the man she recognized from Austin, charged into the room, guns in their hands. The children shrieked and Elizabeth pointed the gun at the men standing gape-mouthed inside the door. "Stop right there. Drop those guns and raise your hands."

The men glared and she shook the gun at them. "Do as I say. I'm losing what patience I had."

They looked at each other. "I didn't come here to shoot no woman. 'Specially not in front of her young 'uns," the man from Austin said.

"Me neither," the other agreed.

"But I will shoot one of you if you don't put your guns on the floor."

With a groan they laid down their weapons.

"Kick them away." She pointed to where she wanted them kicked. "And raise your hands." The men hesitated. Her patience gone, she screamed, "Do you doubt me like Walker did? I *will* shoot you, now kick them away!"

They did as told, as two others skidded to a stop behind them.

Elizabeth thought of nothing but saving her children. Bile rose in her throat, but she kept it down with anger. "You men out there get away from the door!" She didn't want someone using these two as a shield to shoot her.

"And what about the men outside?" one of the men called from the doorway.

"I'll worry about them later. But know this, I have enough bullets to kill all of you if you don't get out of my home and leave me and my children alone!" They didn't know about the extra pistol James had left for her, within easy access inside the top drawer of her bureau. Of course, she had Walker's gun now, too, along with the other two the men had just thrown down.

More men charged into the house from outside and stomped toward the bedroom. Elizabeth glanced between those filling the doorway and recognized Mr. Wilkins, another Austin resident and neighbor. He stopped in his tracks when their eyes met and he lowered his gun.

"Evening, Mr. Wilkins. Are you here to assist these men in killing me and leaving my children orphans?" The children howled behind her. "Are you going to burn our home to the ground to leave them motherless *and* homeless?" she challenged. "We're of no threat to you if you go away and leave us alone." She waved the gun again. "But I am a threat if you don't!"

The two men in front of her inched forward.

"Stop." She waved the gun between their bellies.

"You can't shoot us both," the Austin man said.

Elizabeth chuckled, that same evil sound that had come from her throat the night of the first raid. "I may not get both of you, but is *one* of you ready to die? Which one? Because I swear to the good Lord above, one of you *will* die if you pursue my family further this night!" She swung the pistol back and forth between them again. "Will it be you? Or you?"

"What about the others?" one of the men challenged as he backed up a step.

"I don't know. All I know is young Mr. Walker and one of you will be dead. So it won't matter much to you, will it?" She stared them down and they backed up far enough to block the door so no one else could get inside the room.

"I told you all, my husband is not here! You've searched—and destroyed—the inside of my home. Did you find him? No, you did not!" she answered for them. "So why don't you all just git on your horses and leave us alone? We can't hurt you." The two men looked at the pistol she was holding and she grinned. "Unless you do something stupid and *force* me to." She cocked her head and grinned maliciously.

Silence abounded for several seconds before Mr. Wilkins shouted from the other room, "I think we've bothered Miz Miers enough for one night. You two grab Walker and we'll be on our way."

Elizabeth stepped away from the man who lay motionless in the middle of her bedroom floor, but kept the gun trained on the other two. The children were whimpering, their eyes huge, tears streaming down their faces as the men hauled the unconscious, most likely dead, Walker away.

The men stomped out to the porch, the door in two pieces behind them, one on the floor to the left of the opening, the other hanging lopsided from its leather hinges on the right.

Elizabeth turned to Nora. "Put Joseph down and grab the rifle from the corner. Watch that window and shoot anybody that tries to open it." She pointed at the bedroom window, thankfully shuttered tight.

Nora swallowed and nodded. "Yes, Mama." She, too, had shot her share of squirrels and rabbits with that rifle. She shifted her brother off her lap to Vera, walked to the corner, grabbed the rifle and aimed it at the window.

"Stay there until I tell you it's all right."

"Yes, Mama." Tears streamed down Nora's face and Elizabeth despaired over the fact that at not quite fourteen years old, her daughter was faced with the real possibility of having to kill another human being to survive tonight's ordeal. She shook her head. It couldn't be helped. It was war and she intended to survive it—with her children.

Joseph was snuggled with Vera and Sally, the three in the middle of the bed watching in silence, their eyes puffed and red, cheeks shimmering.

"I'll be right back. Stay where you are. You hear?"

"Yes, Mama," Vera managed. "Joseph and Sally each squeaked out a "Yes, Mama," before she turned and walked through the door into the front room. Before going to the door she checked the children's room to make sure no one was waiting to jump her once her back was turned, but found it empty.

Walking tall back into the front room, Elizabeth went to the window on the right of the shattered door, opened the shutter and laid the barrel of her pistol on the ledge, careful to remain hidden behind the wall. Walker's gun was tight in her other hand, cocked and ready to fire—just in case someone had enough of her rebellious stubbornness and decided it was time to end this by putting a bullet into her.

In a quick glance she spotted at least ten riders, rough men with angry faces, and fear sluiced down Elizabeth's back in waves. The realization of how many men she'd stood up to made her knees feel like jelly and she leaned against the wall to keep from sliding to the floor.

"You're either a very brave woman, Mrs. Miers," Wilkins called, "or a very foolish one."

"I'm a woman intent on saving her children and home from the likes of men intent on destroying it," she called back through the window.

Wilkins pursed his lips and nodded. "Yes, ma'am, I see that, and we'll leave you be—for now." He let the words hang a moment before he viciously jerked his horse's head around and sent the animal bounding away, the other riders behind him.

Elizabeth stood at the window for ten minutes, watching and waiting, frozen in time. Finally giving up her vigil, she slipped to the floor, tried to put the pistols down beside her, and had to pry them from her locked fingers.

Slowly the children came to her side, sniveling and hiccupping. She took them into her arms and kissed them all over their wet faces. They sat on the floor with their mother, crying, kissing and hugging—this little family alone against stronger men bent on destruction. One by one, Joseph and Sally in her lap and Nora and Vera clinging to her arms, they fell asleep huddled together.

They'd been lucky twice. *How long before that luck would run out?* was Elizabeth's last thought before she, too, fell into slumber.

Chapter Five
(Early August, 1861)

Elizabeth did what she could to work the farm on her own. With two small children who still needed a great deal of attention, it was difficult to keep even the few crops not stripped by raiders tended. What stock remained subsisted on the dry, brittle pasture grass, burned up in the summer sun, forage from the trees, and supplemented with a little feed James had managed to hide in a false bottom of the tack locker in the barn.

Joseph and Sally did what little they could to help by carrying small buckets of oats or corn for Poppyseed and Hilda, the only horses left, the others gone with James and Steven or stolen from the pasture. Hilda was old, swaybacked, and blind so of no use to a raider, but Poppyseed was prime horseflesh and escaped thievery only because she was kept out of sight in the trees at the far end of the property. Each morning before the sun came up the two horses and milk cow were led to the creek for water and allowed to graze for a half hour. Once the sun began to rise they were taken back to the trees where they foraged throughout the day on the leaves of low hanging branches and bushes before they were brought back to the barn well after the sun set.

Throughout the day, Nora and Vera took turns sitting in the tree at the back of the house, watching and waiting to give warning if anyone came along the road that might try to steal Poppyseed.

Whichever girl wasn't in the tree watching for thievery hauled water for the remaining livestock—the two horses, one milk cow, four laying chickens and three pigs—from the pump at the back of the house in a rickety wooden wagon James made for Nora when she was three. Inside the barn the animals were more easily tended—and hidden—the horses each having their own stall, the chickens in another enclosure with boards and wire to keep them from wandering away, the cow in another, and the pigs in a larger birthing stall. If they managed to keep the chickens they would, at least, have eggs to eat. With James and Steven gone, they no longer had any meat. Although Elizabeth was quite capable of hunting, she was too busy and too afraid to venture away from the house to do so. The farthest she went was to retrieve Poppyseed, Hilda and the cow in the morning and return them to the trees or barn later.

With the animals inside the barn so much, instead of in the pastures where they were used to roaming at night, the stalls overflowed with waste and had to be mucked daily, a dirty chore that had to be done. It was backbreaking work, especially for children, but everyone did what they could.

Even Walter, the goat, did what he could to help, wandering the property throughout the day eating whatever he foraged, coming to the porch in the evening to get his small share of oats and corn—and stand guard over the house through the night, as good or better than any watchdog.

Water for what was left of the family garden was hauled from the creek. Elizabeth tasked the older girls with keeping it weed-free when they weren't sitting in the tree, watching over the place. The weeding was a daunting job and, along with their other chores and blistering heat and sun, the girls shirked their duties as often as they could and the weeds quickly took over. What wasn't stolen by raiders or dried up by the sun was eventually eaten by grasshoppers.

Elizabeth stood at the counter in the front room kneading a small, thin loaf of bread, using a fraction of the proper ingredients to stretch their dwindling supplies, when the front door squeaked open behind her. The children would have barreled inside, chattering like magpies or arguing, and caution bells rang in her head. She whirled, a knife she kept close for just such a situation in hand, ready to confront whoever was in her home.

"Oh, thank God!" The knife clattered to the floor and she rushed into her husband's arms.

James shushed her with a kiss that left her breathless. "Where have you been?" she asked when she could breathe. "I was beginning to think you were dead. Why did you wait so long to come home?" Her voice cracked on a threatening sob.

"Raiders are everywhere. I had to keep moving to keep from being found."

"Oh, James, it sounds horrible."

He frowned and swung his head up and down. "It is.

There are certainly other things I would rather be doing, but I don't want to talk about that. I'm home, for now, and I want to know about you and the children. What happened here? Is everyone all right?" He thrust a thumb at the door, the broken pieces held together with three wide, thick boards that looked like they came from the fencing around the house, each piece nailed across the door over the broken middle and held tight with a dozen or more nails on each side. He grinned. "Good repair job."

"I learned from the best." Elizabeth grinned back. "The children are fine, aside from doing all the chores and trying to keep this place from falling down around our ears—what's left of it, at least. They're more frightened now than they were before you left. We had another night visit and now they jump and whimper at every sound."

"What happened?" James took her hand and they sat down at the table, worse for wear, but still in one piece, at least.

Elizabeth took a deep breath and launched into a description of the latest raid. James listened, his face a mask of controlled fury, but he remained silent until she finished her tale.

"You kept those men from burning this house down around you and the children?"

She cocked her head and shrugged. "I guess so. I wasn't so much worried about the house as the children. I couldn't think of anything but protecting them."

"Like you did the night of the first raid?" He grinned again.

"I suppose. I know now what a mother bear feels like when her cubs are threatened and why no man should mess with one when she's protecting them. I lost all reason, James—again. All I could think of was keeping them safe."

"And so you have." He sat a moment, his anger simmering, his eyes darkening until he exploded. "Cowards! Making war on defenseless women and children!"

"Not *quite* defenseless," Elizabeth corrected with a grin.

"No, not you Elizabeth, not you. But there are so many women who have no idea how to defend themselves. Who have been burned out, left homeless and destitute with nowhere for them and their children to go. It's not right...."

Elizabeth laid her hand over his. "None of it's right—but this crazy country is at war. Men on both sides believe their cause is right and are doing whatever they deem necessary to win. But it certainly doesn't make it right."

Her husband sucked in a deep breath and Elizabeth saw his weariness. "You must be starving. Let me fix you something." She tried to stand, but he held her where she was.

"Wait. The children will come in soon. I want to tell you what's happening before they do. They don't need to hear."

She settled back on the bench and waited. She knew only what she heard when she went into Austin these days, and only when it was absolutely necessary. In town, she kept her head down, her eyes open, and carried a loaded pistol in her bag. She did her business and left as quickly as possible.

"You remember we took Carthage before I left in early July?"

"Yes."

"Well, there was another battle at Manassas, Virginia, on the twenty-first and, from what I've heard over the last few weeks, we routed the Yanks—sent them scurrying back to Washington with their tails tucked and their brains abuzz."

"That's good, so why the frown?"

"It is good. We took Carthage *and* Manassas, proving this war won't be won by the North's arrogance and hard words. But," He hesitated and Elizabeth squeezed his hand. "It won't help *us* here in Missoura." He took a deep breath. "The same day we won Manassas, Jennison and his Jayhawkers hit Morristown. They skirmished with some locals who tried to keep them out of town. Two of the defenders were killed before the Jayhawkers went in and took everything they could carry out in stolen wagons."

"Morristown isn't that far from here," Elizabeth managed through the fear tearing up her spine.

"That's why you have to be extra careful, Liz. Raiders are everywhere. The Kansas 7th is burning their way south, and Jayhawkers and the Home Guard are raiding on the Missoura side of the border." He stopped and his face went hard. "And what do I do to stop it, Liz? I hide!" His whole body shook with anger.

"There's nothing else to do," Elizabeth countered. "If they find you here you know they'll kill you as easy as look at you. I'd rather have you hiding and alive than dead!" Her heart was pounding. She knew where this was leading.

"I could fight, Liz. I could join the State Guard and fight like a man, instead of hiding like a rat chased by a cat!" He slammed his fist down on the table. "If I was gone, they'd leave you and the children alone," he tried to justify, but Elizabeth knew better.

She snorted. "You don't believe that any more than I do. They've raided the farms of families whose men are off fighting and taken everything. Some they've burned to the ground as the family watched. You being gone wouldn't help us at all, James. Not one bit. The only thing joining up might do is get you killed sooner." She sucked in a breath. They'd had this discussion before and she wasn't about to back down now. "You have four young children and a wife who depend on you. This war will be over some day and we need you back with us when it is. Leave the fighting to young men. What would we do if you got killed off fighting the war?"

He waved his hand at the repaired door. "It seems nothing different than what you're doing right now. You and the children already take care of everything. What's the difference whether I'm hiding—or fighting? If I were fighting at least I'd be useful to the cause."

"You're *alive*." She laid her hand on his cheek. "That's *all* that matters." She took another breath. "Besides, this family has already given one man to the cause and I pray God he survives. I won't give two." The words were said in such a tone they brooked no argument. James looked ready to do just that then snapped his mouth shut and shook his head.

"I never could win with you, Liz."

"No, you couldn't and I don't intend to let you start now."

James shifted on the bench. "There's more."

"More?"

"Much more and none of it's good."

Elizabeth leaned into her husband for support when he said, "Harrisonville has been sacked, too."

Elizabeth experienced that all-too familiar feeling like the ground was crumbling under her. She closed her eyes and clung to James' arm as he continued.

"On the 26th of July Major Dolan and his Home Guard were outside Harrisonville. I heard he refused to allow his men into town to join in the destruction of his neighbors, but there were plenty of others who took up for them. Harrisonville was completely sacked, Liz. Every store looted."

Elizabeth sat in stunned silence, her heart thudding. Tears formed in her eyes then slid down her cheeks. Her mind spun with the ramifications. *Until now, Harrisonville had been pro-Southern. Now it would be pro-Union. What did that mean for the countryside around it? For them?*

"There's even more."

James' voice jerked her back from her frightening thoughts.

"Lincoln has called for the enlistment of 500,000 men for three years."

This time Elizabeth reacted as though struck. She jerked upright feeling like her heart was trying to make its way out of her body through her throat. She stared wide-eyed at her husband, unable to form any words.

"Three years, Liz. Lincoln's so much as admitted this won't be the short war everybody expected—and that it could drag on for as long as three years!"

Elizabeth slumped on the seat, every ounce of hope and energy disappearing like mist on a lake in the morning sunlight. "I don't know if I can do this, James. I'm exhausted beyond reason. I live in fear for myself and the children—you and Steven. We work day and night trying to keep this place up. At least when I thought the war would be short I was able to find the strength to get out of bed and do what had to be done, but if this thing drags on for years, I just don't know if I can do it!" she cried.

"You can and you will." He turned and grabbed her shoulders with his big hands. "You have to. There's no other choice except to lie down and die. I'm not ready to let you do that and I *know* you're not ready to leave our children motherless. You prove that every day by what you're doing here and every time raiders come a-calling."

    She had no words. He was right. She'd do whatever was necessary to protect her children—no matter how long it took. They sat side by side, touching, but neither spoke. Every few minutes Elizabeth shook her head and more tears slid down her face.

    The silence was growing oppressive until James jumped up, pulled Elizabeth up with him, and dragged her off the bench behind him. "No more talk about the war. I've missed you and intend to show you just how much before the children come inside."

    Elizabeth forced everything else from her mind. There was no more war, no more fear, and no more chores or exhaustion. There was only James. He was home and nothing else was important—not how long he could stay nor when he'd come back. Right here and right now was all that mattered.

    She padded after him to their room, closed and locked the door behind them, and let him show her just how much he missed her.

Chapter Six
(Fall 1861)

"They killed Greg." James dropped like a stone onto the bench he and Elizabeth were sharing at the back of the house, his voice dull and cold. He'd appeared from around the front while Elizabeth was scrubbing clothes, scaring more gray into her hair. "Oh dear Lord! Poor Margaret. And the children! What happened?" Like reaching for a lifeline, she grabbed James' hand and held on tight.

"I gather the brothers were warned the Home Guard was targeting them. Victor and Robert left everything behind and high-tailed it out of here, but Greg refused to leave everything he's worked for. He swore he wouldn't be driven away from his home." James took in a deep breath and shook his head.

"They came one night and forced Mr. Josephson, his neighbor, to call Greg out. Of course, Josephson had a gun square in the middle of his back. Hear tell, Greg thought his friend was coming to visit and he was safe, so he put his rifle aside, opened the door, and was shot dead as soon as he did. They killed him right in front of Margaret and the children." James hung his head and ran his fingers through his long, dirty hair.

Tears spilled from Elizabeth's eyes, and she knew they were pouring from James', too. *He'd known Greg for years, they'd always been friends, and now his friend was dead. Ambushed by cowards who used another friend to draw him out then shot him like a dog in front of his family!*

When he could speak again James told Elizabeth what was going on in the war.

"In August General Nathaniel Lyon and Franz Siegel, the same Siegel routed by Governor Jackson at Carthage," he interjected, "met 'Pap' Price's Confederates at Wilson's Creek outside Springfield. Both sides gained ground then lost it just as quickly throughout the day, but when General Lyon was killed that afternoon, the Yankees became disorganized, maybe even unwilling, to keep fighting." He sighed heavily. "By the end of the day both armies were so confused and exhausted they left the field with *neither* side claiming victory.

"After Wilson's Creek came Morristown — again — and a few days later, Lexington."

Elizabeth's mind whirled. Lexington was seventy-five miles away, but Morristown was close, and since the Federal's visit there a month ago, Elizabeth had learned on one of her rare visits to town that it was now a confederate recruiting station for the Missouri State Guard, Tenth Cavalry. *Apparently, the Yankees knew it, too, and decided to shut it down*, she mused. "What happened at Morristown?" Elizabeth's mouth had gone dry.

"The Tenth was camped outside town with about a hundred and fifty men when Lane's Fifth Regiment of Kansans attacked. They came with infantry, cavalry, two howitzers and over five hundred men. We knew they were coming, but were so outnumbered we had no choice but to retreat."

"We?" Elizabeth hadn't missed his inference.

"I fought with them."

"You *fought*?"

"How could I not!" he exploded at her puzzled tone. "They were attacking Morristown—again! I was there when they came. What should I have done? Run away? Hidden in the bushes? Let my friends and neighbors fight while I watched like a coward?"

His face was red with anger and he jumped up and stomped away. Elizabeth realized she was being unreasonable in trying to keep him out of the fight. *She couldn't let anger come between them now. He'd only just come home again!* Emotions pummeled her. *James had fought! He'd survived. He was there when the Kansas Fifth sacked Morristown for the second time in a month, and fought with the Missouri State Guard! He could have been killed! But he wasn't. What else could he have done? James was no coward. He was in hiding only because she wanted it.* Slowly she talked herself through it. James had fought—and survived. There was joy in that. She had to grab it with both hands.

"Stop, James. I'm sorry. I'm just so afraid for you. I don't know what I'd do if something...if you were...."

James stopped, his shoulders slumped, and he came back

to her. He took her in his arms and they stood in silence for several moments before he said, "The Home Guard is sweeping the area more heavily these days. It's getting more difficult to stay near the house, so I headed toward Morristown where I *thought* it would be safe since they were recruiting there." He cocked his head. "Guess I was wrong. It's just too hard to stay close for long periods, Liz. The Home Guard is everywhere and I'm afraid they're going to find me."

"How are you getting around? What are you eating? Where do you sleep?" she asked leading him back to the bench. *She would send him off with what little food they could spare, but how long would it last? A few days? A week at the most?*

"I'm surviving." He ran his fingers through is long, dirty hair and frowned. Deep furrows around his eyes showed Elizabeth how much he'd aged since he left. "As you can see, I came home afoot. There was so much firing and smoke, Solomon bolted in the confusion." He looked up and sighed. "It's getting chilly at night, too, so I intend to grab what blankets I can carry and my heavy coat before I leave again. I have a piece of canvas that keeps the rain off me. As for food, I live off the land. I've become quite adept at finding food left behind by the Home Guard after they visit local farms and I hunt small game. My feet, well, they've become quite accustomed to traveling miles at a time without so much as a twinge of pain." He smiled as though telling her about some great feat he'd accomplished. In essence, he had. He'd survived for months away from his family, in the elements, with no food or shelter to speak of.

"What about other men? Do you see any of our neighbors who are hiding, too?"

He shrugged. "I see some, but I'm never sure which side they're on. Sometimes I don't find out until it's too late."

A chill streaked up Elizabeth's back. "What do you mean, too late?"

"It means I've had to defend myself when a supposed friend was no longer a friend."

"Oh, James, I'm so sorry. Maybe it'd be better if you *did* join up." She shook her head, fresh tears forming. "At least you'd have food and shelter and know who you were fighting."

"Maybe." His voice was tight. "Maybe not," was all he said before he fell silent.

"You said there was a battle at Lexington? What happened there?" Elizabeth hoped to change the subject to anything other than the possibility of James enlisting with the Missouri State Guard.

"Ole Pap marched from Wilson's Creek straight to Lexington and kept it under siege for nine days before the Yanks finally surrendered to Pap's superior numbers, the heat, thirst— and rolling hemp bales," James said with a grin. "The Federals were cut off from the river, their only source of water, and were, literally, dying of thirst under the scorching September sun. Pap's men had them pinned down, picking them off with snipers hidden in the Anderson house whenever they tried to reach the river." He clucked his tongue. "They set up the house as an infirmary at first, but I guess both sides decided it was more useful for its strategic location than taking care of the wounded. So they fought back and forth, both forces gaining and losing control of it over and over throughout the siege. But the final blow came from the hemp bales."

"Hemp bales? How on this earth could hemp bales win a battle?" Elizabeth asked, knowing hemp was the fiber used to make rope.

"The huge bales were soaked with water to be used as shields, and pushed up the hill toward the Union lines."

If it weren't so serious, Elizabeth might have chuckled at the vision in her head of grown men shoving huge, soaking round bales up a hill while being pummeled by Yankee bullets! The big bales would have shielded the soldiers when the firing started, while the water would have kept them from bursting into flame when the bullets hit the highly flammable hemp. Elizabeth couldn't help but grin when the picture flashed through her head again.

"By mid-afternoon of that ninth day," James continued, "with the bales coming up the hill and the sun blazing overhead, that Yankee Colonel Mulligan finally raised the white flag and surrendered." Elizabeth didn't know what to say. War was tearing the country apart. Her husband was in hiding and considering enlisting. She and her children feared for their home and their lives every day. She wrapped her arm around James' and leaned against him, happy for these few moments alone before the children finished their chores in the barn and found their Papa had returned. *This was her time and she was going to suck in every minute of it, whether it was selfish or not!*

James broke the silence with more news. "Two days later, Lane and his men looted and burned Osceola to the ground."

Elizabeth jerked upright, her heart pounding her eyes wide. "The whole town?" She had an aunt and uncle in St. Clair County near Osceola.

James nodded and frowned. "The whole damned town except three buildings. Three!"

Elizabeth couldn't speak. Her throat was closed up with fear. Tears stung her eyes for the second time since James' arrival. His visits brought her great joy—and great sorrow with the news he brought with him.

"They loaded up every wagon they found with all the supplies they could carry and drove out of town leading cattle, horses and slaves away before they put it to the torch." He took a breath then added, "They shot nine men, Liz. I don't know who they were, but they gave them drumhead court-martials and executed them right on the square."

Fear ripped its way up Elizabeth's back. Her Uncle Rupert was a known secessionist—and a hothead. *Could he have been one of the nine men executed?*

James interrupted her thoughts. "That's not the worst of it."

"What could be worse!" Elizabeth couldn't imagine anything else. The world had gone mad and there was nothing they could do!

"That damned, sorry, that Kansas Senator Jim Lane, the self-proclaimed leader of the Kansans, put out a proclamation in mid-September—after General Fremont declared martial law in Missoura."

"There's martial law in Missouri?" Elizabeth interrupted. "And what proclamation are you talking about?" Elizabeth chewed her lip, not knowing about any of it. She rolled her hands in and out of fists in disbelief that things had gotten so bad.

"The kind of proclamation that turns my blood cold, that's what kind." He swallowed. "According to Lane everybody who lives in Western Missoura should consider themselves in occupied territory. Basically, we're in occupied enemy territory, occupied by the Kansas Brigade."

Elizabeth about choked on her sharp intake of breath. "What does Lane want us to do? Leave our homes? What about our children, our farms?" Elizabeth had a feeling that was exactly what he wanted to frighten them into doing.

"He gave us two choices. We can lay down our arms and seek their protection."

"And if we don't?"

"We should prepare for the 'stern visitations of war,' as he called it, to be meted out to rebels and their allies."

Elizabeth had trouble breathing. The news was worse than anything she'd imagined. According to Lane's proclamation she and her children were considered the enemy, living in enemy territory, and needed only wait to be visited by Kansas troops if they didn't go into town and pledge their loyalty to the Union!

"You can pledge...."

"I will not!" she shouted before James could finish the sentence. "After how those Yankees have threatened my children and my home, I certainly will not! We've managed to chase them away twice, I'll do it again if needs be."

"That's what I'm afraid of, Liz. The third time they won't be so forgiving. Lane's men are brutal. They're burning women and children out of their homes without so much as a backward glance. Taking boys as young as ten and holding them until they decide whether they believe they're old enough to fight against them. They took little Willie Sanders and kept him from his mother overnight before they finally let him go. It's shameless what they're doing to the women and children in these parts. I don't want it to happen to you and *our* children."

She laid her hand on his cheek. "I won't let it. They'll have to kill me before I allow that to happen."

James jumped up in front of her, his face a mask of fear. "Don't say that, Liz. They *would* kill you if you tried to stop them from doing what they intend! Those men are ruthless and would burn the house down around you—and the children. They've already done it! Fire is one thing you can't stop." He paused and thought a moment. "Maybe I should come back home."

"You can't. If they find you here there'd be nothing to save you. We'd lose you *and* everything else. You have to stay in hiding—or join up," she added grudgingly, making James' neck jerk back in surprise. "It may be your only chance to survive this war," she added before a sob erupted and James gathered her to him. She cried for a long time in his arms, wishing things were different, wanting only to do what was best for her husband and family, praying whatever that was didn't get them all killed.

The children suddenly appeared in the door of the barn and hurried toward them when they spotted their father. They flew into his arms, crying and kissing him.

Elizabeth drew up her back, dried her tears and smiled for their benefit, even though her heart was breaking.

Chapter Seven
(Christmas 1861)

"Open your present, Mama." Nora slid a box toward Elizabeth. The box was tattered, having been used for many Christmas presents in the past. Elizabeth studied her daughter, quickly becoming a woman, on this solemn Christmas Eve. They were gathered in the front room around a scrawny little cedar tree they'd found in the tree line of their property and was propped up on the end of the table. The children had decorated it with pieces of ribbon and home-made ornaments as they always had, bringing a small amount of normalcy to the holiday. Two candles kept the darkness at bay.

"Go on, Mama."

Elizabeth's heart broke at the weariness in her daughter's voice.

"I wish it were more, but, well," Nora's sentence went unfinished. It wasn't necessary. They both knew there was little to give.

Elizabeth reached out and took her daughter's hand. "Whatever it is, I'll love it." She sat back on her heels, opened the box and pulled out a book Nora had made using two square pieces of leather for the cover and three rawhide strips tied in neat bows on the left to hold it together. On the front, *Elizabeth Miers' Book of Verses,* was carefully etched into the leather in Nora's flowing handwriting. A lump in her throat, Elizabeth opened the cover and read *The Lord's Prayer*, each word meticulously written over the page. On the next page John 3:16 was copied along with two other familiar verses. Flipping through the ten pages was verse after verse of uplifting prayers to help Elizabeth through the days—and nights.

"I thought they'd give you comfort, especially with Papa gone so much," Nora squeaked.

Elizabeth gathered her oldest child in her arms. "I love it, Nora. I love it." Tears brimmed in both their eyes, but the moment was broken when Vera, apparently not wanting to be out done by her older sister, shouted, "Open mine now, Mama!"

Vera's gift brought fresh tears when Elizabeth unwrapped a wobbly picture frame, barely held together with four crooked nails and holding a piece of foolscap with the words: *My Mama*, centered at the top, followed by: "*My Mama is the best Mama in the world. I love my Mama very much.*" Surrounding the neatly printed words were dried flowers of all kinds tied to the paper with pieces of thread. Most were weeds like yellow dandelions, purple thistles, and white and purple clover, but there were shriveled up daisies, black eyed Susan's, and buttercups, too.

"It's beautiful, Vera. What a wonderful job!" she exclaimed with the enthusiasm of any other Christmas Eve celebration.

Sally and Joseph ran over and plopped down on Elizabeth's lap, crushing Vera's handiwork.

Vera pushed her brother and sister off her mother's lap and grabbed the lopsided frame. "Look what you two little brats did! You broke it!" Vera's lips curled in a sneer.

The smaller children burst into tears at their older sister's outburst, but before Elizabeth could speak, Nora shouted, "It's Christmas! Don't fight!" Tears brimmed in Nora's eyes as she stood tall, trying *not* to cry, trying to keep the peace.

Vera's lower lip pushed out into a pout. She plopped down on the floor and crossed her arms over her chest. "They broke Mama's present. Look what they did!" She displayed the frame and Elizabeth quickly took it in hand.

"I can fix this, Vera. Don't you worry. It'll be as good as new. Even better!" Elizabeth put on a happy face and hurried to the table where she twisted, turned and pounded until the frame looked better than when Vera gave it to her. "Look! Good as new."

Vera looked unconvinced. She turned her head first one way, then another to look at it when her mother held it in front of her. "Well, I guess...."

"You guess what? It's better than when you gave it to her!" Nora chastised.

Vera's lips curled tight and her eyes pinched. "Take it back. It's not better. It's just...." The sentence froze on Vera's lips when she looked up. Her eyes widened and she shouted, "Papa!" Vera jumped up, dumping the moments ago precious frame on the floor, and ran into her father's outstretched arms.

She hugged him fiercely, the other children hurrying behind her.

Sobbing with happiness Elizabeth gathered them all to her. "You're here. Oh, thank the Lord, you're here!"

There was laughter in the Miers' home for the first time in months and everyone intended to enjoy it while they could. They exchanged more presents, some James had made, others he'd obtained during his days in hiding. There was a four-inch tall, hand-carved horse made out of a pine branch for Joseph, a corn cob and husk doll for Sally that she grabbed and held to her chest like a real baby, just enough material for Nora and Vera each to make an apron, and a locket for Elizabeth.

After an hour exchanging gifts, laughing and hugging, the smaller children went off and played with their new toys and Nora and Vera worked on their aprons, allowing their parents some time alone.

Raising the locket in her hand, Elizabeth looked askance at her husband. "Where?"

James shook his head and Elizabeth knew he was struggling to keep his composure. "I've had it since September. I found it at a house outside Morristown after the battle."

Elizabeth took her husband's hand. "Tell me."

"The house had been ransacked, the windows busted, walls destroyed. Everything of value was gone—except that. Someone must have dropped it on their way out. Probably had too much in their hands and didn't even realize they'd lost it," he said grudgingly. He squeezed Elizabeth's hand. "No one else was left. The Tenth had moved north and Lane's troops were long gone. There was no one around, except the ghosts of the men killed that day."

He fell silent, the battle obviously looming in his head. He looked up at her, his eyes brimming. "I saw men cut down that day by howitzers, others forced to dig a grave before they were shot and thrown into it, and I ran from former friends who rode with the enemy. It was a day of reckoning, Liz. My reckoning. It opened my eyes to how real the war is and that it won't be over any time soon. And it's not happening somewhere else, it's happening right here—to me. To us." He shook his head. "I don't know why I went to that house. I guess because it was in my path home, so I stopped and went through it. I don't know what I expected to find, but that was lying on the porch outside the front door, well, where the front door had been." He waved his hand at the locket in her hand. "Wear it with pride, Liz, knowing it belonged to a woman who lost her home that day—and who knows what else."

Elizabeth's body stung with guilt and regret. Her back stiffened and her resolve strengthened. Tears filled her eyes and she fought them. Unwilling to destroy the little joy they'd found in the day, she handed the locket to James to put around her neck.

"I promise to wear this locket with pride in memory of its former owner," she promised. Closing her eyes she laid her hand over the blue stone inlaid in silver and prayed no one would find it again someday—in the rubble of *her* home.

Christmas morning dawned crisp and cold. Elizabeth stood at the stove humming, recalling the night she'd spent in her husband's arms, when she was grabbed, whirled in a circle, the breath hugged right out of her.

"James! The children." She extracted herself from his grip with a giggle.

"Let them see some loving, Liz. God knows there's none to be found outside this house."

Elizabeth nodded, leaned in and kissed him full on the lips, drawing oohs and aahs from the children awaiting their breakfast at the table.

"Ewwwwww!" Joseph shouted, drawing snickers from the other children.

Nora jumped up and stepped beside her mother. "May I help you, Mama?"

"You may. Dish out those eggs and I'll butter some bread." Elizabeth's stomach twisted at the knowledge they'd used the last of the flour to make this small loaf of bread for their Christmas breakfast. They did, at least, have cornmeal for cornbread, now that the flour was gone. Scouring the fields after thieves had taken their fill during the most recent raid, Elizabeth and the children recovered several dozen ears that were trampled under the soft dirt. They gathered everything they found, brought it back to the house, cleaned it up and ground the rest into cornmeal to keep it from going bad and getting infested with weevils. So as long as the hens kept laying and the milk cow kept giving milk, they would have eggs, butter and cornbread for a while, even though everything else was running low.

James had come home last night with two turkeys dangling from his back. One was in the oven roasting for Christmas dinner and the other was in the smoke shed, freezing solid in the bitter cold. Elizabeth was aware he'd taken a chance firing a gun to bring them meat. He could have given himself away to the Home Guard or Jayhawkers, but she chose not to remind him of that, happy for the meat and happy her husband had come home to them safely.

Breakfast was loud and full of laughter. Every morsel was eaten, everyone wishing for more, Elizabeth saw it in their eyes and when the little ones had asked for more. Although it was a special day, they couldn't give up what few supplies they had left for one day, so she made enough for the meal, but not overmuch.

Elizabeth slapped James' hand when he tried to steal her piece of bread, then quickly put more butter on it and handed it to him. He was scrawny and she wanted to do what she could to put a little meat back on his bones, and was happy to do it.

After breakfast Vera and Nora cleared the table and washed the dishes, both wearing their newly stitched aprons and using them to dry their hands when they were finished. Throughout the day, James and Elizabeth read aloud in front of the fireplace while Joseph and Sally played with their carved horse and corn husk doll.

Mid-day, peaceful and hopeful the day would remain so, everyone napped.

Elizabeth woke with a start in her husband's arms. He stirred, but was so exhausted he didn't waken. She'd dreamed they were being attacked again and she jumped out of bed and hurried to the other room. She peered out one window and then another before hurrying upstairs to Steven's loft, still empty even after Elizabeth offered it to Nora and Vera. The girls had chosen to stay with each other and the younger children, Elizabeth had mused, for a better feeling of security. She stared out over the farm, convincing herself no one was about. After an hour she decided it *had been* just a dream that awakened her and went downstairs to finish preparing dinner.

"Come on, everyone!" she called to rouse her sleepy family later that afternoon. "Supper's ready!"

The children came to the table rubbing their eyes and James appeared, his hair sticking up on end, his face puffy and red.

"It looks glorious," he whispered, standing at the end of the table staring at the turkey exploding with cornbread stuffing, a huge chunk of cornbread on a plate and butter for it in a bowl. There was a pitcher of fresh milk and honey that, thankfully, seemed to stay good forever. There were canned beets, onions, radishes, and five small sweet potatoes Elizabeth had pulled from their dwindling supplies in the root cellar.

"It looks wonderful, Mama!" Nora trilled.

"Can we eat now?" Vera shouted, settling in her spot on the bench.

"As soon as we pray." Elizabeth took her seat.

Once settled and joining hands, James began. "Thank you, God, for this meal you have provided for us. Thank you for bringing us safely together and I pray you guide us in the coming days. Keep us safe. All this I pray in thy precious name, Oh, Lord." Amen echoed across the room.

They ate until they were as full as ticks then ate more, not knowing when they would have so much again.

Later, after the evening chores were done, James tucked his children into bed, kissed them, and said his farewells.

"When will you come back, Papa?" Vera asked. A shiver of fear ran up Elizabeth's spine watching her husband and daughters from where she leaned against the door, arms crossed over her chest.

He shook his head. "I don't know, honey. It just depends."

"On what, Papa?" his daughter asked, all innocence.

He pursed his lips and shook his head again. "The weather, the Home Guard, lots of things. But I'll be back as soon as I can. I promise."

Vera sniffled and James leaned over and gathered her into his arms, waving Nora, Sally, and Joseph to join their sister.

They remained enfolded in his arms for several moments before he kissed them one last time, dropped Joseph into his cot, and the girls settled in their own bed, sobbing into their pillows.

Elizabeth tried to stifle her tears, but seeing her children's sad goodbyes and the tears that followed was breaking her heart. *If only things were different,* she mused. *But they weren't and they had to make the best of it. And right now, that was saying goodbye to their father—and her husband.*

The children quieted down and James led Elizabeth to their room, closed the door and said goodbye to his wife in a much different way. Breathing hard, he sat up in the bed, pulled his wife up beside him and wrapped his arm around her shoulders.

He swallowed hard and Elizabeth was scared to death of what was going to come out of his mouth.

"Liz, I've made a decision."

Elizabeth's body sang with warning. She sucked in a deep breath for courage. "Yes?"

"I'm enlisting. I tried to do as you asked, but I can't anymore. It's time for me to join up and that's all there is to it."

Elizabeth wanted to scream. She wanted to cry, but sadly, she understood why he had to do this. James Miers was a prideful man tired of hiding, a man who wanted to make a difference in the war. Even though she'd begged him before not to join up, she knew she couldn't stop him now. Knew she *shouldn't* stop him now. It was what he had to do.

"Did you hear me?" His voice was barely above a whisper.

"I did. I'm just trying to absorb it. I know you have to go. I know that now, but it doesn't make it any easier."

They sat in silence for several moments, James holding her tight before Elizabeth broke that silence. "Where will you go to join up? You obviously can't enlist at Morristown and you can't just walk up to someone and say 'I want to join up.' Half the time you can't even tell which side they're on here in Missouri. They'll shoot you just as easy as look at you for your trouble," she said, trying to lighten the ominous feeling in the room.

"They're recruiting in Dayton. Phil Anderson leads one

of the units there from what I've heard. You remember Mr. Anderson, don't you? We met him and his family at the joint picnic last year with the churches from Dayton and Austin."

Elizabeth nodded, afraid to speak, afraid if she did she'd lose what little self-control she had right now.

"I'm going to Dayton and see if I can find him."

He'd obviously done a lot of thinking about this. He planned to join up in Dayton. At least he'd be in the area and might be able to come home occasionally like he did now. Fear gripped Elizabeth and tears filled her eyes, a condition that seemed to be more normal than unusual these days, but she forced them back. She didn't want to send him off with tears. She wanted to send him off with encouragement and faith in him.

She turned her face up to his and kissed him with all the love and passion she felt. Slowly they made love one last time before he gathered what little he was taking with him and said goodbye for only God knew how long.

Chapter Eight
(January 1, 1862)

"Mama, mama! Come quick!"

The urgency in Nora's voice brought Elizabeth from her bed at a run. Her daughter stood at the window of the front room, her hands cupped around her eyes, peering through a spot she'd rubbed clean on the thin, frosted glass.

Nora stepped back and pointed excitedly. "What is that?"

Elizabeth went to the window, looked through, and had to hold onto the frame to keep her knees from buckling. To the south, over what appeared to be Dayton, thick smoke was swirling into the sky, huge and black and spreading itself over the countryside. *What did it mean? There was obviously a fire, but how big was it? Where was it? And was it under control or burning wild in the bitter winter cold?*

"Mama, what is it?" Nora asked again.

"Something must be burning in Dayton, something big."

"That's a lot of smoke, Mama."

"Yes, it is," Elizabeth agreed absently as the black cloud grew and crept north toward their home.

Thankful the younger children were still in their beds, Nora and Elizabeth stood at the window watching the cloud grow bigger and bigger. It encompassed the countryside as far as they could see, plunging the brightening day back into darkness.

"I'm scared, Mama."

Elizabeth laid her arm around her daughter's shoulders, squeezed then kissed the top of her head. "I'm scared, too."

"I miss Papa. Where is he?"

Elizabeth frowned and shook her head. "I don't know, honey. It's dangerous for him to come home, you know that. It's only been a week since he was here for Christmas." Elizabeth hadn't quite figured out how to tell the children their papa was now a soldier. He'd been home so infrequently in the past months she'd decided it didn't make much difference. He'd be home when he was home and that was that.

Nora's lips quivered. "I know, Mama, I just wish he were here."

Elizabeth hugged her daughter again. "I wish he were here, too. We just have to believe God is watching over him and that he'll come to us when he can."

Nora bobbed her head up and down, trying to be brave, but Elizabeth knew she wanted to cry like the little girl she no longer was. Elizabeth wanted to cry, too, but she tamped down her weepiness and turned back to the window.

The day wore on and Elizabeth couldn't stop watching the smoke hanging above her home. Something was going to happen and, although she didn't know what, she was going to be ready. She stood with a pistol in one hand and the rifle in the corner close by. Walker's gun was in the bedroom, James having taken the two left by the other raiders.

Near mid-afternoon movement at the end of the lane drew Elizabeth's attention. Out of the smoke cloud she barely made out a woman with a small child on her hip and two other children trailing behind her. They came on toward the house, their faces black, each step stiff and painful-looking. Drawing closer Elizabeth's uncertainty turned to recognition. It was her friend Mary Case and her children. *Why was she here? Was her home what was burning in Dayton? Would one building make so much smoke? And if hers was the only house aflame, why was she traveling—on foot—ten miles to find shelter? Why weren't her neighbors helping her?* Elizabeth's mind twirled like a child's top. *The only reason she would leave Dayton afoot with three children was if she had no choice.*

Elizabeth leapt into action. "Nora, grab every blanket you can find and meet me at the door when I come back!"

"Mama?"

"No questions, Nora, just do as I say. Quickly now!"

While Elizabeth was giving her daughter directions, she was buttoning up her shoes, pulling her coat around her shoulders, and shoving on a hat and gloves. Prepared to face the cold, she grabbed extra shawls off the pins to the left of the door and ran outside. In moments she was hurrying down the lane as fast as she could go in the bitter cold through the eerie darkness toward her friend.

"Mary! Mary! I'm coming!"

Over the sound of her feet crunching on the icy drive she heard the children crying long before she reached them.

"Mary, what happened?" She skidded to a stop in front of her friend, threw an extra shawl over Mary and her youngest child, Asa, then huddled the other two children under another and hurried them up the lane as fast as they could go in their half-frozen states.

Elizabeth wanted to know what had happened. Mary had come from Dayton. Dayton was where James had gone to enlist. Elizabeth was busting to know, but knew she wouldn't get any answers from her friend right now. Giving up her care and that of her children to Elizabeth, Mary fell apart. She was crying as hard as any of the children as Elizabeth prodded them toward the house. Inside the door they were met by Nora, who immediately covered them with the blankets she had gathered.

"B...blessssss you, Elizabeth," Mary managed through chattering teeth when she sat down on the bench Elizabeth dragged in front of the fireplace, her back soaking in the heat behind her. "I th..thought we'd freeze before we g..got here," she managed before breaking down into sobs again. She pulled her children close and hugged them so hard Elizabeth was afraid she would crush them.

"Quiet now. It's all right." Elizabeth tried to sound reassuring, but the fact they were here told her something very bad had happened in Dayton. All she could think of was James.

"It'll never be all right again," Mary wailed, sniveling.

Elizabeth gathered the distraught woman into her arms and held her like a babe, cooing and trying to convince her everything was all right, until finally, Mary sat up, her eyes afire. "They burned everything, Elizabeth. Everything!"

Forcing herself to stay calm Elizabeth tried to grasp what her friend was telling her. "Who burned what?" She needed to find out what happened to her friend, but she also had to see if Mary knew anything about Phil Anderson's unit—and James.

"Everything! They burned the whole town!"

"All the shops, you mean?"

"No, Elizabeth! I...mean...everything! Every home, every store, every building, every barn, except that damn Mr.

Paul's house! The Yankee that did this! *He* went to Camp Johnson in Morristown and told them we were recruiting for the Confederacy in Dayton. So they came to stop it!"

Mary was rambling now, her children having been hurried to the back bedroom by Nora and Vera. Elizabeth let her friend talk, the only balm she had right now, even though she wanted to ask if any of the Confederate units were, in fact, there. If James was there.

"They came in the middle of the night, Elizabeth."

"Who came?" Elizabeth dared ask, scared to death what the answer would be.

"Colonel Anthony and that damned Kansas 7th Cavalry, that's who! All high and mighty they were, ordering us women and children around, calling for our men to come out and stop hiding behind our skirts." She sniffed and Elizabeth ran for a handkerchief. Mary hiccupped and Elizabeth got her a drink of water to help her friend calm down.

"They called everyone out and went through our homes looking for our men. Looking for the troops Mr. Paul *said* were there." Her face was a mask of rage. Tears streamed down her cheeks as she recalled the terror of the previous night. "Our troops were already gone, having lit out as quickly as they got word they had been betrayed."

"So none of the Dayton units were there?" Elizabeth managed, her throat so tight her voice cracked. *James wasn't there! But was he safe?*

Mary shook her head. "No, they were long gone by the time the Yankees reached us." Her lip quivered and she raised her chin. "But not *all* the men were gone. They found three—three of my neighbors—and dragged them to the outskirts of town where they...where they...."

"Where they what?" Elizabeth dared ask.

"Where they shot them in plain view of everyone in town!" she cried out like a wounded animal. She fell into Elizabeth's outstretched arms and sobbed deep, wrenching sobs. Elizabeth tried to calm her friend, but Mary jerked upright and began again.

"They gave us only a few minutes to gather what we could and leave. Some homes they broke windows and smashed walls before they put them to the torch. They threw our belongings into the snow." She took a deep, shuddering breath. "Old Mrs. Gaines was bedridden, so the men carried her out on her feather bed and set her in the cold before they set her house afire! How could they do such a thing, Elizabeth? How could they be so cruel?" she asked no one before she fell back into Elizabeth's arms.

Elizabeth shook her head, unable to form any words. She, too, was at a loss as to how men could be so cruel.

Mary's head jerked up. "Standing outside the house I was born in, the house my children were born in, I watched it go up in flames, along with every other home in Dayton—save the one." Her eyes pinched with rage and hatred before she continued. "Everything was afire, except Mr. Paul's place, which sat there amidst it all without so much as a new scratch, in spite of the destruction around it. We were warm in the midst of the fires for a spell, downright hot, but as the night wore on and the flames died, the cold crept back into our bones and it was time to go. I grabbed my children and high-tailed it out of there as fast as we could. I wasn't going to wait around and freeze to death trying to figure out what to do. I had no idea where I was going until I landed in front of your house, Elizabeth. I knew you'd take us in. I knew you wouldn't let us stay out in the cold." She broke off into sobs again. Elizabeth led her friend into her bedroom, pulled off her shoes and helped her into bed.

"Everything's gone, Elizabeth. Everything. We have no home, no crops, no livestock. Nothing," she mumbled over and over.

Elizabeth touched her friend's brow. "Mary, everything isn't gone. Your husband wasn't there, so he wasn't killed with the others. You came away with your life and that of your children, that's worth more than any old house or furnishings you might have."

Mary stared gape-mouthed at Elizabeth for several moments before she started screaming. "My children! Where are my children! Bring them to me! I want my children!"

Nora hurried into the room with Asa on her hip. William and Rose ran in behind them, Elizabeth's children at their heels.

Mary sat in the middle of the bed, arms raised,

beckoning them come to her. They climbed onto the bed and she gathered them close, breathing in their scents and kissing their faces and heads.

Mary looked up and the gratitude Elizabeth saw on her friend's face put a lump in her throat. "Thank you, Elizabeth. Thank you for reminding me I lost *things*. Things can be replaced, my children cannot. Thank you," she said over and over before she lay down with her family, murmuring how lucky she was, and telling them how much she loved them before silence descended and they all drifted to sleep, the children wrapped in the protection of their mother's loving arms.

Chapter Nine
(March 15, 1862)

"Thank the Lord it's warming up. I thought spring would never come." Mary's face was red from exertion. She and Elizabeth were butchering one of the two remaining pigs. They'd killed the smallest of the three shortly after Mary's arrival and stretched the meat to last over two months. Feeding nine people took a lot of food, even when four of the children barely ate enough to count. They made the second turkey James brought at Christmas last to mid-January, so there had been a little variety for a short while, at least. As the cornmeal dwindled, pork, milk and eggs became their main staples.

"And now we've got to worry about the spring planting," Elizabeth said. With the weather warming it was time to think about the job Elizabeth dreaded with every fiber of her being, but if they wanted food, it was an undertaking she couldn't shirk. She just prayed *they* would reap the bounty of their work and not raiders. "If we're going to have any produce from the garden, a corn crop and some oats, we've got to get it done. I've got carrots, beets, onions, sweet potatoes, green beans, and tomato seeds in the root cellar. There's even a little rhubarb for a pie or two—if it doesn't all get stolen," she added on a sigh. "There are a couple small sacks of seed corn and wheat seed, too, from what the children and I scavenged in the fields after the raiders took their fill last year. James and I even managed to fertilize a couple small sections last fall. Now all we have to do is till it."

"I'll do whatever needs to be done, Elizabeth. We wouldn't be alive if it weren't for you."

Elizabeth smiled. It had been a long two and a half months since Mary's arrival. Nine people in her home made for close quarters, arguments, hard feelings and hard words. Mary and her children took over Steven's loft, but it was small so they stayed up there only to sleep. Whenever everyone was downstairs they fell over each other, got on each other's nerves, and argued. The smaller children were the worst. They didn't understand what was happening or why their world was being disrupted. What few toys Joseph and Sally had, they didn't want to share after the first few days and, eventually, they fought over them constantly with

Mary's children. Unable to go outside in the bitter cold to relieve some of the tension and release some energy, they were forced to endure. Nerves were stretched to the limit and snapped every day.

"Thankfully we've got Hilda and Poppyseed to pull the plow and till the dirt," Elizabeth said, getting back to what needed to be done. "Otherwise, I don't know what we'd do. Busting dirt by hand with a pitchfork and hoe is the least enticing, most backbreaking chore I can imagine."

"But we'd do it if we had to, Elizabeth. Whatever needs to be done, we'll do to make sure we have food."

Elizabeth hugged her friend. They'd become close during their forced time together, despite the arguments, and Elizabeth was happy for the adult company—and the help.

"We'll have fresh pork for dinner, Mary. Let's pick out the best cut and hang the rest. We'll salt it and put it up tomorrow or the next day after it's all drained."

"That sounds fine to me. I'm exhausted," Mary agreed.

That evening the extended family gathered at the table, enjoying the pork roast Elizabeth and Mary had cut out, when Elizabeth stopped in mid-conversation. Her hands started to shake and her heart thundered, echoing what she heard. Horses were coming toward the house!

Mary's fork halted in mid-air when she heard them, too. Nora and Vera's mouths snapped shut like marionette puppets. The younger children, arguing as usual, kept on.

"Children! Enough. You will be silent. Right now!" Elizabeth shouted.

Mary opened her mouth the protest Elizabeth's harshness, then realization washed over her and she, too, shouted the children into silence.

"Nora, Vera, take the children upstairs." Elizabeth ordered.

"Upstairs, Mama?"

"You'll be safer there."

Mary's face was ashen. Her mouth moved, but nothing came out.

"Mary!"

Mary closed her eyes and shook her head. "Yes, they'll be safer upstairs. Please girls, take everyone up."

As Nora and Vera helped the smaller children up the stairs, Elizabeth ran to the window and peeked out. She had trouble breathing when she spotted five men with beards and long hair tying off their horses to the hitching post. Each man had several pistols strapped across his chest and a rifle in the scabbard of his saddle.

"What should we do?" Mary was shaking and tears brimmed in her eyes.

"Do whatever they ask. Run to the bedroom and grab the pistol beside the bed and put it on the dresser within easy reach. I'll greet our *guests*." Elizabeth swallowed hard.

The men knocked, giving Elizabeth hope they still had some civility in them. She sucked in a breath for courage and opened the door. "Yes, gentlemen, may I help you?"

The first man stepped inside, the others close behind. Each man had a pistol drawn and searched the inside of the room with their eyes before stomping to the table. "You can feed us, ma'am." Their eyes landed on what remained of the meal and glowed with hunger. The way they licked their lips, Elizabeth knew it had been a while since they'd eaten.

"There isn't much left, but whatever there is you're welcome to," she said amenably. Elizabeth suddenly remembered the meat hanging in the shed and her knees almost buckled. *If they went looking for more....*

"Where's your man?" the apparent leader asked, settling on the bench, tearing off a chunk of meat, the others grabbing what they could before it was gone.

Elizabeth's body sang with warning. *Who were these men? Were they Jayhawkers looking for a reason to take what they wanted then destroy her home? Were they southern men, riding to enlist? Or were they men who came to take whatever there was and leave them with nothing—regardless of which side they were on?*

"Where's your man?" he asked again when Elizabeth didn't answer quickly enough.

"He's gone."

"Where?"

Elizabeth didn't know how to answer. The wrong answer and these men might well take revenge on them. She looked up, her heart pounding, and saw seven pairs of eyes staring down at her. At that moment little Asa started to squall. All five men jumped up, guns at the ready and pointed at the loft. "Who's there?"

"It's just children!" Elizabeth screamed, raising her hands to calm them. "Just children. Please, don't hurt them. They're frightened."

"Don't you touch them!" All eyes snapped to Mary, standing in the door of the bedroom holding a pistol on the men. "Don't you dare touch my children!" she shrieked. Her face was no longer parchment white, but flame red. Her lips were drawn so tight they were almost invisible.

"Mary, calm yourself," Elizabeth said as unruffled as she could from across the room.

"I've already had my house burned down around me!" the distraught woman shouted. "I will not have my children harmed further. Now you leave them be!" she yelled at the men standing gape-mouthed around the table.

Elizabeth wanted to run behind Mary and grab the rifle, but she waited. So far the men hadn't threatened any harm and she didn't want to make things worse by pointing another gun at them—but she would if the situation changed.

The men lowered their guns and the leader said, "We don't mean to harm you or your children, ma'am." He cocked his head. "Who burned your house down, ma'am?" His voice was tight but, it seemed to Elizabeth, it was anger at whoever had done the burning and not Mary.

"That damnable Colonel Anthony, that's who!" Mary shrieked, eyes popping. "He burned our whole town to the ground and I will *not* allow my children to become homeless again!" She raised the drooping pistol.

"Anthony," the man growled. "You're from Dayton."

"I am. What does it matter to you?" she challenged, her chin raising a notch.

The man's lips rolled and his head cocked. "Ma'am, we're outriders, together to keep those Kansans from doing what they did to Dayton and Osceola and any number of other Missoura towns again. We're southern boys and we mean you no harm."

"Prove it," Mary challenged. "Put your guns on the table."

The other four men looked at the leader. The man nodded and dropped his gun on the table. Four more followed immediately. "We just need some food in our bellies, some supplies to take with us and we'll be gone." He stepped toward Mary and she waved the gun. "Ma'am, we put our guns down, now you put yours down and no one will get hurt."

Mary eyed them for several moments before she lowered the pistol. "I'll lower my gun, but I believe I'll keep it." She raised her chin again.

"Please, take whatever you want. Just don't hurt anyone," Elizabeth said. "They're innocent children."

The man's head jerked downward. "Yes, ma'am."

Elizabeth hurried to the cupboard and pulled out five plates. Quickly the men filled them with what little was left on the meat platter, stuffing their mouths as fast as they could chew and swallow.

"I'm sorry there isn't more," Elizabeth said. We've been visited more than once by raiders who took what they wanted. They've left us very little."

The men ate in silence.

Mary stood in the bedroom doorway, gun still in hand, eyeing the men suspiciously until the leader finally stood up. "Ma'am, I told you we won't harm you or your children. You really should put the gun away before someone gets hurt."

"The only one who'll get hurt is you or one of your men if you try to hurt any of us. I told you I'll keep it, thank you."

The men chuckled and spoke between themselves before the leader asked, "Where did you say your men were?"

Warning bells went off in Elizabeth's head. *Were they trying to determine where their husbands were for justification to burn the house down, while pretending to be good, southern boys out to protect the women and children of men off fighting for the Cause?*

Mary answered before Elizabeth could decide. "Both our husbands are fighting for the Confederacy," she blurted, her back straightening with the statement.

Elizabeth closed her eyes and hung her head, uncertain if

Mary had saved them or given these men the reason they needed to burn the house down.

"Who they fightin' with, ma'am?" the leader asked Elizabeth.

She swallowed hard before she said, "My husband is with the Dayton Guards. They just made it out of town before Anthony and his men burned it."

"And you, ma'am?" he asked Mary.

"My husband's with Governor Jackson." Her face beamed with pride when her mouth snapped shut.

The men nodded then grew solemn when they reached for more food and it was gone.

The leader stood up, leaving the pistol on the table in, what Elizabeth guessed was, a show of good faith. "Ladies, we're in desperate need of food to take with us, and whatever horses you might have."

They would take Poppyseed! Elizabeth's mind exploded.

"We've told you we won't hurt anyone, but we are in need of supplies and hope you'll help us out willingly."

"I told you, sir, we have very little." Elizabeth thought her heart would pound right out of her chest.

He turned to the man sitting at the end of the table. "Harve, go take a look. See what there is in the barn and in the smoke shed. See if there's anything in the corn crib and root cellar, too." As an afterthought he added, "And check the tree lines around the barn and property."

Mary swung the pistol, but the man was already out the door.

Elizabeth thought she was going to throw up. They were going to find her mare! They'd take the pig she and Mary butchered earlier today, too. And anything else they wanted! "Please, don't take everything. Leave us *something*." Elizabeth heard herself begging, but she couldn't help it. Their lives—all their lives—were at stake. "We have little and many mouths to feed."

"Ma'am, here are your choices. You can willingly give us what we need, or we'll take it. You're two women against five men. You'll be helping the Cause by helping us. If we were Kansans, we wouldn't be askin'. We'd just take and, most likely, we wouldn't even leave a house around your heads when we left. When we do leave it'll be with what forage we take, but no one will be harmed and your house will still stand. You should consider yourself lucky."

Tears welled in Elizabeth's eyes. *Lucky!* She was going to lose her mare and the last of their food and there was nothing she could do about it. *How could that be considered lucky?* she wanted to rail. She waited in bitter silence until Harve came back inside.

"Found two horses. One's a prime piece of horseflesh, but the other is old and blind. Found a hog draining in the shed, too. There're a few chickens, a milk cow, one more pig in the barn and a goat." The man snorted. "Crazy goat chased me!"

Wish he'd run you right off this property! Elizabeth couldn't help think with a slight grin.

"Take the good mare and leave the old one," jerked her back to reality. "Take the pig and goat and half of what's in the shed. Leave the chickens and the milking cow." The leader paused a moment, looked around the room at the women and children fearfully awaiting his final declaration, waved his hand in a circle in the air then shouted, "Gather it up, boys and let's get outta here!"

Before Elizabeth could react, the men had their guns in their hands and were out the door to do what they'd been bidden. A half hour later they left with Poppyseed tied to the leader's saddle, the last pig and Walter trailing behind two other riders, fighting the ropes that dragged them, half the butchered pig tied across Poppyseed's back, and a promise they'd be "around" to look after Elizabeth and her family .

Tears streaming down her face, Elizabeth watched them go, hoping they'd 'look after' her and her family her from very far away.

Hours later and finally calmed down, the families settled in for the night. Elizabeth tossed and turned and when she did drift to sleep, it was to be chased by men with long, flowing beards and hair.

They rose the next morning as usual, gathered the few eggs the hens laid, cut a small chunk of meat from what had been left, and prepared a meager breakfast. No one spoke except, as usual, the children who began fighting as soon as their eyes opened. Elizabeth prayed for patience and separated them until the meal was ready. There'd only been four eggs this morning instead of the occasional five or six, but the meat, once fried, filled some of the void.

In the quiet of the waning meal, Elizabeth's head snapped up when she heard a gunshot not far away. She waited in silence for more. It wasn't long before another shot echoed in the distance, then another until it sounded like a gun fight not far away.

Elizabeth took quick breaths to stay calm and she saw Mary doing the same, her face ashen with fear.

"Where are they?" Mary asked.

Elizabeth shook her head. "I can't tell. Could be a mile away, could be closer." She listened as the firing continued. "Sounds like it might be coming from the Rikker place." She shook her head. "I can't tell."

They sat for fifteen minutes, listening to the gunfire pop in the distance until it slowed and finally stopped. For another fifteen minutes they sat in silence waiting for more, but all remained still.

Elizabeth finally stood up. "I believe it's over. There's nothing to be done about it and we've got chores. Girls, clear the table and do the dishes, but you and the children stay inside. Do not go out for anything, you hear?"

"Yes, Mama," Nora and Vera answered at the same time, their faces showing relief their mother hadn't asked them to do any of their outdoor chores.

"Mary, you and I have a pig to salt—what's left of it anyway—and a cow to milk. We might as well be about it." Elizabeth slapped her hands and everyone scurried to do as told. *They had things to do and a skirmish somewhere in the distance wasn't going to keep them from it.*

The day proceeded mostly in silence with Mary and Elizabeth looking over their shoulders to see if anyone was about. Although chores had to be done, too much had happened to pretend everything was normal. Nothing was normal and wouldn't be again until the war was over.

After a dinner of more pork they read for an hour before everyone retired to bed, exhausted.

Following another almost sleepless night, the next morning began the same with the gathering of eggs, milking the cow and a sparse breakfast. The sun was shining and the temperature rising so Elizabeth shooed the children outside, hoping it would help their dispositions. She and Mary planned to start plowing today. Although Hilda was blind, she could still pull a plow as long as she was led. It would take a couple weeks to get it all tilled and by the time they were done it would be time to plant. She hoped.

Hilda was standing outside the barn, Elizabeth and Mary positioning the plow harness around her neck and withers when they saw it. Smoke. Lots of it.

Mary stood stock still and stared, open-mouthed, at the swirling black cloud rising in the sky not far away.

Elizabeth stood like a post watching the cloud spread as it rose higher and higher in the clear sky. *Where was it coming from? Mr. Rikker's place, it seemed. Just like the shots yesterday.*

"What's there?" Mary managed.

"I think it's old Mr. Rikker's place. I don't know if he's still there or if he lit out. I haven't been away from here in so long I have no idea what's going on anywhere other than right here. James has been the only way I've found out what goes on in the war. If I were to guess, I'd say it's the Rikker place, though."

No shots had been fired. Today there was only smoke. Not smoke like Elizabeth had seen or Mary described after Dayton, more like the smoke coming from a lone house burning to the ground.

Chapter Ten
(March 18, 1862)

"You *can't* go! Where will you go? What about the children?" Elizabeth asked, exasperated.

Mary shook her head. "After what's happened in the past few days I can't stay, Elizabeth. Those outriders made me realize it's not safe here any longer. And after thinking all night about whatever happened at Mr. Rikkers' place yesterday and the day before. It's just not safe. Those men who came here could have easily taken everything and burned your house down around us, like Anthony and his men did to Dayton and my home. I can't risk my children's lives by staying here." She paused and took Elizabeth's hands in hers. "We're going and you should come with us." Mary released Elizabeth's hands and stood firm at the front door, her children huddled around her.

Elizabeth's head was spinning. *Go? Leave her home and everything she and James had built? Go where?*

"Where will you go? Your family is all the way in South Carolina. How will you get there?" Elizabeth asked.

Mary shook her head. "I'll get there some day, perhaps. All I'm worried about is today and my children." She laid her palm on Elizabeth's cheek. "You taught me that." Mary smiled, as much as anyone could smile these days and continued. "I'm going to Harrisonville."

"Harrisonville!" Elizabeth exploded. "Why would you go there? It's a Union fort now. You'll be a pariah, chastised. You can't."

Mary rolled her lips. "I've made up my mind, Elizabeth. I'm going to town and give my loyalty pledge so we'll be given shelter. It's the only thing I can do to keep my children safe."

"But Bob is off fighting for the Confederacy. Don't you think they'll know that?"

Mary closed her eyes and sighed. "I'm sure they will, but what other choice do I have? We can't walk to South Carolina. And I'm too scared to stay here." She looked down at her children and tears formed in her eyes. She dashed them away. "It's what I have to do, Elizabeth." She raised her chin. "I can't thank you enough for what you've done for us, but it's time to go. And I still think you should go with us."

"How are you going to get there? It's fifteen miles! Do you intend to walk?" Elizabeth couldn't believe her friend was planning to walk to Harrisonville. To put her children in harm's way of both the weather *and* raiders who roamed the countryside unmolested. Although it was mid-March the weather this time of year was unpredictable. It could be warm one day and snowing the next. And the thought of running into raiders made Elizabeth's skin crawl.

"I was hoping you might help me." Mary's gentle statement snapped Elizabeth back to the situation at hand.

"What do you want?"

"Blankets, in case it does get cold again and a wagon to carry the children, perhaps?"

She paused and it seemed to Elizabeth her friend was deciding whether she should ask for something else.

"Hilda?" Mary blurted.

"Hilda!" Elizabeth couldn't believe her ears. *The blankets and wagon she would give her friend happily, but Hilda? Anger tore through her and Elizabeth was suddenly hopping mad. Mary had no right to ask such a thing! She knew Hilda was all Elizabeth had left to plow the fields for what little crops they might grow. Mary was the one who wanted to walk away—so walk she would!*

"No. You cannot have Hilda. She's all I've got to keep this farm going. She's the only thing I have to get these fields tilled. You're the one who wants to leave, but you're not leaving with Hilda. I'll give you the children's wagon to carry Asa and Rose. William is old enough to walk, but you cannot have Hilda." Anger guided her harsh words, but again, Elizabeth couldn't believe her friend had asked such a thing.

"I understand." Mary's voice was tight, controlling her own disappoint and, perhaps, anger?

Elizabeth still didn't think it was the right thing for Mary to leave, but she didn't want to send her friend off with harsh words, regardless of her outlandish request. "I'm sorry, Mary. I wish I could give you what you ask, but I just can't."

"I understand, but I had to ask, for the sake of my children." Mary shrugged then smiled.

"What about raiders?" Elizabeth reminded her friend of the most dangerous obstacle in her path to Harrisonville. "Have you thought about what might happen if you run into any? Jayhawkers are all over the place. They were probably involved in whatever happened yesterday and the day before at Mr. Rikker's place. Have you thought about that?" Elizabeth had to keep trying to dissuade Mary from leaving, she couldn't let her leave without doing everything she could to change her mind. *It was just too dangerous for a woman and three small children on the road to Harrisonville!*

Mary frowned. "I have thought about it, but we'll be safer in town than here."

"But you have to *get* to town, Mary."

Mary sucked in a deep breath. "I'm a lone woman with three small children. I have to believe there are still virtues left among the men running around the countryside—despite this war. No one will harm us. There's no cause. We have nothing to take and can hurt no one."

"They could hurt you out of sheer cussedness!" Elizabeth spat. "It doesn't matter what side you're on. They'll take what you've got and leave you on the side of the road with absolutely nothing!" Elizabeth had to take a deep breath to calm down. *James had told her too many stories of murder and thievery on the Harrisonville-Dayton Road and she didn't want her friend and children to become one of those stories!*

"All I'll have is a broken down child's wagon and three young children. What's to take?"

"Your virtue?" Elizabeth hissed through gritted teeth.

Mary's lip trembled and she remained silent, pondering Elizabeth's statement. "No!" she burst out. "No! I won't believe it could come to that. Not with my children right there. I cannot believe all morals have fled. I won't, Elizabeth. I just won't."

"I pray you're right," Elizabeth said, resigned to the fact Mary had made up her mind. She hugged her friend again, opened the door and stepped onto the porch. "Come on then. Let's get you ready to go since I can't seem to change your mind."

A half hour later Elizabeth waved goodbye to the Case family. They headed down the lane toward uncertainty with

Mary in front pulling a small wagon carrying two children huddled in the back and William walking beside her.

Elizabeth and her children watched them go, Sally and Joseph sniveling now that their playmates were leaving, Elizabeth wondering whether Mary had gone mad in the aftermath of everything that had happened. *Or was she the strongest, bravest woman she'd ever met?*

Chapter Eleven
(May, 1862)

The backbreaking work of planting was done. Between Elizabeth, Nora, Vera, and of course, poor old Hilda, they managed to get enough corn, oats, radishes, cabbage and potatoes planted to fill their needs—if it wasn't all plundered. Without Hilda Elizabeth knew they'd never have completed their task and was thankful every day for the old mare, and the fact she was already blind and useless to anyone intent on stealing her. While Nora led the old mare, Elizabeth guided the plow and broke the soil, and Vera took care of Joseph and Sally. Once the weather warmed enough, Nora and Vera took turns helping Elizabeth with the planting and watching the children. Their hands were raw and their skin burned, but they'd have food to put in their bellies when the crops came in. Now all they needed was rain and to be left alone.

It seemed to Elizabeth that things had quieted down. There'd been no sounds of shooting in the distance for weeks, she'd seen no smoke and prayed, perhaps, the war was waning. She had no way of knowing what was happening outside their little world, never venturing farther than the fields and tree line—not even to Austin.

Late in the afternoon, taking a break from the daily chores, Nora read to the children in the shade on the porch. Elizabeth was doing some much needed mending in the front room, listening to Nora through the open window. She was trying to stretch what little clothes they had. Joseph was busting out of everything. All she had were girls' clothes for him to grow into, so Elizabeth was altering what she had to make it acceptable for a boy to wear. At three, he was sprouting like weeds in a garden and it was all she could do to keep ahead of him. Sally had Vera's clothes to grow into, and Vera wore Nora's hand-me-downs. Nora was able to wear some of Elizabeth's dresses, dresses altered to her petite size, but there were few between the two of them that weren't growing worn and shabby. The aprons the girls had been so proud of after their father's return last Christmas had become patches for the fraying material on everything they wore.

"Mama?"

The fear in Nora's tone brought Elizabeth to her feet. She dropped her mending on the floor and hurried outside to stand beside her oldest daughter.

"Who is it?" Nora asked, pointing to a man coming up the lane toward the house.

Elizabeth shaded her eyes and stared at the lone man. There was a familiarity about him. If he was a raider, why was he alone? *Who...?* Her jaw dropped and she stepped to the top of the stairs. In a heartbeat she was running to him.

"James!" she laughed and cried at the same time, slamming full force into his arms. "Oh, James, you're home!"

He squeezed her so hard she squeaked. Their mouths met in a kiss that took her breath away and he held her until they realized the children were gathered around, hugging him, too.

"Papa, papa!" they shouted, grabbing at him for their turn.

He swept Joseph into his arms. "Look at you! You're so tall!" He twirled the boy in a circle making the child giggle, a welcome sound, having been gone from their lives for so long. "And Sally." He put Joseph down, lifted his youngest daughter and squeezed until she squeaked, too.

"Papa!" Vera threw herself into her father's arms as soon as he set Sally on her feet and buried her face in his chest. Nora waited like the adult she almost was until everyone else said hello before she hurried into her father's embrace, tears streaming down her cheeks.

The greetings complete, James hurried his family out of the open and into the house. He visited with, hugged and kissed the children for over an hour before he pulled Elizabeth next to him on the bench and told her of his comings and goings in the last months, and Elizabeth told him about Mary and all they'd endured since his last visit.

"We heard they destroyed Dayton after we left. Most of the men in my unit were from there and had families and homes there. A lot went back, but it was too late."

"We saw the smoke from here. It was horrible. We had no idea what happened. Then Mary showed up. I couldn't believe they burned the entire town to the ground. Put families, children and old people out in the snow!"

"It's what they do, Liz. They take what they want then burn whatever is left." He looked around, assessing the house and children. "How have you all fared?"

Elizabeth cocked her head. "The best we can." She told him about the outriders' visit and how they took Poppyseed, part of the meat and the last pig, but had the decency to leave them some of the meat and seeds they'd found.

"They called themselves outriders, eh?" James asked with a smile.

"Yes, why?"

"They're more commonly being called bushwhackers, and they're all that stands between the farmers in these parts and the Kansans."

"What about the Home Guard?"

"They've been disbanded. Most of the men re-enlisted with the Missoura State Militia, though, and are still in these parts."

"And the Jayhawkers and the Seventh?"

"They're still raiding, but aren't sanctioned by the Union Army. They plunder and burn wherever they want. They've murdered and destroyed so indiscriminately they've driven many loyal Unionists into the arms of the Confederacy." He shook his head. "They've burned many a family into destitution — regardless of which side they were on."

Elizabeth swallowed, trying to take in everything he was telling her. "What about Steven? Have you heard anything from him?" She was hopeful for some word about her oldest child, having heard nothing since he left them.

James smiled the smile of a man proud of his son. "He's with D Company, 8th Battalion of the Missoura Infantry. We've been able to communicate by courier between our regiments and he seems to be doing well. The army, apparently, suits him," he said with a cock of his head and raised eyebrows. "Who would have thought?"

Elizabeth sighed heavily, relieved and happy to know her son was safe, so far, and doing well. "And what about you? You're thin as a rail post." She squeezed his shoulder. "Don't they feed you? Isn't that why you enlisted, so you'd be housed and fed?" She shook her head and pursed her lips.

"Things are tough, Liz. We mostly forage for what we get, from people just like us. It pains me mightily, but it's all we can do to keep from starving. Last winter we took hundreds of fence rails for the fires." He waved his hand outside. "Looks like we've lost a few here." He sighed. "Both Yankee *and* Confederate forage teams took thousands. Families like ours give what they can, or it's just taken, but there's not much after they've been raided so many times by both sides. But we've got no other option. We have to use what's available whenever and wherever we can find it."

Elizabeth was beginning to understand more of what was happening. Both armies were stripping the countryside of food, horses, mules, and anything else that could be supplied by local farmers, including wood and fencing. It didn't matter what side you were on. If you were visited by raiders who fought against what you believed, they took without a care and left you with nothing. And if you were visited by men from your own cause, you gave what you could to help the Cause, whether you had it to give or not. Oftentimes, it didn't matter which side you or they were on, they took whatever they needed leaving many a family destitute and homeless. Elizabeth shook her head, not wanting to think about it anymore. James was home and she was going to enjoy every minute he was here, for however long that was.

"How long before you have to leave?" she asked, dreading his response.

He took her hand. "I requested a furlough, but it was denied. I don't know if or even when they might allow me to come home for any length of time. Furloughs aren't very high on their priority list, Liz."

"So how long do you have now?"

"Till tonight."

Her shoulders slumped with disappointment, but she didn't voice it.

"The only way I could see you was to come ahead of my unit and rejoin them as they pass through here later." He frowned. "I had to get special permission, but I *had* to. We were going to be so close I had to make sure you and the children were all right."

"We're surviving, James, just like you. We even got some crops planted. We put in a garden and managed some corn and wheat seeds that we can plant later from what we scavenged out of the fields last year. As long as we can keep what we've planted, we'll be fine. We'll have vegetables and corn and wheat for bread. As long as the hens keep laying and the milk cow keeps giving milk, we'll be in fine shape." She put on a brave face, hoping her husband would believe they were surviving well.

He smiled, a smile that said he knew they were anything but fine, but appreciated that she tried to make it seem so.

She touched his cheek. "I've missed you so much."

He covered her hand with his dirty, calloused one. "I've missed you, too."

Having forgotten them in their intimate moment, they glanced up and noticed the children sitting on the bench listening to every word.

Nora jumped up. "Come children. Let's play in our room."

"I don't want to play! I want to stay with Papa!" Sally, sitting across from her parents shouted.

Joseph's lip puffed out and his arms slapped across his chest. "I want to stay with Papa, too!"

"So do Vera and I, but Mama and Papa need some time alone—to talk," Nora was quick to add.

"About what!" Sally shouted. Almost five years old now, she'd become quite vocal about her feelings. "I want Papa to stay with me!" Her lip pooched out like her brother's and the two sat side-by-side, legs dangling from the bench with their arms across their chests.

Elizabeth sat in rapt silence as her oldest daughter smoothly took charge. "I would rather go outside to play, but it's raining, so we must go to our room. Only for a little while so Mama and Papa can talk."

"No!" Sally swung her head back and forth, her curls bouncing around her face, her legs swaying back and forth. "I want to stay here with Papa!"

"I don't want to play!" Joseph shouted. "I want Papa, too!"

Nora sighed and thought a moment before her eyes brightened and she went to each of the children and whispered in their ear. Within seconds all three younger siblings bounded into their room.

"What did you say?"

Nora smirked. "It's my secret Mama, and my gift."

Elizabeth opened her mouth to speak, but found she couldn't think of a thing to say. *What would she ask? When did you become a woman? How do you know these things?* She decided it was something she really didn't want to know and watched Nora walk to the bedroom where the other children waited, a smile of knowing on her face. She pulled the door partway closed then stopped. "I give you thirty minutes," she said before the door closed with a gentle thump.

Elizabeth stared at the door, again wondering when her daughter had become a woman, with a woman's knowledge—and wondering what in the world she'd done to bribe the other children so easily.

James sat in stunned silence beside her, his mouth working, but nothing coming out. Their befuddlement lasted only a few moments more before James shook his head, jumped up and offered his hand to Elizabeth the way a king would to a lady. He bowed deeply. She laid her palm into his, looked into his eyes, and was lost in a love she prayed would last her lifetime.

Mischief twinkled in his eyes before he yanked Elizabeth to her feet and hurried her to the bedroom like a new bride. The door locked behind them and in the precious thirty minutes their daughter had given them, they proceeded to show just how much they'd missed each other.

Chapter Twelve
(Later That Night)

Elizabeth and James stood hidden in the shadows, but Elizabeth was still afraid someone might spot her Confederate soldier husband. They'd said goodbye a dozen times already, but each time he stepped out the door she pulled him back, unwilling to let him go.

"How long before you return?" she asked for the tenth time.

He smiled a patient smile, one she knew he was hard-pressed to give. He had to be on his way. His unit was waiting for him just beyond the trees. He'd been watching and listening for the appropriate signal and it had come twenty minutes ago. They were waiting and it was time for him to go.

Elizabeth was trying not to cry, but it wasn't working. *She wanted her husband with her and the children!* She took a deep breath for strength. "I'm sorry for asking again and again. I know you have no idea when you'll be back." She slapped her hand against her leg. "I'm just blurting whatever comes to my mind to keep you from going. I don't want you to go." Her voice cracked on the words.

He opened his arms and she fell into his chest sobbing. She cried for a minute or two before she jerked away and viciously wiped her wet cheeks. "Is this any way for me to act? A grown woman, married these many years already, sending you off with tears and acting like a schoolgirl! I'm sorry, James. I don't mean to be difficult. I'll do better the next time you come home." She stammered to a stop and prayed there *would be* a next time. She blinked her eyes, swiped at her nose and realized what a fright she must look. She moaned. "And I'm sending you away looking like an old washer woman!"

James cupped her chin in his hand and gently raised it, forcing her tear-filled eyes to meet his. "Elizabeth Miers, you're the most beautiful woman in the world...even now."

"What?" She blinked, sputtered and stumbled backward, never having heard such words from her husband before, not even when they were courting, and she was completely unbalanced. She smoothed her hair and tried to dry her cheeks.

As she did, a giggle bubbled up. "My eyes are puffed out like a prairie chicken's chest, my nose is running like a pump with a broken handle, and I'm crying like an infant, yet you say I'm beautiful?" She cocked her head, a wide grin across her face. "What are you about James Miers?"

His smile was wicked and there was a devilish glint in his eyes. "I'm about telling you you're beautiful because I know those tears, those puffy eyes, and that runny nose are for me. They're a testament to how much you still love me after all these years."

Elizabeth fell back into his arms and cried until her throat hurt and she could barely see. She finally drew up her back, dried her eyes, and blew her nose on a handkerchief she'd been crushing in her hand. "I'll be good from now on, I promise." She smoothed her dress and hair again.

"And *I* promise to be back as soon as I can."

"I'll hold you to it," she whispered, stepping on her toes to capture his lips one last time. "Now go before I change my mind, tie you to a chair and keep you prisoner from both armies!" She tried to grin, but failed when she saw the reluctance in his eyes as he turned to leave. Halfway through the door he turned back and lifted his hand to her. She reached out, able only to curl her fingers around the tips of his. Their eyes met and held until his gentle tug told her it was time to let go. Their fingers slid apart, his eyes still locked on hers, when he stepped onto the porch.

"I love you, Elizabeth Miers," the brave soldier said with tears in his eyes.

"I love you, too, James Miers," she answered, rolling her simple gold wedding band between her fingers.

"I'll be back as soon as I can." Then he was gone.

Would she see him again? If so, how long would it take? A month? Two? Ten? She poked her head out the door in time to see him melt around the corner of the house before she ran to the bedroom to watch him as far as she could. He crept along the wall below her, hidden in the shadows and close enough to touch before he hurried toward the barn like the devil was after him. Once he made the barn he'd hurry out the back to the newly planted corn field, what there was of it, keeping low in the little cover it provided, before disappearing into the trees.

Elizabeth watched until she couldn't watch anymore, hoping for some sign he was safe, knowing there'd be none, waiting anyway. She was thankful the children were all abed, although it had been much against their wishes. They'd sobbed themselves to sleep after their Papa had said his first three goodbyes, become stern and told them it was time for sleep. He promised he'd see them soon and shooed them off to bed with tears dripping from their cheeks and chins, Joseph and Sally, clutching the horse and doll he'd made for them last Christmas like lifelines.

Standing sentinel her grief became so much she broke down into sobs. Her knees gave way and she slid to the floor. She pulled her knees to her chest, wrapped her arms around them, and cried until she couldn't cry another tear.

Nora found her there an hour later. "Come on, Mama. It's time for bed." She pulled the linens back, helped her mother to her feet then guided Elizabeth to the bed where she fell into it heavily.

"Thank you, Nora. I don't know what I'd do without you." Their tear-filled eyes met.

"I hope we never have to find out."

Pounding at the front door brought Elizabeth awake like she'd been shot out of her squirrel rifle! Unwilling to make the mistakes she'd made before, she took the moment to throw on her wrapper and grabbed the pistol and rifle before running into the front room. The children met her outside her bedroom door, shaking with fear, their eyes wide.

We've already done this! Elizabeth wanted to scream. *I'm only a woman with her children here. Leave us alone!* She wanted to rail at the men threatening her home and children. But she couldn't. She had to face what was in front of her and do whatever was necessary to protect them.

"Who's out there?" she cried, the children around her.

"Open the door!" came a voice she recognized, but couldn't place—yet.

"I will not! It's the middle of the night and my children are frightened out of their wits! I will not open the door!" she shouted in defiance.

"We know he's in there."

"Who's in here? The only *he* in here is three years old!"

"Your man is in there. We know he is. Someone seen him 'round here this afternoon."

Elizabeth's body stung with anger and betrayal! Someone had seen James—and reported it! The skies would rain down on them now. If she opened the door they would surely destroy what remained of their home looking for him. When they found he wasn't here, they'd destroy what was left just for spite.

"I would hate to call that person a liar, but James is *not* here."

"So you say. Why should we believe the wife of a traitor?" came the scorn-filled reply.

"Because it's the truth—Mr. Bartlet." The name snapped to her lips like lightning striking. "My husband is not here."

Mr. Bartlet sputtered outside the door at Elizabeth's recognition, but he regained his composure momentarily. "Well, Miz Miers, we want to see for ourselves. Open the door!" His fist slamming on the wood made Elizabeth and the children jump, but she stood firm.

"You may pound all you want, Mr. Bartlet, but I do not intend to open my door to wastrels like you! Go away, leave us alone! There's no one here but me and the children." Her heart was hammering like a mallet pounding railroad spikes, but she *would not* back down. Everything was at stake. "That door is sturdier now than the one you and your ruffians broke down on your last visit! It's been replaced with thicker, heavier oak and your incessant pounding will *not* bring it down—sir!" she added by way of an insult.

The pounding intensified and Elizabeth prayed she was right. It was the same door that had been broken in two when they came the last time. She'd stripped the flattest, straightest, strongest boards she could find from what hadn't been stolen of their fencing, stretched them and strong pieces of leather across the broken door, and nailed them so tight there was no space between them. Even James had commented on what a good job she'd done when he came home after that attack. She prayed now her lie was convincing and that the repair would hold up to the heavy pounding.

The children clutched her skirt and Elizabeth knew she had to get them into the back room. "Nora, Vera, take Joseph and Sally to your room and stay there until I call for you. Understand?"

"Yes, Mama," four children squeaked, hurrying for the back bedroom.

Left to challenge the men alone, Elizabeth was able to think more easily. At least the shutters were already closed. With the constant threat of raiders always on her mind, despite the warming weather it had become a nightly ritual for the shutters to be closed and latched. The only way into the house was breaking through the shutters or the front door, and she had no intention of allowing that. If they got in, it was because the door came down—again.

"You men might as well give it up. That door is stronger now than it ever was. You can pound until your fists are raw!" she shouted with bravado, still hoping to convince them her lie was true.

"We know your man is in there and we aim to git him!" came another voice Elizabeth recognized, but couldn't put a name to yet.

"You're wasting your time! He's not here and you're not coming in. Go break down someone else's door!" She tried to sound bored, even though she was ready to fall on the floor with fright! She raised the pistol and yelled. "And just so y'all are aware, the first man through that door or one of those windows will get a bullet for his trouble!"

The renewed pounding of fists brought her heart into her throat. She watched the door, waiting for it to buckle. "Please, Lord, make it hold," she prayed over and over as she watched and waited, pistol aimed and ready.

Finally, the pounding stopped. There was silence until Mr. Bartlet shouted, "Miz Miers, we aim to get inside that house whether you open this door or not!"

The next instant both windows in the front room shattered and the shutters were being pummeled. The latches holding them closed gave way and they flew open. Elizabeth stood in mute silence as her home was being invaded by men who were her neighbors! She ran to the shutters and tried to relock them, but it did no good. They were broken and wouldn't keep a bluebird out.

"Why are you doing this?" she cried. "James is not here!"

"Then let us in and prove it."

"I will not! And I remind you I have a pistol in my hand, aimed at the first man that crawls through either of those windows. He'll make an easy target, all stuffed into that little bitty frame."

There was mumbling outside and Elizabeth felt a small sense of victory. *These men weren't complete idiots, ready to lay down their lives to get into her home and find James.*

That sense of victory was lost in the next heartbeat. "We'll burn 'em out then," came another voice. "If'n she won't open that door, fire is the only way to get 'em out."

Elizabeth swallowed the lump in her throat and knew she was in serious trouble now. Fire was the one thing she couldn't stop with wood, words or bravado. *Think, Elizabeth, think!*

"Come on, Henry, fire it up!" wafted through the busted window.

"Yes, Henry Watkins, fire up that torch to burn out a defenseless woman and her children!" Elizabeth yelled in response.

The men stopped talking and all she heard were boots moving back and forth on the porch between the front and side windows. "Come on, hurry up," someone mumbled.

The next instant a burning torch was flung through the broken window and landed on the floor at her feet. Elizabeth reacted without thinking. She grabbed the handle and threw it into the empty fireplace.

Another rolled inside from the side window and then another from the front.

"Nora!" Elizabeth called.

"Mama?" Nora skidded to a stop in the doorway, her eyes wide.

"Here!" Elizabeth shoved the pistol into her hands. "Shoot the first man that comes through either of those windows!" Elizabeth yelled loud enough so every man outside knew what she was about.

Nora didn't have to be told twice. She raised the pistol and moved it from one window to the other. Elizabeth talked as she grabbed up burning torches. "I might remind you men that Nora is a crack shot. I wouldn't test her mettle or her aim."

At that moment a man poked his head through the front window and got a splintering of wood in his cheeks. He fell backwards screaming in pain.

Two more torches were flung through the windows and rolled to the middle of the floor. Elizabeth grabbed one and tossed it into the fireplace with the first then grabbed up the second and threw it in with the others after stomping out the threadbare rug that had caught fire.

"Keep 'em coming, Mr. Bartlet! We can do this dance all night!" Elizabeth challenged.

Men grumbled outside and the fireballs stopped. Elizabeth took a deep breath, pushed her drenched hair off her forehead, and retrieved the pistol. Nora stepped beside her mother and the two stood ready for whatever was to come next.

"What's going to happen now, Mama?" Nora barely asked.

Elizabeth swallowed. "I don't know, Nora. We just have to wait."

"Damn it, Miz Miers! We know that no good Reb husband of yours is inside. Just let us come git him and we'll leave you and the children alone. Better yet, just send him on out and we'll be on our way."

"And you're a lying bastard!" It was Nora who had screeched the response, and in that moment Elizabeth knew Nora was no longer *trying* to become a woman, she *was* a woman. With all the instincts of survival and protecting her family her mother had. Despite the severity of their situation Elizabeth grinned with pride.

"You heard my *daughter*, gentlemen," Elizabeth drawled with scorn. "You've done nothing but prove your intentions to harm me *and* my children. You're despicable liars and we will fight you until, well, until we no longer can." Elizabeth straightened her back and Nora did the same beside her.

Again there was silence outside. The only sound in the

front room was Nora and Elizabeth's labored breathing as they waited.

Then they heard it, the thump, thump, thump of torches hitting the roof. Mother looked at daughter and the fear was unmistakable in their eyes. They stood in the center of the room waiting for the smoke to swirl in and drive them from their home then force them to watch everything burn to the ground. But the smoke never came. Only more thumping until Elizabeth heard someone grumble, "We ain't got no more torches."

"Have any of 'em caught?" Elizabeth recognized Mr. Bartlet's voice again, the apparent leader of this gang of ruffians.

"Not a one. They just sputter and go out. It's too wet. We can't burn it, leastwise not tonight," came Henry's response.

Elizabeth couldn't help it. She laughed out loud then laughed harder and louder so the men outside couldn't help but hear her. "You fools! It rained all day. Those torches won't catch. You've wasted your time and been bested by two women intent on keeping the likes of you out of their home!"

At the same time Elizabeth remembered the covered wood pile at the back of the house and a chill ran up her spine. If they ventured around back they'd find plenty of dry wood and kindling to set the house afire. She had to keep their attention here in front.

There was grumbling and the scuffing of boots on the porch then silence.

"Nothing more to say, Mr. Bartlet? Don't you think it's time for you and your men to leave? We'll let you go. We won't even shoot you when you turn around." That statement made, she slid the barrel of the rifle out the front window and Nora stood with the pistol ready at the side window. "Go on now, git on outta here and I won't shoot you, Mr. Bartlet, since you're the one in my sights, *again,* right now." She waited a moment before she continued. "And if you doubt my intentions or my words, remember Mr. Walker and his reluctance to listen to me." She paused and took a deep breath. "James is *not* here, I've told you that time and again. If he *were* here he'd have shot every one of you dead from that loft above where my son could have done that very thing the first time you all came here!" she cried, letting them know she knew who every one of them was and that this wasn't the first time they'd come. "That's proof enough he's not here."

"Fine, Miz Miers. You win—this time. I didn't want to shoot no women tonight anyway. Come on boys, let's ride." Bartlet jumped into his saddle, sawed his horse's reins viciously, and turned the animal down the lane, his men following until they were all out of sight.

Elizabeth and Nora stood at their respective windows for fifteen minutes watching and waiting in case the men returned. Finally, Elizabeth laid the rifle against the wall, stepped back and plopped onto the bench in front of the table. Nora slid down next to her. Elizabeth put her arm around her daughter and the two sat in silence for several minutes before Vera called from the back room, "Mama, can we come out now?"

"Yes! Yes, you may come out." She gathered them around her and hugged them so hard she thought they'd pop. But none of them protested, each of her children hugging her and Nora back as hard as they could.

James had missed being caught by only a few hours and they'd only narrowly survived being burned out because it rained all day. *Her body sagged at the prospect of how differently this night* could *have ended.*

Chapter Thirteen
(Fall, 1862)

In August of 1862 the towns of Independence and Lone Jack became synonymous with battle. On August 11th Federal and Confederate forces met at the Battle of Independence. William Clarke Quantrill and his men met the Federals, led by Colonel James T. Buel, where Quantrill's Confederates out-fought and out-maneuvered the Union forces and left the field of battle victorious. That Confederate victory, however, charged the countryside like a lightning rod. Union troops scoured the land hunting rebels, sending hundreds of undecided men to join up with the Confederate cause.

In the wake of Independence came Lone Jack, a brutal, bloody battle fought on a dusty, oppressively hot August 16th. Sweat and dust covered the men who fought on the main street of the little town that became a field of battle between neighbors, friends, and family who faced each other from opposite sides of the war. The blood of men and horses, Yankees and Confederates, mingled together on the street that day in a battle that meted out death and destruction and left ninety local men dead, their wives widows, and their children fatherless.

"Take what you want, but please go." Elizabeth was beside herself. There were five men in her home, eating whatever was to be found, gathering whatever they could carry. The *same* five men who had visited them earlier this year, taken Poppyseed and a good portion of their food. Why was this happening *again*? This was the fourth time they'd been visited in less than a year. At least these men wouldn't leave this time with her more precious items—like her wedding ring and the locket James had given her, both hidden in a pouch and buried behind the barn, along with several sentimental tintypes of her family, a broach not worth much besides being her mother's, and an old pocket watch of her father's that still worked when it wanted.

"Ma'am, I told you before, we'll leave when it's safe. And that won't be till dark. So calm yourself and everything will be fine."

Elizabeth looked at him like he had two heads. *How could she possibly be calm with bushwhackers in her home! Again!* Forcing herself to gather her wits, she decided if the men were going to be here for a while, she must make the best of it. She wouldn't invite more trouble than was already here by getting hysterical.

"Are you or one of your men still riding the mare you— took when you came before?" she dared ask the same man who had led them on their prior visit. If he still had Poppyseed, she wanted to see her.

The man pursed his lips and nodded. "She's a fine mare, ma'am. She's in the barn out of sight with the others until we light out. If you'd like see her, I've no quarrel with it."

Elizabeth managed a smile. "I'd like that. Thank you." She turned to Nora and Vera. "Girls, take Sally and Joseph into your room and stay there." She turned back to the bushwhacker. "I have your word as a gentleman the children will be left alone while I'm outside?"

The man's head jerked back, as though insulted. "Of course, ma'am. We don't harm children like Lane and his bunch. We formed to *stop* his raiders, remember? We just want food and rest before we're on our way when the sun goes down."

The children safely in their room and trusting the man to his word, Elizabeth stepped onto the front porch in the clear, crisp day. She took a deep breath of the coming winter air and soaked in the sun on her face. Anxious to see her mare, Elizabeth hurried to the barn.

"Poppyseed!" she called halfway there.

There was an answering nicker from inside.

She ran through the doors where five additional horses stood inside stalls munching on corn and hay stored in the barn Elizabeth and the girls had cut for Hilda and the milking cow. A backbreaking chore that gave her pause knowing it'd have to be done all over again after these men left, *if* there was any to cut this late in the year.

Poppyseed's head bobbed up and down over the stall rail, waiting for Elizabeth to reach her.

"Hello, girl," Elizabeth cooed when she reached the mare. "You're so thin," she whispered. The horse nuzzled her former owner and Elizabeth laid her head on the mare's neck. "I'm so happy you're all right."

"She's a good animal." The calm statement behind Elizabeth startled her. She whirled to face the bushwhacker leader.

She rubbed Poppyseed's nose. "Yes, she is. She always was. I miss her sorely," she couldn't help say.

"She's saved my bacon more than once, ma'am," the man said. "Wouldn't be here today if she weren't as fine an animal as she is. She's got stamina and speed, a good combination in a horse."

Elizabeth rubbed between the mare's ears and down her neck, kissed her nose and snuggled up to her. "I've missed you, girl." She hugged the horse for several moments before she straightened and asked, "I know it's not my place to ask, but I'm curious. Why are you here? Where did you come from?"

The man cocked his head. He thought a moment, Elizabeth guessed, trying to decide whether he should answer her question or not. Finally, he said, "We ride with Quantrill. We were with him at Independence and took care of those damned Yankees while we was there." There was a queer gleam in his eyes.

Whether it was anger or excitement that sparkled in his dark eyes, Elizabeth didn't know and didn't want to know. She was sorry now she'd asked the question. It was probably better not to know who these men were, who they fought for, where they'd been or where they were going. She kissed Poppyseed one last time and decided she'd best get back to the house to ensure her children were safe, even though she'd only been gone five minutes. She turned to leave, but the man stayed her with a hand on her arm.

"Don't worry ma'am, the children are fine. I've given strict orders for my men to leave them be and my men follow orders. Now, you asked me a question and I intend to answer."

Elizabeth swallowed, wishing she weren't so curious. *These were Quantrill's men!*

"A couple days ago we were camped at Big Creek north of Harrisonville," he continued. "When we broke camp to head south we come on a Federal train."

He stopped speaking and that gleam came back into his eyes.

"What did you do?" She swallowed hard, uncertain she wanted to know the answer.

"We attacked it."

Elizabeth felt sick. *How many men had they killed in that attack? And why were these five here and not with Quantrill and the rest of his men? Her curiosity gnawed at her, but she was loath to find out. Whatever had happened, it couldn't have been good.*

"We got separated from Charley and the rest of the boys after the fight," he said. "We remembered your place, knew we were close, and headed this way. We know where Charley and the boys are headed so we'll just meet up with 'em later."

Dear Lord, these were Quantrill's men! her mind screamed again. *Some of the most ruthless bushwhackers roaming the area according to James! And they were in her home! With her children!* Fear bubbled up in her throat and she took big gulps of air to keep it tamped down.

"I have to get back inside." She didn't give the man a second chance to waylay her. She ran from the barn to the house as though the devil were on her heels. Perhaps he was.

She shoved through the front door and four guns turned on her, hammers cocking.

"Put your guns down." The leader pushed through the door right behind her. He stomped past Elizabeth, standing frozen in the middle of the room.

"You boys find a bed and catch some sleep. Walt, you keep watch and Harve will relieve you in two hours." He turned to Elizabeth. "Gather your children and go up to the loft. We're going to rest and be gone by nightfall. We'll take a few supplies before we go, but I'm sure you'll be happy to give us whatever you've got—for the Cause."

Elizabeth closed her eyes and nodded. "Of course, for the Cause. Take whatever you need." She walked to the bedroom where the children were huddled together on the girls' bed. "Come children. Up to the loft as Mr.? May I ask your name?"

"Todd. Just call me Mr. Todd."

"Do as Mr. Todd says children. Come along."

They hurried to her side and climbed up the stairs to the loft, Elizabeth close behind them. The ladder was removed to deter any attempt to run away while the men slept, and Elizabeth and her children crowded on Steven's little bed to wait until the men had rested and went on their way.

As the sun began its decent into darkness the men roused, went out and gathered everything they could carry from the corn crib, the root cellar, the smoke shed and took all the canned vegetables Elizabeth had put up in the cupboard, leaving very little for the Miers family for the coming winter. They put a rope around the milk cow's neck and led her from the barn. *Meat on the hoof,* Elizabeth mused. As Mr. Todd waited for the others to gather the rest of what they would take with them, Poppyseed twirled in circles and fought the bit. Eventually Mr. Todd got her under control and she fell into step behind the others.

Inside the barn, Hilda acted more like a young colt than an old mare, kicking the walls of the stall and bellowing as the men and Poppyseed rode away.

Elizabeth felt sorry for Hilda. The old girl would have to learn just like she and the children had that no matter how much she fussed, kicked or bellowed—it didn't change a thing.

Chapter Fourteen
(Winter 1862)

"It makes my skin crawl and my pistol finger itch." James closed his eyes and shook his head. He'd finally gotten his furlough and arrived home a few days ago gaunt and exhausted. He rested, but didn't really sleep the first two days, bucking and mumbling, fighting unknown enemies Elizabeth couldn't see. He left the bedroom only long enough to eat what little Elizabeth scrounged up before he went back to fight more battles in his sleep. "Knowing that man is living right next to us. After all he's done...."

Elizabeth laid her hand over her husband's where he stroked her shoulder. She was stretched across James' chest his arms wrapped around her. The children had gone to bed long ago, leaving their parents some much needed time alone. They'd made love like young lovers, something they did as often as possible these days whenever James was home, not knowing how long he would be there nor when he would come again. "How do you know Newton is living in the Dewey place?" she asked.

"It's common fact among the ranks that he's settled into a farm 'vacated by a rebel family,' as he refers to it." James almost spat between clenched teeth.

"He's made no secret of where it is or that he's living there. He's quite proud of it."

"I'm glad I didn't know. I haven't left this farm in so long I don't know if I could find my way home. But if I'd known he was living right next door, I might never have gone out of the house!" The thought of former Colonel Andrew Newton of the Cass County Home Guards living right next door made Elizabeth more than uneasy. *Commander of the* same *Home Guard that attacked their home not once, not even twice, but three times!*

Silence descended, both lost in their own world of war and survival. They lay in each other's arms, just being together, until they fell asleep. Elizabeth didn't sleep long, awakened by her husband's violent jerking and pitiful cries.

"James. James!" She pushed at him to wake him up until

his hand snapped around her wrist in a bone-crushing hold.

"I'll kill you, you damned Yankee!"

"James!" Elizabeth shoved at his chest with her free hand.

He jerked upright and his eyes popped open. They were glazed with sleep and hatred, mingled with fear, his chest dotted with sweat, rising and falling quickly as he gasped for air.

"James, you're home. It's Elizabeth." She laid her cool hand on his hot chest and unwound his fingers from around her wrist as he came to his senses.

"Oh, Liz! I'm so sorry. Did I hurt you?"

There were tears in his eyes. She didn't know if they were left from his dream—or because he might have hurt her. Elizabeth laid her fingers across lips as hot as his chest. "I'm fine, James. I'm not worried about me. I'm worried about you. Do you have these dreams every time you sleep?" She'd seen him wake up bucking and shouting too many times to count in the few days he'd been home. *How did men rest during wartime if every time they closed their eyes they relived the fighting?*

He wrapped his arms around her, squeezed, and sucked in a deep breath. "That's about right. Every time I close my eyes I'm back at Morristown and every other place I've been and relive every horrible thing I've seen—and done."

Elizabeth wanted to weep, but she'd save that for after her husband left again. *She needed to be strong while he was home. The last thing he needed was a weepy wife!*

"Well, you're here now and you're safe."

His body jerked again, almost dumping Elizabeth off the bed. "Safe? Am I safe? Are you and the children safe?" He scrubbed his hand across his face then through his hair. "Nobody is safe, Liz. Nobody. It may be winter, but the cold doesn't stop those damned, yes damned, Yankees from raiding. They're out there, somewhere, right now, just waiting for an unsuspecting soul to appear so they can kill him."

Elizabeth gently pushed her husband back down onto the bed, but not before she noticed his heart was beating like thunder rolling across the empty plains. *She had to calm him down.*

"James?"

His head snapped toward her, as though he'd forgotten

she was there, lost in another world.

"James?"

The clouds fell away from his eyes and he curled his arms around her again. "Oh Liz, will I live through this horror? Will I come back to you and the children? Will any of us survive?"

He squeezed her and she squeezed him back. They lay in silence, Elizabeth not knowing how to answer his questions—not wanting to know the answers—answers that too often came up "no."

Elizabeth stayed in his arms, and each time James began to dream she was there to bring him back to the present by whispering his name in his ear and giving him a gentle push. The night passed and James Miers finally slept without Yankees and demons chasing him.

Elizabeth did not.

For the first time in too long to remember there was joy in the Miers' home since their father's return. The younger children laughed and played with him whenever they were awake. Little Joseph, Sally and even Vera wrestled with him in front of the fireplace, giggling as though all was well. They snuggled on their father's lap in the big chair, pushed from the corner into the winter sun where he read book after book. He made faces, became the characters he read about, bringing his children's laughter back into a home empty of it for so long. They sang silly songs and told silly stories and the days passed with great enjoyment.

"Do you know how the Barrows are faring?" James asked Elizabeth one morning at breakfast.

"No. I haven't left the farm in so long I haven't seen or heard about anyone. They're probably hole-up just like we are, trying to stay out of sight so they'll be left alone."

"Maybe we should pay them a visit?" James suggested.

Fear raced up Elizabeth's spine. "Leave here to go visiting?"

"Why not? They're only just next door."

"Yes, and Newton is 'just next door' on the other side.

What if he's watching us? What if...."

James shushed his wife with a kiss. "It'll be fine, Liz. The children will enjoy an outing. They've been stuck in this house for months and need to get out. We'll follow the tree line. Nobody will even know we're gone—if they're watching, that is." He smiled, seemingly to allay Elizabeth's fears, but Elizabeth noticed a twinge of unease there.

She thought a moment, her fear still there, thinking how nice it would be to get away from the house, if even for only a few hours. "I would like to see Rebecca and find out how they're faring," she admitted. "See if everything is all right at their place."

"It's settled then. Gather the children, tell them what we're about and we'll go a visiting in half an hour!" He slapped his legs, jumped up and headed for the bedroom.

"Come children, you heard your father. We're going visiting!"

A half hour later, everyone dressed in their heaviest coats even though the weather was mild, they scurried for the tree line between the Miers and Barrow places. An hour later they were laughing and enjoying the companionship of neighbors Thomas and Rebecca, whom they hadn't seen in too long to remember.

The men spoke in muted conversations about the war. Elizabeth and Rebecca fussed with Robert, only two weeks old, and the children played like they hadn't played since Mary's children left last year, only without the fighting. It was a beautiful afternoon, the weather held, and both families almost forgot there was a war on. Almost.

"Why are you going?" Elizabeth was sure her husband had lost his mind. "You do *not* need to see Thomas again. We just saw him and his family a few days ago."

"I said I'd meet him before I leave and I intend to keep my word." He pulled on his heavy coat, ragged from excess wear, his boots even worse.

"It's not necessary, James. Please don't go. I have a bad feeling. We spent a lovely day with Thomas, Rebecca and the children, why take another chance? You do *not* have to go.

You're leaving tomorrow; please don't jeopardize your last day by going out into the open." Elizabeth's heart was racing. She did *not* want her husband to go traipsing off to meet their neighbor for God only knew what! He was risking his life—and Thomas'. If the Yankees knew Thomas was even visiting with a known Rebel, they'd kill him out of sheer meanness, regardless he had a wife and nine children.

"I'll only be gone a little while, not even an hour. I can make it to the property line a lot faster than we did dragging four children along. I'll visit a few minutes and come right back." He kissed the top of her head where she stood in the doorway of their bedroom as though to block his way. "Come now, be a big girl and let me pass."

"Do *not* patronize me James Miers! I'm too afraid of becoming a widow and of your children becoming fatherless."

He shook his head and smiled as men do when trying to placate a distraught woman. "I'm not patronizing you. Everything will be fine. You'll see in less than an hour. You and the children just go about your business and I'll be back before you even know I've left."

"You'd better be fine James Miers or I'll never forgive you!"

Elizabeth puttered as much as she could for the next half hour. Shooing the children away, she cleared the breakfast table and washed the dishes, needing the diversion to keep her from her dark thoughts. There was little to do after that. Having been stuck inside as long as they had the house was already spotless, everything mended, books read and reread. She felt like a mouse rattling around in a big glass bowl, waiting for *something*, not knowing what it was, and fearing it greatly.

A shot from the direction of the tree line brought her upright. She stopped breathing and waited. Moments later there was a second shot then two more. Without thinking she threw open the front door and ran. Coatless she ran past the barn toward the fence line where James and Thomas were supposed to meet. The sound of horses working their way through the woods in front of her stopped her cold half way between the barn and the trees. She stood stone still out in the open until six riders crashed through the foliage in front of her. They were laughing and congratulating one another—and Elizabeth knew.

"What have you done!" she shrieked, lifting her skirt and running as fast as she could toward the riders. "What have you done?"

The men raised their guns, but held their fire as she ran into the trees as though they didn't exist.

They were by the fence line. James lay at the base of the fence and Thomas was draped across it as though he'd tried to jump it and run toward home, struck down before he could clear it. James' gun lay in his open hand, stretched out beside him.

Elizabeth scooped her husband into her arms. "No!" she wailed like a wounded animal. "Oh, James, why did you come here?" she cried. "Why weren't you afraid like I was? Why didn't you listen to me!" she wailed to no one as she rocked her dead husband. She rocked and rocked until she heard someone coming through the trees from the other direction. Grabbing James' gun she waited for whomever was about to accost her. Red-hot anger coursed through her, giving her the strength needed to shoot whomever it was if he intended to do her harm—and she would do so without remorse or thought.

The gun fell back to the ground when a puffing Rebecca pushed through the foliage, her face wild, cheeks red and soaked with tears. Like Elizabeth, she knew what had happened before she reached her husband.

"No!" Rebecca screamed. "No, no, no!" She stepped to her husband and lifted his face with both hands before she wrapped her arms around his head, his face in her chest. "Thomas! What am I to do without you?" she cried. "Murdering Yankees!" she screamed in agony. "Murderers!" she shrieked to the skies, sobbing.

Elizabeth rocked James and Rebecca railed against the Yankees, the Kansans, the Home Guard, and anyone else she could think of for murdering her husband, until both women fell silent, their voices and tears spent.

Having sat in silence with their dead husbands for almost an hour Rebecca staggered to her feet and stepped back, her face awash with tears. "We can't leave them like this. What are we to do?"

Elizabeth couldn't speak. She had no words to describe her grief or intentions. *What would she and the children do now that James was gone? Where would they bury him?* How *would she bury him? And what of Rebecca, left with nine children to raise on her own, and one a newborn?*

"Why didn't you listen to me?" she sobbed again, wrapping her arms around her dead husband's shoulders, rocking, rocking, rocking. "Why did you come?" she whispered.

"Help me, Elizabeth." Rebecca's quiet statement drew Elizabeth's attention. "Help me get him down."

Carefully, as though not to harm him, they pulled Rebecca's husband from the fence, nearly dropping the dead man more than once before they laid him on the ground.

"We'll bury them here," Elizabeth said. "There's no help for it. We have no way to move them."

Tears streamed down Rebecca's face when she nodded her head in agreement. "Yes, Elizabeth," she answered woodenly.

Elizabeth looked at her husband on the other side of the fence. She climbed over and fell to her knees beside him again. She lifted his head and settled it onto her lap as she brushed hair and dirt from his face. "Sleep now, my love, and dream in peace."

The two women finally stood and embraced each other in pain and uncertainty across the fence. They had to bury their husbands and no amount of crying or denying it would change it. They'd survived much since the start of this war. *How much more would they have to endure before the senseless killing ended?*

James Benton Miers and Thomas Barrow were buried almost where they fell beside the fence that divided their properties, James on his side and Thomas on his. Stoic, trying to stay strong for their children, Elizabeth and Rebecca buried their husbands where they were murdered until such time as they could be moved to a final resting place when the war ended. *If* the war ended.

Twelve children sobbed loudly as dirt was thrown into the graves, dug with pick axes to hack through the frozen ground, their fathers covered only by the thin shrouds Elizabeth and Rebecca found to bury them in.

"I don't know how I'm going to survive, Elizabeth," Rebecca lamented after the final prayer over James and Thomas was said. "We managed to escape the raider's wrath, but only because Thomas spent most nights in the woods hiding. These same woods where he was murdered!" She fell into Elizabeth's arms, almost crushing a slumbering Robert, and cried for several minutes before she stood up and dried her eyes. "Oh, we were visited more times than I care to remember by raiders who took whatever they wanted, but we still had Thomas. Now we've got...." She broke down again before she could finish the sentence.

"Rebecca, we have to be strong for the children. They're frightened and look to us. Stop your crying now and be strong. Thomas would want it that way. He wouldn't want you crying over him, frightening the children now, would he?"

Rebecca shook her head. "No, he wouldn't. He'd want me and our children to survive." She looked up and raised her chin. "And that's what I intend to do. Survive with our children." She waved them to her. "If you have need of me, Elizabeth, I'll be in my home. I will not run and I will not hide and someday, folks will know our men were killed by murdering Redlegs!" she shouted in the direction of Andrew Newton's home.

"Rebecca, stop! You're frightening the children again."

Rebecca's face crumbled into tears before her back straightened and her arms went out, gathering her children to her. "Come, it's time to go home." She turned, eight children beside and behind her with Robert cradled protectively in her arms, and began the trek from the grave back to a fatherless, husbandless home.

PART II
YANKEES AND DEMONS
AND
HELL ON EARTH

Chapter Fifteen
(September 1, 1863)

THE ORDER
Day 1

Winter passed into summer, Elizabeth and her children barely surviving the season *and* the loss of their husband and father. The children, especially Nora and Vera, were often found sitting in a corner with silent tears streaming down their cheeks, Vera asking more than once, "Why did they murder Papa?" Nora, however, stayed silent as a stone, having fully learned the realities of the war, knowing her father was killed because he fought for the Confederacy.

As the weather warmed, Elizabeth turned her thoughts again to survival. Crops had to be planted in the hope they would survive another year of brutal weather *and* raiders.

Small fields were tilled, the family garden planted. Seeds sprouted, but as the summer wore on, the temperature rose and stayed there. July was relentless and passed into an August that cooked the corn right on the stalks, evaporated creeks and streams, and dried up wells. Fortunately, James had dug their well deep and they were still able to get water from the pump, but it became gritty and brown as the drought dragged on. There was no rain, only heat, and the creek became an overlarge mud hole, the corn stalks turned brown and curled up after the ears fell off, and the oats died long before it could be harvested. And as the year before, what the weather didn't kill the hoppers took care of, jumping from one stalk to another like a living wave to feed on and destroy what was left.

Sitting in the shade on the front porch, Elizabeth wiped sweat off her neck and shoulders with a wet cloth in a futile attempt to stay cool when she spotted them—a contingent of riders heading up the road. Her heart stilled then raced when they turned up the lane. She stood on wobbly legs as they approached, the children gathering around her as the men drew closer.

They were soldiers, Yankees in uniform. *What did they*

want? Were they here to complete the job other raiders hadn't? They'd already taken her husband, stolen their crops and livestock. What else was there? She drew the children close, felt their trembling and heard the fear in their cries as they waited beside her.

"Ma'am," a captain Elizabeth thought from the insignia on his uniform called as he drew his horse to a halt in front of the porch.

Elizabeth wasted no time with pleasantries. "Why have you come, captain?"

"We're here to inform you of the vacate order."

Elizabeth tried to stand straight, but her body sagged, scared to death of the man's next words. "And what order is that?"

"General Thomas Ewing of the Union Army has issued General Order No. 11, which states..." he pulled out a piece of well-used parchment and read:

"From the Headquarters, District of the Border in Kansas City, Effective August 25, 1863, 'all persons living in Jackson, Cass, and Bates Counties, Missouri,'" he looked up at Elizabeth, "that's you and your family, ma'am." He paused a moment before he raised the paper again. "I shall paraphrase the rest for the sake of expediency, 'you and your family are hereby ordered to remove yourselves from your present place of residence within fifteen days from the date hereof.'" He looked up, "And should you, during this time, go into Harrisonville or Pleasant Hill and swear your oath of loyalty, you and your children will be allowed to remain there under the protection of the military." He waved his hand to encompass the entire farm. "Whether you go into one of these forts and swear loyalty to the Union, or simply remove yourselves from this place, all your grain and hay, your crops and your residence will be forfeited." He took a breath before he finished. "You are required to remove yourselves by September 9th, 18 and 63."

Elizabeth felt like a bolt of lightning hit her where she stood. *They were going to lose everything! But what had she told Mary? As long as her children were safe she would lose* things. Things *were unimportant. The children were all that mattered.*

"Why has this General Ewing put out this Order? We

haven't done anything?"

"You don't know?"

"Of course I don't know. If I knew I wouldn't be asking." The captain shifted, having been chastised like a little boy, but regained himself quickly. His back straightened and his face hardened. "Before sunrise on August 21st William Clarke Quantrill and his murdering bushwhackers rode into Lawrence, Kansas and murdered almost two hundred men and boys. They burned over a hundred buildings to the ground—some with their owners still inside. The cowards struck before most of the town's inhabitants had even risen for the day!"

His voice had grown hard with the telling and Elizabeth thought she'd be sick. *Quantrill's men! Some of the same men who had sat at her table, eaten her food, and slept in her beds!*

"And because of folks like you and every other farmer in these counties, those murdering outlaws have been able to hide and stay fed so they could keep on murdering and thieving their way to Lawrence!"

Bile rose in Elizabeth's throat. This man made it sound like folks around these parts had a choice in helping Quantrill and his men. *They did not!* she wanted to scream in his face, but held her tongue, not wanting the man to know she was among those who had harbored Quantrill and his men—albeit against her will.

Forcing the bile down, her lips trembling in her effort not to cry, she asked, "What is today's date?"

"The first day of September. That gives you eight days to vacate."

"Eight days! How can I gather everything and leave here in eight days?" she cried.

"Ma'am, we don't care what you gather or how you gather it. The Order is that you and your family be gone from here by September 9th."

Elizabeth felt like she'd been struck again. It took all her strength to keep upright. Unwilling to show her fear, she drew her back straight, sucked in a huge breath of air for courage and said, "I understand."

The soldier's head snapped down then up again.

"Where are we to go?"

The captain shrugged. "It's of no matter to us where you Rebs go. The Order simply states you are to vacate the premises, leave the county, and do so by September 9th. You just have to go—we don't care where." He waved his gloved hand as though he were batting at a persistent fly.

Elizabeth almost doubled over, but she forced herself to stand straight in the face of her enemy. *What would they do? Where would they go? How would they get there? And do it all within eight days!* She looked down at her children, wide-eyed with fright, huddled together beside her.

Raising her chin she asked, "I have until September 9th to vacate?"

The captain nodded. "Yes. Do whatever you must until that time, but after that, everything left here will be confiscated." His hand encompassed the farm again.

"Stolen and burned," she corrected loud enough for only the captain to hear then quickly added, "And until such time as the deadline has passed this is still *my* property, correct?"

"Yes."

"Then you and your men are trespassing. Kindly leave right now. You have done your duty and informed us of the Order. As you stated, until the given date to vacate this is still our home, so be good enough to leave it. Now!" She raised her hand and pointed toward the road.

Her statement made, she turned her back on the gaping soldiers. She gathered her crying, shaking children and walked into what was still their home, praying she hadn't angered these soldiers enough to give them cause to burn it down around them right now for her arrogance.

The door closed behind her and her knees gave way. Elizabeth slumped to the floor, the children grabbing for her and sobbing. Her heart was pounding and she couldn't think. *What were they to do? How would they survive? They'd been stripped of almost everything they had, by raiders or the weather—and now the army would take their share! Where would they go?* Her children huddled around her, asking questions she couldn't answer.

"Mama, at least get into the chair." Nora and Vera helped

their distraught mother slide down into the chair, her head shaking in disbelief. "How is this happening?" she asked no one. "When did the world go so crazy that it would turn women and children out with nothing?"

Nora shook her head. "I don't know, Mama."

Elizabeth laid her hand on her daughter's cheek. "What would I do without you? Both of you?" She put her hand on Vera's cheek, too. "You two are my strength." She smiled sadly. "And that strength will be greatly tested in the coming days. You're going to need to be tougher than you ever dreamed—for me *and* for Joseph and Sally."

"We can do it, Mama," Vera said before Nora could answer.

"Yes, Mama, we'll do whatever we must. We've survived so much already." Nora's voice trembled and Elizabeth knew she was thinking about her papa, moldering in a grave at the edge of their property.

She once again gathered the children around her, hugged them, and together they sobbed for what they'd lost and what they were sure to lose in the coming days.

THE ORDER
Day 2
(September 2, 1862)

Sleep eluded Elizabeth. She tossed and turned the entire night, her mind spinning, trying to decide what to do, where to go, and how to get there. By night's end, she had a plan.

The Yankees would *not* win this battle. They'd already taken too much from her and her children. They would not break her into complete submission, it was not in her nature and she would not allow it.

Elizabeth got up before the sun came up, everyone else in the house still asleep. She slid a threadbare dress over her head, taking note of how the material sagged on her thin frame. Her bosom, usually generous, was all but gone in her food deprived, overworked state. Her hip bones jutted out, and her thighs, normally overlarge in her assessment, were almost shapely in their thinness. Unwilling to ponder her dwindling form further, she trod to the barn to begin her work.

After lighting a lantern and feeding Hilda from the pile of hay she and the older girls had cut and stored in the barn, she threw the remaining two chickens a handful of feed and began her well-thought out task.

She positioned herself in front of the empty stall, raised the hammer above her head, and swung it as hard as she could at the corner. Her arms stung and reverberated painfully with the impact, but nothing budged. Not so much as a creak. She dropped the hammer and stared down at it like it had turned into a slithering snake. She was already sweating in the stifling heat of the barn and she wiped her forehead with the back of her hand. With a deep breath, she looked up at the stall again. Eyeing the structure more closely to find a weak spot, she stepped to the corner where the nails were bent and stuck out of the wall at odd angles. She studied the connection to decide where best to strike, took a deep breath, and imagined that Yankee captain was standing right there. She picked up the hammer and swung it as hard as she could, the anger she'd kept at bay exploding like a Confederate cannon. Again and again she slammed the hammer against the wood until it broke free from the wall. Panting, every nerve in her body vibrating, she stepped to the corner post, imagined a Yankee uniform draped over it and, with every ounce of strength and rage she possessed, laid the hammer against it. Again and again she hit that board until the nails backed out and the board hung limp. Grabbing the middle of the plank she jerked. There was a long screech, like fingernails scraping over a chalkboard, as the nails pulled free. Sweat was beaded between her breasts and on her forehead. She wiped it away with the inside of her elbow and grabbed hold of the board. With one final jerk the last of the nails pulled out and it dropped to the ground. She stood sweating and breathing heavily, knowing it was going to be a long tedious process, but one that had to be done to make her plan work. One by one she pounded each board until it was loose enough to yank away from the rest of the stall. One board at a time the sides of the stall fell away. Hours later the stall was gone, replaced by a stack of wood.

By the time she finished tearing down the first stall, she was soaked clear through and smelled like James used to when he'd been hunting all day in the heat. But there was no help for it, the job had to be done and she was the only one to do it.

"Mama?" came Nora's trembling voice from outside the barn.

"I'm here, Nora."

Her oldest daughter ran inside, her face white with fear. "You weren't in the house. I looked and looked, but couldn't find you. Then I heard the pounding in here. I was so afraid Mama!" She fell into her mother's arms, sobbing.

"Shhhh. I'm sorry, Nora. I didn't want to wake any of you. You're going to need all the rest you can in the coming days."

Nora pulled away. "What are you doing?"

"I'm tearing down the stalls."

"Why?" Her face showed her confusion.

"Because when we leave here everything in our home, this barn, the smoke shed, fields, everything will be destroyed by those men who came here yesterday. I intend to leave as little as possible. I'm going to take as much as we can carry and destroy the rest. Right now I'm taking down the stalls so I can use the boards to build a sled."

"You're building a sled?"

Nora's obvious surprise made Elizabeth grin. "I am. I helped your Papa put up fence when we first came here, and I helped him build these stalls, too. Did a pretty good job I'm thinking, since I'm having a hard time getting them apart." She smiled, hoping to allay some of her daughter's fear. "And I repaired that door that held against Mr. Bartlet and his raiders when they came the last time didn't I?"

Nora smiled and her head bobbed up and down in agreement. "Yes, you did, Mama." She looked around and a grin came to her lips. "Can I help?"

"Of course you can." Elizabeth looked around the barn for another hammer she knew was there somewhere. When she found it she handed it to Nora, who could barely lift it let alone swing it. Elizabeth giggled and Nora giggled back.

"It appears I'm too much of a girl," Nora groaned.

"You can help me stack the boards when I get them apart, how does that sound?"

Nora nodded. "How many stalls are you going to take down?"

"As many as it takes. I have no idea how to build this thing, but I'm sure going to try. It may be a wasted effort if I can't get it to stay together, but I won't leave here without trying."

As the sun rose higher, so did the temperature, the air unmoving and stifling in the barn. Elizabeth was soaked from head to toe from her continued exertion, Nora the same beside her. About eleven o'clock Elizabeth had Nora gather the other children and bring them to her. The older girls did whatever they could to help their mother while the younger two played, jumping in the small hay pile or chasing each other. If Elizabeth hadn't known better, it might have been any other day of chores in the barn.

After noon Elizabeth quit—at least for the time being. She was exhausted and could barely lift the hammer to lay another blow. Nora ran to the pump and brought back a pail of water that Elizabeth dumped over her shoulders, gasping and shrieking when the cold water hit her hot skin. The children laughed and Elizabeth laughed with them. For the second time that morning, if Elizabeth hadn't known the severity of their situation, she might have thought it was a normal day of chores in the barn.

After a lean mid-day meal that was by no means satisfying, she was at it again, pounding the boards with all her strength—and anger. Every board was a Yankee soldier or one of Jennisen's Jayhawkers or one of the damned Redlegs that had killed her husband. The hammer became her only weapon against those bent on destroying her home and family. Sensing her mood, the children disappeared and left her to her business until she was so exhausted she slid to the floor and slept where she fell.

Nora found her mother late that afternoon, cheeks soaked, eyes puffy and red from her crying and exertion. Helping her mother to her feet, Nora and her mother made their way to the house where Elizabeth fell into bed and slept as she hadn't the night before.

It was dark when Elizabeth woke. She sat up in bed, her body singing with uncertainty, every muscle throbbing. She tried to determine what time it was, but had no idea. She was in her own bed, but had no remembrance of getting there. There were soft voices in the front room, as though conspiring, and fear washed over her.

Shaking sleep away, she shoved back her soaking hair and peeled her dress from her sweat-soaked skin. The barn. Nora. Slowly she remembered where she'd been and what she'd been doing. The children! Uncertain who was in her front room she slid out of bed, her arms and legs screaming painfully, grabbed the squirrel rifle, inched her way out the bedroom door—and stopped in her tracks. Sitting around the table were the children, plates in front of them with what passed for supper, talking quietly.

Nora spotted her and came to her, took the rifle, put it back in the corner, and led Elizabeth to the table.

"We just finished supper, Mama. Are you hungry? Do you want a plate?"

Tears welled in Elizabeth's eyes. Never had she been so proud of her children, each one of them.

"What do we have?" Elizabeth asked, as though there were a choice.

"We saved you the last of the rabbit stew." Elizabeth knew there was barely enough for the children, let alone her, too. Their meat supplies gone, Elizabeth had taken to hunting in the woods at the back of the property. She did so when she went to visit James' grave. She made good use of the visit by hunting rabbits, the occasional turkey, coons and, when the meat supply became very limited, possum, its meat so oily Elizabeth wanted to vomit with each bite. But it was sustenance and necessary when there was nothing else. Initially the children refused to eat it, but as their hunger grew they gave in with as much grumbling from their mouths as in their bellies.

Staring at the ceiling, Elizabeth recalled coming upon a young fawn. Her mouth watered, thinking about the tender meat it would have had. She'd sighted the small creature down the barrel of the rifle, but hadn't been able to pull the trigger and the animal had darted away into the trees. *Have you allowed an animal to live while your children go hungry?* she berated herself.

A gently spoken, "Mama?" brought her back to the present. She sat down at the table and took a mouthful of the stew Nora put in front of her. The children watched each bite she took and Elizabeth saw in their faces how hungry they still were. She pushed the plate away. "I don't know what's wrong with me, but I just can't seem to eat all this. Would anyone like to help me?"

"I'll help you, Mama!" Joseph shouted, unabashed.

"Me, too," Sally piped up.

"I think that's a good idea. Nora, why don't you split what's left between you and the other children?"

Elizabeth saw tears in Nora's eyes, well aware of what her mother was doing.

"Mama?" She cocked her head in question and protest.

"It's fine, Nora. I've eaten enough. You children finish it."

Nora closed her eyes and drew in a deep breath. "Yes, Mama." She took up the plate and dished another small portion onto the other children's plates, but not her own. "I don't know what's wrong with me, either," she said with a smile. "I've had enough, too." An unshed tear slid down her cheek.

For the second time that night great pride washed over Elizabeth. They *would* survive this ordeal. She would not allow herself to surrender to anything else.

THE ORDER
Day 3
(September 3, 1863)

Elizabeth was up again before the sun. Although every muscle in her body ached, she didn't let it deter her from the task at hand. She was already hard at work tearing down the last of the stalls, leaving only the two that held the chickens and Hilda. The stack of boards was three feet high and she was sure she would complete her task.

She'd decided they would go to her Aunt Pearl and Uncle Rupert's in St. Clair County. It was sixty miles, give or take, and she was confident they would make it—now that she had a plan. Having visited her aunt and uncle many times since she and James moved to Austin, she was familiar with how to get there. They would head east on the Austin-Wadesburg Road then south toward Clinton and St. Clair County. There were several creeks to cross along the way, but with the heat and drought that had plagued them these past weeks, Elizabeth hoped they'd be low enough to be easily crossed, yet still have some water for the weary travelers and their animals.

Elizabeth stared at the pile of lumber, uncertain where to begin. Her first thought was to build the frame. She chuckled when Vera's picture frame popped into her mind, lopsided and wobbly and she hoped to do a better job than her daughter.

Nora had taken to keeping the younger children occupied and out of her mother's way, once she realized how inept she was at wielding a hammer. The children brought Elizabeth big glasses of water from the pump, filtering out the grit by letting the water drip slowly through a piece of thin cloth, and put wet towels around her neck and face to keep her temperature down in the soaring heat. Regardless of their efforts, by mid-day Elizabeth was soaked from the water to cool her and her own sweat.

Standing in front of the pile of wood, hands on her hips and head cocked to one side, she thought out loud, "What now? I have enough boards to make *two* sleds, so I can choose the best. They're eight feet long and an inch thick, so how do I put them together?" She stepped over and inspected a couple then dropped them back onto the pile. "Hmm, most are straight, but some are bowed so badly they're useless," she reported to herself. "Might as well separate them right now." She bent to the task, reminding herself that whatever she did, the sled had to be light, or else the strain of pulling it might become too much for poor Hilda.

Sweat poured into her eyes so she wrapped a kerchief around her forehead to catch it. Her hair, in a bun in the middle of her head, allowed what little air there was to flow across her neck and shoulders, but gave little respite to the heat and humidity inside the barn. She'd discarded propriety and put on a pair of James' denim trousers, the children laughing hysterically when they'd first seen her. The legs were rolled up to her knees and she kept them from falling down around her ankles with a rope around her waist.

Wielding the hammer with strength borne of desperation and rage, she began building the sled. She laid out a frame on the ground with the straightest boards she could find. Using two eight foot boards at the top and bottom, she placed them about four feet apart over two eight foot long side boards then hammered them together. Then she laid another eight foot board over each of the side rails and hammered them all together with lots of nails to make sure it was sturdy. The eight foot boards at the top and bottom had an excess on either side of about two feet that should be cut away, but Elizabeth would worry about that later. The only thing that mattered right now was that she got the frame built and that it was solid.

After breaking for water and a sponge bath to cool down, Elizabeth ate some eggs Nora brought out then searched the barn for leather and rope to help brace the floor of the sled. In her plan to keep the conveyance light, instead of using wood she would stretch leather and rope from one side of the frame to the other, in the same way bed ropes were stretched under a mattress. In her search she found some thick, discarded plow reins, a couple leather cinches that would fit almost perfectly across the bottom, and a coil of heavy rope she could cut as necessary. Once the makeshift floor was in place, she would cover it with canvas. Only the smaller children would ride in the sled and only when necessary, along with Hilda's feed and hay, and what few household items they would bring. One of the mattresses would be folded and placed over the floor as a cushion, the other two mattresses lashed across the top of whatever else they carried and easily dragged off each night for sleep.

Elizabeth spent the afternoon nailing the leather and rope pieces to the side runners. Placing them close enough to give good support, she stretched and pulled and crossed the pieces until she couldn't stretch them another inch, and then jerked them one last time. Some she nailed, dependent upon how thick they were, and some she wrapped and tied. By day's end a lightweight, solid leather and rope floor stretched across the bottom of the sled.

Although exhausted beyond thought, her mind continued to whirl on what needed to be done and how little time she had to do it. Entering the house she sat down to a meal of cornbread and turnips. Until she hunted again, they were out of meat and whatever she caught would have to be cooked and smoked to keep it from spoiling in the brutal heat. Maybe tomorrow she'd take a break from her carpentry and do some hunting. She'd visit Rebecca and let her know her plans and invite her friend to join them on their journey.

Elizabeth stared down at the plate of bland, uninviting food. Despite the fact her ribs were scraping her spine with hunger she pushed the uninviting fare away. Too tired to keep her eyes open, she laid her head down on her arm and fell asleep.

An hour later, Nora woke her, gathered her into her arms, and led her to the bedroom. Elizabeth fell into bed fully clothed and slept until long after the sun rose the next morning.

THE ORDER
Day 4
(September 4, 1863)

Elizabeth stood on the porch under the roof and out of the mid-day sun, her children beside her, always with her in these uncertain days. Hilda was tied to the porch rail, also with them wherever they went these days. Elizabeth knocked on the door.

"Yes?" came Rebecca's frightened response from the other side.

"Rebecca, it's Elizabeth and the children."

The door swung open and a startled Rebecca stood in the opening. "What are you doing here?"

"Let us in and I'll tell you."

Her face reddening, Rebecca moved out of the way and waved Elizabeth and her family inside. "I'm so sorry. Come in, come in."

"Rebecca, it's all right." Elizabeth stepped inside, the children behind her. She looked around. Everything was as it had been when they'd visited back in February.

"Rebecca? Aren't you getting ready to go?"

"Go where?"

"What do you mean, go where? Go anywhere but here."

Rebecca looked away. "I don't know where to go."

Rebecca's oldest daughter Helen, a tall, thin girl of about fourteen with curly brown hair, stepped beside her mother. "Where are we going, Mama?"

"Are we going somewhere, Mama?" Clara, a younger daughter asked. She waited for her mother's response, her dark eyes pinched and her lips pursed.

"Helen, Clara, you and the children go to the back room and play," Rebecca said.

"But we want to know where we're going, Mama." Helen crossed her arms over her small chest and stared hard at her mother.

"And I told you to take the children to the back room."

"But I want to know where we're going!" Helen stomped her foot.

"Do not question me, child!" Rebecca snapped. "You will find out when I am ready for you to know. Now all of you— go to the other room. And no more questions."

Helen looked wounded. Her lower lip trembled and her eyes filled with tears. "Yes, Mama." She and Clara quickly gathered her brothers, sisters and the Miers children and herded them toward the back room.

Once they were out of hearing distance, Elizabeth took her friend's hand. "You know about The Order, don't you?" Elizabeth couldn't believe Rebecca was just sitting around, waiting for the Yankees to come and burn her home down around her!

"Yes," Rebecca managed. "I've been completely unnerved since the soldiers came and told me. I'm the mother of nine children without a husband, how am I to comply with such an order? They'll have to realize I can't go anywhere. I have nowhere to go."

"Rebecca! You have no choice," Elizabeth snapped. "They're coming back and they're going to burn this place down. And if you don't leave, they'll burn it down with you and the children inside!"

"They wouldn't dare!" Rebecca's back stiffened and her chest puffed out as though Elizabeth had hurled the worst of insults at her.

Elizabeth shook her head. "They have and they will, Rebecca. You must go. There *is* no other choice. All you have to decide is where."

"Where can I go, Elizabeth, with nine children? Both mine and Thomas' people are in Tennessee. How can I get there with no transportation and no food!" Tears brimmed in her dark eyes and slid down her cheeks. "What am I to do?"

"Come with me."

"Where?"

"We're going to my Aunt and Uncle's place in St. Clair County, *if* they survived the burning of Osceola back in '61. If so, they'll take us all in. At least you'll be able to decide where to go from there. There's no way you can reach your people in Tennessee alone. You *must* come with me."

"What if they didn't survive the burning and there's

nothing for us when we get there?"

"We'll face that if or when we get there. Right now, we have no choice but to leave."

Rebecca shook her head in bewilderment. "Since the soldiers brought me the news I've been trying to decide what to do. I have no way to get anywhere, Elizabeth. The raiders took everything. There's barely any food. What am I to do? Where am I to go? And what about little Robert? He's still suckling!"

"It doesn't matter what you do or where you go, but you can't stay here. They'll burn the place down around you, I tell you. Those men don't care about you *or* your children. They've made more widows and orphans in this county than I care to contemplate. You *must* leave, Rebecca. There *is* no choice. Right now your only choice is to come with me."

"I don't know, Elizabeth, I just don't know."

"I'm building a sled for Hilda to pull. Even though she's blind she'll go where I lead her. The smallest children can take turns riding Hilda or on the sled. We'll put little Robert in the sled when you're not carrying him and we'll stop for you to nurse whenever it's necessary."

Rebecca stared at her friend. "You're building a sled?"

Elizabeth couldn't help but smile at Rebecca's shocked expression, remembering Nora's bewildered face when she told her the same thing. "I am. It may look a sight, but it'll be functional and carry what we need." She took Rebecca's hand. "You must come with me, Rebecca. This house and everything you own will be destroyed, period. It doesn't matter if you don't *want* to go or whether you have some place *to go*—or not. You can't stay here. If you do one of your children could be hurt—or worse."

A sob bubbled up from Rebecca's throat and exploded. "Oh, Elizabeth, I must protect my babies!"

"Then come with me. There's no help for it. We've been given the order to leave and that's what we must do. We can't discuss it. We can't cry or yell or stomp. We just have to do it. And I intend to make the best of it in the doing. With the sled the littlest children will be able to ride when they get too tired to walk. We'll carry what is necessary—nothing more and nothing less. Each child will carry one bag and will be responsible for that bag, so they shouldn't put too much in it. We must travel light. If we do, we should make about ten miles a day and reach my aunt's place in six or seven days."

Rebecca stared at her friend. "You've got it all planned."

"I do. And we only have a few days to get ready, so we mustn't dawdle."

Rebecca continued to gaze at Elizabeth before she asked, "When did you become so strong?"

"When they took food out of our mouths, robbed us of everything they could carry away in their saddlebags, and murdered my husband. That's when, Rebecca. I *will not give up*, for my children, myself—or James."

It didn't take much more to convince Rebecca she had no other option than to travel with Elizabeth and her family. The Barrows were to come to the Miers home in five days' time and their journey would begin. Prior to that they were to set aside one bag each of what was most important to carry with them. Each person, no matter how old, would be expected to carry their own burden. They would leave at dawn on September 9th.

That afternoon Elizabeth left the children with Rebecca and took to the woods. She spent four hours in the brutal heat hunting and returned later that afternoon with two squirrels and a fat turkey. She stomped in through the door of the Barrow cabin and was surrounded by Rebecca and the children.

"Mama, can we eat them now?" Vera shouted.

The Barrow children eyed the food from a distance, uncertain whether they would be allowed to partake of the feast.

"They have to be cooked first," Elizabeth laughed. "Rebecca, I imagine you can help out with that?"

"Oh yes, I can do that. But the turkey will take a while to cook."

"Let's fry up the squirrels for tonight's supper—for all of us," Elizabeth said to assuage Rebecca's children's worried looks. "It isn't much between all of us, but the turkey will fill our tummies tomorrow." She rubbed her stomach, crossed her eyes, and smiled a silly smile, causing the children to giggle uncertainly.

"I have some turnips, radishes and a few ears of corn that were missed the last time we were raided that I've been saving. I'll make some cornbread and between that and the squirrel, we should be able to calm the rumblings in our stomachs until tomorrow, at least," Rebecca said with a matching smile.

"Good, let's get these critters cleaned so you can get to frying them. While you're cooking I'll clean the turkey to cook over night. The children and I will come back tomorrow and we'll have a feast! How does that sound everyone?"

The room erupted with joyous shouts and cheers. It brought another smile to Elizabeth's lips and saddened her at the same time. How far they had fallen when the promise of a meal that used to be commonplace brought as much joy to these children as Christmas did.

After their sparse supper, each adult and child getting barely a taste of the meat, the children were shooed off again and Rebecca and Elizabeth made plans for the coming days. The sun would be setting soon and Elizabeth and the children needed to get home, but they'd return in the morning. The children would stay with Rebecca and Elizabeth would hunt again. She wanted to get as much meat as she could to build their strength before the long journey and more to cook and dry and bring with them.

There was much to be done and little time to do it.

THE ORDER
Day 5
(September 5, 1863)

Taking advantage of the slightly cooler early morning air, Elizabeth was up and building her sled before the sun rose. It was brutal work and her back, arms, hands and legs screamed with pain, but she kept on. Their lives depended on it. She would work until the heat became oppressive then head back to Rebecca's where she and the children would enjoy a long-anticipated meal of wild turkey with Rebecca and her family.

Right now, though, she had work to do and she got to it, stretching the canvas over the leather and rope bottom of the sled and nailing it tight. The conveyance was as ugly as a boar and looked like a gross misrepresentation of a wagon without wheels, but it would suffice for their needs. She cut the extra length from the bottom cross-board, but left the excess at the top. She could use it to wrap Hilda's reins, hang water jugs, lanterns, and anything else that had a handle and could be hung out of the way.

She stood back, crossed her arms over her chest, and surveyed her handiwork. If the situation weren't so dire, she'd have had a good laugh! It was the ugliest thing she'd ever seen and she prayed it didn't fall apart in the first hole it hit.

Exhausted beyond reason, a full day yet ahead of her, Elizabeth pumped what little water she could get to come up and let it run over her exhausted body. Her back and arms railed against the exertion, but the cool, although gritty wetness helped reinvigorate her. She put her head under the thin stream of water and let it sluice through her hair, trying to rinse out the dirt and sweat clinging to her. Standing upright the water slid down her body and she felt an odd satisfaction at the completion of her task. She looked up to the Heavens and raised her hands in supplication.

"Give me strength, Lord! *Please* give me strength and I swear on my love for my children and my murdered husband— *we will survive!*"

James' wet clothes shed and back in one of her few

remaining day dresses, Elizabeth gathered her family for the short trek to their neighbor's house. The children chattered like magpies, anxious to reach the Barrow's and the turkey dinner waiting for them.

Stomping onto the porch they were met by a sweaty, red-faced, yet smiling Rebecca before Elizabeth could even knock.

"You look wrung out," Elizabeth commented stepping inside the cabin. "Oh my, it's so hot in here!" She fanned herself with her hand.

"That's what happens when you keep the fire going all night when it's already a hundred degrees outside. But the turkey is cooked. It's falling apart in the pot," she beamed.

"Then what are we waiting for?" Elizabeth grinned.

The table was set, the children already waiting in their seats, but the oppressive heat put an edge on Elizabeth's buoyant mood. She pulled Rebecca aside.

"Why don't we all eat outside? I've spent so much time in the blistering heat of my barn, and you look as used up as an old wash rag. I don't know if I can stand another minute inside— not that it's really any cooler outside," she added, "but it's not *quite* as hot as it is in here and there's, at least, a breeze." She looked around at the anxious children. "Why don't we fill our plates and eat on the porch?"

The children all nodded and Rebecca agreed. "All right then, after we pray you'll get your food and take your plates outside."

The children waited anxiously as Elizabeth offered up a prayer for their food and guidance then grabbed their plates and hurried to be first in line, pushing, shoving and yelling as children did in their excitement. Joseph, Sally, and Rebecca's little boy, Andrew, wound up in the middle of the room crying, empty plates in hand, before Elizabeth and Rebecca shouted everyone to silence.

"Now then, Joseph, Sally and Andrew, go to Rebecca," Elizabeth instructed. "Then we'll go by age, youngest to oldest." The older children groaned, but did as Elizabeth told them. Within minutes plates were filled and everyone was on the porch, their legs hanging over the sides, lustily eating more food than they'd had in a month, the oldest helping the youngest. Rebecca and Elizabeth helped themselves to what was left of the turkey and cornbread without a word, thankful to fill their bellies to overflowing for the first time in too long to remember.

After the meal the children split up to play and do whatever children did, and Elizabeth went into the woods to hunt again. Ammunition for the rifle was dwindling, so she had to make every shot count. Walking through the brush, her mind drifted to years past, wondering if her son was still alive, and missing her husband so much she staggered as she approached his and Thomas' graves.

Kneeling beside James' overgrown plot, tears filled her eyes. *Would there ever be a time when she came here and didn't cry?* she wondered, absently pulling weeds from the ground above him. "I miss you so," she whispered. "Why did you go that morning?" she asked, having asked the question hundreds of times already. "Why didn't you listen to me and stay home, then you'd still be with us...maybe," she amended, knowing he could have been killed any time during this seemingly unending war. Elizabeth sat with her eyes closed in oppressive silence for several minutes, running things over in her mind, wishing things were different, aware wishing did absolutely nothing. Things were as they were and couldn't be changed. Her husband was dead. There was a war on and her son was out there still alive somewhere, she hoped, still fighting. And she and her children had only four days before everything she and James had built together would be left behind to be destroyed. Elizabeth laid her right hand on the grave, swallowed hard and whispered goodbye, perhaps for the last time. She pushed to her feet, turned—and froze. In the distance stood what looked like a yearling deer munching on what there was of a shriveled up bush. Her mind flashed to the fawn she'd let escape last year and wondered if this could be the same animal. *That was then and this was now. This time she would not be so foolish. Its meat would fill hers and Rebecca's family's bellies in the days before they left, with enough to dry and bring with them on the long journey. She would have one shot. She had to make it count.*

Slowly and quietly she raised the rifle, sighted the animal's chest, aiming for the heart, then brought the hammer back and locked it, careful to keep it steady with the animal in view. The deer stopped eating when the hammer clicked into place. It lifted its head, sniffed the air, and spotted her. Before it could leap away, the rifle exploded and the deer crumpled to the ground, legs thrashing.

Joy washed over Elizabeth. This one kill would sustain them for a long time. "Thank you, Lord!" She ran to the fallen creature, still now. Its eyes were glazed in death and for an instant Elizabeth felt regret, but she pushed it away, knowing how long this one gift would feed hers and Rebecca's children.

It looked to weigh about a hundred pounds. *How would she get it back to Rebecca's? She couldn't leave it here to run and get help. The four-legged predators in the woods would steal it away before she got back. She had to lighten it so she could drag it by herself. That was all there was to it.* As distasteful as it was, the first thing she had to do was gut it. She'd watched James and Steven do it many times when she'd hunted with them. Now it was her turn.

Steeling herself to what must be done she pulled a knife from her boot and, with great difficulty, cut the length of the belly. Elizabeth barely had time to stagger away before she threw up. Her guts twisting, talking herself through what she must do, she wiped her mouth on her shoulder and finished the miserable chore, stopping twice more to throw up.

The deer's insides cleaned, the next thing she had to do was remove its head, lightening it enough that she could drag it back to Rebecca's. Forcing down the bile threatening to come up again, she bent to the wretched task.

An hour later she stood up and wiped her hands on the back of her skirt, the only spot that wasn't bloody. She swung the rifle across her back, shoved her sweat-soaked hair off her face, and grabbed a leg. Mustering all her strength of will, she pulled—and wound up on her fanny in the dirt with her legs spread. The dead weight was more than she'd imagined. *After all she'd done she* would not *leave this animal here for wolves or coyotes to drag away!* Taking a deep breath she pushed back to her feet, grabbed the legs again and tugged until the carcass moved—then moved again and again with each pull. It was going to take a long time to get it back, but there was no help for it. Her only hope was that Rebecca would come looking for her before it got dark and help her with her burden, but until then all she could do was pull.

She'd been dragging the carcass for what seemed like hours when she heard Rebecca calling in the distance.

"I'm here, Rebecca! I'm over here!"

Rebecca crashed through the bushes and ran to Elizabeth. Spotting the burden her friend was lugging she laughed out loud and clapped her hands like a little girl. "Oh, Lord, Elizabeth! You've shot a deer!"

"Yes, and I'm about spent dragging it. Run and get a rope and some help so we can drag it home before it gets dark."

Rebecca didn't hesitate. She was running before Elizabeth could say another word. Elizabeth slumped to the ground, so exhausted she could barely lift her head, knowing help would be back soon.

Rebecca returned twenty minutes later, rope in hand, Nora and Rebecca's twelve-year old son, Joshua, with her. Nora and Joshua gushed with excitement over the fact there would be more meat before their long journey and each grabbed the rope after Rebecca tied it to the back legs of the deer. Elizabeth was so spent she just watched.

An hour later, the deer was safely at the Barrow house. Having regained a little of her strength with the others dragging the carcass the rest of the way, the four of them managed to get it hung in the smoke shed to drain overnight and into tomorrow. Once drained, they would cut out a few choice cuts for upcoming meals and slice what was left into strips to dry for the journey.

They would survive this ordeal, Elizabeth mused in her bed that night in the same spot she'd landed earlier, unable to move. *It would take more grit and perseverance than she'd ever thought possible, but they* would *survive.* She vowed it on all she held dear—her children.

THE ORDER
Day 6
(September 6, 1863)

Elizabeth could barely move. Every muscle in her body hurt like she'd been tortured, but there was more work to be done. She rolled out of bed with a groan before gaining her feet. So exhausted she couldn't even lift her arms to pull her dress off, she'd fallen into bed with the bloody thing on and woke up this morning in the same spot. *What did she care if the linens got dirty? She'd replace them with clean ones when she got home tonight. Everything would be destroyed and burned when the Yankees came back anyway. Why should she care if the bedding was soiled?*

Nora came into the room. "I thought I heard you stirring in here." She flung open the shutter to let in the day, Elizabeth squinting against the abrupt bright light.

"Oh, I was stirring all right—like a broken pot. What time is it?"

"Almost ten."

"Ten! There's no time to waste then. We need to get to Rebecca's." She rubbed her aching back. "You shouldn't have let me sleep so long."

"Mama, you're played out! Look at you. You're obviously paining—I *heard* you get out of bed," she over-emphasized. "You're in that same awful dress from yesterday." Nora scrunched her nose in displeasure. "And your eyes are as red as the blood on your dress!" she finished louder than was necessary.

"And I'll be more played out by the time we reach Aunt Pearl's. I have to keep going." She cupped her daughter's face in her hands. "*We* have to keep going. I'm sorry, but..."

"I know, Mama. There's no help for it. I understand."

Elizabeth took Nora in her arms and hugged her. "I know you do. I don't know why I felt the need to explain." She pushed her daughter to arms' length, her hands still on her upper arms. "You're a woman, full grown now, with a woman's heart and mind."

Nora blushed and smiled.

"And I want you to know how very proud I am of you." Elizabeth pulled her back into another embrace until Vera charged into the room.

"Are we going yet?"

"Yes, after I change my clothes." Elizabeth gave Nora one last glance, telling her in silence how very proud she was.

Joseph and Sally rode Hilda to the Barrow's house, Elizabeth unwilling to leave anything of value behind—Hilda being the most valuable thing they had left—excluding the children, of course. Leading the mare through the woods, the Miers made the short trip quickly and Elizabeth found Rebecca had been up and busy for a long time. The deer was drained and her friend had already cut out several choice pieces for their meals in the few days before their departure. Elizabeth's mouth almost watered at the thought of venison steaks and stew.

"You did the really hard work yesterday," Rebecca explained when she saw how relieved Elizabeth was. "It was my turn to shoulder the burden. Especially since more of the mouths to be fed are mine." She blushed. "So here I am and by day's end, we'll have the best cuts of meat for a few days, with the rest drying for our trip."

Elizabeth hugged her friend. "Thank you," was all she could manage, still so exhausted she'd wondered on their way here how she would keep going. *At least some of that burden has been relieved*, she thought, gazing at her friend. She and Rebecca had always been friends because of the proximity of their homes, but were growing closer every day in their mutual need for survival and companionship.

"We're in this together, Elizabeth," Rebecca continued. "Now that I've resolved to myself this is the only choice I have, I intend to do my part."

Elizabeth waved her hand over the disappearing carcass. "It's a good start."

Rebecca sighed and smiled. "I'm not as afraid as I was. This one deer will give us meat for our trip, so six or seven days traveling doesn't frighten me like it did before. I believe we'll make it now, Elizabeth. I didn't before."

The two women embraced again, nodded their acknowledgment that they were equals in this venture and both intended to survive, and got back to work.

The day continued with slicing the meat into eight inch strips to be smoked and dried, or jerked as it was more often called. It was brutally hot inside the shed. As it had been for weeks the temperature was close to a hundred degrees and the smell of the carcass was overpowering, forcing them outside often to keep their stomachs from coming up. They took to wearing a kerchief over their noses in a mostly futile attempt to keep out the stench.

With the middling children supervising, they and the younger boys and girls went off to gather wood for the fire, as well as straight, green branches about a half inch around and five or six feet long to build a rack for hanging the meat. Once the meat was cut and hung the fire would be started and kept going throughout the night until the meat was fully dried, making it easy to carry, giving it a better chance of surviving the heat on their journey.

The youngsters brought armloads of kindling and small branches, dropped their loads and ran laughing back into the trees for more, with a stop along the way in a barely trickling stream to cool down. Their joyous laughter in the distance buoyed Elizabeth and Rebecca through their own difficult work. While mothers and youngsters continued their tasks, Nora, Helen, Clara, and Vera prepared the mid-day meal from the venison steaks Rebecca had cut out that morning.

Agreeing to only one meal a day to stretch the venison as long as possible, work stopped about three o'clock to eat. Following yesterday's routine, the youngest children filled their plates first then on up to the oldest before Rebecca and Elizabeth finished what was left. Rebecca had estimated what she thought was needed for the meal and only that much was prepared. Once it was gone, that was it. She'd estimated well, because everyone went away satisfied—at least for today.

There was laughter and smiles, the meal eaten knowing there'd be more tomorrow and the next day. No one would be hungry—at least not until after their journey began.

The meal over, Elizabeth and Rebecca returned to their work slicing the venison and preparing it to dry. That evening, the meat sliced and hung, the fire going with Rebecca's promise it wouldn't go out until the meat was fully dried, Joseph and Sally mounted Hilda and Elizabeth and her family went home for some much-needed rest.

Tomorrow would be another grueling day, but for the first time since this ordeal began, Elizabeth had real hope. There was plenty of food for the trip. If they drank sparingly, the water, too, might last, and they had the means to carry it easily with a sled and a horse. She still had the squirrel rifle and two pistols and could defend what was theirs if the need arose. They were better off than most, she convinced herself, because everything was so well-planned and they were so well-prepared, that once they got started the worst would be over.

She'd never be more wrong.

THE ORDER
Day 7
(Morning)
(September 7, 1863)

Morning came long before Elizabeth was ready for it. Every inch of her body still ached and she never stopped thinking about what needed to be done. Sleep had eluded her most of the night so she was already awake when Joseph and Sally charged into her room in the pre-dawn hours.

"Mama! Mama!" Joseph bounded through the door, Sally right behind him, each clutching their precious wooden horse and cornhusk doll Papa made for them.

"Mama! They're back, Mama! The Bogeymen are back!" Sally's frightened voice penetrated the darkness like a bolt of light as she and her brother scrambled into their mother's protective arms.

Elizabeth knew what had frightened them. She'd heard the slap, slap, slap, throughout the night, but was too tired to get out of bed to do anything about it. So exhausted when she got home, she forgot to secure the shutters in the front room and when the wind came up in the night, they banged and thumped against the window frames.

Elizabeth welcomed her children to her. Despite their agitation they were a soothing balm in a world turned upside down. She calmed them with quiet words—wishing she could promise the Bogeymen would never come again—knowing she couldn't. She wouldn't lie. Besides, Bogeymen *did* exist. They were real men who went by the names of Redleg, Jayhawker, bushwhacker, and Yankee.

"I'll go make sure there are no Bogeymen." She extracted herself from their hold and headed into the front room.

"Be careful, Mama. Don't let him get you!" Joseph said with a loud sniffle.

"No, Mama, don't let him get you," Sally echoed in an equally frightened voice.

Elizabeth smiled. Her eyes already adjusted to the darkness she saw her children huddled together in the middle of the bed. How she wished the expulsion of real Bogeymen was as easy as bracing a shutter against the wind.

Nora and Vera met her outside her door. "Is everything all right, Mama?"

"Yes girls. The children were frightened by the shutters flapping. Go on back to sleep. Tomorrow will be another long, hard day."

"Yes, Mama." Without hesitation the older girls disappeared back into their room.

Elizabeth padded to the farthest window, locked the shutter, and checked the other one before she crawled back into bed between Joseph and Sally.

"Did you get rid of him, Mama?" Sally squeaked.

"I did. I told him to go away and never come back!" Elizabeth tweaked each of their noses, wrapped her arms around them and squeezed until they squeaked. In minutes they were asleep beside her and, finally in their comfort, she, too, slept.

When the sun came up a few hours later, Elizabeth woke more tired than when she'd fallen into bed the night before. But there was work to be done. Reminding herself there is 'no rest for the weary' she rose and steeled herself for another hard day.

There were two days left and much still to be done. When the deadline was up, regardless whether she was ready or not, her home and farm would be robbed of everything of value and burned to the ground, even if she and her children sat right in the middle of it.

All the meat was cooked, dried and ready to be sacked. That task could be done any time in the next two days so Elizabeth opted to do what needed to be done now—finish the sled.

Leaving the children asleep she dragged herself out of bed. Keeping her groans to herself she dressed and went to the barn to decide what to do next on the sled. The heat was already building and she was sweating by the time she reached the barn. Hilda nickered when she entered. Elizabeth greeted the mare with a nose rub, a little corn and some hay. The horse quickly forgot Elizabeth and ate greedily, her usually round belly showing lots of ribs these days.

"You're welcome." Elizabeth grinned and went about

her business. She circled the sled, banged it, shook it, and jumped up and down on it. It held firm. She'd done all she could and now it was time to load it.

The sun was almost up. It was time to wake the children. Nora would help her finish the sled while Vera took charge of Joseph and Sally who *tried* to help, but only got in the way.

On her way back to the house in the peaceful, dawn stillness, Elizabeth took her time surveying everything she and James had built. She remembered the parishioners from surrounding churches helping them erect the barn—some of the same parishioners James told her he'd met in battle and some who had attacked their home. Reverend Newton and Reverend Dolan had blessed the land for them, while she and James lived in a tent until the two-room cabin with a loft was finished a few months before Steven was born. Her eyes fell on the few remaining fence rails, broken and strewn about by foragers and recalled dragging and notching them under James' direction. She glanced over the fields she, Nora, Vera, and a blind horse had plowed and planted, only to have the yield stolen. She gazed into the brightening barn to where the stalls she helped build were now a sled that would carry her family and all that remained of this life away from here.

She was struck with such a violent sense of loss she went to her knees. "Oh, James, I miss you so!" Tears streamed down her cheeks. "We've lost so much and now we're going to lose our home. Even the weather is against us! There's been no rain to relieve the oppressive heat, and the smoke from burning homes or prairie fires, I don't know which, hovers above like a black shroud waiting to drop." She sighed and her shoulders drooped. "I'm so weary! It takes all my strength to rise in the morning and put one foot in front of the other and keep going." A sob tore from her chest. "But I do it for the children. I'll protect them with my life, so help me, James. I swear I will." She put her face in her hands and rocked back and forth, crying until she couldn't cry any more. Her tears spent and painfully aware how much more there was to be done, she wiped her face, took a deep breath, regained her feet, and went inside.

"Nora." She shook her daughter's shoulder until her eyes opened, fuzzy with sleep. Nora groaned and tried to roll away.

"I'm sorry, sweetheart, but it's time to get up. There's work to do."

"But I don't want to, Mama. I'm so tired. I can't do anymore."

It was the first time Nora had tried to shirk her duties since the evacuation order and Elizabeth realized just how tired her oldest child was. But there was no help for it. The work had to be done if they were going to be ready in time.

"Come on, honey. Get up. We have things to do."

Nora rolled on her back and stared at the ceiling for several moments before she turned to her mother. "Yes, Mama, I'm coming."

"Wake your sister and tell her to get in my bed with Joseph and Sally. When they wake she's to keep them out of our way so we can finish the sled."

"What's left to do?" Nora sat up, stretched and wiped the sleep away.

"We're going to drag Steven's mattress out and put it on the bottom of the sled. Then we're going to pack it."

Nora groaned again and pushed out of bed.

"I know you're tired. I'm tired, too, but...."

"I know, I know, there's no help for it," Nora finished with a grin.

Elizabeth grinned back. "No, there is no help for it. So come on, get dressed and let's get to it."

"Yes, Mama." Nora began to dress as Elizabeth climbed the stairs to the loft.

A few minutes later, Nora poked her head over the edge from where she stood on the ladder. "What do you want me to do, Mama?"

In the light coming through the window, Elizabeth noticed for the first time how drawn her daughter was. Her cheeks and eyes were sunken with dark rings, her collarbone pronounced at her neck. It may just have been more noticeable in a child so slight naturally, but it gave Elizabeth pause. Once they reached Aunt Pearl's she hoped they would *all* regain their strength.

"Get everything off the table. I'm going to pull Steven's mattress off the bed and throw it down so we can drag it to the barn."

"Yes, Mama." Nora's reply was wooden and without protest, seemingly resigned to the fact things needed to be done—regardless whether she wanted to do them or not. Ten minutes later the mattress lay across the table. "Grab the other end and we'll drag it outside."

"But it'll get all dirty, Mama."

"It doesn't matter. We're going to fold it, so we'll put the dirty part inside. Besides, it's going to get dirtier on our trip."

Nora swallowed as though unable to grasp what her mother had just said. Everything in their home had always been kept clean and tidy. "It really *doesn't* matter, does it Mama?" Her voice quavered. "Nothing matters except leaving in time."

Elizabeth wrapped her arms around her daughter. "The only thing that matters, Nora, is you, your brother and sisters. All this," she waved her hand to encompass the house, "all this can disappear, but as long as you children are safe, nothing is lost."

Tears stood in her daughter's eyes and rolled over onto her cheeks. "I'm scared."

"I'm scared, too, but we're doing everything we can to help make our trip as tolerable as possible, with enough food and minimal comfort to reach Aunt Pearl's. We're going to make it just fine, Nora."

Nora smiled. "If you say it's so, Mama, I believe you. You've never lied to me and I don't believe you'd start now."

Elizabeth crushed her daughter to her again and tears slid down her face. "We will make it, Nora, I promise." Elizabeth hoped with all her heart it *wasn't* a lie.

THE ORDER
Day 7
(Late Morning)
(September 7, 1863)

With much less effort than it took to drag the deer carcass through the woods to Rebecca's, Elizabeth and Nora hauled Steven's mattress to the sled, laid it on the bottom, folded and nailed it tight. Looking down at their handiwork they grinned.

"That'll suffice," Elizabeth said, hands on her hips.

Nora sat down on the end and laid back. "It feels good."

"Don't get used to it. It's not for us, it's for the little ones, most specifically little Robert, Andrew, Joseph, and Sally. They'll walk as long as they can, but being so young they won't last long and will have to ride to keep us from losing time. Each of you older children will be responsible for one of the smaller ones. You'll have Joseph, because he's bigger than Sally now, Vera will take care of Sally, and Rebecca's children will pair with their younger sisters and brothers. That way you older children can watch over the little ones and make sure they don't fall behind. If they do start to lag behind, you'll let me or Rebecca know, and we'll decide whether to put them in the sled or on Hilda."

"Yes, Mama."

"Each of you will be responsible for your own bag, as we already discussed," Elizabeth continued. "The little ones included. Hilda will have enough dragging the sled behind her carrying the food, water, and necessities for the trip like pots and pans and blankets and doesn't need any additional, even if it is just a small child, but we don't want to overburden her. I'll hunt when I can, but there's no guarantee I'll get anything, not when so many people and animals will be around, which is why we're bringing the jerked meat."

Nora nodded her head in understanding and pushed herself up out of the sled. "What now?"

Elizabeth thought a moment. "It's time to gather what we need from the house and load it." She took Nora's hand. "Come on, let's get started."

They trudged from the barn back to the house, where Vera sat in the chair reading to Joseph and Sally.

"Mama!" the smaller children squealed, sliding out of the chair and running into their mother's arms.

She hugged them tight, praying the war and this journey wouldn't scar them for the rest of their lives. They were already as skittish as young colts. Every bump and thump sent them screaming into her arms.

"Hello children. Are you being good for your big sister?"

"Yes, Mama."

"They are, Mama," Vera confirmed.

"Good. Keep them busy a little longer while Nora and I pick out what must be loaded on the sled," Elizabeth told Vera.

"Yes, Mama." Vera took the children's hands, got comfortable in the chair again, and continued her story.

The sound of Vera's voice soothed Elizabeth as she and Nora went through the cabin deciding what to take. Nora pointed and Elizabeth said yes or no, or Elizabeth pointed and Nora retrieved it. An hour later a stack of pots and pans, metal dishes, the earthen jugs to hold the water, the few blankets they'd managed to hide from raiders, lanterns, and any other items that might be useful on their trip were crowded on the table. Knowing the value of their mattresses, both monetarily and for what little comfort they might bring during their journey, they would be put on the sled last to cover and hold everything securely, but easily pulled off at night for sleeping.

"Can I help load the sled, Mama?" Vera asked.

"You may," Elizabeth agreed.

Vera beamed. "What about Joseph and Sally?"

"They can help, too, as long as it's unbreakable and small enough for them to carry out."

The smaller children jumped up and down, happy to be included in the preparations.

"Take what you can and bring it to the barn. Nora, help Joseph and Sally choose then help them outside."

Joseph and Sally ran to the table, taking a moment to decide before they each took a metal plate and hurried out the door. Nora grabbed a lantern and a heavy metal pot and hurried behind them.

Elizabeth remembered a tintype of her and James on the dresser. She went to retrieve it leaving Vera to decide on her own what to carry. A minute later, Vera screamed and Elizabeth heard the shattering of glass and what sounded like the crash of heavy cookware. She ran to the porch where Vera lay sprawled at the bottom of the steps, two cast iron pans lying on either side of her, and a shattered earthen water jug beside her.

"What have you done? Those jugs aren't supposed to go to the sled! We only had three and now you've broken one!"

Nora, Joseph and Sally ran from the barn, came to a skidding stop, and watched in silence, their eyes wide with sympathy for their sister.

Vera sat up, legs spread, her dirty dress tangled around her ankles, her hair a wild mess. "I'm sorry, Mama. I didn't know. They were on the table with everything else so I thought I could take one. I couldn't see where I was going and I fell."

"I can see you fell, Vera, trying to do more than you should!"

Vera's lips trembled and tears streamed down her face. "I'm sorry, Mama. I'm sorry. I didn't know."

Elizabeth looked at her other children, each with tears in their eyes. *What was she doing? She hadn't even asked Vera if she was hurt!* She hurried down the steps, plopped down in the dirt beside her sobbing daughter and pulled her into her arms. "No, Vera, I'm the one who's sorry. I'm so sorry for worrying more about a water jug than whether you were hurt. I'm sorry for what's happening, for what you have to deal with, what you all have to deal with living in such terrible times." She hugged her crying child tighter and cried right along with her.

The other children came and put their arms around their mother and sister, giving comfort as best they could until the weeping stopped, the broken jug was forgotten, and work began again. There was no time to grieve over a lost water jug. If this was the worst that happened on their trip, Elizabeth welcomed it, fearful this would be only one of many mishaps that would plague their journey.

The rest of the morning was spent gathering and loading what Elizabeth had decided to take with them. Afraid of pulling the sled out into the open, they brought everything from the house to the barn, exhausting work for mother and children already spent in their continuous efforts in the ever-present heat preparing for their trip. Under Hilda's watchful scrutiny from her stall, they piled everything onto the sled, lashing it as they went, the stack growing higher and higher as the morning passed. Room was left up front for weary children and sacks of meat and, by the time it was all loaded, the contents in the sled stood four feet high.

"We can't put another thing on here except the mattresses." Elizabeth studied their handiwork. "I hope this isn't too much for Hilda to carry." She shook her head. "There's so much more than I thought." She pushed a sweaty lock of hair off her forehead, puffed out her bottom lip, and blew up to try and cool her face.

"I'm hungry!" Joseph shouted from the other side of the barn where he and Sally played in the small, dwindling hay pile, both children bored fifteen minutes into their packing.

"Me, too!" Sally agreed.

Elizabeth took one last look at the sled. "There's nothing else to be done except load the mattresses and we won't do that until tomorrow morning. I won't take our last night of sleep in our own beds away from us."

"Can we go to Rebecca's for supper now? We're having the stew Helen, Clara, and I made yesterday." Nora fairly beamed.

"Don't forget me! I helped, too!" Vera shouted indignantly.

"And Vera, too," Nora added grudgingly.

Elizabeth's heart broke at the joy the promise one good meal brought to her daughters. How sad their dreary lives had become in the wake of General Order No. 11 and a war that seemed to go on forever. Absently, she stroked Hilda's neck, the mare standing inside her stall. Since beginning their daily trek to the Barrow home, Nora, Vera, Helen, and Clara had fashioned a new rope corral every day in the trees behind the cabin so Hilda could forage throughout the day. With little grain or corn, what the mare found inside those makeshift corrals had become her main food supply, regardless the foliage and grass was dry and brittle in the continuing drought.

"Mama, supper?" Nora broke into her musings.

"Yes. As soon as I change out of Papa's dirty trousers we'll go." She kissed Hilda on the nose. "And how about you, girl? Are you ready to go, too?" The mare bobbed her head up and down as though in response.

A half hour later, Elizabeth led Hilda along the now well-worn path between theirs and the Barrow home. Her mouth almost watered in anticipation of another good meal and her step quickened. Then she remembered what would follow the meal. More work. Always more work. She sighed heavily and groaned out loud. Her shoulders slumped and her pace slowed.

Would they ever know rest again?

THE ORDER
Day 8
(September 8, 1863)

Time was ticking away. The Miers arrived early at the Barrow house to begin the final day of preparations. The jerked venison was put into empty feed sacks to be separated into what would go on the sled or taken home to be put into the individual bags for each family member. Everything that could be done was done and the two families sat down to their final meal in Rebecca's home.

"We should eat at the table today." Rebecca pushed a sweaty lock of hair off her brow. "I know it's hotter inside than out, but I want us all to be together. It's the last time we'll have supper here and I want everyone around me." Unshed tears glistened in her eyes and Elizabeth touched her shoulder.

"I think that's a fine idea."

"Children, gather round the table. We'll eat inside today." Rebecca's voice caught as she said the words.

The children scrambled to find a seat, Helen with little Robert on her lap so her mother could help Elizabeth serve. Elizabeth and Rebecca went to opposite ends of the table where Rebecca stood unmoving, staring down at the chair, tears spilling over her cheeks.

Without speaking the words Elizabeth knew Rebecca was thinking of her husband, whose place she was about to sit in.

Her own thoughts turning to James, Elizabeth forced a wavering smile of acknowledgment, and bowed her head. "Shall we join hands?" Everyone joined hands and Elizabeth prayed. "Dear Lord, we thank you for and ask your blessing on this food. We ask that you might guide us through our coming journey. Lay your cloak of protection upon us and lead us to our destination in your keeping. We pray these things in Thy precious name. Amen."

"Amen," was whispered around the room.

Elizabeth and Rebecca distributed the stew rationed for the meal, having put aside enough for tomorrow's breakfast at their respective homes before their departure. One ladle full was given to each child, the younger children receiving half.

Whatever was left after the first time around was equally split until it was gone. Each child watched intently as the stew filled their bowl, hoping for a few extra spoons full. It went farther than anticipated and everyone wound up with almost two ladles full before it ran out. The room was quiet throughout the meal. Thoughts of what lay ahead weighed heavily on the minds of those who understood what tomorrow would bring—the smaller children silent in their ignorance.

"We'll be at your house by dawn, Elizabeth." Rebecca stood on the porch above the steps. Because the sled was at Elizabeth's, the Barrows would go to the Miers' and they would depart from there.

Elizabeth turned in a circle below the porch, surveying the area outside Rebecca's cabin. There was nothing left to do. The meat sacks were tied to Hilda's saddle to carry home for loading in the sled and packing their personal bags. Two empty earthen water jugs waited on the porch for Elizabeth and Nora to carry home, giving them four for the trip. Everyone had eaten their fill of stew, and perhaps a little more, giving them a good start on their way.

Saying goodbye until tomorrow, the Miers family headed home. Trudging through the trees, approaching where the fence *used to be* that separated the two homesteads, Elizabeth felt such a sense of regret and longing she almost went to her knees like she had the other morning. *She had to stay strong for her children. It was no time to show weakness. The only thing that mattered was keeping them safe when everything they loved was left behind tomorrow.*

The family stopped and stared across at the ground where their father and husband lay. Even Joseph and Sally, on either side of their mother, hands tight in hers, understood to some degree that their Papa was sleeping under the ground and they'd never see him again.

In silence the family stood lost in their memories of James Miers. Finally, Elizabeth stepped over where the fence had been and knelt beside her husband's grave. She pulled the weeds that had sprouted since her last visit, already withered in the heat. She threw the dead weeds aside, wishing they were the Yankees that had killed her husband. She stared down at the ground, her thoughts tumbling in her head, until a gentle hand on her back startled her back to the present. Nora knelt beside her, a handful of scraggly flowers in her hand. Swallowing, her daughter laid them atop her father's freshly cleaned grave.

Again wishing things were different, knowing wishing wouldn't change a thing, Elizabeth straightened both her back and her resolve and stood up, Nora rising beside her.

They joined hands around the gravesite and let their tears flow without restraint until Elizabeth cleared her throat. "James, you were a good husband and father. We miss you every day and wish you were still with us." Hearing her children sniffling and crying, her voice broke and she took a moment to regain herself. "We won't be back to visit for a while. An order has been issued forcing us to leave our home. So the children and I are going to Aunt Pearl and Uncle Rupert's until this crazy war is over," she whispered her voice shaky. Tears streamed down hers and her children's cheeks. The mourning family stood silent a few more minutes before Elizabeth announced it was time to go.

One by one they told their Papa how much they loved him and missed him, touched their fingers to their lips in a kiss then laid them on the grave, and started for home, their sniffles the only sound in the otherwise quiet woods. *If only things were different,* Elizabeth mused for the thousandth time since burying her husband, turning for one last look. *'If only' counts for nothing,* she snorted through her sadness. *Absolutely nothing!*

Arriving at home with several hours of light left, Elizabeth and Nora got back to work. Vera took charge of Sally and Joseph and kept them occupied while their sister and mother did what was necessary to finish preparing for tomorrow.

All four water jugs were filled to the brim. Nora put on the metal lids then Elizabeth wrapped them with rope from top to bottom. She fashioned a handle and hung them deep in the well to stay chilled until morning, the wet rope keeping the water inside cool against the brutal heat once the journey began.

That task done, Elizabeth and Nora went inside to help the children pack. They carried in four sacks of meat so the night creatures wouldn't find them. Elizabeth set another bag of meat on the table.

"Nora, split the venison evenly between you, me and Vera. Give half portions to Joseph and Sally. Put it in piles on the table then wrap it and set it aside." She turned to the other three children, each holding an empty ten pound flour sack, waiting for instructions on what to put in it.

"Vera, you and Sally choose four dresses to wear tomorrow. I'll choose what Joseph will wear."

"Mama? We're going to wear four dresses?" Vera asked her face twisted.

"Yes. You'll fill the pockets of the first dress you put on with jewelry and medicine then you'll put on another dress over it and another and another. Nora and I will do the same."

"Why, Mama?"

Elizabeth put her hands on Vera's confused face. "You've seen what the Yankees do. They'll steal anything we have, even our clothes. If they don't know we have them, they can't take them."

"But it'll be so hot, Mama!"

"And we'll bear it, Vera. If we want to keep what little we have, we must be smarter than those who would steal from us."

Tears streamed down Vera's cheeks and Elizabeth didn't know whether it was because her daughter did—or did not—understand.

"You may bring one item that isn't clothing or food," Elizabeth continued. "Everyone run and get the most important thing you want to bring with you."

Joseph and Sally returned quickly, Joseph with the wooden horse and Sally with the now raggedy cornhusk doll their Papa made them.

Vera brought out a wooden cross James had made when she was baptized at eight years old, and Nora lovingly held a small piece of material, all that was left of the cloth her Papa gave her and Vera for their aprons last Christmas, now used as patches for disintegrating clothing.

Inside Elizabeth's bag she put *Elizabeth Miers' Book of Verses*, Vera's poem in the lopsided frame, the tintype of her and James on their wedding day, and her portion of the jerked venison. The locket James gave her after the fight at Morristown was sewn inside the pocket of the dress she planned to wear under her other clothes, along with her wedding ring, her father's watch, her mother's cameo pin, and several other pieces of jewelry of sentimental value that she'd dug out of the hidey hole behind the barn. Other than the children, of course, of all she had left, these items meant the most to her. In another pocket she put some Confederate bills James gave her on his last visit, just in case. Going south she hoped they might be used as viable currency, but knew they'd probably be better served as kindling to start a fire.

The evening was spent cutting and sewing straps from top to bottom on each of their bags so it could be slung across their back or chest for easier carrying.

After eleven o'clock, Elizabeth looked around at her home and children. The cabin looked nothing like it had only days ago, empty of everything that made a house a home. Joseph and Sally were sound asleep in the chair, Joseph stretched across one arm and Sally lying across the other. Vera was slumped over the table, her head on her arms, eyes closed and breathing evenly. Only Nora and Elizabeth were still awake.

"I guess this is it." Nora tried to push back the tears Elizabeth saw in her eyes, but they spilled over and down her cheeks. Nora fell into her mother's arms weeping. "I'm so scared, Mama."

"Shhhh, I know. I'm scared, too, but I promised we'd make it. And we will."

Nora pulled away, wiped the tears from her cheeks and smiled. "And I still believe you."

"Very good then, let's wake up your brother and sisters and get to bed. It's going to be a hard morning."

Nora swallowed and nodded then went over and lifted a sleeping Sally in her arms as Elizabeth gathered up a slumbering Joseph. Putting them into their beds for the last time, both Joseph's and the girls' beds stripped of the already packed linens, Elizabeth kissed each of them good night with a cheerful face. Their understanding limited to what the sun would bring they smiled back, rolled over and went back to sleep.

Elizabeth woke Vera and she and Nora went to bed with lips trembling, trying hard not to cry, with the knowledge this was the last night they would ever spend in their home. Elizabeth tried to encourage them, but her older girls knew better.

"We have to look at our journey as an adventure," she told them. "If we don't, we may get discouraged and that will be of no help. We have to stay true to our task, and that is reaching Aunt Pearl and Uncle Rupert's."

"But I don't *want* to go, Mama," Vera whined. "I want to stay here."

"But we can't and you know it," Nora interrupted, her voice stern. "None of us *wants* to go, but we have no choice. There's no help for it."

Elizabeth watched the exchange between sisters and smiled sadly. Nora had a full understanding of what was happening. At ten Vera tried to comprehend everything that was going on, but it was still difficult for her to grasp the fact that tomorrow everything they knew and loved would be left behind.

She kissed her children one last time and padded to her own dismal room. She blew out the candle, lay down on her bed for the last time and closed her eyes, knowing there would be no sleep. With a heavy sigh she thought of the preparations. There was nothing left to be done—except the leaving.

THE ORDER
Day 9
(Departure Day - Morning)
(September 9, 1863)

Breakfast in the pre-dawn was solemn. No one spoke, not even Joseph or Sally who eyed their older siblings and mother, waiting for some clue of what to do. Tears brimmed in silent faces, brushed away harshly when they spilled over so no one else would see, but soon it didn't matter and the silent tears flowed.

"Finish up children, there's work to be done." The short sentence had been among the hardest Elizabeth ever spoke, signaling the completion of their last meal in the home they would leave behind and the knowledge that once said, there was no turning back.

Nora and Vera got up, bowls in hand, to put on the counter to be cleaned as they had every day of their lives in this place.

"Leave them there. If the Yankees want our home so badly they can have it with dirty dishes."

The girls looked down at their bowls then back at Elizabeth with the first smiles on their faces in a very long time. "Yes, Mama."

"And after we drag the mattresses out and tie them to the sled, we're going to come back inside and have a party." She clapped her hands and smiled like it was the most natural thing in the world to do.

"What kind of party?" Vera's voice belied her puzzlement.

"Yay! A party!" Joseph and Sally, doing everything in unison these days, jumped up and down, clapping like their mama.

"What kind of party?" Vera asked again.

"A destruction party," Elizabeth answered, her voice now solemn.

"I don't understand, Mama." Vera's head cocked to the side again showing her bewilderment. Only Nora seemed to understand her mother's intent with a slight grin and a gleam in her eyes.

"We're going to break everything those dirty, stinking, thieving, rotten, low-down, murdering Yankees can steal." Even that didn't seem to be enough vile names to call the men coming to destroy her home and what was left of their lives.

Vera swallowed. "Everything?"

"Yes! And we're going to have fun doing it." She picked up an empty glass pitcher, looked at it one last time, turned and threw it against the wall where it shattered with a thunderous crash.

Joseph and Sally, uncertain what was going on, sat in silence, eyes bulging, lower lips trembling.

"And when we come back inside you can break things, too!" she told them. The two youngsters looked at each other then back at their Mama before a cautious smile broke across their faces.

"We can break things, too?" Sally squeaked.

"On purpose?" Joseph asked after his sister.

"Yes, so let's get Hilda harnessed and pull the sled in front of the porch so we can finish packing it." She waved her hand around the interior. "We have some breaking to do when we're done!" If she made it a game, perhaps it wouldn't hurt so badly. Deep down, she knew that was a lie, but maybe she could convince her children otherwise, *at least* Joseph and Sally.

Hilda stood in front of the porch, the sled behind her loaded to overflowing with what remained of the combined households of two families, the three sacks of meat, swaying water jugs, pots, pans, linens, blankets, and whatever else had been deemed necessary for the long trip, the last two mattresses slung over the top of the huge pile and lashed down tight to keep everything from falling off.

Elizabeth stood at the top of the steps, her arm around Joseph and Nora on one side of her and Sally and Vera on the other, all staring down at the ugliest conveyance she'd ever seen, piled high with what remained of their lives. Ugly as it might be, she prayed it would survive the trip intact. If it didn't, an already grueling trip would get much worse.

With everything loaded and the sun rising, Elizabeth

knew it was time to finish it. She intended to leave absolutely nothing behind for the Yankees, except the shell of what had been their home.

"Who's ready to have that party now?" She clapped and smiled happily. "Who wants to break things?"

"I do! I do!" Joseph and Sally shouted, still not realizing what it meant.

Tears pooled in Vera's eyes, but she nodded, as did Nora with equal solemnity.

"Let's go then!" Elizabeth shouted happily, trying to keep the tone fun.

They spent the next half hour destroying everything inside their home that could be broken, bent or split. Joseph's bed was pulled off the wall, breaking into pieces when the older girls hung on it and bounced up and down. Joseph and Sally had fun destroying crockery and glassware, throwing it into a pile in the corner of the front room, giggling with uncertainty with each piece they flung against the wall. Mirrors were shattered, the dressers in Elizabeth's and the children's room toppled, the drawers pulled out, jumped on and broken, clothing ripped and shredded. Using a hatchet Elizabeth had kept back for this occasion, she hacked hers and the children's bed frames to uselessness, scattering the pieces around the rooms. Racks and shelves were pulled off the walls, shutters torn from the windows until the cabin was a ruined mess.

Elizabeth stood in the middle of the destruction, sweating and breathing heavily from the exertion. "Our party is all over now, children."

"Aw, I want to break more!" Joseph shouted.

"Can we do it again?" Sally yelled.

Elizabeth tried to keep a happy face, while praying they never, ever had to do something like this again in their lives. "No children, we're all done and we won't do it again. Ever."

Speaking to Nora she said, "Come up to the loft with me." She turned to Vera. "Take Joseph and Sally outside and don't come back in no matter what you hear. Do you understand?"

"Yes, Mama." Vera shuffled Joseph and Sally out the front door.

Without question Nora followed her mother up the ladder, one of the few remaining things in the house still in-tact.

"Help me turn the bed over."

Between the two they upended Steven's bed and pushed it close enough to the edge so its weight carried it over the side. It landed on the table with a resounding crash, broke into pieces, and split the table under it.

Nora and Elizabeth stared down over the remains of their home. Everything of worth or necessity to them was already packed in the sled or hidden in their clothing, each wearing at least four layers. What they didn't have in the sled or wear was shattered, broken and worthless on the floor.

Nora suddenly started tearing at the collar of her multiple layers of clothing and gasping. "I'm so hot, Mama."

"I am, too, Nora, but we have to hide our valuables on our person if we want to save them. It won't be much longer. In a week we'll be at Aunt Pearl's and Uncle Rupert's. We'll be safe there. Until then we must be diligent in keeping anything of value out of sight.

Nora leaned into her mother. "It's the next week I'm worried about, Mama. We'll be sleeping outside! There'll be bugs and animals and it's so hot!" she wailed.

"Shhhh, Nora. Yes, there will be all those things, but we're going to make it. Haven't I promised you that?" Again she prayed a silent prayer she wasn't making false promises.

Nora sucked in a deep breath and managed to nod her head. "Yes, Mama."

"Well, I meant it. We're going to make it and we're all going to be fine."

Nora broke down into sobs and Elizabeth held her daughter until the tears stopped.

"Come on now, it's time to go outside and wait for the Barrows. They should arrive any minute and there's nothing left for us in here."

Nora nodded again, unable to speak.

They climbed down from the loft and shoved the ladder over, hoping it would break when it landed, but James built things to last. It bounced and settled on the floor intact.

"Wait." Elizabeth retrieved the hatchet and hacked at one of the rungs until it broke in half.

"Can I do some?" Nora's eyes almost gleamed.

"Of course, here." Elizabeth handed the hatchet to Nora who timidly struck a rung like she had when trying to tear apart the stall only days ago. Today, the more she swung the weapon the harder it hit, shattering rung after rung. Tears streamed down her cheeks as she destroyed the ladder, it having become a substitute, Elizabeth presumed, for those who were hurting her family.

When the ladder was nothing but shards of wood, Elizabeth laid her hand over Nora's. "That's enough."

Her daughter looked up, eyes red-rimmed and full of pain, her cheeks flaming and soaked with tears. "Oh, Mama!" She fell into her mother's arms and wept bitter tears, and this time Elizabeth cried with her.

Regaining their composure Elizabeth and Nora linked arms and stepped out the door of their home for the last time. They were met by an anxious Vera, Joseph and Sally. "What was all that noise?" Vera asked.

"Did you break the rest of the house, Mama?" Joseph bounced from foot to foot, energized by the excitement of the morning.

Elizabeth forced a smile. "We sure did Joseph. We broke the rest of the house."

Rebecca and her family arrived a few minutes later, quiet and withdrawn. Little Robert was in a sling-like carrier Rebecca had fashioned much like the bags Elizabeth and the children made for their belongings. The baby was slung across his mother's back, sound asleep. Elizabeth almost envied the child, oblivious to what was happening and protected by his mother.

"Well, I guess this is it." Rebecca's eyes pooled with tears and she swiped at them angrily as they slipped down her cheeks. "I don't know how I have a single tear left in my head! I've been crying since last night. I cried in mine and Thomas' bed for the last time, then I cried through our last breakfast, and I cried the whole way here. I can't believe I still have more."

Elizabeth laid her hand on her friend's shoulder. "We're going to be all right, Rebecca. We're better prepared than most so we're going to be fine. We just have to stay strong and not let it break us down."

"I hope you're right. Remember the other day when I said I wasn't afraid anymore? Well, I'm afraid again. I can't stop shaking. I'm afraid something bad will happen on this trip. Afraid one of my children...."

She stopped, unable to utter the unspeakable words that something might happen to one of her children.

"We're going to be fine," Elizabeth promised again, hoping to make Rebecca feel better. *Why did she always have to be the strong one? Once, just once, she wished someone would hold her up, tell her not to worry, and promise they would come through this safely. But it was not to be. Her rock and strength was gone, and now she had to be that rock and that strength for her family.*

Elizabeth looked around what had been her home, now an empty shell devoid of the love and happiness that had built and filled it. The barn stood empty. The fields were burned up from the heat and crumbling in the wind, the creek a mud hole. The house, although it looked normal from the outside, was a shambles inside. Nothing remained that had been loved by her family or her. All was lost except what they carried with them.

Rebecca did a head count of her children then stepped up beside Elizabeth. "I guess it's time."

Elizabeth pursed her lips. "You're right. There's no reason to linger—and nothing left here for us. I've destroyed everything inside the cabin so those thieving blue bellies won't have a thing to take away with them. They can burn the house, but that's *all* the satisfaction they'll get from this place!"

Rebecca smiled then actually giggled. "We did the same thing before we left. We destroyed everything. I'll be...darned if I'll let them have anything of ours worth having!"

Rebecca and Elizabeth actually laughed before reality struck again. It was time to go. There was nothing to hold them here.

"Well then, let's be on our way." Elizabeth raised her hand toward the road. "Shall we?"

"Come children, it's time to go." Rebecca's children gathered around her, the older ones with red, puffy eyes knowing what was happening, the youngest ones oblivious to what lie ahead. Elizabeth's children walked beside her, Nora and Vera quiet, their cheeks glistening from the tears they'd already shed, holding tight to the hands of their younger siblings, silent in their ignorance.

Elizabeth took Hilda's bridle and clucked her forward. With effort, the mare took one step then another until the sled jerked forward.

It was really happening. They were leaving behind everything they'd built and loved. Heading toward what, Elizabeth didn't know, but whatever it was it would not be easy getting there. This journey would be the most difficult thing she would ever do. More difficult than destroying her home, more difficult than leaving everything she loved, possibly even more difficult than burying her husband, regardless what she and Rebecca told the children to bolster their spirits.

"Don't look back children. We must look forward—only forward."

Doing exactly what she told her children not to do, she looked over her shoulder as though to speak to everyone again so she could take one last look at what had been her home, her life, where she had cared for and loved a husband, and birthed and raised five children. Turning forward so the children wouldn't see her pain, she walked on, her legs like wooden pegs, saving her children the only goal.

PART III

THE ROAD
DUST, DEVILS,
AND DESPAIR

Local Refugee Routes
August through September

Map reprinted (with permission)
from Cinders and Silence by Tom
A. Rafiner, page 238.

THE JOURNEY
Departure Day 1
(The Austin-Wadesburg Road)

They headed east toward the Austin-Wadesburg Road that would meet with the road toward Clinton.

"Mama, I'm so hot!" Vera's face was scarlet, her mouth tight with frustration as she tore at her sleeves and collar.

"I can't breathe," Nora whined, not as loudly as Vera, but in just as frustrated a tone, ruffling her four skirts to allow air beneath the layers.

Joseph started to cry. "I'm hot, too, Mama." Big tears slid down the boy's no longer chubby cheeks, bright red from walking two hours on the churning, dusty road in the soaring temperature.

Sally mewled like an injured cat, yanking at her collar and skirts like her older sisters.

Rebecca's children voiced their displeasure loudly on the other side of the sled.

"It's hot!"

"My feet hurt!"

"I want to stop!"

Elizabeth brought Hilda to a stop. "Enough!" she shouted loud enough for everyone to hear.

"But it's so hot, Mama. I can't take another step!" Vera stomped her foot, making dust puff up in little clouds around her ankles.

"And you're going to get much hotter and more tired before we get where we're going." Elizabeth stepped in front of her daughter, while Rebecca tried to quiet her children on the other side of Hilda and not doing much better. Several clusters of travelers behind them halted and waited as Elizabeth spoke to her daughter.

"Vera, we talked about this—about all this." Elizabeth waved her hand at Hilda and their surroundings. "We haven't really even started our journey and you're already complaining."

"What do you mean we haven't even started?" Vera's eyes were wide and her nose flared. "We've been walking forever! My feet hurt and I'm sweating like, like a stinky ole boy!"

Elizabeth put her hands on Vera's shoulders. "Listen to me. This is hard for all of us, but we have no choice, just like Rebecca and her family have no choice, and the folks behind us have no choice. We have over ten miles to go before we even reach the Clinton Road.

"Ten miles!" Vera shouted. Tears brimmed in her eyes. "I can't do it, Mama, I can't!" she wailed dramatically.

"You can and you will, Vera. If we don't make at least six or seven miles a day, it'll take two weeks to reach Aunt Pearl's house, and I don't want that, and I imagine you don't want that either, do you? To be on a dirty, dusty, hot road for two weeks?"

Vera's chin dropped and she stomped her foot again. "No Mama. I want to be there now."

"You know we can't, so you're going to have to be strong. And you don't want to frighten the little ones, do you?" She waved her hand at Joseph and Sally, standing beside their big sister with lips quivering.

Vera sniffed and shook her head. "No Mama."

"Good girl. Tomorrow we'll reach the main road and head south to Clinton. And once we're on that road we'll be one of hundreds of other families with their animals, their slaves, their carts, *and* the heat." She smoothed her daughter's sweaty hair off her forehead.

The look on Vera's face almost broke Elizabeth's heart before the girl fell into her chest and wrapped her arms around her mother's waist. "I'm sorry, Mama. I'm just so scared and tired, but I'll try and be brave," she promised, sniffling loudly.

Nora stepped up and put her arms around her mother and sister. Joseph and Sally wrapped themselves as far as they could around their family. Elizabeth, at the center, gave encouragement until she realized this coddling had to stop or the children would protest often and expect the same kind of pampering. Pampering that would make them weak. They'd complain more and it would slow them down. She pushed to her feet, forcing the children away from her. In her sternest voice she said, "Children, this is the last time we will feel sorry for ourselves. I've said it a hundred times and if I have to, I'll say it a hundred more. We—have—no—choice in what's happening. It is going to be hot, our feet will hurt, and we'll be more tired than we've ever been in our lives. But we're going to bear it with dignity and strength and we're going to make it to Aunt Pearl and Uncle Rupert's. I want no more crying and no more complaining. If the little ones get too tired, they'll ride Hilda or on the sled until they're able to walk again."

"What about *us*?" Vera slapped her arms across her chest and her lips curled into a sneer. "Why do *they* get to ride and not us? I'm tired, too."

So much for being brave. Elizabeth grabbed her daughter by the shoulders again and shook her. "And you're going to get so much more tired, Vera. There's nothing to be done about it. How many times must I tell you? The more you complain, the worse it'll be. Cry if you want, but cry in silence. I won't have you sniveling about, making everyone unhappier than they already are."

"Mama, that's cruel," Nora said for the first time since they'd stopped.

"Perhaps, but it's no more cruel than what we're facing. There'll be no mollycoddling from now on. We *must* be strong. You'll do what you're told when you're told to do it." Her voice caught, thinking of everything that could go wrong. *Soldiers, raiders, wild animals.* "If you don't...." She stopped short of saying someone could die. "We must be stronger than this." She waved her hand at everyone standing around sniveling. "There's no help for it."

"But Mama," Vera tried to say one last time, but Elizabeth cut her off.

"No, Vera! There will be no more discussion. Right here is where the self-pity ends!"

The children snapped straight, their eyes wide, lips trembling, but stayed silent. One by one they ran a hand under their nose, sniffed a last time, and nodded.

Rebecca's children were still complaining until Rebecca shouted, "Enough! There'll be no more whining or complaining. We can't go anywhere but where we're going. There *is* no home to go back to. There's only forward and that's where we're headed. Is that clear?"

"But Mama...."

"No Helen! There will be *no* more whining and *no* more complaining. You will be responsible for yourself and whomever you've been paired with, and you *will* be silent in your miseries, just as everyone else will."

Rebecca's children grew quiet and Elizabeth turned back to her own. "You see. There will be no tolerance for complaints or whining or crying from anyone. *Everyone* must do their part, carry their own loads, and be silent in the doing."

"Except the little ones," Vera sniped.

Elizabeth lost her patience, grabbed Vera by the shoulders and shook her again. "Stop being so selfish! Joseph and Sally and Andrew are little! They can't do what you older children can. They tire more easily. Maybe you would like to carry them? Or should we leave them by the side of the road when they can't walk anymore?"

Vera's eye's pinched. "Leave them? Of course I don't want to leave them!"

"You should carry them then?"

"No!"

"What's left?" Elizabeth asked her tearful daughter.

"We can stop when they get tired."

"And how often do you think that will be, Vera? Every ten minutes, every hour, every two hours? They can't keep up with everyone else. So what else is there to do?"

Vera sniffed. "Let them ride Hilda or on the sled until they can walk again."

Elizabeth smiled. "There, you've worked it through and solved the problem yourself. Now do you understand?"

"Yes, Mama."

"And will you help me with the little ones instead of being mad because they get to ride when you have to walk with sore feet?"

"Yes, Mama."

"Very well then, consider this today's lesson!" she shouted to everyone.

Rebecca's children were gathered around their mother on the other side of Hilda, their mouths shut their eyes wide.

"So children that was our first rest," Elizabeth said loudly. She looked over Hilda's back at Rebecca. "Are you all ready to get moving again?"

"We are."

Elizabeth clucked the mare and the sled jerked forward, the small troupe of vagabonds walking beside and behind her in silence.

Elizabeth's mind spun like a child's top. They'd gone perhaps a mile and the children were ready to give up already. *They had sixty to go!* She hated being so stern, but that was the only thing that would get them through this ordeal—that and a stubbornness not to give up or give in. They *would* reach their destination and her children would thank her—someday.

Hours later Rebecca took off her hat and ran the back of her hand across her forehead. "We have to stop, Elizabeth. Even I don't know if I can take one more step."

Elizabeth nodded. "I know. I'm exhausted, too. As soon as we find enough shade we'll take a rest and eat. I'm sure the children won't protest," she added with a forced smile. It was so hot she felt like a pig roasting on a slow-turning spit.

Twenty minutes later they came to a big grove of cottonwoods and pulled off the road. Some of the travelers behind them pulled off, too, to take advantage of what shade there was when it was there. Settled on stumps and fallen limbs, equal portions of meat were pulled from the bag and passed out, along with small cups-full of water from the rope-wrapped jugs. The meat was hard, but helped fill some of the void in their empty stomachs, the lukewarm water gritty, but better than hot or none at all.

Barely lifting her eyes, Elizabeth ate and studied the other travelers who had stopped around them. Some nibbled on hardtack like she did, but most just rested, hunger and thirst obvious on their faces. Some watched hers and Rebecca's families eat, and she warned herself to be leery they might try and take what wasn't theirs. She was sure each family on this road had a sad story, much like their own, but she didn't want to hear it or know it. All Elizabeth cared about were hers and Rebecca's children, not someone else's—regardless the story.

Sitting beside her mother Nora interrupted Elizabeth's musing when she whispered, "I'm still hungry, Mama."

"Me, too," Vera said from where she sat beside Nora on a fallen branch. Across from them sat Rebecca, Helen and Clara on another limb under a huge dead oak, the smaller children on their laps or playing in the dirt as though nothing were amiss.

"I'm still hungry too," Elizabeth admitted, "but we must eat sparingly, especially so early in our trip. We have a long way to go and if we've misjudged our rations we'll be in serious trouble if they run out too soon."

"I know, Mama, I just couldn't help saying it." Nora looked up, blinking away the tears pooling in her eyes to keep them from falling. "I...I...." She snapped her mouth shut and scrubbed at the threatening tears.

Elizabeth sucked in one last breath of the stifling, hot air. It was time to move again. They probably hadn't made three miles yet and she wanted to try and reach Sugar Creek before nightfall. It would be a good stopping place and meant they needed to keep going. Of course, she had no way of gauging how far they'd gone already, but *hoped* they'd make it to the creek before they stopped—and that there was water in it when they got there.

Rebecca had finished feeding little Robert, the babe asleep at her breast in his sling. "Are you ready?"

"No, but we have to keep going, I know that." She cocked her head in acceptance of the painful fact and took a long, deep breath.

"I'll gather the children." Elizabeth set Joseph on his feet, the boy holding her hand as he gained his balance. She stood up and almost went to her knees. Her feet hurt so badly she didn't know if she'd be able to take one more step let alone thousands. Her back ached like someone had used a wheelwright's hammer on it, and her inside skirt was so wet with sweat it clung to her inner thighs. Keeping a wince of pain to herself she gained her balance, and her inner strength, straightened her back, and called the children together.

"Everyone, I know you're not ready to continue, but as has become my favorite saying, there's no help for it. Gather your things, it's time to go."

There was groaning, grumbling, and lots of silent tears, but no one voiced their objections aloud. Pulling Hilda from where she'd been foraging, the little troupe started off again. They had lots of miles to make and the sooner they were about it, the sooner they would get where they were going.

THE JOURNEY
Departure Day 1
Evening (Sugar Creek)

Elizabeth thought her mind was playing tricks, but there it was. Sugar Creek—and there was water in it! She pulled Hilda to a stop and waved at Rebecca. "Look! Over there! The creek, with water! We can stop, refill the jugs and cool off." She covered her eyes with her right hand and studied the sun. "Looks like there are still a few hours of sunlight left, we could keep going if we...."

"Elizabeth." Rebecca interrupted. "We're done in. This is as far as you wanted to get today. We got here and we're going to stop. We can refill our water, the children can cool off, Hilda can drink her fill and forage, and we can *all* rest. We can put the mattresses right there." She flung her hand toward the trees lining the bank.

Elizabeth noticed a number of old fire pits, left by travelers ahead of them on their journeys to who knew where. *It is a good spot, but if they could just get a little farther.* "But we have more daylight and could get closer to the road if we keep going."

Rebecca came around Hilda and stepped in front of Elizabeth. "Why? Is there a rule that says we have to get so far before we can stop for the night? Elizabeth, this is a good place. There's water and shade, and safety in numbers. Other people have stopped here before and are stopping behind us." She waved at several families who were traveling the road behind them who were stopping, as well. "The children are finished, Elizabeth. You may not hear them, but I do. They're stiff, sore, and crying their little eyes out, but afraid to say anything. Even the little ones who have ridden on the sled for the last hour are whimpering like lost puppies. It's time to stop."

Rebecca laid her hand on Elizabeth's forearm, heat building under it. Elizabeth looked back over their ragged families and a cry of realization almost tore out of her throat. *They were beaten, at least for today. They'd done well,* she told herself. *If they'd reached Sugar Creek, they'd gone as far as she'd hoped they would on their first day. They were done in. It was time to stop.*

Elizabeth nodded. "You're right. It's time to rest and this is the best place we've come upon. We can bed down under the trees, refill the water jugs, Hilda can drink her fill from the creek and forage along its banks, and we'll be refreshed and ready to go in the morning."

Rebecca forced a smile, grunted and shook her head. "I don't know about refreshed *or* ready, but it'll have to do."

Elizabeth laid her hand over Rebecca's. "I know I push too hard sometimes. Keep me from it, Rebecca. The days are too long to go from sun up to sun down. We left almost twelve hours ago." Elizabeth smiled. "Keep me from pushing too hard."

Rebecca squeezed Elizabeth's arm and pulled her hand away. "I will, and you do the same for me. You're not the only one that can get pushy." She grinned again and both women nodded agreement to keep each other in check. They were traveling with children and, regardless how far they had to go, they didn't want to break the spirit of those children before they got there. They would survive—one day and one mile at a time.

The children rolled up their pant legs or hiked their skirts to their calves to play in the shallow creek. They plopped down into the water, soaked their hot, tired bodies and cooled their sore feet. They drank all they could, and when they felt like children again, splashed each other with squeals of laughter.

Elizabeth watched the children play from where she pulled the water jugs off the sled to refill. *A good soaking would do them all good.* She smelled her own stink and vowed to visit the creek, too, before the sun set. Children from other families camped nearby played together in the shallow water, while the mothers set up camps.

Knowing the children were safe under Nora and Helen's watchful eyes, Elizabeth and Rebecca set about getting ready for the night. Rebecca took a squirming Robert aside to nurse, while Elizabeth unlashed the ropes that held everything in place on the sled. When Rebecca returned, leaving Robert sleeping on a blanket under a nearby tree, Elizabeth said, "Grab the top mattress and let's slide it down."

They each grabbed an end and it slid off the top with a

few hard tugs. *Getting it back up was going to be the hard part,* Elizabeth mused.

"Let's put it over there." Rebecca pointed to a tall oak, its wide branches offering lots of shade.

"Wait!" Elizabeth yelled when Rebecca grabbed the mattress and started pulling it across the rocky ground. "It's too heavy for just the two of us. They'll be worthless in two days if we drag them from one place to another every time we take them down. We need help." She called Nora and Vera and Rebecca called Helen and Clara, leaving the middling children to watch their younger siblings in the water.

When the girls gathered around them, Elizabeth explained what needed to be done. Nora and Vera grabbed one end of the mattress, Helen and Clara took the other, and Rebecca and Elizabeth took the other two. "On three," Elizabeth said. "One...two...three!" With a grunt they hoisted the mattress and staggered forward.

"Over there." Elizabeth headed toward the tree she and Rebecca had decided upon. Although everyone tried to move together, they dropped their burden several times before they made it to the allocated spot, everyone sweating again before the second mattress rested beside the first.

Breathing heavily, Elizabeth stared down at the two mattresses, a common commodity in what had been a normal life in what seemed like another lifetime, now a blessed respite for the days to come.

"I could curl up and go to sleep right now," Nora announced sitting down on the corner of the makeshift bed, testing its softness with her fingers. She took off her wet shoes, peeled off the top layer of wet clothes, shoved them aside, and scooted onto the mattress. She lay down, closed her eyes and became still as a post.

"She hasn't even eaten," Elizabeth said to Rebecca standing beside her.

Rebecca shook her head. "I know how she feels. As hungry as I am, I could curl up right next to her." She turned to Elizabeth. "Should we wake her to eat?"

Elizabeth pursed her lips. "I don't think so. If she sleeps through the night she can have a double ration in the morning.

I'm afraid once we try and bed down the little ones, she may not *stay* asleep." Looking over the expanse of the mattresses, Elizabeth knew she and Rebecca might well have to find someplace else to bed down. There just wasn't enough room for all the children *and* them. The children needed their rest more than they did. She sighed. "I'm afraid we may be finding someplace else to sleep, Rebecca."

Rebecca surveyed the bed. She frowned and nodded. "I thought the same thing—too many children and not enough room." She glanced at Elizabeth. "These are your mattresses. You and your family should sleep on them. We can find someplace else."

"Don't you dare tell me you and your children will find someplace else to sleep Rebecca Barrow. The children will sleep on those mattresses—all of them—yours and mine together. If there's room for one or both of us, we'll sleep there too, if not we'll take turns and do whatever is necessary to ensure the children are rested." She laid her hand on Rebecca's cheek, seeing tears rise in her friend's eyes. "This is going to be a long, grueling trip. We both knew that before we started, but we'll do whatever is necessary to make sure the children arrive as hale and hearty as possible. Right?"

Rebecca swallowed and nodded gratefully. "Right."

"Then let's get to it. There's food to be broken out and a fire to build so we can boil water and soften the jerky. It'll be easier to eat and taste better, too. So let's get the children gathering wood and get that fire started." She paused, again watching the children giggling and splashing in the creek, happy and wet from head to toe. "They'll be cooled off and feeling better by now. There's plenty of wood here with all the downed branches from the drought."

The children set upon the task of gathering wood and dumped armload after armload where Rebecca and Elizabeth started a fire in a previously used fire pit. Within an hour, deer bacon was popping in the pan and everyone was anxiously looking forward to the meal. A few hard biscuits they'd brought with them were pulled out of the sack and passed around for their first evening meal on the trail.

It wasn't so bad, Elizabeth thought, *at least not so far.*

Surprisingly, they'd reached the creek, which she hadn't been sure they could do. Not bad for the first day. Other travelers were camped all around them, with the jingle of animals being unhitched and clatter of pots and pans being pulled out for cooking. They weren't alone. Tomorrow they would reach the road that led to Clinton.

She paused in her musing and took a deep breath. *When we reach the Clinton Road, that's when things will really get rough.* The fear of fellow travelers, some thrown out of their homes only days or hours before the deadline, with no time to prepare as they had, possibly trying to take what they had, caused Elizabeth's stomach to clench. She sucked in a breath at the thought of someone stealing the food and water they'd so carefully prepared and brought with them. And the thought of soldiers and raiders nearly made her gag.

But she put on a happy face, ate her meal with gusto, and bedded down on the edge of the mattress in front of Nora, who hadn't stirred since she lay down. Vera, Joseph and Sally were huddled together behind Nora, with Rebecca's children front to back beside them. Rebecca lay cross-wise at the foot of the makeshift bed, Robert at her breast. The child had suckled himself full, the effort becoming more painful and taking longer each time he nursed, Rebecca's milk drying up from her lack of food and water and the heat.

How long could Rebecca feed her son if she didn't have food and water herself? What would they do then? They would pass no towns between Wadesburg and Clinton to buy some. Maybe a local farmer, a Yankee if needs be, who hadn't been forced to leave his home like she and so many others, would open his home and give them milk for the child? She snorted at the thought. *No Yankee would help them out, even if there were any between here and the Clinton Road, for fear of reprisals from their own soldiers and raiders!* She sighed again. *They'd be hard-pressed to keep Robert fed if Rebecca's milk dried up.* The thought of that happening almost made Elizabeth sick.

"Oh dear Lord, please bring us through this. Please keep us safe with food and water until we reach our destination. Protect us, O' Lord," were her last thoughts before sleep claimed her—dark and black and empty.

Elizabeth jerked upright, the yipping of coyotes cutting through her exhausted sleep like a saber thrust. Rebecca was sitting up, too.

"They're close." Rebecca didn't tell Elizabeth anything she didn't already know. She knew the sound of coyotes well. They were in the timber all around the farm and yipped and yapped some nights for hours. On occasion, a lone young one would venture into the barn looking for easy food before Walter the goat, hooves thrashing, sent it running back to the woods, tail tucked between its legs.

Elizabeth wasn't afraid of coyotes—unless there were lots of them and they were hungry. It sounded like there were lots of them tonight and she prayed they weren't hungry. She got up, every muscle in her body screaming, knees and back snapping, her head spinning at the abrupt awakening. Hilda nickered from the timber not far away where they'd tied her for the night to forage. The sled only a few feet away, Elizabeth pulled out the rifle from under a piece of canvas on the side close to the edge.

"I'll stand guard." Elizabeth noticed other travelers stirring in their camps, too. *There'd be safety in numbers,* she thought, getting comfortable on a log near the mattresses. *They'd have to go through her* and *her squirrel rifle to reach the food* or *the children.*

"I can do it," Rebecca offered.

Elizabeth shook her head, wide awake and alert now. "I'll do it. You need your rest for Robert. Go back to sleep."

"I can't sleep now," Rebecca griped. She stood up with a groan, her body snapping and popping like Elizabeth's had, and plopped down beside Elizabeth on the log. "We'll keep each other awake," she said as another round of yipping and yelping ensued.

"How could I go back to sleep with *that* going on?" Elizabeth snorted.

"I'll feel better if we both watch."

"You're going to regret it tomorrow," Elizabeth said with a grin.

"I regret a lot of things, but this won't be one of them. We're in this together, Elizabeth. You can't take all the responsibility all the time."

Elizabeth nodded and sighed. "I know and I appreciate you staying with me. There's no telling how bold they might get if they're hungry."

Rebecca shook her head. "They shouldn't be hungry, not this time of year, but with the drought, who knows? They sound like young ones, though. Hopefully, they're just testing out their new found ability to make lots of noise." Rebecca grinned and smiled.

"I hope you're right. But I'm not leaving anything to chance." Elizabeth got up and pulled a pistol from its hiding place on the sled and handed it to Rebecca. She settled the rifle on her lap and tried to stay alert—until the coyotes quieted and exhaustion claimed her.

Elizabeth and Rebecca woke the next morning, back to back astride the log, the rifle locked in Elizabeth hands, the pistol in Rebecca's, neither able to remember how they got that way.

THE JOURNEY
Day 2
(The Austin-Wadesburg Road)

Elizabeth finished harnessing Hilda. Although the sun had only been up a short time, the heat and humidity were already building. They'd eaten a quick breakfast, filled the water jugs to overflowing, dumped mud from the creek on the smoldering embers of the fire so it wouldn't start a blaze in the trees, reloaded and re-lashed the mattresses to the sled, and were sweating again within minutes.

They stood at the lowest edge of the creek where it looked like it had been crossed many times. Other families waited for Elizabeth and Rebecca to lead the way. Elizabeth was on one side of Hilda, Rebecca on the other, each with a grip on the mare's bridle to guide her through the water and up the bank on the other side.

"Are you ready girl?" Elizabeth whispered to the horse, her ears twitching. "Then let's get on with it. Ready?" she called to Rebecca.

"As I'll ever be."

"Then let's go." They clucked Hilda down the embankment, careful to keep her from going too fast and upsetting everything on the sled, avoiding rocks and protruding trunks that could break it apart. Moving slowly, they guided the mare through the knee deep water, Joseph, Sally, and Andrew on her back, Andrew in front clutching her mane, Joseph and Sally clinging to him and each other to stay on. The other children, except Helen who was carrying little Robert, were lined up around the sled, holding it up as much as they could to help float it across. As soon as Hilda reached the other side they hurried her up the bank to get the sled out of the way as quickly as possible. They guided Hilda down the road before they stopped and inspected everything to make sure all was well. The items on the bottom of the sled were soaked, but aside from the mattress that would dry quickly, the pots, pans, and metal dishes, it didn't matter. Other than some wet spots on the mattresses on top from Hilda's splashing, everything came across intact.

Elizabeth breathed a sigh of relief. "I hope the rest of our journey goes as easily as this water crossing did." Elizabeth knew it was a big hope and one that, most likely, wouldn't be realized.

Clothes dried, feet got sore again, legs stiffened, and the heat soared. *One day, just one day, couldn't the temperature stay below ninety, rain fall, or a breeze blow?* Elizabeth shook her head at her silly musing. It had been this way for weeks. Wishing would do nothing to help them or their miseries.

The day progressed and the heat rose, along with their tempers.

"Hurry up!" Nora shouted at Vera.

"I'm going as fast as I can. My feet hurt!"

"So do everybody else's, but you're the one slowing us down."

"Leave me alone." Vera's nose was running and tears streamed down her cheeks.

"You're such a baby," Nora taunted.

"And you're not Mama!" Vera was in her older sister's face, hands on her hips, eyes wide and angry, lips tight. "You're not Mama and I'm tired of you telling me what to do all the time!"

Helen and Clara were bickering, too. Even the little ones had taken to sniping at each other. They had to stop soon, Elizabeth knew it. The children were exhausted—she was exhausted. The sun was almost straight up in the sky. It was a good time to stop for the noon meal.

"Everyone stop their fighting right now!" Elizabeth yelled. "As soon as we find a good place, we'll stop. Until then, everyone keep their mouths shut and their thoughts to themselves. Is that understood?"

Mouths snapped closed, but tears flowed. That's when she heard it, horses coming from the road behind them. Fear ripped through her like tearing cloth.

"Get off the road!" she screamed, pulling Hilda to the right side of the thin road. "Nora and Vera grab the babies and get off the road! Get off the road! Now!" she shrieked.

The girls grabbed Joseph and Sally's hands and ran beside their mother. Rebecca and her children ran behind them,

Robert clutched to Rebecca's chest, the others huddled around their mother. Families behind them hurried off the road, too. Moments later, Union soldiers were on them, their horses barely slowing down as they thundered past.

"Get out of the way!" soldier after soldier shouted, reining his horse only long enough to keep from running over a woman or child who couldn't get out of the way fast enough. "Get out of the way you worthless rebel trash or we'll run you down like the garbage you are!" Oxen and cows bellowed as they were forced off the road, the wagons and carts they pulled tumbling down the hill on the side of the road, scattering their contents.

Elizabeth's heart pounded, her breath labored she was so afraid. The children huddled close to her and Rebecca, their eyes wide with fear. No one spoke as the riders pushed their way through the line of emigrants behind them before kicking their horses back into a run. They raced past Elizabeth and Rebecca, the horses gaining speed with each thrust of their powerful legs.

The road had been mostly deserted until now. The farms they'd passed empty, everything stripped, nothing left behind and deserted the same way hers and Rebecca's had been. *Why were the soldiers in such a hurry? No one came behind them. They weren't being chased or running from someone.*

Then she looked into the sky in the direction they'd come from and she saw it. Smoke! Black, billowing smoke, and she knew. The soldiers were burning the farms between Austin and here and were on their way to the next one. She couldn't breathe with the realization that her farm, her home, was probably already in flames, part of the growing black cloud in the distance. Rebecca knew, too. Tears streamed down her face and her lips quivered. Everything they'd loved was gone. It was fact now. There was no hope they'd return some day to a home spared the torch. It was gone. All gone. There was no sense denying it.

Later that day they stood, staring in silence, the emigrants behind them staring, too. Flames danced and popped and smoke billowed into the sky. Through the ever-present swirling soot from the road and smoke from the fire, Elizabeth stared at what had once been a thriving farm. It was the home of a family she, James and the children had visited on their many trips to St. Clair County, now ablaze, the soldiers who had set it long gone on their way to the next farm to burn.

Elizabeth shook her head. Rebecca stood beside her, her face a mask of disbelief, little Robert in his sling across her back, the other children gathered around them. Tears dried as quickly as they were shed, leaving long streaks on their soot-covered cheeks.

"Why are they doing this, Mama?" Nora's voice caught with the question.

"It's what they promised they would do, Nora. They gave us fifteen days to leave or go into the forts at Harrisonville or Pleasant Hill and take the oath of loyalty—which I would never do—then promised to burn whatever was left after we were gone. I had no doubt they'd do what they said, but seeing it," she shook her head, "seeing it is confirmation of how bad this war has become." She sighed. "And it didn't matter whether we were Confederate or Union folk, there was still no choice in swearing loyalty at the forts. Everyone had to go." She looked around, wondering just how many of her fellow travelers were Yankees, displaced from their homes just like they were. She raised her chin. "They'll not break us, Nora, I swear they won't. Someday we'll go back, reclaim the land and rebuild what they've taken."

Nora cried quietly beside her mother as Vera and the other children stood staring at the blaze, the heat from the fire adding to the heat already roasting them.

"Come along children, it's time to go. There's nothing more to see here."

Prodding Hilda ahead, Elizabeth started forward, one step at a time, wondering what other horrors they would see before reaching their destination.

That night the families huddled together on the mattresses on the side of the road. There was no creek or even a small stream to wash up in or refill their jugs and, after a sparse meal and small ration of water, everyone went to bed. No words were spoken, but children cried and whimpered in their sleep while Rebecca and Elizabeth took turns watching over them.

They were only two days into their journey and were already beaten down. *Would they survive what was yet to come?* Elizabeth wondered, taking her turn perched on a rock in front of the children, rifle in hand, waiting for anything that might threaten them. Be they man or beast, she was ready for whatever evil they brought.

THE JOURNEY
Day 3
(The Road to Clinton)

The sun was high in the sky, the heat oppressive, when they reached the road that headed south to Clinton. In gut-twisting silence, Elizabeth watched the dust swirl above the heads of the seemingly endless line of bedraggled souls trudging down the road going — where? *Did they know or were they just going somewhere — anywhere — as ordered, just like she and her family? Forced to leave their homes, land, and everything they'd worked for and built. To disappear from the land they loved, just go, it didn't matter where?*

Many were barefoot, so deeply layered in the grime that had once been the road everyone looked alike. Be they white or black, beast or fowl, woman or child, all were the same gray-black, ashen color. She stared down at what was left of a broken fence line, the dust so thick you could scrape it off like snow and make a ball with it—*if* you were of a mind. But there was no cause for such frivolity and Elizabeth was of no such mind. All she wanted was to be far away from the powdery gray-black stuff clinging to every part of her body in the intense heat—but that was not to be. Soon they would join the line of refugees with all they had.

The road stretched as far as she could see, the undulating line of refugees reminding Elizabeth of a snake slithering its way across the land in search of what, she didn't know. What it really was, was an army of lost souls, trying to salvage what was left of their lives in the wake of General Order No. 11.

Elizabeth turned to Rebecca who stood like a stone, staring at the mass of people and animals trudging mindlessly forward.

Elizabeth glanced at her children, wide-eyed and silent. After everything they'd already endured, even they knew the hard part of the journey started here. Rebecca's children clutched each other, silent, too, with the knowledge of what was ahead. Only little Robert made his displeasure loudly known.

"Are you ready?" Elizabeth asked Rebecca.

"I'll never be ready." Her statement merited no response.

Both knew they had no choice.

"Children, it's time to go."

The children groaned but said nothing as they slung their belongings across their backs and went to whomever they'd been paired with to begin the next part of their journey.

Elizabeth clucked Hilda forward and walked woodenly toward the line of refugees. Dust, many times worse than what they'd already encountered, swirled under her skirt, settling on her sweat-soaked clothes and limbs like a second skin. The smell of smoke hung over the land and she wondered how many lives and homes had already been destroyed by this senseless war—hers included. Elizabeth pulled her scarf up over her face, but not quickly enough before taken by a fit of coughing as the billowing silt went into her mouth and up her nose. Her eyes watered. *Would she and the children survive what lay ahead?* she wondered for the thousandth time since leaving their home only days ago.

"Mama! I can't breathe!" Sally cried from beside her.

"Me neither!" Joseph yelled, coughing and spitting next to his sister.

"Quiet children! There's nothing to be done about the dust. It's everywhere and covers everything. We must continue to be strong. Keep your scarves over your faces and don't speak," she managed through coughs of her own.

"But Mama, I can't breathe!" Sally shouted before launching into a coughing fit. "I need water, Mama!" The little girl gagged and spit.

"Not yet." The words were said gently. Elizabeth patted the child's back, wiped her mouth with her skirt, and tried to soothe her, but saw her little girl wasn't going to easily accept it. "We must save what water we have." Elizabeth pushed an errant strand of sweat-soaked hair off her daughter's forehead.

"I want water, too!" Joseph shouted.

"You may not." Elizabeth became stern. "We must save what we have for later. It'll be worse as the day wears on."

"I don't care! I'm thirsty now!" Sally stomped her foot like she'd seen her older sister do many times. Dust puffed up in little clouds, swirled into her mouth and nose, and she coughed again.

"You will wait, as will we all, Sally. Now stop talking, both of you. There's nothing I or anyone else can do." She looked over at Rebecca, at the same time dealing with a squalling Robert and her two youngest children, protesting the dust as loudly as Joseph and Sally.

"Children!" Elizabeth shouted, her nerves already worn. "There's nothing to be done. Stop talking and keep your mouths closed."

Their muted whining told her the children understood her meaning and wouldn't argue, but that they didn't like it much.

"I'll take care of Sally, Mama," Nora murmured.

"Come on, Joseph." Vera grudgingly took her little brother's hand.

"Why don't we hum a song?" Nora suggested.

"That's a wonderful idea. Let's hum," Elizabeth almost shouted, hoping her children might be distracted from their unhappiness.

Watching Nora and Vera, Elizabeth thanked God again for her two oldest daughters, who did whatever they could to help with their younger siblings. Without them, Elizabeth feared she wouldn't have made it as far as they'd come, nor would they make it through what they yet faced. Certainly they had their moments, especially Vera, but for the most part they helped more than anything. Her thoughts flashed to Steven, fighting somewhere for the Confederacy. *Was he still alive? Would he come home bitter, beaten, and whole? Or was he one of the many men who would return without an arm or leg from this damnable war? Would he come home at all?* Afraid her thoughts would take her down a dark path she didn't want to travel she smiled at her daughters—although neither saw it beneath her scarf. She looked over at Rebecca for additional support.

"Yes, children, hum a song!" Rebecca shouted. "And be sure to keep your mouths closed when you do. Hum for us, children. Hum!"

Slowly, the notes to *My Bonnie Lies Over the Ocean* began as Nora and Elizabeth started the song. Vera joined in and soon Rebecca and her children were humming, too. They sniffed and coughed as they walked toward the dust-laden road, but continued the song, defiant of their dreadful situation.

Reaching the stream of refugees, Elizabeth Miers, Rebecca Barrow, and thirteen children waded into line, still humming, the cheerful song wafting over them and the other refugees like a talisman, spurring them all to keep going.

With feet as heavy as rocks and fearful of what was down this road for her and her family, Elizabeth thought back to what brought them to this place. *In a country blessed with freedom, how had everything unraveled so quickly? How could brothers, fathers, and cousins fight on different sides of this war? How could a conflict expected to last weeks, drag on for years? And how could one man hold the lives of thousands of women and children in his hands by ordering them from their homes in the heat of a brutal Missouri summer? Some were given fifteen days' notice—many only fifteen minutes—before their homes were put to the torch, as their owners watched helplessly. Most were forced to leave everything they loved with little more than what they could carry and their children.*

She cursed General Thomas Ewing and his damned General Order No. 11 for what it was in her mind—a proclamation of death and destruction, a license to murder and plunder in the name of the Union cause, and an invitation for men to be just plain mean.

The Barrows and Miers trudged along with the other refugees. Dust, even thicker than what they'd experienced on the Austin-Wadesburg Road, swirled around them like a fog. The heat and closeness of the other emigrants clung to them like sap on a tree. Although they'd been on the road for two days, the other families that traveled behind them had done so at a relative distance, not right beside them or behind them as these people did now. *There were so many!* Elizabeth watched them, staring enviously at Hilda and the sled, and she feared for all they could lose.

She peered over Hilda's back. "Pssst, Rebecca."

Rebecca turned, her face revealing the same fears.

"We have to keep our eyes open. We have much more than many here and I'm not about to lose it to thieving."

Rebecca nodded. "I noticed more than one jealous look

in our direction when we joined the line. So many of these people have nothing more than the clothes on their backs. We have to be careful, Elizabeth, and always watchful nobody tries to take what's ours. We worked too hard to prepare for this."

"Those were my thoughts, too." Elizabeth looked ahead, careful not to push Hilda too fast and run over the family of six slogging ahead of her with a thin, haggard-looking mother and five children about the same ages as her own. They were all bare-footed, wore ragged, dirt-covered clothes, their faces smeared with the silty dust that hung around them like a low-hanging cloud. The children walked backward more than they walked forward, watching Hilda and the swaying water jugs at the front of the sled and licking their cracked lips. They stared at the mattresses as though imagining how soft they'd be to sleep on or trying to see the treasures hidden below them.

Elizabeth turned to her family to make sure they were all together. Nora and Vera both had a tight hold on their younger brother and sister, eyeing those around them, also leery of what they saw.

"Stay close to the sled, children," Elizabeth said, hearing Rebecca give the same order from the other side of Hilda.

The day continued in a haze of pain, exhaustion, thirst, and disbelief that this was really happening. The road was much wider than the Austin-Wadesburg Road, without the benefit of any shade unless you went off the road. The sun beat down on them so hard Elizabeth was sure she knew what it felt like to be an egg frying in a pan. Arms where sleeves were rolled up for some relief from the heat turned bright red. Although everyone, including the boys wore overlarge hats, noses and cheeks grew crimson and lips cracked. Shoes were removed, the heat so intense it seemed to cook the already bloody blisters on heels and toes rubbed raw by the leather. Tops of feet turned pink along with any other areas left uncovered like necks and hands. Little Robert squalled. He squalled from the heat, squalled when he was hungry, and squalled when he was uncomfortable until he finally exhausted himself and slept, leaving everyone's nerves raw.

On they went. Silt filled their mouths, lungs, hair, ears, and anything else it could stick to or fill. Their stamina and hope dwindled with each step, knowing it would be the same thing—or worse—tomorrow, the next day, and the next.

"Mama?" Nora called several times before her mother acknowledged her. "Mama!"

"What is it, Nora?" her mother groaned.

"We *have* to stop. The children can't go any farther. We have to eat. My stomach is grumbling like thunder across the plains and everyone else's are, too."

"Just a few more miles."

Her mother didn't even turn her head to speak or look at Nora when she answered. She just looked forward, always forward, and kept walking.

"Mama! Stop!" Nora had never seen her mother like this. It was like someone else was inside her, making her keep going. Everyone was tired. They *had* to stop. She had to make her mother realize that. "Please, Mama. We can't keep going without some rest and food. It's got to be close to mid-afternoon by now and we haven't eaten since early this morning. Please Mama."

Elizabeth's head snapped around and she looked deep into Nora's eyes. Nora noticed a tear slip from one of the corners before her mother wiped it away with an angry swipe. "You're right, Nora. It's time to stop. As soon as we find someplace agreeable, we'll do just that."

"Right over there is a good spot." Nora pointed at a small, empty, grove of trees. She'd noticed families dropping out of line along the way to take food or rest, but this spot was empty—at least right now. "Mama?"

Her mother shook her head. "You're right, Nora, it's time to stop." Elizabeth turned to Rebecca. "Are you ready to rest a while and take some food?"

"I'm more than ready and so are the children." Rebecca's back sagged with her statement.

"Nora found a spot for us." Her mother waved at Nora and said, "Lead the way."

Nora suddenly felt very grown up. It felt good, despite the hardship, and she led them to the small cropping of trees where everyone found a spot to sit and her mother led Hilda to some bushes where the mare immediately began stripping the mostly brown, curling leaves.

"After we've eaten and rested a while, we'll get going again," Elizabeth said.

"Aw Mama, can't we stop for the day?" Vera whined. "I'm so tired I don't think my feet will work anymore." The girl looked down. "My blisters have blisters!" she cried.

"Me too!" Sally yelled from the sled where she, Joseph, and Andrew were still squished in front.

"I don't want to go anymore, Mama!" Joseph cried beside his sister.

"We want to stop, too!" Clara cried from beside her mother, Joshua, Francis, Edna, Richard, and Benjamin all shouting agreement.

Nora wanted to yell at all of them that she was tired, too, but she wanted to keep that grown up feeling, even though she really wanted to curl up at the base of a tree and go to sleep. "You know we have to keep going," she said before her mother could say a word. "Mama and Rebecca know what's best for us, and right now that's to rest some, to eat and then be on our way again."

Nora looked over at her mother and Rebecca, standing together in front of the sled, her mother beaming with pride, Rebecca's eyes wide with surprise. "Isn't that right?"

"Of course it is, Nora. So come now children, it's time to eat and rest a few minutes before we continue," Elizabeth confirmed.

Amidst much grumbling and whining, the children waited for Elizabeth, Rebecca, Nora, and Helen to distribute the jerky and small cups of water between them.

Nora suddenly realized the road behind them had grown quiet. The rumble of crooked wheels and lopsided wagons had stopped. The lowered voices of people talking, chickens clucking and broken down horses, mules and cattle snorting had ceased. She turned to look. Those on the road closest to them were watching them, licking their lips, their eyes wild with hunger and thirst and, although she always believed what her mother told her, for the first time Nora truly understood her mother's fears. Even those they traveled with were potential threats to take what they had. Now she knew what drove her mother's great desire to be prepared and ready for anything—in any form.

Noticing the line of travelers had stopped to watch them take their meal, Elizabeth went to the sled, covered the bags of meat, and closed the lid to the water jug. She walked to her friend. "Rebecca," she whispered.

"I see them. What should we do?" Rebecca clutched a sleeping Robert to her chest, the boy having nursed while they walked and quiet for the first time in hours.

"There's nothing we can do except hope they keep their distance and don't try to take what we have. We worked long and hard to ensure there was enough for this trip and by damn I won't let anyone take it. Nobody, Rebecca."

"So, what do we do?"

"There is something we can do." Elizabeth hated the thought of it, but she walked to the sled, pulled the squirrel rifle out of its hiding spot, and laid it across her elbows in plain view of those passing. What was theirs was theirs—and only enough to get them where they needed to go. She was unwilling to share and put her children's well-being at risk for anyone. For sure, there were sadder stories than hers and Rebecca's right there in that hoard of destitute emigrants, but she didn't want to know or hear them. Her only goal was to protect hers and Rebecca's families, and she would do so at any cost.

"Move on!" She raised the rifle so any one who hadn't seen it saw it now. "We're of no interest to you. Keep moving."

Slowly the wagon wheels creaked, animals squawked and snorted that their short respite was over, children whimpered and protested, and the line moved on.

Rebecca took charge of feeding the children, while Elizabeth stood guard. Their journey had only just begun and Elizabeth would not allow their provisions to be taken—by anyone. No matter what it took, she would protect what was theirs.

That night Elizabeth slept on a soft patch of dirt next to the sled, the rifle in her hands, jumping at every sound around her. In and out of sleep, she felt, more than heard, something moving beside her. Her eyes popped open and she found herself staring into the face of a big, fat raccoon, his round eyes glowing in the moonlight. Childhood memories of a raccoon just like this one struck her and she lay frozen as those memories surged, bringing both comfort—and fear. Although these creatures looked cute and cuddly, able to open barrels and doors one thought only human beings could maneuver, they became vicious when cornered.

"Oh Papa, please let me take care of it," ten year old Elizabeth cried, trying to stop her papa from tossing the baby raccoon he'd found into the creek. "I'll call him Henry and we'll become great friends!"

"Elizabeth, that's not a good idea. These are wild animals and not meant to be pets."

"Please, Papa. I can do it, I promise."

She begged and begged, which usually made her papa very angry, but she couldn't help it. She wanted to save the life of this tiny little creature that fit in the palm of her papa's hand. He finally sighed, went to one knee, and looked her square in the eye. "It goes against what I know I should do, but I'll allow you to keep it. From now on, Liz, this tiny little creature is your responsibility." He stood up, patted Elizabeth on the head, and lowered it into her hands. "I imagine it'll die in a week."

Her father's challenge ringing in her ears, Elizabeth watched him walk away and vowed to nurse the babe put in her care until it was fat and healthy—which was exactly what she did. Every morning before doing her chores she went to the barn, opened Henry's pen, and nursed him with a bottle her mama fashioned for her. The creature held her finger and the bottle just like a human baby while it drank its fill. Once his tummy was round and full, Elizabeth played with and cuddled him until chores or her mama called.

That raccoon didn't die in a week like her papa predicted. A year later he was fat and playful and followed Elizabeth everywhere she went when she was outside. She had his full adoration, her older brothers and sisters vowing never to go near him, allowing her to have Henry all to herself.

Of a morning she went to the barn to let Henry out of his cage, feed him and do her chores with him following her like he did every other day, but the latch on the cage was already open and Henry was gone. Elizabeth searched the barn, called for him, and looked in every corner and behind every barrel and bale of hay, although she already knew in her heart he was gone. She even went up into the loft. *If a raccoon could open barrels and doors, maybe he could climb a ladder, too.* She searched for almost an hour before she sat down in the very corner her papa had found him over a year ago and cried. She felt abandoned and kept on crying for weeks until another morning she went to the barn to do her chores and found Henry sitting in the hay waiting for her. She ran toward him. "Henry, you came back!"

The raccoon stood up on its hind legs, spread its little arms, curled its lips back, and snarled at her! Confused why her beloved pet would snarl at her she stepped closer with her hand extended. The raccoon swiped at her with his paw and bared his teeth even more. Only then did Elizabeth realize it wasn't her Henry and she stood frozen as the animal growled and snapped in front of her. Every time she tried to step back to run away the creature lunged and ran in circles around her. With tears streaming down her face she screamed and screamed for her papa.

Her father came to a skidding halt behind her a few minutes later. "Don't move, Lizzie."

"Yes, Papa," she stammered, more afraid than she'd ever been in her short life.

The explosion of his rifle sent her to her knees clutching her ears with her eyes closed, and when she finally opened them she was staring right into that raccoon's dead eyes. She scrambled to her feet, ran behind the barn, and vomited.

Betrayed by her beloved Henry and scared to death by another, ever since that day Elizabeth hated, and feared, raccoons.

Now she was face to face with another one—this one very much alive and of a mind to steal their precious food—if he didn't take a chunk out of her first. Uncertain where her strength came from, other than knowing she could not let this animal pillage their supplies, her fingers tightened around the barrel of the rifle clutched at her chest and she slammed the stock into the animal's head. With a dog-like bark, the raccoon scrambled away faster than Elizabeth ever saw Henry move. She jumped up, breathing hard and wide awake. She scanned the area for other predators, but saw only the back-end of the raccoon as it waddled away into the trees. After standing guard for several minutes in front of the sled, legs spread, rifle at the ready, Elizabeth decided the raccoon, and any friends it might have had, were long gone. Exhausted by her lack of sleep, her heart finally slowed enough that she didn't hear it pounding in her ears anymore, she plopped down beside the sled and leaned back, laid the rifle across her lap, and waited for morning.

THE JOURNEY
Day 4 – Morning
(The Road to Clinton)

Rebecca found Elizabeth slumped against the sled before daybreak, sound asleep, the rifle tight in her hands.

"Psst, Elizabeth."

Elizabeth jumped up and swung the rifle, barely missing her friend with the barrel as she jumped out of the way.

"Whoa, Elizabeth, it's me."

Elizabeth thought her heart was going to explode it was racing so fast. "Rebecca, I'm so sorry." She plopped to the ground again, trying to calm down.

"Why were you sleeping there like that? Did something happen last night I don't know about?"

Elizabeth nodded, unable to speak yet. She took a deep breath, licked her dry lips and tried to swallow, but there was no saliva in her mouth to do so. "We had a visitor," she managed, her voice cracking.

Rebecca's eyes grew wide. "What kind of visitor?"

"The kind on four legs that'll rob you blind before you even know it. A coon."

With a sigh of relief, Rebecca plopped down beside her. "I was afraid you meant one of our traveling companions, or worse yet, raiders. What happened?"

Elizabeth recounted the events of the evening. "I promise, Rebecca, I won't let anyone or anything steal our food or water, at least not without a fight, whether they're human or animal, they're going to have to go through me to get it."

Rebecca laid a hand on Elizabeth's shoulder, smiled and nodded. "I believe you."

Needing to start the day, Elizabeth turned to put the rifle down, but her fingers were locked in place around it. She looked up at Rebecca, grimaced and shook her head. "I told you, I wasn't going to let anything get our supplies."

Giggling with uncertainty, she and Rebecca pried her fingers away, the joints aching and popping with each finger removed and straightened. "Can we do this, Rebecca? Can we *really* do this? I'm so tired and scared, and I hurt in places I never knew *could* hurt." Unwilling to show weakness, Elizabeth wiped her nose with the hem of her dirty skirt. She waited for a rebuke from Rebecca, but her friend only shrugged.

"What does it matter? Our clothes are filthy, they smell—we smell—even though we tried to clean up in that stream yesterday, it isn't enough to get the stink of sweat and dirt out of our clothes. Rebecca tugged at her collar. "We go to bed sweaty, sleep sweaty, if we sleep at all, and wake up sweaty. It's already trickling down my chest and the sun isn't even up yet!"

Trying to sound cheerful despite her tears and runny nose, Elizabeth said, "At least we made it through another night with no *real* incident. Only five or six to go."

"*Hopefully* only five or six," Rebecca interrupted. "Have we planned correctly, Elizabeth? Are we going fast enough to reach your aunt and uncle's place in five or six more days?"

Rebecca was voicing fears Elizabeth had had since they left. *Had they allotted enough provisions? Was her aunt and uncle's farm only sixty miles, or was it more and she'd made a grave miscalculation? Would they run out of food before they reached it?* Elizabeth's mind suddenly whirled with questions she couldn't answer and she felt tears threatening before she shook her head and willed them away.

"We'll be fine," she tried to reassure her friend—and herself.

"And what will we find the further south we go, Elizabeth? They burned Osceola almost to the ground for recruiting confederate soldiers. Is your folks' place even standing?" Again Rebecca was voicing fears Elizabeth didn't want to speak aloud. *Could her uncle have been one of the nine men James told her had been hanged when Jim Lane and his men raided and burned Osceola back in '61? Was their farm close enough to town that the raiders burned it, too? Were they heading toward more heartache and destruction?* Elizabeth heaved another heavy sigh, something she seemed to be doing a lot of these days. "I don't know. All we can do is pray their farm is still standing and that they can offer us shelter until this is over." She felt her blood starting to boil, like it did every time she thought about what this war had cost her.

Rebecca pursed her lips and nodded agreement. "I guess

we'll find out when we get there, won't we?"

"That we will, but right now we have to get moving before the sun is full up and it gets so hot we can't breathe—again." Elizabeth turned to the line of emigrants, already moving steadily. "Looks like the parade has already started."

Rebecca grunted and again nodded agreement. "Shall we?"

With groans and popping knees the two women stood up and began preparations for the day. They pulled out the morning ration, took one of the water jugs from the sled and walked to where the children slept. Again she envied their innocence. Although frightened and they knew everything about their lives was different, they had their mommas to tell them what to do and when to do it. Elizabeth wished again there were someone here who could tell her what to do and when to do it. But it was not to be. She was the rock of the family now and it was time to get about their business. The sun was rising and it was going to be another long, hot, grueling day.

Little Robert cried. Joseph and Sally whined. Andrew sucked up snot running from his nose from his continued whimpering. The older children grumbled. They didn't complain out loud, no, their mommas would get after them if they did, so they did so under their breaths, loud enough for Rebecca and Elizabeth to hear, but not loud enough to draw a reprimand.

Elizabeth gnashed her teeth when Rebecca stepped up beside her, a screaming, wriggling Robert in her arms. "Elizabeth, we've *got* to find some milk. I'm dried up and he's hungry. I don't know what to do to make him stop."

The desperation in her friend's voice made Elizabeth's irritation with the screaming baby dissolve like rain on a hot roof, even though each of Robert's shrill screams were like knives in her back. *Where could they find milk? And if they didn't find any, how long would he scream or, worse yet, how long before he perished?* She couldn't think it, wouldn't think it. *They could try and feed him some softened jerky, but he was only nine months old with a few front teeth. His momma had been his only nourishment so Elizabeth held little hope for that idea. They* had *to find milk, that was all there was to it.*

"Quickly, get everyone out of line." Elizabeth led Hilda off the road, the little troupe behind her. Everyone plopped down on the ground and groaned with gratitude they were stopping. Elizabeth tossed a rein at Rebecca. "Hold Hilda and wait here with the children."

With a puzzled look Rebecca took the rein and nodded, Robert still squalling in the sling across her back.

Elizabeth took a deep breath and headed toward the road. Robert's constant screaming was driving her mad. *If she didn't find a way to stop it....* She pushed the thought from her mind. He was a babe—a hungry babe—who needed milk. Standing along the edge of the road watching the other travelers slog past her, her heart broke. There were mostly women and children much like them, but many with only what they carried and what they wore. Most were shoeless, as they were. Some had rickety old wagons or hastily built sleds like theirs, piled high with what was left of their lives, but most had nothing. She saw sadness, fear, and hunger in their eyes. The few animals in the procession were old, sway-backed, lame, and blind—of no use to the raiders who patrolled the countryside wreaking destruction upon the innocent. Mismatched teams of the smallest donkeys, old cows, and broken-down horses led the way for their owners. And a milk cow was what Elizabeth sought now. She watched and waited for nearly an hour before her patience was rewarded. Coming toward her was an old, crippled man guiding a wobbly cart led by a thin cow. A milk cow.

She fell in beside him and the old woman walking with him. "May I have a word, sir?"

"Go on, I ain't got nothin' fer ya."

"But I have something for you."

The man's head jerked up with curiosity. "What you got?"

"May we stop and talk? Please?"

The old man groaned as though she'd asked for his last breath, but he led the cow and cart off the road a short way from where Elizabeth's family waited.

"Sir, we have a babe that needs milk."

"Ain't got none." The old man had the cow turned back toward the road before Elizabeth could say more.

"Sir! Please! You must listen."

"Ain't gotta do nothin' of the kind. Me an' the missus here ain't got much. All we got is ole Bess an' what's in that bitty cart, an' we ain't givin' none of it away."

"But I'm not asking for you to give it to me. I want to trade."

The man jerked the cow to a halt again and his head swung back to Elizabeth. "What you got to trade? You ain't carryin' nothin' an' you don't got no cart or horse. What do you want to trade fer, anyways?"

"I want milk and, believe me, I have plenty to trade."

"Like what?"

"Meat? Water?"

The man licked his lips and his wife grabbed his arm and squeezed.

"Albert, she's got water," Elizabeth barely heard the woman say.

"Meat an' water ye say? How much?"

"Enough."

"How do I know? What if I give you milk an' you don't give me no meat or water?"

"I'll give you the meat or water first. My family and our belongings are over there." She waved at Rebecca and the children close enough to see them. "Bring your cow and come this way."

The man and woman eyed each other a few moments before he jerked the cow back around and headed toward Rebecca. "Come on then, let's git about it," the old man drawled, a lightness in his step that hadn't been there before.

The man stopped the cart beside Hilda, Rebecca and the still crying Robert. He eyed the baby then seemed to dismiss him. "You got quite a pile a stuff in that there sled, ma'am. I see the water jugs, but I don't see no meat."

Again Elizabeth saw the hunger in the man and woman's eyes, but she wasn't about to show him what they had. "It's hidden."

"O'course. How much milk you wantin'?"

"In this heat anything more than what he takes in a couple hours will go to waste, so I'd like to walk with you all and milk Bess whenever we need more."

The old man pondered her words. "An' what is it we git?"

"Whenever we milk, you get one cup of water and a strip of jerky."

"Two strips of jerky."

Elizabeth gritted her teeth. The old codger was going to try and get more than he deserved because he knew how much they needed the milk for Robert. "Look around, mister. We've got all these children to feed and barely enough to make it to our destination. Would you take food out of their mouths?"

"Ain't my problem. My problem is me an' the missus here. Ye can take my offer or be on yer way—without the milk." He looked at Robert, squirming and squalling in his mother's arms, his sooty face red and tear-stained.

Rebecca swallowed and her eyes begged forgiveness that she was causing this worry, but Elizabeth knew they had no choice. Robert needed milk. Then she thought out loud, "Maybe I'll just wait for someone else to come along with another milk cow then. Bess won't be the only milking cow on the road."

The old woman jerked on her husband's arm. "Albert," she hissed. "Take what she's offerin' and be done with it."

"But Meg...."

"Not this time, Albert. You ain't gonna take more'n you deserve. Take that woman's offer. We both git somethin' an' that chile will stop his squallin'!"

Elizabeth could see Robert's crying was already getting on the woman's nerves, enough so that she was ready to do whatever it took to get him quieted down—without taking more than they deserved.

"Do it, Albert. Now."

"Dang it, Meg, all right." The old man turned back to Elizabeth. "You got yoreself a deal. One cup o' water an' one strip o' jerky for every time you milk ole Bess here."

Elizabeth stuck out her hand. "Deal."

An hour later Bess was milked, Robert was fed, the old man and woman were given their water and meat, and all were back in line, trudging along with the other refugees.

One crisis averted, Elizabeth thought, enjoying the

silence that went with a sated, sleeping Robert. She didn't even let her sore feet and aching back detract from the peace and quiet. *Ah silence, blessed silence.* She was smiling, enjoying that silence when she heard them. Horses were coming—lots of them. Her smile disappeared and her guard snapped into place.

THE JOURNEY
Day 4 – Afternoon
(The Road to Clinton)

The Union soldiers thundered to a halt along the road beside the frightened refugees.

"What we got here, Billy? More ref-u-gees from Rebel Land?" The eyes of the soldier who spoke sparkled with malice. "Y'all havin' a niiiice day?" he drawled in an exaggerated southern accent.

Elizabeth's heart was hammering as the children gathered around her, Rebecca's family doing the same on the other side of Hilda. Nora grabbed her mother's arm. "Mama?" Vera grabbed her other hand and even Joseph, Sally, and Andrew, sitting atop Hilda, looked as though some unknown artist had drawn fear on their little faces with lips trembling and eyes as wide as walnuts.

"What should we do?" Rebecca asked over the mare's back.

Elizabeth shook her head. "I don't know. All we can do is wait and see what they want."

"You know what they want. They want whatever they can ride away with or destroy to make our journey more difficult," Rebecca snarled.

Elizabeth's lips grew tight. "I know," she snapped. "But what can we do?"

Rebecca offered no response.

The troop of about ten Yankee soldiers walked their horses along both sides of the road, eyeing the travelers, spreading out amongst them. A soldier on a tall sorrel stopped his horse in front of Elizabeth and the two girls. His eyes grew wide in appreciation. "What do we have here? A picture of southern loveliness?"

"There's nothing here for you," Elizabeth managed through a dry throat and mouth. Her tongue felt three times its normal size and it seemed like her heart would jump right out of her chest. Nora squeezed her arm, turned her head away from the soldier, and slid closer. Vera moved closer, too.

The soldier just sat there, staring at the three of them.

Elizabeth could almost see him salivating.

"Charley! Lookee here what I found," he called to another soldier who rode up beside him.

"Um, um, um, you did find a bevy of lovelies, didn't you Randall." The second soldier stared at Elizabeth's family until her anger turned to rage.

"How dare you!" she shouted, wiping the smiles from the men's faces. "You are soldiers and should comport yourselves as such! You should be ashamed!" she shouted in a show of bravado, hoping to dissuade them from causing trouble, noticing the other soldiers had stopped their mischief down the line, albeit momentarily.

Nora and Vera had strong grips on Elizabeth's arms, but were shaking, and Joseph, Sally, and Andrew whimpered from atop Hilda. Rebecca's children stared, their mouths and eyes tight with fear.

"We got us a fighter here, boys," Randall, the first soldier, tall in the saddle with dark hair and dark, evil eyes shouted. There was a long scar across his chin and Elizabeth wondered at it. *Was it a scar he got in battle from a Confederate saber? Something from his childhood? Or from a woman perhaps?*

Elizabeth thought she'd jump right out of her skin when the soldier dismounted and walked toward them. He eyed the sled then turned abruptly to Hilda and grabbed the reins from Elizabeth hands. The mare jerked in surprise, but Elizabeth grabbed her bridle and put a hand on her neck to keep the horse calm. "Shhhh, girl. It's all right." *She might be blind and old, but she could still do a lot of damage in the midst of all these people if she took off, dragging the sled behind her—with the children atop her!*

Randall stepped close to the mare and looked in her eye. "Old is she?"

"Isn't it obvious?" Elizabeth couldn't help say.

Randall grinned. "Blind, too?"

"Again, isn't it obvious?" Elizabeth shook her head as though dealing with someone who was dull-witted.

Randall's face turned hard. "Did you blind it your own self?" he snarled.

"I did not!" But Elizabeth knew to what he referred. A

blind horse was useless to a soldier and, as brutal as it was, James had told her stories of farmers who purposely blinded their horses so they wouldn't be confiscated by soldiers or raiders, be they Yankee or Confederate. Although useless in battle, a blind horse could be led where it needed to go, and many a farmer's field was plowed by one. Knowing Poppyseed's worth, Elizabeth had even considered for a short moment blinding the mare so as not to lose her to raiders or soldiers, but couldn't do it. She'd rather have lost her than do her harm, which was exactly what had happened, and she snorted with this soldier's snide reminder. *But if she hadn't had Hilda, how desperate might she have become?* Her skin pricked at the thought.

Randall cocked his head and stepped toward Nora, her face still turned away. He touched her hair and she jerked back with a whimper.

Elizabeth slapped his hand. "Do not touch my child!"

The soldier threw his head back and laughed. "She got spunk, don't she boys?" he yelled at the two others still on horseback behind him. He grabbed Nora's hair and forced her head around.

She spit in his face.

The two men howled. Randall did not. There was rage in his eyes. Elizabeth's rage exploded to the fore and she shoved him aside. "Do not touch my child, I told you!"

Laughter erupted behind Randall again and he stepped back, his mouth tight his eyes pinched. "Why I'll...." He raised his hand to backhand Elizabeth when another rider jerked his horse to a halt beside the angry man.

"Randall!" the officer barked.

Randall snapped to attention. "Sir!"

"Remove yourself. Now!" the officer commanded.

"Yes, sir!" Randall snapped a salute, remounted, and waited.

The officer stepped down from his horse and doffed his hat. "My apologies, ma'am. These men have been away from civilization too long. Although not an excuse, it is an explanation. Again, my apologies."

Elizabeth swallowed. "Thank you, captain is it?"

"Yes ma'am, Captain Howard, at your service." He bowed low and swept his hat across his waist. When he stood Elizabeth saw regret on his face.

"I find I must apologize again, ma'am."

"For what?" Ripples of foreboding swept up Elizabeth's spine.

"My men and I are on a foraging mission, ma'am."

If Nora and Vera hadn't been holding onto her, Elizabeth might have fallen down. *They were going to take their supplies!* She looked up and down the line of other refugees and her fear was confirmed. Soldiers were tearing into all the wagons and sacks pulling out clothing, food, and anything else that might be of use.

"Sir, please...."

He raised a hand to stay her plea. "I have my orders." He put his hat back on, remounted and whirled his horse to face the men awaiting his orders. "Take whatever is of use." He wheeled his horse back, cocked his head as though in a last apology, and disappeared up the road.

The mattresses were yanked from the top of the sled and dragged away by Randall and the two other soldiers.

"Better make sure they're not hiding anything inside these mattresses," Randall yelled, slicing into one with his knife. Feathers billowed like a snowstorm into the air before settling along the side of the road, the remaining bits and pieces of mattress material discarded on top.

"Guess there wasn't anything inside." Randall stood grinning over the shredded material and sea of feathers. He turned and glared at Elizabeth then strode back to the sled. "Let's see what else we got here." His eyes fixed on the sacks with the meat in them and Elizabeth thought she was going to be sick.

"Please," she heard herself whimper, but knew her plea fell on unhearing ears.

"Ooh we! Looky here. We got us a passle of jerky! Grab ye some boys!" He and the others reached in and grabbed handfuls of the meat that was meant to sustain Elizabeth and Rebecca's families for the next week. *What would they do now?*

Elizabeth and Rebecca stood frozen, unable to do or say anything to stop the soldiers from ransacking the sled and taking what they would. Pots and pans were thrown over their shoulders as non-useful items, clunking and clattering as they rolled away. Lanterns were smashed, the dry ground soaking up the leaking oil like a thirsty sponge. Blankets and linens were draped over saddles and the water jugs were slung from saddle horns. Elizabeth looked away, tears streaming down her face. She glanced at Rebecca, her face as white as parchment, little Robert clutched close to her breast, whimpering, the other children wide-eyed and crying silent tears.

"Will you leave us nothing?" Elizabeth asked. "That's everything we have."

"Then you should have been nicer to me, shouldn't you?" Randall spit, turned and shattered a mirror that had been hidden in the sled.

Elizabeth stopped breathing when they found the squirrel rifle and pistols tucked between the two boards that made up the side panel.

"And what do we have here?" another soldier asked.

"Please!" Elizabeth cried. "You've taken all our food and water. How are we supposed to hunt if we have no weapons?" Her stomach felt like it had fallen out onto the road.

"Please!" Randall mimicked. "Please!" He and the others threw back their heads and laughed.

Elizabeth had that feeling again. Rage was creeping up her spine—rage she couldn't stop. She stalked over to Randall and slapped him in the face. Silence fell over him and the others, who stared wide-eyed at the soldier and woman facing off. "You sir, are no gentleman! You shouldn't even be allowed to call yourself a soldier! You are shameful, all of you!" she shouted.

Randall looked up the road and, noticing the captain was nowhere to be seen, did what he'd intended to do earlier. He drew back his hand and laid it across Elizabeth's cheek. She went to the dirt, holding her face. Tears threatened, but she refused to let them out. She would show these—men—she was better than they were. She raised her chin and stood up. "Do you feel better now?" she challenged.

He stepped toward her again, but Nora threw herself in front of him, her arms protecting her mother. "Don't you dare you vile piece of horse dung," she snarled through gritted teeth.

Randall stopped and stared, his eyes belying his rage. His hand was raised to strike Nora this time, when the captain's bellow came from up the road. Captain Howard rode between Randall and Nora and Elizabeth, almost knocking them over, but Elizabeth was grateful for his intervention.

"Enough!" he yelled. "Private Randall you're done here. Move on."

Howard looked down at Elizabeth and Nora, holding each other for support. "Again I apologize for my man."

Elizabeth could only nod.

"We're through here." The captain wheeled his horse around. "Mount up!"

In minutes they were gone, the remains of the travelers' lives left in shambles—again. Wagons were broken, their now-worthless contents strewn about. Women and children whimpered as they gathered whatever was recoverable, knowing it would be precious little. Others walked in circles with glazed eyes, speaking to no one, asking questions that had no answers.

Sniffling and whimpering, Elizabeth, Rebecca and the children set about gathering what little was salvageable. Thankfully, the sled was spared destruction by Private Randall and his cohorts with Captain Howard's timely rescue. And they still had Hilda.

The meat and water were gone. Not a morsel or drop was left. Two of the three mattresses were shredded, blankets stolen, lanterns shattered, everything else broken and worthless. Worst of all, the guns were gone. *How would she replace the stolen food? How would they survive the rest of their journey with no food and no means to hunt?*

For a few minutes Nora was a hero amongst the older children, having spit right in the face of that Union soldier and blocking him from hitting her mother. "How brave you were!" Helen congratulated, but Elizabeth saw the fear her daughter hid. Her celebrity passed quickly and Nora and the other children finished gathering what was left of their supplies and put it beside the sled for Elizabeth and Rebecca to repack.

The day had started poorly and slid downhill since then. *Could it get any worse?* Elizabeth worried, gazing at the destruction ahead of and behind them. *Of course it could! The day was only half gone.* A chill raced up her spine, despite the sweltering heat.

THE JOURNEY
Day 4 – Early Evening
(The Road to Clinton)

"Mama?"

Nora was shaking and Elizabeth gathered her daughter in her arms. "I'm here, Nora." Disheartened and exhausted, they'd stopped for the night long before sundown in a small copse of trees that offered some shelter and some spindly bushes for Hilda to forage on. Many of the travelers continued past, but as the day wore on other families, seemingly as lost and disheartened as Elizabeth and Rebecca, stopped close by. Elizabeth was relieved to see Meg and Albert were close, but she was sure they'd stopped only because Meg insisted. Thankfully, there would, at least, be milk for little Robert.

"I'm afraid." Nora was still shaking.

"I know, but you're safe now," Elizabeth lied. She knew it and Nora knew it, but there was nothing else she could say to assuage her daughter's fears. They wouldn't be safe, any of them, until they reached their destination. Even then, *what would they find? Were they walking toward more heartache?* Elizabeth's fear and uncertainty were beginning to take root, and she had to stop it—now—for the children's sake.

"We'll be fine." Elizabeth's body stung with the added lie, but she'd sworn to do whatever it took to keep them safe and that's what she intended. She wouldn't quit. Not now, not ever.

Nora looked up, her eyes brimming with tears. "We won't be safe again until this war is over, Mama." Nora said the words without emotion. They were just fact.

"Shhh," Elizabeth cooed, unable to refute her daughter's words. They had to live day by day in the shadow of their fear until this war ended. Until that time, Elizabeth did not plan to let that fear get the better of her. She stiffened her back and hugged Nora again. "We're going to be fine and we're going to survive. We'll figure out what to do." Nora nodded and buried her face in her mother's chest like she used to when she was a little girl. How Elizabeth wished she were that little girl again, of no interest to roving soldiers. But she wasn't a little child. She was a blossoming young woman and that scared Elizabeth as much as anything about this miserable war.

Although the sun was still a few hours from setting, everyone tried to relax and keep their minds off how hungry and thirsty they were. The older children sat under a tree, shoulder to shoulder, whispering, while the younger children, despite their exhaustion, played in the sand giggling in their ignorance. Rebecca had coaxed some milk from old Bess and was sitting on a rock in the shade under a tree feeding Robert. Elizabeth sat in what little shade a leafless tree offered and watched Hilda. The mare ate everything her nose touched—bark, branches, dead grass, and curled up brown leaves—and Elizabeth realized the mare needed water more than she did food. She was already showing signs of dehydration. There were little white flecks of spittle around the corners of her mouth, she was wobbly on her feet, and her belly was tightening. If she went down, she'd never get up again. The mare's nose disappeared into a shriveled bush, but Elizabeth knew she needed more. Combining her age, the heat, and the extra exertion from pulling the sled, Elizabeth feared Hilda wouldn't last another day without water—if that long.

"I'll be back soon. I've got to find water for Hilda or she won't make it much longer," she told Rebecca.

Rebecca nodded solemnly.

"If I can't find water, maybe I can find some trees that still have green leaves she can reach." Elizabeth wiped her brow. "This damnable heat!" she growled, unable to stop the words from bursting out of her mouth, feeling slightly better for having said them, voicing what everyone *wished* they could say. "I won't go far," she promised at Rebecca's questioning look. She shaded her eyes and looked up at the sun. "There're still a few hours before dark. Don't worry."

Walking into the trees lining the road, Elizabeth scanned the area for still green foliage. Despite what she'd told Rebecca, the sun would go down soon. She didn't want to go too far and wind up lost, but Hilda *had* to have moisture of some kind, so she plodded forward. Anything would help. Mostly what she saw were shriveled up bushes and shrubs, the drought having taken its toll. Remembering trees had deeper roots than bushes and would generally take longer to show the effects of the drought, she looked up to see some still green leaves on the branches of a few cottonwoods! Her excitement was short-lived when she realized the branches were way too high for Hilda to reach. She thought a moment then hurried back to camp.

"Nora, Vera, Helen, Clara, and Joshua, come quickly!"

"What's the matter?" a puzzled Rebecca asked. "Did you find water?"

"I didn't, but I found a few cottonwoods that still have leaves on them. Green leaves."

"But what do you need the children for?" Rebecca cocked her head, even more confused.

"Gather round," she told the children when they reached her. "I have a chore for you."

They groaned and, as had become her way, Vera was the one to voice her displeasure.

"We're too tired, Mama."

"You'll be more tired if we lose Hilda. She needs water and there is none to be found, so we have to do something else."

"What, Mama?" Nora asked.

"I found some cottonwoods that still have green leaves on them." Elizabeth pointed to the woods she'd just come from.

"So?" Vera asked annoyance in her voice.

"Hilda needs water—badly. If she doesn't get some, she won't last another day in this heat."

"You said you found leaves, not water, Mama," Vera sounded annoyed *and* confused.

"Yes, and green leaves hold moisture. Precious moisture Hilda needs."

"What do you want us to do, Mrs. Miers?" Joshua asked.

"I want you all to climb the trees, break off the smaller limbs that still have green leaves on them, and drag them back here to Hilda. It's the closest thing we can get to water and, hopefully, it'll keep her going until we find some."

"Climb trees?" Vera sounded incredulous.

"Yes, climb trees. And don't act like you've never done it before, Vera. Pretend you're climbing the big tree in our yard to watch for Yankees, like you used to before your Papa was killed." Elizabeth eyed her daughter, daring her to challenge her.

"We can do it, Mrs. Miers. Can't we?" Joshua asked the other children.

Everyone, including a reluctant Vera, agreed they could.

"Good, then let's go." Elizabeth turned to Rebecca. "Again you're stuck behind with the smaller children, but there's no help for it. We have to do this or Hilda...."

"I understand, Elizabeth," Rebecca interrupted. "Take the children and go. You're losing daylight. And don't get lost!" Rebecca turned Elizabeth toward the trees and gave her a shove.

Elizabeth made their quest for leaves a game and for the first time in days the children laughed, and Elizabeth laughed with them. It took fifteen minutes to reach the trees she had found and one by one they climbed to where the green leaves clung.

"Be careful!" Elizabeth shouted to the giggling children as they shinnied up the trunks as easily as cats.

"Yes, Mama," and "Yes, Mrs. Miers," was shouted in unison by the five children.

One by one they reached a limb that held the promise of moisture for Hilda.

"Break off as many branches as you can and drop them. I'll gather them down here to drag back. Go as high as you can and get as many as you can. The more we get the better off we'll be. We can drag any extra behind us to give to Hilda tomorrow."

The children worked for almost an hour, clinging to the larger branches, jerking and breaking smaller branches still heavy with leaves, letting them fall for Elizabeth to gather in piles below.

"It's time to come down, children!" Elizabeth called up when she realized the sun was starting to set. "We don't want to get caught away from camp in the dark."

Five minutes later they were headed back, each dragging a load of leafy branches behind them. *At least Hilda would have food and moisture tonight*, Elizabeth thought almost grudgingly. *It was more than the rest of them would get.*

THE JOURNEY
Day 4 – Evening
(The Road to Clinton)

The two families did their best to settle in for the night. The temperature cooled somewhat, and for once Elizabeth didn't curse the heat. They might be hot, but they wouldn't shiver without blankets, stolen by the Yankee soldiers. After pulling their supplies from the sled and assessing what little they had left, they put the smallest children on the mattress floor to sleep. Andrew, Joseph, and Sally were squeezed up front, while young Benjamin, Richard and Francis were squished at the bottom. Against the side of the sled, Nora, Vera, Helen, Clara, Joshua, and Edna, sat huddled together on a bed they fashioned by stripping leaves off nearby bushes, Joshua's intention made plain he intended to guard the girls. It seemed to Elizabeth he'd taken a bit of a protective fancy toward Nora since the incident with the soldiers.

Joshua was the first one asleep.

Elizabeth and Rebecca sat on salvaged mattress pieces, talking quietly not far from the sled. Little Robert was in his sling at Rebecca's breast, finally having cried himself to sleep after finishing a small bit of milk they'd managed to get from ole Bess amidst much protest from Albert.

"What are we going to do? We need water and food." Rebecca put her finally slumbering son beside her on another small piece of rescued mattress.

Elizabeth shook her head. "I don't know. Without a gun, I have no idea how we're going to replenish what we've lost." She looked over at the sled, arms and legs and feet sticking out all over it instead of the bags and jugs of meat and water that should have been there. Meat and water they'd worked for days cutting, curing and bottling so they'd have plenty for their journey. All gone. Anger simmered so strong in Elizabeth's belly she wanted to lash out and hit someone or something. She wanted to scream. Her hands were rolling in and out of fists when Rebecca spoke again, drawing her attention from her anger.

"What?"

"I said maybe someone will be kind enough to share."

Rebecca sounded hopeful.

Elizabeth snorted at Rebecca's naiveté. "No one is going to share—if there were anything *to* share. How many farms have we passed since we left?

"A few," Rebecca stammered from the hostility in Elizabeth's voice.

"And what did they look like?" Elizabeth pressed.

"Deserted—or burned." Rebecca's voice broke. "And those that did have people living there had signs out telling us rebels to keep going, that they wouldn't help folks *like us*," she said, her voice cracking on the realization.

"And how many folks *like us* do you think have already walked by those deserted farms, looking for food? There's nothing for us and no one to help us, Rebecca." She drew in a deep breath. "We're on our own."

"There might be something, somewhere Elizabeth. If we just look...."

Elizabeth's patience snapped. She sat up and almost shouted, "Rebecca, have you not been paying attention? We're alone." She waved her hand at the camps nearby. "Amidst all these people—we are alone. No one cares what happens to us. We don't care about them and they don't care about us. There's nothing to be found anywhere. We have to take care of ourselves," Elizabeth ground out, trying to stay calm.

Rebecca's lips flexed and tears slid down her cheeks. "Yes, apparently we are. Now what?"

Elizabeth shook her head again. "We have to find water and a way to hunt."

"But how?" Rebecca sounded lost, defeated.

"Any way we can." Elizabeth looked over at the slumbering children. "We can pull some of the rope from the bottom of the sled to make a bow or some kind of a snare. We have to do something; otherwise, we're going to be very hungry by the time we get where we're going. *If* we get where we're going." She snapped her mouth shut, sorry she'd uttered the words, afraid by having said them they might come true.

Both women were pondering their difficult situation when Nora joined them. "I can't sleep."

Elizabeth raised her palm to her daughter. "Wait." She

unrolled another piece of salvaged mattress and laid it on the ground next to hers. She patted the shredded cloth. "Come on."

Nora scooted down beside her mother who wrapped her in her arms and pulled her close. "We'd better get some sleep." Nora was cradled in the crook of her arm and using her shoulder as a pillow. "Daylight will be here before we know it and it'll be time to move out."

"But what about food?" Rebecca whined like one of the children.

Elizabeth sighed. "I guess we'll have to figure it out in the morning, because I'm out of ideas right now."

Unwilling and unable to think any more on their situation, it wasn't long before exhaustion claimed them and all three were sound asleep next to a Heavenly silent Robert.

Elizabeth jerked awake. It was still dark and her mind buzzed with warning, but she didn't know why. A twig snapped nearby confirming someone or something was close. They had nothing left to steal. What could they want? She squeezed Nora and the girl sputtered awake, but it was too late. A pistol was waving in front of them as Rebecca and Robert still slept beside them.

"Git up," came the whispered command from the familiar voice of the soldier bent over in front of them. Randall!

"Quiet like. If one of you screams, I'll shoot you both. And the babe," he added to shock them into doing what he said.

"Mama?" The fear Elizabeth heard in her daughter's voice mirrored her own and made her shudder, but she gathered her wits, what was left of them, and took Nora's hand.

"Shhh, we'll be all right." Elizabeth tried to sound confident, so as not to frighten Nora more, as they got to their feet.

Randall chuckled. "Yep, you'll be all right, darlin'. Right between my legs." He ran his dirty fingers across Nora's chin. She jerked away and turned her head. The gleam Elizabeth saw in his eyes in the moonlight, and knowing what he wanted to do to Nora, made Elizabeth want to retch.

"Do not touch my daughter," Elizabeth growled. She put

her left arm across Nora's chest and pushed her behind her.

"You are a feisty wench, ain't you?" Randall spit and wiped his mouth with the back of his hand. "I hate to inform you, lady, but you got no say. Cap'n Howard ain't here to rescue you tonight an' me an' that pretty thing got business."

Nora sagged against Elizabeth's back, clinging to her mother to stay on her feet.

"You will not touch her."

"An' what you gonna do to stop me?" He waved the gun in her face.

What could she do? Elizabeth was deciding when she raised her chin and took a deep breath. "Take me instead."

Nora slid to her knees behind Elizabeth gagging.

"She's a child. You don't want a child. You want a woman. She'll fight. I won't." Elizabeth thought she'd be sick right next to Nora, but she kept her stomach down and her chin up.

Nora continued to gag and Elizabeth prayed her daughter understood what she was offering to do. She would do *anything* to protect her daughter from this man and any others like him. Anything.

Randall eyed her a few moments before he grabbed Elizabeth's arm and put his face into hers. She forced his putrid smell out of her mind and stood tall in front of him, blocking his way to her daughter.

He stepped back and leaned around Elizabeth to peer at Nora, still on her knees behind her mother. "I prefer the young, pure one, but it was a nice offer." He tapped the gun barrel against Elizabeth's chin. "Don't want you interferrin' though, so I'm gonna tie you up, gag you, and set you down over there." He waved to the spot he suggested about ten feet away. "You can even watch—if'n you want," he leered, pulling a piece of rope from an inside pocket of his uniform and dangling it in front of Elizabeth.

Elizabeth wanted to scratch his eyes out. She had to do *something* to keep this vile man away from Nora—but what? He laid his finger across his lips, reminding her to be quiet then waved the gun to where he wanted Elizabeth to go so she wouldn't interfere with his rape of her daughter. *Like she was going to allow that to happen!* His eyes sparkled with lust and Elizabeth knew she had to do something—right now—before she was bound and gagged.

In the short seconds the gun was pointed away, Elizabeth threw herself at him, screaming at the top of her lungs. She hit Randall with the full force of her body, grabbing for the pistol. He dropped the weapon and, taking advantage of his momentary confusion, Elizabeth raked his face with her broken fingernails, satisfaction racing through her when he screamed.

That satisfaction was short-lived. He threw her to the ground like he was shrugging off a heavy coat, the breath knocked out of her. Trying to catch her breath, he yanked her back to her feet. She staggered, gaining her balance just before he backhanded her and sent her sprawling into the dirt again.

There was movement in the camps around her. *If she could keep him busy until others arrived to help, she might come out of this alive.*

Rebecca suddenly screamed at the top of her lungs and flung herself onto Randall's back. She scratched at his face and pulled his hair before she stuck her fingers in the corners of his mouth and pulled his lips so hard blood spurted out. With a shriek he threw her over his shoulder like a sack of potatoes. Rebecca hit the ground and didn't move.

Other travelers had gathered, but one voice stopped everyone from coming closer.

"You stop right now or I'll blow a hole right through you." Nora stood behind Randall, her legs braced, his gun pointed at his back, her voice deadly calm.

The soldier straightened to his almost six foot height and raised his hands. "You think you're gonna shoot me little girl?" He threw his head back and laughed then whirled to face Nora.

She jumped, but held kept the gun trained on him.

"You think you got the sand to pull that trigger?" His voice was deadly and he took a step forward.

Gulping in the tepid air, Elizabeth scrambled to her feet and grabbed the gun from Nora's shaking hand. "She may not, but I do. Believe me, I have *more* than enough sand to pull this trigger." Elizabeth shook her head. "And do not doubt me. I've already put one man in a grave because he didn't think I would pull the trigger. A no good Yankee, just like you." She cocked her head. "Will you test me, too? Will you force me to shoot you or will you take your leave and never come around again?"

Randall stood still, his eyes darting between the three women standing side by side. Rebecca stood on Elizabeth's right, Elizabeth pointing the cocked pistol at Randall's heart. Nora stood on Elizabeth's left, clinging to her mother's free arm, as more refugees gathered behind them.

With a hard set to his face, Randall took a step forward.

Elizabeth waved the gun. "I wouldn't if I were you. I promise I *will* kill you if you press me. I know you blue bellies bleed red, just like we do, and believe me I have no care whether you live or die." She cocked her head, realizing how much she meant what she said. "Maybe I should just kill him so he doesn't bother us again. He's becoming quite a nuisance. What do you think, Rebecca? Should I shoot him and be done with it?"

Nora jerked upright in surprise, but Rebecca grinned. "I think that's a fine idea, Elizabeth. Don't want to have to look over our shoulders from now on. Maybe you *should* shoot him and be done with it—just like those no good Yankees shot our husbands."

The man snorted but looked uncertain.

"You ain't gonna shoot me."

"Are you willing to bet your life on that?" Elizabeth challenged. "That man I killed. Well, I killed him in my own home when he didn't heed my words. Shot him twice, actually. Blew his elbow apart the first time he doubted my words, and when he came back the second time, the damned fool still questioned whether I'd shoot him and, well...." She let the words hang a moment before she continued. "I'll do no less now when you threaten my child. Yankees killed both our husbands." She jerked her head toward Rebecca. "You Yankees have taken our homes, land, husbands, and everything we hold dear, so you better believe I'll shoot you right here and right now." She paused again, pursed her lips and added, "So if I was you, I wouldn't press overmuch and make up my mind for me."

He took another step toward her. There was a collective gasp behind her.

"Don't do it, soldier boy. I'm telling you, I *will* shoot

you if you take one more step." Elizabeth's heart was pounding. *Could she pull the trigger again, knowing another man would die?*

Doubt must have shown on her face. He looked away as though to contemplate her words—and charged.

The gun exploded. He slammed into Elizabeth, almost knocking her over, before he slumped to the ground, blood gushing from the wound in his stomach.

"I'll be damned, you did shoot me." The surprise in his voice and in his eyes made Elizabeth smile despite knowing she'd killed him.

"I told you I would." Elizabeth started to shake, but it didn't matter now. The deed was done. All that was left now was the waiting.

Blood soaked his shirt and pants, but neither Elizabeth nor Rebecca or any of the others who had gathered moved to help him.

"You'll be dead in a few minutes with a wound like that, Randall. You should have listened to me, but you men are foolish, prideful creatures. You think all women are weak. Someday men will learn. But *you* learned today, didn't you?" Elizabeth felt like someone else was inside her body. She was cold and uncaring what happened to this man. He'd threatened her daughter and she'd done what was necessary to remove that threat.

Nora was crying beside her and she laid her free arm over her shoulder. "I told you we'd be all right, Nora. I'll do whatever it takes to keep you safe—*whatever* it takes."

The other travelers converged on the wounded man. Some spat on him and hurled insults. Some asked him about how it felt to die at the hands of a Rebel—and a woman no less—or who had taught him to be such a devil? Others stood in silence, waiting. Ten minutes later he was dead, surrounded by those he'd demeaned and stolen from earlier in the day.

"We should bury the body," a woman with three young children beside Rebecca said. "Shouldn't leave him where the Yankees can find him. Let them think he ran away like the coward he was."

There was general agreement from those gathered. Even

old Albert and Meg agreed.

"Did them blue bellies leave anyone with a shovel?" another woman asked.

A young woman raised her hand. "I saved a small garden spade, but it's better than nothing."

"We'll use sticks and rocks if we have to, but let's get a hole dug so we can get rid of this trash," an old woman with a bent back shouted, hobbling toward the trees.

Everyone turned at the ready when someone crashed through the bushes leading the soldier's horse. The woman led the animal to Elizabeth and put the reins in her hand. "She's yours now, since you killed the vermin that rode her."

Elizabeth was staring at the small chestnut mare standing in front of her, wondering how she could take on the care of one more living creature, when a tall woman stepped out of the crowd toward the horse.

"Molly? Molly is that you?"

Elizabeth watched the young woman with two small children beside her walk toward the animal.

"I think that's my Molly. The Yankees stole her months ago. I thought I'd never see her again." Tears streaked the woman's cheeks. The children reached for the horse and she bobbed her head and nudged them with her nose in recognition.

"She's yours then?" Elizabeth asked.

The woman sniffed. "Yes. These same soldiers came to my farm a few months ago and took everything we had, including Molly. She was all we had to keep the farm going— but they didn't care." Her voice was hard now and the tears seemed to have frozen on her face. "They took everything except my girls." She was lost in a world of hurt and memories as everyone listened in silence. "When they rode in they taunted my husband, Carl. They called him a coward because he wasn't off fightin'—for either side. Told him he was as worthless as teats on a bull." Her lips trembled and fresh tears slid from her eyes. "Until he charged and they shot him. Right there in front of me and my girls. Shot him dead. And then they laughed." Her children buried their faces in her dirty, threadbare dress, and the three wept. Folks in the crowd wept, too, reliving their own similar stories. The woman finally straightened her back, raised her chin, and sniffed. "You should have her."

Elizabeth shook her head. "No. She's yours." The surprise on the woman's face reminded Elizabeth how little kindness there'd been in a long time. "Take her, please." Elizabeth laid the reins over the woman's hands.

"Thank you," the woman whispered, her voice cracking. The woman and her children turned and started away, the mare following behind them, still nudging the children in familiarity as they went.

"Wait!" Elizabeth stopped the woman before she got too far. "We should check the saddle bags." Elizabeth lifted one flap and Molly's owner lifted the other.

"Find anything?" Elizabeth asked.

"There's some hard tack and a couple hard biscuits, but nothing else in this one," the other woman responded.

Elizabeth felt around inside the bag and pulled out some coins, a dirty handkerchief, an extra box of cartridges for the pistol, some extra leather piggin' lines that might come in handy later, and a smaller bag. Inside the bag were several pieces of jewelry.

"That's my husband's watch!" shouted one of the on-lookers when Elizabeth dumped it all out in a pile in the middle of the crowd.

"And that's my weddin' ring that varmint took right off my hand!" shouted another woman.

Elizabeth spread everything out. "Take what's yours and give the hardtack and biscuits to the children. I'll take these." She slid a Springfield rifle from the saddle and unwrapped another ammo pouch from around the horn.

Their prayers had been answered. They had weapons again to hunt and replenish their food supply. She looked around at the hungry, expectant faces and raised Randall's rifle above her head.

"Tomorrow, we hunt!"

Two hours later Randall was buried in a shallow grave Elizabeth knew would be desecrated by wild animals within hours. But she didn't care. She'd done what had to be done to keep him from defiling her daughter.

THE JOURNEY
Day 5 - Morning
(The Road to Clinton)

None but the younger children slept the rest of that night. Nora curled into a ball at the base of a tree as Helen, Clara, Vera, and Joshua tried to raise her spirits. Rebecca fought with an unruly Robert, awakened by the ruckus, who squalled all over again. If anyone other than the little ones *had* wanted to sleep, he kept them from it. Elizabeth was too charged from having killed another man in defense of her family and didn't even try. But it wasn't to be helped. She swore on everything she loved she would do whatever was necessary, whenever necessary, as many times as it took, to protect her children. Foolish men had taken more from her than she could ever take back and they would learn the hard way she wasn't weak.

Long before the sun came up she and a tall woman named Betty, professing to be a pretty good pistol shot despite her scrawny body, set out in search of game. Molly was recruited to carry anything they shot back to camp and both were optimistic when they set out that they would return with food to fill their empty bellies.

They tromped through the woods in the building heat as the sun rose, leaving signs along the way so they could find their way back, neither seeing nor hearing anything that passed for game. They saw a turtle—one turtle—and a couple of fast moving squirrels, but aside from that, nothing. They re-joined the group at mid-morning, surrounded immediately by their fellow travelers.

"I'm sorry. We didn't see one deer, one turkey, or even a miserable possum." Elizabeth felt weak from the lack of food and water, as well as impotence at not being able to find any game.

"Maybe we'll have better luck later," Betty said, hopeful, a dull look in her eyes that told Elizabeth how hungry and disappointed her fellow hunter was.

"And maybe the skies will open and it'll rain!" the bent-over, gray-haired woman grumbled from the crowd that had gathered on their return. She waved her hand dismissively, slung her raggedy bag over her shoulder, and headed for the road, leaving a dust cloud swirling behind her.

Amidst more grumbling, the others gathered what little they possessed, sent whiny children ahead of them, and lit out again.

"You found nothing?" Rebecca asked when she sidled up to Elizabeth, little Robert crying and squirming in her arms, as had become his usual state. Although Meg had forced Albert to allow Rebecca access to old Bess without getting anything in return, the child still screamed. He had developed a horrible rash and nothing Rebecca did helped ease his discomfort. Naked in his mother's arms in her effort to make him feel better, he still screamed.

Elizabeth swallowed, trying to keep from reaching out and shaking him. "Can't you make him stop? Even for a few minutes?"

"I don't know what to do for him, Elizabeth," Rebecca groaned. "No matter what I do, he screams." Her lip quivered before she added. "I know how he feels. I want to scream, too."

"Helen!" Elizabeth shouted. When the girl ran up Elizabeth snatched Robert from his mother's arms and handed him to his older sister. "Give him some more milk, but take him over there to do it. He's wearing on everyone's nerves. Play with him, do whatever you must, but make him stop crying." Elizabeth's teeth were grinding. She was at the end of her patience.

Helen stood with her unruly brother in hand, waiting for her mother to tell her it was all right.

"There is no more milk." Rebecca's voice was flat with exhaustion and defeat. "He drank the last of it this morning after you left and I haven't asked for more."

"Then you and the other children play with him, Helen. Do whatever you must to make him stop his caterwauling!" Elizabeth said louder than she intended.

Helen looked askance at her mother, who swallowed and nodded. "Do as Elizabeth says."

"Yes, Mama." Helen walked to the other side of the quickly disbursing camps with the wiggling boy in her arms. Soon, only the Miers, Barrows, and Molly's owner, Annie, and her two children, remained. Even Meg and Albert had slipped away unseen.

Elizabeth sighed. "What do we do for milk now?" She looked over at Helen, trying to keep her baby brother quiet. Nora, given a distraction from her own worries, tried to help in the cause, as did Vera, and Clara, but nothing they did seemed to quiet his ear-splitting cries.

"We'll have to catch Albert and Meg, it's the only thing we can do," Rebecca said.

"Or wait for someone else to come along," Elizabeth said.

Rebecca shook her head. "I don't know. We could wait for hours, even days, before someone else comes along with a milking cow—one that still has milk. Old Bess was drying up. I could tell. With no water to speak of she was giving less and less every time I milked her." Rebecca looked down at her breast. "I know the feeling." She sighed. "And what if we do find a cow that still has milk, but the owner is greedier than Albert and won't give us any unless we give them something in return." She shook her head again and added, "Something we don't have."

Elizabeth thought again. Albert and Meg were a sure thing, well, somewhat sure. Meg would make Albert give them milk as long as Bess produced it. "I think we should catch up to Albert and Meg. They're old and move slower than everyone else. They can't get too far ahead. It shouldn't be hard to catch them."

"I agree, but that still doesn't take care of finding food for everyone else. What're we going to do?" Rebecca's eyes glistened with uncertainty.

"I'll hunt again later," Elizabeth promised as they hitched a steadier Hilda to the sled, the mare having munched on cottonwood leaves all night. A few minutes later, ready to go, she clucked to the mare and the sled jerked forward, what few belongings they had left stacked at the top and the smaller children riding at the bottom. Randall's pistol was tucked in the pocket of her skirt and she carried his rifle at the ready in the crook of her elbow, in case a deer, or two-legged vermin, came into view.

They fell back in line with the slogging emigrants,

moving as slowly as those in front of them. Dust swirled into their eyes and mouths, their handkerchief masks doing little to keep it out.

The day progressed in slow, mindless boredom. They put one foot in front of the other, chanting quietly as they did so, making it a game to help them keep going. The sun roasted them, as it had every day for the last few weeks. Clothing was soaked and smelly, feet blistered and raw. Lips were cracked and bled. The children begged to ride Hilda, their feet so sore they swore they couldn't take another step, but were told no—the mare was too weak—and Robert continued to shriek his hunger and displeasure. Elizabeth thought she'd go mad from the constant screaming and crushed her skirts in her fists to keep from grabbing the boy and shaking him into silence.

The scraggly line of emigrants suddenly came to an abrupt stop. Elizabeth pulled Hilda to a halt and craned her neck to see ahead, but saw nothing but others trying to see what was happening, just like her. *What was going on? Had more soldiers come? Were they looking for Private Randall? Would they destroy what little they had left?* Her mind was buzzing crazily when she heard the word that made her knees go weak.

Water! *There was water ahead. Was it a creek or stream? A well, perhaps, that someone had opened up to them? How long would it take to reach it? What did it matter?* she berated herself. *It was water!*

"Did you hear that?" Rebecca asked over Hilda's back. "There's water ahead!"

"Don't get too excited." Elizabeth shook her head to contain her own burgeoning excitement. "Whatever it is will take a long time to reach. It could be dry by the time we get there with all these people and animals in front of us." She was trying not to get too hopeful only to have her hopes dashed. "And," she continued, keeping a tight rein on her emotions, "it's going to cost us a lot of travel time to get there."

"I don't care what it takes. I'm going to drink until I bust!" Rebecca shouted.

"And then you'll get sick," Elizabeth reminded her friend. "Be smart, Rebecca, drink your fill, slowly, but no more.

We have to make sure the children don't drink too much, too fast, either, or they'll get belly aches. And we especially have to watch Hilda. She'll go down if she drinks too much too fast and she'll never get back up." Elizabeth thought a moment then strode to the sled. "We have to find something to carry water. There must be something the soldiers didn't destroy."

"I think we saved a couple pots that aren't bent too badly. If there are lids, they're bent even worse. How will we carry the water and keep it from sloshing out without lids that fit properly?" Rebecca asked.

Elizabeth sucked in the dusty, hot air. She coughed then coughed more before able to spit out what she'd brought up out of her chest. No one looked at her with reproach or turned away in disgust. They only waited until she could speak again. She wiped her mouth and grinned under the kerchief. A few years ago she would have been chastised harshly for what she'd just done; a woman who spit was most unladylike. Today it meant nothing more than clearing her throat so she could continue her journey.

When she spoke again, her voice gravelly, she said, "We have to carry whatever water we can. We'll have to find something to cover the pots. There must be *something* in here." She dug into their belongings and pulled out two pots. There were dents on the bottoms and the tops were no longer round, but they were salvageable. "These should work. Maybe the lids aren't as bad as you remember. Did we keep them? Oh, please tell me we did," she jabbered more to herself than to Rebecca. Again she went through what was on the sled and found one lid, so badly bent there was no way it would keep the slightest drop of water inside the pot. She held it up for Rebecca to see. "If nothing else the soldiers were thorough in their destruction. How will this be of any use?"

"We can pound it and the pots back into shape with a heavy rock," Rebecca suggested.

Elizabeth nodded. "Good idea. We have to find one rock big and flat enough to use as a base and another to use as a hammer."

"Then what?" Elizabeth started to take another deep breath then thought better of it. She remembered the broken mirror that might have been laid across the top to cover one of the pots, shattered in pieces on the road behind them. They had the shredded mattress pieces, the cinches stretched across the floor of the sled, and what else that might possibly work? She dug into the things scattered on the sled again, hoping to find something she'd missed that could be used as a lid, but gave up. There was nothing. Absolutely nothing.

They moved when the line moved and Elizabeth pondered what to do. It was several minutes before an idea struck. If she cut off the extra pieces of wood the water jugs had hung on at the top of the sled, they could lay them across the pot and hold them in place with a heavy rock. It was worth trying. Now all they had to do was figure out how to cut the wood.

"Rebecca, I'm going up the line to see how far we are from the water and to try and find a saw."

"A saw? What for?"

"If we cut the excess wood from the top of the sled, maybe we can lay it across the second pot as a lid."

Rebecca cocked her head. "It's worth a try. Anything is worth a try." She looked at the line ahead of them and then at the children, enjoying their forced rest. "We'll be fine. I'll take the children into the bushes while you're gone and get that business out of the way for a while."

Elizabeth nodded and hurried away. Ten minutes later she reached a wide creek that ran parallel to the road. It was shaded by huge willow trees on both sides and a dam had been built on the south end to create a pool. Glancing north of the stream, Elizabeth saw the burnt remains of a house and presumed the dam was constructed by the former owners of the property. A small spring of water trickled over an outcropping of rocks at the far end of the stream that kept the water circulating so it hadn't become stagnant in the merciless heat and extended drought. The pool of water was still half full and people and animals clamored over its banks and into the mud to reach the water. Animals bawled and broke their tethers to reach it as quickly as they could. Carts and wagons shattered as cows and goats shoved people and smaller animals aside, falling into the mud and covered in black slime when they regained their feet. The dusty, exhausted travelers slogged their way through the soft, calf-deep mud to wade into the water where they splashed each other, soaked their clothes, and drank until they looked like they'd pop, their eyes wild and joyous at the same time. Along with green moss, downed branches, and dead leaves, a layer of gray slime floated atop the water, attesting to the travelers' large numbers and the filth that washed off them. But no one cared. The slime was splashed aside until clean water was accessible and swallowed as fast as possible before the filmy gunk slid back into place. Anything that held water was filled to the brim. If someone lingered overlong, they were badgered by those behind them until they moved along, the routine repeated over and over. Many a horse, cow, goat, and chicken, still weak from exhaustion and lack of water, got stuck in the sucking, cloying mud and had to be dragged out.

Although the pool was only ten minutes normal walking distance from where Rebecca and the children waited, Elizabeth knew it would take hours to reach at the rate the people and animals were moving in and out of it.

"That'll give us time to straighten the lid, find a saw, and cut the wood to fashion a cover for the second pot," Elizabeth said to herself, heading back. "That is, of course, if I can *find* a saw and I'm *allowed* to borrow it," she qualified.

Asking every family she passed, Elizabeth finally found a mother and son who had a small hand saw they would let her borrow, as long as the twelve or thirteen year-old boy went along to ensure its return.

The boy, named Wallace, turned out to be more helpful than Elizabeth could have hoped. He was immediately love-struck when he spotted the girls. Learning of their dilemma, he stepped up and cut the wood from the sled, then cut it in two pieces that fit over the pot and would keep the water from sloshing out when a rock was set on top to keep them in place.

While Wallace worked on the wood, Rebecca and Elizabeth found a flat rock to pound the bent lid and round out the tops of the pots. They weren't perfect, but it was better than nothing at all.

They moved slowly toward the water and as they did, Hilda grew more and more anxious, smelling it long before anyone saw it. Once she broke away from Nora, dragging the sled behind her, dumping everything on it as she ran toward the creek. Elizabeth managed to grab her before she got far and from then on, Elizabeth held her with a strong hand and a firm voice. Three hours later, they reached the pool and finally had their turn.

Hilda was unhitched, the sled left on the right side of the road with Rebecca guarding it and the four youngest children waiting with her. Elizabeth led Hilda, more accurately Hilda dragged Elizabeth, toward the water. The older children slipped and slid their way down the embankment and were covered in black slime by the time they reached the pool, enjoying the cooling mud on their heat-soaked bodies, even though they protested. The girls screeched when they sank to their calves with their first step, and Joshua and Benjamin laughed aloud as they slogged their way forward. Nora had one of the pots and Helen had the other, both trying not to drop them while keeping their balance in the sucking ground. They squealed and laughed with each misstep, winding up on their bottoms more than once.

Elizabeth was up to her knees in the water before Hilda stopped dragging her. The mare put her nose down and sloshed it back and forth before she put her snout fully into it and drank. While Elizabeth watched Hilda drink, she splashed herself and drank what she could cup in one hand. She had to be very careful, allowing the mare to drink only a little at a time. If she drink too much too fast, her guts would twist and she'd go down. A minute later she jerked Hilda's head up. The horse tried to drop her nose back, but Elizabeth slid her shoulder under her chin and kept it out of the water. She stroked the mare's neck and head before she let the horse drink again, feeling the pressure of the other emigrants behind her, wanting her place in the water.

"Hurry up!" a woman shouted from behind her, anxious for her spot.

Elizabeth whirled. "Wait your turn, just like we waited ours!" she yelled in response.

Nora and Helen stopped splashing beside her. "Vera, Clara, come on over here," she called to the two girls still splashing on the other side of Hilda with Edna, Joshua, Benjamin, and Francis. "It's time to fill the buckets."

"But," Vera opened her mouth to protest, but was cut off immediately.

"Do not argue," Elizabeth growled. "Our turn is up."

The two girls sloshed their way around Hilda to Elizabeth, their wet dresses sagging around their ankles. "Fill those pots to the brim," she told the four girls, the other children gathering behind them. "And be careful carrying them. Try not to spill it all by the time you get back."

"Yes, Mama," Nora said, bending to the task.

"Yes, Mama," Vera groaned, doing the same.

A few minutes later with barely three-quarters of the water left in the pots, they were back at the sled, covered in mud again. Hilda shook, spraying everyone with droplets of water, but no one groaned or fussed, instead they laughed and soaked in every drop.

One pot was drained by the smaller children, who drank lustily. What they didn't drink was dribbled over them to cool them down. Even little Robert drank.

"My turn," Rebecca said.

Elizabeth nodded and handed her the empty pot. "Go and enjoy the water. Bring back as much as you can. There's no telling how long it'll be before we find more."

"I know, Elizabeth. I'll do my best."

Rebecca made her way to the water and returned with an almost full pot, much to everyone's delight. The lids were put on and rocks set on top to keep them seated. With luck they'd have water for a few days—at least enough to keep Hilda going. They could last longer than the horse without water. That was the way it was and the children would have to accept it. There was just no help for it.

THE JOURNEY
Day 5 – Evening
(The Road to Clinton)

The children were already sniveling and grumbling again, having forgotten their refreshment in the water only hours ago. Their feet hurt, they were hungry, tired, hot, and thirsty already.

Elizabeth stopped Hilda and looked over at Rebecca. "We'll stop as soon as we find a good spot." She *had* to hunt. Everyone was giving more than she'd imagined they could. "I have to find food. And soon." Relief jumped into Rebecca's eyes.

"That would be wonderful. I don't know how I'm still walking and I know the children are beyond exhausted. We could all use the rest." Rebecca closed her eyes and sighed. "But what about catching up with Albert and Meg? We lost so much time at the water, if we stop, they'll get even farther ahead of us. We should have caught up with them by now."

Elizabeth shook her head. "I don't understand how we haven't caught them. They would have stopped for water the same as we did. They've got to be moving slower than we are, even with the children. And I didn't pass them when I went ahead to find a saw or the water."

"Maybe they're going faster so we *don't* catch up. Robert has made himself unwelcome among the other travelers." Rebecca grimaced. "I've seen their looks. They hurry past us as fast as they can. I try, Elizabeth, I really try to make him stop crying."

Elizabeth shushed her friend to silence. "I know. He is a bit—distracting," she said instead of annoying, "but there's nothing to be done. You're doing the best you can, we're doing the best we can, but there are other forces against us." Elizabeth shaded her eyes against the sun, looked ahead then scanned the sides of the road for any place they could rest and she could hunt. There was nothing but dust and open sky for at least another mile.

"What are we going to do?" Rebecca whined like one of the children again.

"Keep going, it's all we *can* do, until we find someplace you can rest with the children and I can hunt.

Rebecca closed her eyes and nodded. "I guess it's all we can do."

It was another hour before they found a place to stop, Robert making his displeasure loudly known.

"Stay here and do whatever you can to quiet him down," Elizabeth instructed a frazzled Rebecca. "Watch the road for someone who has a milk cow. It looks like we're not going to catch Albert and Meg. Wiley old coot," she grumbled. "Who would have thought they could move so fast?"

Rebecca snorted. "Trying to outrun Robert's crying, I can understand it. He's driving me mad, Elizabeth.

"Then watch close and don't let a goat or cow pass without asking for milk."

Rebecca pursed her lips and nodded. "I'll keep a close watch. You be careful, too. There's no telling what is in those woods."

"I will. I hunted often enough with James to know the signs."

"I don't mean to be careful of the animals. I mean men. Soldiers or raiders could be anywhere."

"I know. I'll be careful."

Rebecca switched a crying Robert from one shoulder to the other, patting his back to silence him. But he cried on.

"What if you find a deer?" Rebecca asked. "How will you get it back here? You were about done in by the time I found you the last time, and I can't come looking for you now."

"If I get that lucky, I'll come and get Hilda to drag the carcass back."

"With what? There isn't even any rope."

Elizabeth sighed. "We can pull some from the bottom of the sled if necessary. We'll figure that out *if* we have to."

Rebecca nodded.

Nora stepped beside her mother. "I'm going with you, Mama." The words were said without question.

Elizabeth opened her mouth to tell her no, but decided there was no reason for her not to. She pulled the pistol from her pocket and handed it to Nora. "Remember how to use this?"

Nora cocked her head as though she'd been asked if she remembered how to breathe. "Of course I do."

"Then let's get about it." She looked over at Rebecca, the other children huddled around her. "We'd better go. Keep a watch out for that milk cow. Give them whatever they want in return, not that we have anything, but if they want something we do have, give it to them. We won't go far and we'll be back as soon as we can."

Rebecca laid her hand on Elizabeth's shoulder. "Be careful."

"We will. Are you ready?" she asked Nora.

Nora nodded.

"Let's go."

They returned two hours later with nothing. Walking into camp, their feet swollen, hot and burning, any exposed skin caked with dust and sweat, Elizabeth and Nora plopped down beside Rebecca and little Robert. The boy was lying on his belly on the small mattress piece beside his mother, squirming and whimpering, but at least he wasn't squalling. Elizabeth noticed Molly's owner, Annie, was close by with her two children. Perhaps they were willing to suffer little Robert's screaming in the hope of getting some food if Elizabeth was successful in the hunt.

Rebecca looked at Elizabeth with wide, questioning eyes, but didn't even ask.

"Nothing. Just like this morning there wasn't a turkey, raccoon, or a squirrel to be found. No deer or even a greasy old possum. Nothing," Elizabeth grumbled through swollen lips and an enlarged tongue she was so thirsty. Her cheeks were red from exertion and heat to match Nora's.

"What are we going to do? We need food, and we need water even worse. What we've got isn't going to last. Especially if we give what we've got to Hilda."

Elizabeth snorted. "You think I don't know that Rebecca?" she snapped. "We found a couple streams, but every one of them was dried up. Not one more than a mud hole. Not even enough to soak a rag." She shook her head and forced back tears. "I'm sorry I snapped at you, I feel so helpless. I've never been unable to care for my children before."

"I know. Now you understand how I feel being unable to quiet Robert." Rebecca forced a smile.

"I do, but no more of that. We're doing the best we can." Elizabeth swallowed. "Hopefully, it's enough."

"Mama?" Vera slid down beside her mother, the other children gathering around them and Rebecca. "What did you bring to eat?"

Elizabeth grimaced and tried to answer her daughter, but the words wouldn't come. *How could she tell her, all of them, there would be no food tonight or tomorrow morning—again? How could she tell them they'd found no water, either?* She saw the hunger and thirst in their eyes, felt it in her own belly and on her lips, but try as they might, they'd found nothing.

"Oh, Mama!" Vera fell into her mother's arms. "I'm so hungry," her daughter wailed. The other children, seeing Vera's reaction began to snivel and cry, too. Soon, thirteen children and two women sat in the middle of a clearing along the side of the road, crying. But they didn't cry silently as they'd done the past couple of days. They cried aloud, wailing their fear of how they'd starve to death before they reached Aunt Pearl's.

Guilt washed over Elizabeth like a hot, drenching rain. Not cool or refreshing rain. Not even a warm, comforting rain. Instead it burned like fire making her skin prick and her head hurt.

"We're losing so much time," she said quietly to Rebecca, sniveling right along with the children. "We have to get moving soon or we'll never reach my aunt's."

"But we're so tired."

"Don't say it Rebecca. We're all tired *and* hungry. But we can't stop or this is where they'll find us." She thrust her finger at the ground where she stood to make her point. "Right here, dead from starvation!" Her voice had grown loud and angry and she tamped it down so as not to frighten the children more than they already were. "Unfortunately, we can't go anywhere tonight, it's too late, but Nora and I will hunt again in the morning."

Rebecca drew in a deep breath, wiped her eyes and cheeks, and straightened her back. "I'm sorry, Elizabeth. I'm becoming as much of a burden as the children."

"We're all having a difficult time, Rebecca, but you and I must stay strong. We have to give the children hope when there is none and smile when we want to weep."

Rebecca swallowed and nodded. Robert started to scream again and Elizabeth thought she'd come right out of her skin. *God give me strength....*

Rebecca jerked her son off the ground, making him cry harder. She pulled him to her chest and sobbed, "I'm sorry Robert, I'm so sorry. I know you can't help it." She kissed the top of his head, his face and neck as she held him to her, his legs and arms flailing wildly. Still he cried.

Rebecca turned to Elizabeth. "He's so hungry. He doesn't understand." Tears ran down her cheeks and pity for this small babe welled up inside Elizabeth's belly—despite her wanting to sew his mouth shut.

"I'm going to try and feed him." Rebecca's face was tight with determination. "There's nothing else I can do. Maybe if he just suckles he'll be quiet."

"He'll tear you up." Elizabeth knew Rebecca's breasts were beyond tender. She'd confided to Elizabeth they were cracked and bleeding from the heat and Robert's suckling *before* her milk dried up. Elizabeth couldn't imagine trying to nurse a child in her condition.

"There's nothing to be done. I have to try." Rebecca walked away with the screaming Robert and went behind a tree. She returned a few minutes later, her face awash with fresh tears, Robert screaming as loudly as he was when they walked away.

Elizabeth laid her hand on her friend's shoulder.

"I have nothing for him and it hurt *so* badly." Rebecca's voice caught on the words.

Elizabeth pulled her friend to her chest. Robert cried harder, crushed between his mother and Elizabeth, who cried right along with him.

THE JOURNEY
Day 6
(The Road to Clinton)

Light from the rising sun streaked through the defoliated timber like bright, beckoning fingers. Outlined in its light, Elizabeth saw them. Six turkeys roosting on one of the bare branches and she thought her heart would explode with hope.

Elizabeth laid her finger over her lips and pointed. Nora looked up, nodded, and raised the pistol as Elizabeth sighted the rifle. "One, two, three," Elizabeth mouthed.

The guns exploded. In a massive flurry of squawks and flapping wings the turkeys soared into the air, save one, which fell to the ground not far from Nora and Elizabeth.

Despite their sore feet and exhaustion, Elizabeth and Nora jumped up and down then ran to where the bird lay. They stood over it, almost reverent in their excitement.

"We did it, Mama! We did it! We got a turkey!" Nora shouted.

Elizabeth couldn't stop the smile that came. "Yes we did." She sighed. "I wish we'd killed two, but we'll be happy with what we got." She took her daughter's chin in the palm of her hand. "Let's get it back to camp. The sun's almost full up and it's going to be very hot soon."

It was a large bird and, grabbing the feet, Elizabeth realized she couldn't lift it alone. "Help me settle it on my shoulder." Nora did as she was asked and the two set off toward camp.

As they walked, Elizabeth recalled their last turkey dinners. It had been during one of James' last visits when he'd strode in with two of them slung across his back. Despite her happiness at knowing they'd have food, tears welled in her eyes. *How she missed her husband!* Unwilling to let her sadness overshadow her joy, she tamped it down, buried her face in the crook of her arm to wipe away the tears, and slogged ahead.

They hadn't gone far when Elizabeth heard it—the muffled sound of branches breaking and leaves crunching in the woods. She grabbed Nora and stopped, listening only a moment before she shoved her daughter behind the closest bushes.

Elizabeth clung to the turkey with all her strength to keep it from dropping in their haste.

Crouched behind a bush with barely enough foliage to hide them, Elizabeth spotted the riders.

"I'm telling ya, I heard shots," one of four men said, their horses passing so close Elizabeth's breath caught. She studied them as they went by. They weren't soldiers, marking them as raiders and making them as dangerous, or more so, than Yankees. She clutched the turkey's feet, the bird getting heavier by the second, and prayed for strength not to drop it, alerting the riders to their presence. She glanced a look at Nora, stone-faced on her knees beside her, shaking.

"Damn, Darby, we could search these woods till we're blue-faced and not find a thing. I'm hot and I got better things to do."

"Like what, Ned? What the hell you got so all-fired important to do?" the man called Darby asked.

"Damn, I don't know, but I sure don't want to spend the day wandering around looking for something we ain't gonna find."

"So, where would you rather be, Ned? Tell us," one of the unnamed men challenged.

The man called Ned stopped his horse right in front of the bushes that hid Nora and Elizabeth! The others did the same.

Elizabeth thought she was going to fall over. Beside the fact she felt like she was holding a hundred pound weight on her shoulder, she was terrified Nora might make a noise in her fear. She shook her head at her daughter, wanting more than anything to take her hand, aware if she did the turkey would fall to the ground, alerting the men to their presence. She closed her eyes, prayed for strength and forced herself to breathe evenly.

"Forget it! We'll do what Darby says and keep looking. I just don't think we're gonna find a damned thing. Not a damned thing," the man named Ned grumbled. Elizabeth almost groaned at how close the men were to finding exactly what they were looking for. And more.

"Come on boys. The shots were over there." Another of the men clucked his horse in the direction Elizabeth and Nora had come from.

Elizabeth and Nora sat in paralyzed silence as the men walked their horses past them, through the woods, and out of sight.

Dropping the turkey and slumping to the ground, Elizabeth sucked in a deep breath. Nora slid down beside her mother, breathing heavily, her eyes wide and brimming with tears.

"We're all right," Elizabeth tried to assure her daughter as she attempted to stand up.

Nora grabbed her mother's hand and jerked her back down. "We should wait. They might not be far enough away and hear us. They didn't see us before, so they won't see us again. We should wait."

The fear on Nora's face and in her voice made Elizabeth wince, but they had to leave now to outdistance those riders and make it back to camp undiscovered. Elizabeth shook her head and tried to ease Nora's fears. "They went in the other direction and we're going to be very quiet the rest of the way. Help me with this bird."

Her hands shaking, looking all around her, Nora resettled the bird on her mother's back. Elizabeth looked at her daughter, took another deep breath, and stepped out into the open, Nora so close Elizabeth felt like she had just put on another layer of clothing.

Nora looked around nervously. "Hurry Mama, before they come back."

Elizabeth nodded, anxious to be as far away from the men as quickly as she could. They arrived back in camp a half hour later, immediately surrounded by their little group. Their excitement obvious, Annie made her way toward the returning hunters, hope in her eyes she and her daughters would be allowed to share in the bounty Elizabeth and Nora had returned with.

"Let's start a fire and cook it right now," Rebecca almost shouted.

Elizabeth shook her head. "We can't. Not yet."

"Why in Heaven's not?" There was anger in Rebecca's voice.

"Because there are raiders out there," Elizabeth hissed,

swinging her head toward the woods they'd come from. "We were lucky not to be discovered. If we start a fire they'll smell it or see it and find us for sure. We can't let that happen, not even for food. We have to wait. And we have to go."

Everyone who understood groaned but held their complaints, except Vera. "But we're hungry now," she grumped.

"Yes, we're all very hungry right now, Vera, but we cannot risk discovery by those raiders, who will take not only the turkey, but ...." She couldn't finish her sentence, which would have been, *and any* one *they looked upon favorably*.

Vera's lip puffed out, but she remained silent.

"Gather everything. We can wrap the turkey in the mattress pieces so it looks like a big bundle of rags, in case we're stopped. We must get well away from here before we build a fire—which can't be until tonight. This bird will have to cook all night before we can eat it anyway, so it's just as well. Otherwise, we'd lose a whole day while it cooks if we started it now. But we'll have turkey tomorrow!" Elizabeth tried to sound cheerful, but everyone groaned again instead.

She shook her head and began preparations to leave. It was going to be another long, hot, hungry day.

They'd gone a few miles when Elizabeth heard the all-too-familiar sound that turned her blood cold every time she heard it. Riders. *Had the raiders from the woods found them?* She tugged Hilda to a stop and, realizing it was too late to hide Molly or the guns, quickly instructed everyone to gather around the mare to conceal her as much as possible. She yanked the pistol out of her pocket and threw it and the rifle into a ravine on the side of the road, hoping to retrieve it later. She could *not* be found with Randall's weapons. If she were, she could be prosecuted as a spy! Or worse yet, murder if these were soldiers and they'd found his body!

Her knees almost buckled when Captain Howard and his men rode up a few minutes later. *They were looking for Private Randall!* she was certain.

"Ma'am." Captain Howard touched the brim of his dusty hat.

"Captain." Elizabeth stood rooted to the spot, silently praying to survive this latest incident.

The captain turned to his men. "Search them," was all he said and the men fanned out along both sides of the road, dismounted and began looking through the traveler's belongings.

"There's nothing left, captain," Elizabeth couldn't help saying, hoping against hope they didn't find the hidden turkey. "Your men were quite thorough the first time you—*foraged*—from us," she said, instead of *stole* like she wanted to.

"Got something!" One of the men shouted, drawing everyone's attention. "Isn't that Randall's horse?"

Elizabeth felt the blood drain from her face. The captain dismounted and made his way through the travelers to the mare, Elizabeth close on his heels.

Howard ran his hand over the mare's neck, down its back and over its rump. "I believe it is Private Randall's mount." He swung back toward Elizabeth. "Where did this horse come from?"

Elizabeth was trying to think of what to say, thankful they'd disposed of Randall's saddle and everything else he'd carried except his weapons, when Annie stepped forward.

"She's mine. Always has been and always will be—mine," the woman growled. Hatred glowed in her eyes and she held her back straight in defiance. She laid her hand on the mare's neck. "May I explain, captain?"

"Please do." The captain cocked his head and waited.

"Me and my girls have been traveling with these folks for a ways now. We were walking, as we've been walking since we were ordered to leave our homes, when this horse crashed through the trees and I recognized her as my Molly. She must have been looking for us, caught our scent and, well, here she is. She was born at our farm, the one we were driven from back there," she added as a second reminder as to why they were here, before she continued, "and has known only us. Maybe your private Randall didn't treat her too well and she ran away."

"That doesn't tell us where Randall is."

Annie raised her shoulder and cocked her head again. "Well, how would we know? Maybe he got tired of soldiering and ran away, too?"

"Deserted? No sir," a man Elizabeth recognized as having been with Randall when he attacked Nora shouted.

"Randall may be a lot of things, sir. Lazy, a shirker, but he ain't no deserter and he sure wouldn't go nowhere without his horse."

"So where is he then?" Howard asked the soldier pledging Randall's loyalty to the uniform. "Perhaps these women killed him and took this horse?" Howard joked.

Elizabeth thought she'd fall down and prayed Annie and Rebecca held steady following Captain Howard's jovial statement. She smiled to match Howard's grin. "What a silly notion, captain," Elizabeth trilled like a fluffy-headed female. "How could we do such a vile thing?" She giggled, her heart slamming in her chest like a blacksmith's mallet.

The captain eyed her a moment and she kept the smile on her face as though nothing was amiss. "Truly, sir, the mare busted through the trees looking for Annie and her girls, just like she said."

Elizabeth chanced a look at the children, huddled around Nora and Helen who were shushing them to silence. Elizabeth prayed they wouldn't, in their innocence, betray their secret to the soldiers.

Captain Howard grinned again. "I'm more apt to believe Private Randall deserted than a bunch of women and children killed him and relieved him of his horse. If that *did* happen, the man was no soldier and *should* be dead." He let the words hang and Elizabeth thought she'd turn to stone. She swallowed then smiled again.

"It is a silly notion. How could *three* women and *fif-teen child-ren*," she drawled, "kill an armed, trained soldier and take his horse?"

The captain studied her face. She saw his doubt, but held to her story. Shrugging her shoulders, she shook her head and said, "I truly can't imagine what happened to your soldier, Captain Howard. All I know is what Annie has already told you. Molly came crashing out of the woods to find her family. We have no knowledge of anything more than that."

He stood a moment longer before he shouted, "Owens, take the mare! Men, remount!"

"Please, no!" Annie protested loudly when the soldier grabbed Molly's rope and led her away. Annie's two girls cried aloud as their treasured mare was taken from them a second time, while Elizabeth and the others looked on, helpless.

The soldiers started up the road, Owens leading Molly behind him with a long rope. They'd gone only a short way when the mare dug all four feet into the ground, jerked to a stop and reared up on her hind legs, pawing the air. The rope burned through Owens' hands and, with a shriek, he let go.

Elizabeth grinned at the memory of Poppyseed rearing up and breaking away from her would-be thieves the same way in the raid on their home in what seemed like another lifetime.

In a blink the mare whirled on her feet and ran bucking and kicking to a skidding stop beside Annie and her girls, her ears forward, nose flared and eyes wild. The family welcomed her back, but it wasn't long before another soldier, this one wearing thick gloves, came to retrieve her again. Molly dug in all four hooves again. Everyone watched the mare fight every effort to be taken away. She was like a ship aground in the mud, unwilling and unable to move—until another soldier laid a whip across her backside. She jumped forward, prancing behind the second soldier's horse. He tied her rope around his saddle horn and kicked his mount forward, not giving the reluctant Molly time to dig in again. The soldiers moved out, Molly fighting the rope behind them, throwing her head back and forth, snorting and kicking, trying to break away, unable to do so. Shrill whinnies of protest floated behind her.

Elizabeth had a tight grip on Hilda's bridle; otherwise, she might have taken off after Molly. The mare tossed her head back and forth, snorted and whinnied in response to Molly's fading calls. She swung her butt back and forth and pranced in place before she reared up, everything on the sled sliding off.

It wasn't until the soldiers were out of sight that Elizabeth slid to the ground. Anger, frustration, and helplessness bubbled in her belly like a gathering storm. Her hands rolled in and out of fists and her anger built. She slammed her right fist into the ground, then her left, then her right again until she was pounding the earth, screaming her frustration and anger for everyone to see and hear.

THE JOURNEY
Day 7 – Morning
(The Road to Clinton)

The previous day ended without further incident. At dusk the travelers started a fire and put the turkey on to cook, which they were enjoying this morning.

"Oh, Mama! This is wonderful. Can I have more?" Vera licked her fingers.

Elizabeth looked at Rebecca and Annie. "Are we ready for seconds?"

Both women nodded. "They'll have to be small. There's not much left," Rebecca said.

Without fussing or argument, everyone lined up behind Vera to wait for another small portion of the quickly disappearing turkey. Elizabeth felt like she could eat at least two more plates full, but held back so the children could get their fill. Even little Robert gnawed on a slice of dark meat, sucking out the juices and gumming the tiny pieces Rebecca cut for him, quiet for the first time in too long to remember.

The sun was full up, the heat building, but no one seemed to notice as they stripped every ounce of edible flesh off the bird, leaving only the white carcass behind when they left camp that morning.

Everyone was sated, happy and seemingly content for the first time in days. No one complained about the heat or their sore feet or being too tired to take another step. Happy to have a full belly, they walked without complaint. They didn't even grumble about being thirsty, having gotten one swallow of tepid water after their meal, finishing the last of the water they'd gotten two days ago, most of it having gone to Hilda.

Having retrieved the pistol and rifle after the soldiers left, Nora and Elizabeth struck out that evening when they stopped for the day to find more game. Luck held and they returned before sunset with a fat raccoon.

Everyone gathered around as they displayed the kill and the promise of food for tomorrow. "We should start a fire to cook it overnight like we did the turkey so it'll be ready in the morning." Elizabeth dropped the raccoon at her feet.

"I'll do it." With a smile on her face and a hitch in her step, Rebecca handed little Robert to Francis, recruited Helen and Clara, and started off to gather wood.

She didn't get far before Elizabeth stopped her with a hand on her arm, busting to tell her friend what she and Nora had found while hunting.

"What is it?" Alarm jumped into Rebecca's eyes.

Quick to allay her friend's fear, Elizabeth shouted, "We found water!"

Everyone looked back and forth at one another, silent only a moment before they hooted with joy and danced in circles.

"Where?" Rebecca clutched her throat, as though to confirm her thirst.

"Not too far." She looked up at the sky. "It'll be dark soon, but I think I can find my way back."

"Alone?" Nora asked.

It was Elizabeth's turn to sigh. "I can't risk anyone else coming with me. If I get lost I'll find my way back in the morning."

"But," Nora tried to interrupt.

"I'll be fine."

"You're being foolish, Elizabeth." Rebecca's voice was stern. "It's getting dark and with no lanterns, you'll get lost for sure. We can wait until morning for more water. No one should leave camp until then."

"I agree." Annie stepped beside Rebecca.

"Me, too." Nora joined the other two women.

"We're all thirsty, Elizabeth, but it's not worth you getting lost out there in the dark." Rebecca raised her chin as though daring Elizabeth to protest.

Elizabeth smiled and shook her head. "You're right. You're all right, it's foolish of me to consider going into the woods now. We'll wait until morning."

Annie jerked her head. "Agreed."

"We'll wait until morning then," Rebecca said, as well.

There were no further protests. A fire was built and the raccoon was cleaned and put in a pot to cook overnight.

Everyone settled down with hope in their hearts and more to look forward to than they had in a long time.

THE JOURNEY
Day 8
(The Road to Clinton)

The day dawned as each one had before—hot and muggy with the promise of more heat and dust. But the families woke happy, knowing there was food to eat and water to drink and wash. It would be a good day.

"We should go in small groups instead of all at once," Elizabeth said, getting ready to lead the way. "There's only a small pool of water in the middle of the creek bed that hasn't dried up. It'll be easier with only a few of us at one time."

"I want to be in the first group!" Vera shouted.

"You and everyone else wants to be in the first group, but I'm going to take the smaller children first."

"It's *always* the little children first!" Vera pouted. "Why can't *we* ever go first?"

"Right now, because *you're* acting like a baby, Vera," Elizabeth scolded. "You're old enough to understand what's going on and *should* be able to contain yourself, whereas the little ones *don't* understand and just do as they're told."

"But I'm so thirsty, Mama. I need water now!" Vera stomped her foot.

Elizabeth stared at her daughter, deciding what to do. She put her hands on her hips. "Because of your attitude, young lady, you'll go in the last group."

Vera's eyes and lips pinched with anger before she ran behind some bushes, crying loud enough for everyone to hear.

"Does anyone else want to question how we conduct our trips to water?" Elizabeth asked.

The other children remained silent. She gathered Joseph and Sally, Andrew, Benjamin, and Caroline, Annie's six year old and, holding hands, they started off toward the creek she and Nora had found. It was about a quarter mile from the road and walking with the little ones in the growing heat took a while, but their trip was rewarded when the children fairly fell into the shallow stream, giggling and sucking down water so fast, Elizabeth had to physically drag them out to keep them from drinking too much and get a belly ache. They played and floated then drank some more before Elizabeth ushered them back into a line and headed back to camp.

Annie joined the next group. She, Eleanor, Annie's eight year-old daughter, Francis, Benjamin, Joshua, and Edna, left as soon as the first group returned. They moved quicker since they were older and spent more time at the creek splashing, drinking, and soaking every layer of clothing they wore until they could hardly move when it was time to return to camp.

Finally, Nora, Helen, Vera, Clara, and Rebecca with Robert in tow, joined Elizabeth and made their way to the creek. After drinking their fill, the four girls sat down in the water side by side and laid back to let it cascade around them, soaking themselves from top to bottom. Robert, sitting naked in the shallow water beside his mother, splashed happily. Rebecca poured water from her cupped hands over his head and he squealed in delight. While he played, she laid back and let the water surround her. Elizabeth cleaned her hair as much as was possible then soaked in the water to cool her heat-exhausted body.

"We should get back," Rebecca finally sighed. "Annie is probably tired of watching the other children by now."

Elizabeth groaned. "I suppose you're right. Come on everyone, it's time to head back."

Groaning, the children slogged from the water, got into line and followed Elizabeth back to camp.

By the time everyone had visited the creek and returned to camp it was almost noon. Nora, Helen, Clara, and Vera had carried the two pots full of water back between them. The camp buzzed with excitement when everyone returned. The meat was falling off the bone. They were clean and now had water to wash down their meal. They'd spent the morning cooling off and felt refreshed and ready for the day. Again they would walk, but their feet would be light, their stomachs full, and their hearts hopeful—for the second day in a row.

It was early afternoon when they got back on the road with the non-stop flow of refugees. Dust clogged their throats and filled their noses and ears, but they had food in their bellies and, for a short time, they forgot their thirst.

By late afternoon, however, their carefree morning was long forgotten as the drudgery of the road regained its hold on them. They remembered how badly their bare feet hurt, they coughed and their eyes watered from the dust, and hunger and thirst once again nipped at their heels, despite the meal they'd eaten before they left.

Nora sidled up beside her mother. "I'm hungry again, Mama, and thirsty."

"So am I. Seems our stomachs remember what it's like to have a full meal every few hours and wants more, but we have to keep going. When we stop tonight Annie and I will hunt again.

"But we're hungry and thirsty now," Vera whined, falling into step beside her mother and sister.

Elizabeth bit back a hard reply to her younger daughter who seemed to voice her discomforts more often than anyone. "Everyone will get their ration of water when we stop and we'll hunt again when we stop, too, but not before. Right now we have to keep going so we can reach Clinton as soon as possible. We're already seven days into this trip and once we reach Clinton we still have twenty miles to go."

"Twenty miles?" Vera shouted. "We should be there by now! You told us we'd be there by now!"

"We might have been if we hadn't been slowed down," Elizabeth answered through grinding teeth. "We've not gone as fast as I hoped, and losing our food and taking so much time getting water hasn't helped."

"But I'm hungry and thirsty, and I'm *so* tired. Can't we stop now so you can hunt and we can have our water?" Vera pressed.

Elizabeth took a deep breath for patience. "No, we cannot. Not yet. We ate and drank earlier till we were full and now we have to walk to make up the time we've lost. We'll stop later like we always do."

Vera looked as though she would argue more, but thought better of it. She crossed her arms over her chest and stomped away, puffs of dust following her.

"I'm sorry, Mama," Nora said. "I'll talk to her."

Elizabeth reached out and stroked her oldest daughter's

face. "You know there's nothing that can be done. Vera is high-strung and speaks her mind."

"Yes, she does," Nora agreed before she dropped back beside her pouting sister.

The day continued in its dogged boredom until Elizabeth heard the familiar sound that almost brought her to her knees. Moments later four ragged, bearded men who looked like they hadn't bathed in a very long time, crashed out from the tree line. These weren't regular Union soldiers. They were raiders from the looks of them, *but were they Jayhawkers or bushwhackers? If they were Jayhawkers, the refugees were in as serious trouble as if they were Union soldiers. They would take what little there was, and just for sheer cussedness, destroy what was left. If they were rebel bushwhackers, they might be sympathetic, but would still take whatever they wanted, whether it left its owner more destitute than they already were. Regardless which side they were on, these men meant trouble.*

Confirmation came fast and swift.

They pulled their mounts to a stop in front of Hilda. The mare jerked to a halt, the sled rocking behind her, tossing the three children off. Elizabeth had a good hold on Hilda's harness and kept her from rearing, but the mare stepped nervously in place as the raiders' horses danced around her.

"Nora, Vera, get the children!" Elizabeth shouted, ignoring the studying glares of the scruffy men. Rebecca and Annie gathered their children and waited with wide eyes. Travelers ahead hurried on and those behind waited for their turn to be abused or, when the men looked away, skulked into the woods to avoid it.

The children safely removed from the proximity of the sled, Elizabeth unleashed her fury at the riders. "How dare you! Have you no sense? There were children on that sled when you charged in here and frightened my mare. They could have been hurt!"

She stopped short of calling them buffoons, deciding it wouldn't help to insult them. "We're not soldiers and should be treated with due accord!" She almost stomped her foot like Vera might, but contained herself.

The man closest to Elizabeth snorted. "We know who

you are. You're rebs fleeing from up Cass County way." He leaned over the saddle and eyed the sled. "What you got there?"

Elizabeth thought her heart stopped beating. "Nothing of value. Soldiers have already taken everything we had."

"There's something in there. I see it." He pointed at the mound under the shredded mattress.

"It's only empty pots." She tried to sound unconcerned, but her heart was pounding now, praying they would look past the pots that held their water. *If they found it they would surely take it. And the rifle and pistol, hidden under the sled and in the pocket of her dress!* "There's nothing there, just the pots." She threw back the material to show him nothing else was hidden there, hoping they wouldn't search underneath and find the rifle. She laid her hand over the pistol in her pocket, hoping they wouldn't search her or see the outline through her dress.

"I don't believe you, woman, so just get out of the way and let me inspect it my own self."

Elizabeth thought her knees would buckle when he dismounted and shoved her out of the way. Unable to keep her grip on Hilda, she stumbled away and was quickly surrounded by the children. They held on tight to each other as the ruffian tossed off the rock holding the makeshift lids on the pots holding their water.

"Boys, I found us a treasure!" He waved the others to his find. The men dismounted and yanked the pots off the sled, water slopping over the side.

"Please, that's all we have," Elizabeth begged, knowing her words fell on deaf ears.

The leader swung toward her. "I told you, we don't care. We got some rough riding ahead of us and need water to do it—and here it is."

Elizabeth grew numb watching their hard-earned water disappear—again. The children squeezed closer and tighter, Annie, Rebecca and their children cowering on the other side of a still jittery Hilda. The people on the road in front of them were far ahead and those behind who hadn't sneaked into the woods stood wide-eyed, unable to do anything to assist, waiting.

"Let me look at that beast." The raider grabbed Hilda's bridle and jerked—hard. The mare reacted as though stung. She reared up, kicked out her front legs and caught the man in the side of the head, knocking him over. Dazed, he sat up and ran his hand over his forehead, pulling away bloody fingers. Screaming with rage he jumped to his feet, stomped back to the shaking Hilda and swung his fist into her nose as hard as he could. The mare reared again, shrieking and shaking her head back and forth, the man careful to get out of her way this time. When her feet hit the ground, he punched her again. She reared a third time then kicked out at the confining sled behind her until it shattered, dumping what little was left, the rifle included, the stock broken. Free of the restraint behind her and without Elizabeth beside her to calm her, Hilda bolted, dragging what was left of the sled down the road after her.

Elizabeth stood in shock only a moment, watching people ahead scatter in front of the terrified mare, before she regained her senses and took off running. Elizabeth ran around the people and their scattered belongings, screaming Hilda's name. *She* had *to reach Hilda before the animal did more damage—to herself or someone else.*

She forgot her blistered feet as she ran after the out-of-control horse that charged on blindly. Hilda stayed on the road a short distance then suddenly veered right—straight into a tree. With a heart-sickening thud, she went down, her legs thrashing wildly.

Elizabeth ran as fast as she could. "I'm coming, Hilda. I'm coming!" Tears streamed down her face and her heart felt like it would explode from the exertion in the staggering heat. The blisters on her feet tore and her mouth was as parched and dry as a dead well. She finally reached the horse, grabbed the bridle, and cradled Hilda's head in her chest. "I'm here, Hilda, I'm here. Shhhhhhh." Elizabeth rubbed the mare's nose and tried to comfort her.

The mare lay still a moment before her nose flared and her eyes went wild. She snorted and tried to get up. Her whole body shook and her legs pumped, but she didn't have the strength to get to her feet. Her blind eyes were crazed and fearful. The muscles in her belly constricted. She was more dehydrated than ever after her run and hitting the tree with such force must have severely injured her inside.

She was done. As the thought struck Elizabeth, the mare stopped thrashing. She lay still her breathing labored and shallow.

"Hilda!" Elizabeth held Hilda's head in her hands and tried to coax the mare back up, but she lay there. Elizabeth tried and tried to get her up, but it was impossible. The mare was finished. All she could do was hold her head on her lap and talk to her, until, with a shudder through her body, Hilda breathed her last breath.

Shouting and laughter came from up the road. The riders were back on their horses, coming toward Elizabeth. She wanted to hit them. Wanted to hurt them for what they'd done. To make them realize they'd cost Hilda her life, until she realized—*they did not care.* To these men they were Rebs, the enemy, and it didn't matter whether they were women, children, horses or chickens. To these hard, cruel men, it just plain didn't matter.

Fury bubbled up from the pit of her stomach and she reached inside her pocket for the pistol. *She would teach these men a lesson! Show them she was not weak!* Her eyes flew open. The gun was gone!

The men hooted with laughter as they reined in around her.

"Looking for this?" One of them waved Randall's pistol in the air in front of her. "Should have been more careful on your run down the road," the man goaded before they all laughed again.

All the starch went out of Elizabeth. She felt beaten down and defeated. Her back sagged and she sucked in a deep breath to keep from crying out.

"What else do you want?" she barely managed. "We've nothing left. You've taken everything, even our mare. Please, leave us be." She was begging and she hated it. *Hated them for making her do it.*

She was suddenly surrounded by her children and Rebecca and Annie. They covered her like a human blanket, as though daring these vile men to attack her further.

Minutes passed until one of the raiders finally yelled, "We're done here, boys. There ain't nothin' left to take." He spit a stream of dark tobacco juice on the ground, jerked his horse's head around, and thundered away down the road, the others following.

Elizabeth sagged to the ground and let her tears flow for several minutes before she regained her wits.

They gathered up the mattress remnants strewn along the road after Hilda's wild run and covered her with them. Looking down on the shredded material, Elizabeth likened it to her shredded heart. They'd taken her husband, her home, and now the mare she loved like one of the family. There was nothing left, save her children and her life and she prayed to God he would allow them to reach her kin with both.

Then she realized there was one more thing they hadn't taken, and she intended to arrive with it in tact—her pride. This war had taken almost everything she loved, but it would not break her. She wouldn't let it. No matter what happened she was proud of who she was—and she'd smile, or spit, in their Yankee faces to prove it.

With tears flowing, the Miers, Barrows, and Annie and her children said goodbye to Hilda before continuing on their way with nothing more than the clothing on their backs. On a day that began with food, water, hope, and promise, it ended with rage, hunger, and the gnawing fear of what tomorrow would bring.

THE JOURNEY
Day 9 – Morning
(Clinton)

Elizabeth's whole body felt numb. The three families stood at the top of Clinton's main thoroughfare, the town and street pulsing like a beating heart. The dusty road churned with carriages, soldiers, local citizenry, animals, and refugees. Union soldiers rode beside and behind cowering travelers shouting insults and easing them off the road with their horses. They laughed as women and children stumbled and scurried out of the way, losing what little they carried to be trampled under the horses' feet. High-classed citizens, showing their Union support with red, white, and blue sashes and Union flags, sat inside carriages with their noses in the air, as far away from the refugees as possible, as though unwilling to breathe the same air. Infantry soldiers stomped the sidewalks, taunting whomever they could, whenever they could, bringing many dirty, barefooted women and children hoping only for a little food or simple pity, to tears. Food and pity that came at a price.

Elizabeth turned to her companions. "We've got to find food and water."

"Of course we do, but how?" Annie's reply was sharp. Everyone was on edge since the raider attack. They'd camped for the night down the road from where Hilda had fallen and, although Annie and Elizabeth tried to hunt, with only their wits and their bare hands, they came back with nothing. It had been a long, anxious night with little sleep for anyone other than the little ones, snuggled in the protection of their mothers' arms.

"No one is going to give us anything here. Soldiers are everywhere. Even if there are some sympathetic citizens, they won't help us. If someone found out they'd be punished," Annie added tersely.

"I know, I know. Let me think," Elizabeth snapped. They had nothing left, nothing except the few confederate bills James had given Elizabeth, worthless in this Union town, and the few things she had hidden in her clothes and most precious to her. Her father's watch and her mother's cameo, the locket James had given her, and her gold wedding band, all sewn inside the pocket of her dress. She thought about each piece and what it meant to her. She'd lost the tintype of hers and James' wedding day in their first encounter with the soldiers and swore she would *not* lose her wedding ring. It was just a plain, thin gold band, but it was all she had left of her husband. She refused to give up her father and mother's keepsakes, either. The locket James had brought her from Morristown, although it meant a lot to her, she would part with it, along with a few other smaller pieces of jewelry, if necessary. It would have to be enough. She would *not* give up the only remaining links she had to her parents and husband.

"What can we do? We have nothing to give." Rebecca sighed.

"I do." Before Rebecca or Annie could question her, Elizabeth continued. "We'll find a mercantile store and trade for what we need."

"With what?" Annie almost snarled.

"I have some things. A few pieces of jewelry a shop keeper might be interested in."

Rebecca shook her head. "Not your wedding band? Tell me you're not thinking of trading your wedding band!" Rebecca said, horrified.

"No!" Elizabeth was quick to respond. "I won't trade that for anything. There are a few other pieces I brought for such a situation."

Rebecca's shoulders slumped in relief. "Good. I won't trade my wedding ring for anything, either. Not even food or water." Rebecca glanced at her children, staring at her wide-eyed, and trembled. "Not unless it is absolutely necessary," she amended with another shudder.

Annie nodded agreement, the fingers of her right hand circling where a ring should have been on her left.

"Come along. Standing here talking about it isn't going to get us anything." Elizabeth straightened her back, took Sally's hand on her right and Joseph's hand on her left. Nora and Vera fell in behind her as she stepped onto the sidewalk and started forward.

Annie and her two girls walked behind Nora and Vera and Rebecca and her children were behind Annie. Other refugees followed at a distance behind them.

Slowly, they made their way into Clinton. Heads turned. They were greeted with sneers and cat calls by passing soldiers and still Elizabeth walked tall with her head high. They would not break her. She and her family had survived too much to allow harsh words or withering looks to give them pause.

They hadn't gone far on the sidewalk when Elizabeth stopped. Everyone stopped behind her. She pointed to a sign on the right that said *Owens Mercantile*. "Here. I'm going in and see if I can trade for supplies. You all stay out here. Whoever I'm dealing with doesn't need to see how desperate we are so wait over there." She pointed to an open section of sidewalk with a small alley in between. "Nora, Vera, take hold of Joseph and Sally and wait with Rebecca and Annie. I'll be right back." She handed off the younger children to their older siblings and turned toward the store.

"Are you sure about this?" Rebecca asked, concern on her face. "I don't like it."

"There are a lot of things I don't like about what's happening, but we have no choice. We need food and water and I intend to get some."

Rebecca sighed and nodded. "I know. I'm just worried."

"I know," Elizabeth interrupted. "You're scared. I'm scared, too, but I have to try. Wish me luck?"

"Good luck." Rebecca grabbed Elizabeth's hand and squeezed. Annie did the same before they gathered the children and went into the alley.

Her heart hammering, Elizabeth pounded as much dust as she could off her dress, smoothed her hair, and slouched down to let her dresses cover her bare feet. Taking a deep breath, she pushed through the door. A bell sounded overhead, announcing her entrance.

The shopkeeper, an older, gray-haired man with a rough gray beard, stood behind the counter. His eyes grew hard when he saw Elizabeth.

"Good morning, sir. I...."

"I know what you want. You want a hand out. Well, you won't get one here." He waved his hand at her, but Elizabeth wouldn't be put off.

"Please, sir, my family needs food and water. We had plenty before we began our journey, but the Yank...but it was lost along the way," she corrected.

"I know your story. It's the same as all them others that come through town. You're no different."

Elizabeth looked down at the floor and noticed her toes sticking out. Uncaring now whether the man knew she was bare footed or not, she straightened her shoulders, took a deep breath for courage, and stepped toward him. "Sir, I don't want a hand out. I can trade."

The man perked up. "Trade?" He looked her up and down. "What do *you* have to trade?" Scorn was heavy in his voice. He thought a second and a gleam came into his eyes before shouting, "I don't take favors in trade for food!"

"No, sir, no! That's not what I mean. I have things—to trade."

Elizabeth saw she'd piqued his interest and hurried on. "I have a few pieces of jewelry I can trade."

The man waved her closer, his eyes almost glowing. *This man is a viper, an opportunist just waiting for someone desperate to come into his shop and steal what little they have. He's no better than those Yankee soldiers or raiders that had accosted them on the road!* She forced herself to step closer.

The man looked around the store, as though to confirm they were alone. He waved her closer until she was just across the counter from him.

Shaking Elizabeth asked, "Will you trade? Please?"

The man leaned over and Elizabeth steeled herself for his verbal attack. Instead he whispered, "I'm a friend. Don't be afraid. My attitude is for anyone passing by to keep them convinced I'm a Union man."

Elizabeth was uncertain, but stayed where she was as he continued. "I'll shout at you one minute, but listen carefully to what I say in between."

Elizabeth barely nodded understanding.

"You Rebs come into my store looking for something for nothing. Why don't you git on outta here!" He waved his hand toward the door and Elizabeth turned to see two soldiers peering in through the window.

"Old man Green is at it again," one howled with laughter, loud enough for Elizabeth to hear.

"Glad I ain't no Reb looking for a handout!" his acquaintance agreed with the same loud hilarity.

"Please, sir. My family needs food and water. And milk for a small babe," Elizabeth continued in a tight, controlled voice.

"I don't care what you need, Missy, git on outta here!" The man waited until the men passed by then whispered. "What you have to trade is on your person?"

Elizabeth nodded slightly.

He shook his head. "Don't let anyone else know that." Then he shouted, "I told you there are no handouts here so turn yourself around and git on outta here!"

"But my children!" Elizabeth cried, sounding desperate.

"Don't care about you or your dirty Reb children!" He leaned in and in a soft voice said, "Go south to the next block, Jefferson, then turn east," he whispered in a rush. "Make sure you go right and not left or you'll run smack into Judge Dorman's house, the biggest Union man in town. Lucky for you you stopped here and not at his store. He'd have run you out of town." The storekeeper stepped back and shouted, "Go away. I don't want to deal with you or your kind anymore. You're a pestilence on society! A tick, sucking the blood out of this country! Git on outta here," he finished with a flourish of hands.

Elizabeth wasn't sure what to do, so she waited until he whispered.

"Go right on Jefferson till you come to a run-down barn on the north side, on your left, about a half mile. Behind the barn is a hidden well." He spoke quickly and Elizabeth nodded to let him know she understood. "Look for a burned down shed. Under it is the well. Have a care to put everything back for the next traveler I send there. It'll be of no use if discovered."

Trying to contain her excitement she smiled and nodded. She reached for his hand and he exploded.

"Don't offer me favors, I told you! Just git on outta here and be on your way!"

"What about food?" she asked in a rush as he came around the counter to shoo her out of the store.

"There'll be a bag of jerky hanging from a rope on the side of the well. Leave the rope and take the food."

"And payment?"

"I don't want payment. It's the least I can do to help you folks displaced by that damned General Ewing. I got no love for that man, his Order *or* the preservation of the Union," he fairly spat. There was hatred in his eyes now and Elizabeth knew there was a story behind that hatred she would never know.

"Damn you woman! Quit pestering me. I'm telling you there's nothing here for you! I'm tired of hearing you beg." He leaned in and said, "When I turn my back, grab one of them cans of milk for the babe, but make sure my back is turned so I don't have to chase you out. Now go on, git!" He shouted, shoving her before he turned away. She stumbled as though pushed roughly.

Elizabeth hurried toward the door, but not before she grabbed a small can of milk and shoved it into her pocket. Tears streamed down her face, but they weren't tears of defeat or humiliation. They were tears of joy. Tonight they would eat and little Robert would have milk.

"What happened?" Annie asked through gritted teeth.

"Mama, why are you crying?" Nora grabbed her mother's hand. "He wouldn't give us food, would he?" Defeat was heavy in her daughter's voice.

Elizabeth didn't know whether to tell them about what had transpired in the shop or not, afraid if they knew, one of the children might unwittingly betray the man's secret. Instead she told them, "He refused us anything. Wouldn't even look at the pieces I had to trade." She felt guilty for lying, but she wasn't *totally* lying. He *hadn't* allowed her to show him anything. "He kept shouting for me to get out of his shop and that he was tired of us Rebs coming in looking for handouts."

"But you weren't looking for a handout," Rebecca hissed. "You had things to trade."

Elizabeth shook her head. "He wasn't interested."

Rebecca and Annie clucked their tongues and shook their heads in defeat.

"But...."

"But what?" the two women asked at the same time.

"I stole this when he wasn't looking."

Rebecca looked at the can like it was gold.

"Oh, Elizabeth, thank you!"

Elizabeth shoved it back into her pocket. "That's for later."

"And what do we do now?" Annie asked.

"We find a place to camp."

"Camp? But it's morning," Nora said, confused. "We never camp until late afternoon or early evening."

Elizabeth sighed and ran her hand over her daughter's head. "And we've traveled some hard road and deserve a rest. We'll find a good spot," she covered her eyes to the glare of the sun and pointed down the road at Jefferson Street, "down that road there. Perhaps someone outside town will be more helpful, but at least we can rest for the day before starting out again tomorrow. Robert will have milk and all will be quiet."

Everyone eyed her with uncertainty. "I know you're wondering why I'm not rushing to get through town and on our way. I told you, we've had a rough couple days and we need rest. It's as simple as that."

A quiet cheer went through the children and even Annie and Rebecca made their pleasure known. With happy murmuring behind her, Elizabeth headed south toward Jefferson Street, as directed by the shopkeeper. When they reached it she turned right and out of town.

"Why that way?" Annie challenged. "Maybe we should go the other way." Annie pointed west, where the shop keeper had expressly told Elizabeth *not* to go.

"We *have* to go this way." Elizabeth swung her hand in the other direction.

"Have to? Why?" Annie challenged again.

"Because we *have* to, that's why."

Realization began to dawn on Annie and Rebecca's faces that the shopkeeper must have told her something she wasn't sharing.

"Fine, we'll go that way, but I hope you know what you're doing," Annie grumbled, taking the lead out of town.

"That shopkeeper told you something, didn't he?" Rebecca slipped up beside Elizabeth with a squirming, unhappy little Robert on her hip.

Elizabeth nodded then quickly added. "I can't tell you till we get out of town. I don't want to chance one of the children blurting something out before we're clear."

Rebecca's eyes sparkled with understanding. She smiled and said no more.

They walked until they were well out of town, passing several acceptable camping spots until everyone started grumbling. Elizabeth finally spied a spot not too far from where she hoped the well and barn would be. She didn't want to camp too close and draw suspicion, but close enough so they didn't have to carry the full water pots too far. Tonight she and Annie would slip away, get the water and food and surprise the children. For now, they would set up camp like always. Robert cried and the children grumbled, but today there was nothing else to do. Other than the pots Elizabeth insisted they keep there was nothing to set up. There were no mattresses to put down, not even the shreds of what hadn't been destroyed. There was nothing to cook and nothing to drink. So for today, setting up camp meant finding a place to sit down and rest and wait for morning.

As usual, the children gathered in little groups by age. They talked and grumbled and cried, but kept their displeasure from their mothers. Once the children had settled, Elizabeth called Rebecca and Annie over.

"I know where there's food and water."

"What!" Annie nearly shouted. "And you didn't tell us?"

"Shhhh," Elizabeth hissed. "I couldn't risk one of the children letting it out before we were out of town. I couldn't put the shopkeeper at risk—or us. If anyone found out he helped us, it wouldn't be good for him."

Annie frowned, but nodded.

Rebecca nodded too. "Tell us."

"There's a barn up the road with a hidden well. And food."

"But is there water?" Annie wondered aloud.

"There must be or he wouldn't have sent us. From what I could gather he's sent other travelers like us there. He keeps the meat replenished, so I can't imagine he'd send us to a dried up well." She thought a moment then continued. "He has no love for General Ewing *or* his Order either. I don't know the shopkeeper's story, but it was obvious he has a deep hatred for both." She sighed. "In a Union town it must be difficult for him and he's doing what little he can to help those of us turned out by the Order—without getting caught. He's playing a deadly game, but thank God he is, or we'd most likely have passed through with nothing."

Rebecca and Annie agreed with nods and smiles.

"How do you plan to get the food and water?" Annie asked.

"You and I will tell the children we're going to hunt and we'll go find the barn. Once it gets dark, we'll go back and retrieve the water and food."

"It's a sound plan," Rebecca said, but I want to go with you instead of Annie.

"You can't, Rebecca. You have to stay with Robert. You have milk for him now and you need to tend to him."

Rebecca looked away, but not before Elizabeth saw the anger on her face. There was only so much she could do with a babe to take care of.

Elizabeth laid her hand on Rebecca's arm. "I know you want to do more, but Robert needs you more than anything."

"Helen and Clara can feed him while I'm gone." Rebecca was adamant.

"And what if someone comes by and he's screaming and they ask where his mama is? Can you be certain one of the little children won't innocently give us away? Tell them his mommy 'went away in the dark.' You can't, Rebecca, that's all there is to it. This is something Annie and I must do. If it came to it and someone questioned you, you can tell them we went hunting while it was still daylight. We must have gotten lost, but you can't do anything because you must stay with the children."

Rebecca hung her head in defeat. "I know you're right, Elizabeth. I'm just so tired of being left behind. I want to do something more than take care of the children."

Elizabeth squeezed her arm. "I know. You're helping by keeping Robert quiet and the other children safe. How could we leave them any other way?"

Rebecca frowned, but nodded. "I understand. I'll keep them safe while you're gone."

"I have no doubt of that, which is why Annie and I will be able to do what needs to be done with no worries."

Rebecca sniffed and smiled a tremulous smile. "Thank you for that."

"Here." Elizabeth handed Rebecca the can of milk. "Take care of him."

Rebecca looked at the can and a puzzled look came over her face. "How do I open it? We don't have an opener or even a knife to put a hole in it."

Elizabeth sighed. She hadn't thought beyond what was inside the can. "Do the best you can. Use a rock to break it open or look around for a piece of metal to put a hole in it, just do the best you can."

Rebecca shook her head. "Can't *anything* be easy?"

Elizabeth grimaced. "Apparently not."

Annie stepped up beside Elizabeth. "Are you ready?"

"I am, but I don't know how we can pretend to hunt without a gun or anything useful toward that end." She paused in thought then said, "I suppose we can pretend the animals know we're hungry and will come to us, right?"

Annie grinned at Elizabeth's attempt at humor.

Elizabeth smiled back and soon the two were headed along the road under the pretense of trying to hunt. It wasn't long before they came upon the ramshackle barn on the north side of the road.

"There it is!" Elizabeth held down her excitement, but her heart was hammering and she felt light-headed.

"And I see the burned shed behind it!" Annie almost shouted.

"Shhhh, we have to be quiet and act like it's just another broken down barn. Someone could suspect the shopkeeper and be watching. We have to believe someone is always watching. It could be disaster for him if someone learned he was sending starving refugees here," Elizabeth pointed out.

Regaining herself, Annie agreed. "How much farther do you want to go before we turn around?"

"A little farther. Let's, at least *try* and look like we're hunting—in case someone *is* watching." Although her bare feet pained her badly from her run after Hilda, Elizabeth tried to ignore the stones and twigs poking her and continued on.

Two hours later they returned to camp. Rebecca and the older girls had gathered wood for a fire and everyone was sitting around it.

Rebecca jumped up and met Elizabeth and Annie. "Did you find it?"

"We did. After it gets dark and the children are asleep, Annie and I will go back. It's not far from here, maybe a quarter mile. We should be able to get there and back in a couple hours."

"Should we tell the older children?" Rebecca asked.

"No," Annie answered before Elizabeth could. "They can't know anything. If they should wake and ask where we are, just tell them we'll be back soon. They have to be completely ignorant of what we're doing." She looked pointedly at Nora and Vera and Helen and Clara.

"She's right. They can't know anything. Not even what direction we went in. That way they can't give us away if someone comes by and asks questions."

Rebecca nodded agreement, repositioning an unusually quiet Robert on her hip.

"Did you give Robert the milk?" Elizabeth noted how pasty he looked.

"I tried, but I couldn't get the can open. I tried rocks and sticks, but nothing worked. I finally smashed it with a really big rock, and everything spilled out before I could get any of it into a cup.

Looking at the child again, Elizabeth was afraid for him. He'd had no real nourishment in days and, although he had water yesterday morning and some bits of turkey and raccoon, as young as he was he needed lots of milk to stay healthy.

"Is he all right?" Elizabeth asked a nervous Rebecca.

"He's fine," Rebecca answered quickly, her voice strained. "He's quiet for once. Be thankful for it."

Fear streaked up Elizabeth's spine. *Was Robert dying? They'd done everything they could for him, but would he reach their destination with everyone else?* She refused to accept the child wouldn't survive the trip. They'd get the water and food at the well and he'd gnaw on jerky, drink lots of water, and regain his strength like everyone else.

Elizabeth started to say something more, but was stopped cold.

"He's fine, Elizabeth," Rebecca assured her, but there were tears in her eyes.

THE JOURNEY
Day 9 – Night
(East of Clinton)

Each carrying a salvaged pot and lid, Annie and Elizabeth slipped away from camp a few hours later. Staying close to the road, but not on it, they easily found the barn again. Using what little light the moon gave they hurried behind the dilapidated structure and started pulling the burned boards and foundation rocks from the hidden well.

They'd moved rocks and boards for only ten minutes or so before Elizabeth's lower back throbbed so badly she felt like it could snap as easily a dry twig. Rubbing her muscles to help ease the pain, she jerked upright when she heard noise on the road. She waved her hands at Annie and laid a finger across her lips. "Shhhh."

Annie stopped pulling at the board she had in her hands. "What?"

"Horses."

Annie carefully put the board back down and looked up the road and around them. "Where do we go?"

Elizabeth scanned the area. Although there was little light from the moon, there was enough to give them away if they stayed where they were. They had to get to what was left of the barn. "This way." Lifting her skirts above her ankles Elizabeth sprinted away, Annie close behind her. Moments before the riders came into view, they slid lengthwise as close as they could next to the crumbled remains of the foundation, their bellies to the ground their faces hidden.

Unable to see the riders, they listened instead. From the conversation that floated through the night air, it seemed to Elizabeth they were just a couple of locals on their way home from a day's visit to town. They passed without incidence, but it left Elizabeth and Annie shaken.

Elizabeth rolled onto her back and sucked in deep breaths of the tepid air to calm her frayed nerves. Annie lay where she was, her face hidden in her arm, hiding the tears Elizabeth knew she wept. They lay still a few minutes, unable and unwilling to move, before Elizabeth finally got to her feet.

"They're long past. We have to get back to it or we'll be here all night."

Clearing her throat and swiping at the tears she'd tried to hide, Annie stood up, her still wet cheeks glistening in the moonlight. "I was so scared."

"Me, too, but we're all right. We have to finish what we started and get back to camp. Come on."

It took another hour to clear away the debris. As the kind-hearted shopkeeper had said, a bag hung from a rope on the side of the well, but in the darkness they couldn't see what was below.

"Is there water down there?" Annie asked. She and Elizabeth peered over the side into the dark depths.

"I can't tell. It's too dark. Wait." Elizabeth found a rock, tossed it in, and waited. Seconds later they heard a splash.

"There's water!" Elizabeth breathed, her heart hammering again. "It's low, but there's water!"

Retrieving the meat was no problem. They simply pulled up the bag, untied it, and let the rope drop back into the well. Retrieving the water was something else. There was no bucket like there would be in a functioning well, only a deep, black opening into the earth.

"How are we going to reach it?" Annie asked Elizabeth, on their knees peering over the edge again.

Elizabeth thought a moment then untied the rope that had held the meat and tied it around the handles of one of the pots. "I hope it's long enough." She snapped the knot to make sure it was tight, unwilling to lose the pot.

She held her breath and lowered it down, but it stopped short of the water.

"What now?" Annie clasped her fingers together. "What do we do now?"

The normally unflappable Annie was showing a side tonight Elizabeth hadn't seen, making her jumpy. "Give me a second to think," she snapped. Elizabeth thought several moments then realized they had plenty of material to *make* a rope. She lifted the first three layers of dresses she wore and tore off the hem of the one closest to her body. She wound it tight, knotted it to the end of the existing rope and let it slide through her fingers until there was no resistance. "It's long enough!" she almost shouted to Annie's immediate shushing.

"I know, I know, I'm sorry."

"Can you get it to fill?" Annie asked.

Elizabeth rocked the rope and pot back and forth until the pot slid under the water. She left the line slack until there was pressure again and pulled it up. Careful not to spill any, she and Annie lifted the pot over the side and set it on the ground. The water looked black in the darkness, but neither cared as they cupped their hands and drank. It was gritty, wet and wonderful.

"Oh, I never thought water could taste so good — even bottom of the well water," Annie whispered.

"Me neither. Drink what you can then let's get this other one filled." Elizabeth untied the first pot and retied the rope around the second, lowered it like she had the first, and brought it up again when it was full.

They seated the lids as best they could, put rocks on them and set them aside. As quickly as they could, they retied the original rope on the well wall where they'd found it and built up the rocks and boards as they'd been when they found it, leaving everything looking like it did when they arrived.

"Now comes the *really* hard part," Elizabeth groaned. "We have to get these back to camp without spilling it all. They're so much heavier now and will be awkward to carry. And we can't forget the bag of meat. How are we going to get all this back to camp without losing half of it?"

The two women thought a few minutes until Elizabeth grabbed the remnants of material she'd pulled off her dress and used for rope. "I'll make a sling for the meat and we can take turns carrying it."

Annie sighed and nodded. "This is *not* going to be easy."

"It never is."

Minutes later the two women set out with the bag of meat slung across Elizabeth's back and each of them carrying a pot. They went slow and sure, daring not to go too fast and lose any of their life-saving water. They could lose the food and survive, but not the water. It only took days to die of thirst in this relentless heat, a young child much less.

They arrived back at camp, met by a squalling baby, and

an almost-crazed Rebecca. "I was so scared! What took you so long? I thought you were lost or got caught, or a wild animal got you!"

Elizabeth raised her hand. "Stop, Rebecca. You're getting hysterical. A couple locals passed on their way home and we had to hide is all that happened. And we had to go very, very slow on the way back with the water. These pots are heavy and we didn't want to lose any of it going too fast."

Rebecca took a deep, calming breath. "Was there meat, like the shopkeeper said?"

"Yes." Elizabeth's eyes gleamed with joy. She didn't know what or how much was in the bag. All she knew was they had food and water thanks to the kindness of one man. If they were prudent and didn't eat everything tonight, maybe there'd be enough for tomorrow. And they had water. They would certainly finish one pot tonight and have to rig a way to carry the other to take with them. It would be a challenge, but Elizabeth was up to it. She refused to let one drop of water be wasted. But that was later. Right now, it was time to enjoy what had been given to them.

"Let's wake the children and enjoy what we've been given." Elizabeth headed for her children, anxious to share their good fortune.

When the children saw what Annie and Elizabeth had brought with them, they laughed and cried with excitement. Elizabeth explained how being frugal with the food tonight would leave enough for tomorrow and they took what they were given without complaint.

Elizabeth watched everyone dig into their portion of the jerked meat and small piece of the six hard biscuits that were also in the bag. There were smiles on the children's faces, the hardship of the journey forgotten for the moment. But it was a fleeting moment. Tomorrow would bring another day of sore feet, sweaty, blistered skin, and aching bodies. But they were close. Their destination was within their grasp. *Would they reach it without losing any more than they already had?*

THE JOURNEY
Day 10 - Morning
(South of Clinton)

By firelight the night before Elizabeth had fashioned a carrier for the water pot using a three-foot long, two-inch round branch for the holder. The rope she'd made from the hem of her dress came in handy, looped around the pot handles and across the top. Even Randall's confiscated piggin' lines helped secure the lid. Satisfied it wouldn't leak with the swaying motion, she pulled out the pieces of rope she'd salvaged from the destroyed sled and fashioned handles so the pot hung freely when the branch was lifted.

The carrier had to be held between two people. If they went through town in the daylight they would be easily noticed, increasing the odds of being set upon by soldiers or townspeople, and most likely losing the water as a result. So they left camp long before the sun was up. Using the fading moonlight to guide them, they went straight down the main street as quickly and quietly as they could with their heavy burden and fifteen sleepy children. They were *almost* out of town when four soldiers rode up in front of them.

"What have we got here?" The lead rider, a tall, thin, dark-headed and heavily bewhiskered man jerked his horse to a halt ahead of Elizabeth and Annie, the pot swinging back and forth with their abrupt stop. Elizabeth's skin pricked, noting the gleam of mischief in the man's eyes in the moonlight.

"We're leaving town, sir." Elizabeth's throat was tight.

"And what's that?" A second, heavier soldier leaned forward and pointed to the swaying pot, his saddle creaking under his shifting weight. "Looks like a heavy burden. Maybe we should relieve you of it." The men chuckled.

"It's just water," Elizabeth said through clenched teeth. The bag of what was left of the jerky was slung behind her back and she knew it was only a matter of time before they found it and threatened to take it, too.

"Where you going with that water and this brood?" a third, seemingly well-fed and clean-shaven soldier, drawled.

"South," was all Elizabeth said. She dared not mention

Osceola.

"How far south?" The first rider took over the questioning again.

"Just south."

The rider eyed Elizabeth. He knew she wasn't giving him the full truth, but she didn't want to stir their ire by telling them exactly *where*.

"I asked *how far south?*"

"Twenty miles." Elizabeth's skin pricked with warning, but there was nothing she could do.

"Twenty miles?" the first rider shouted, a grin of knowing on his face. "Why boys, that's where Osceola *used to be*—before we burned it to the ground and her rebel pride with it!"

The soldiers hooted with laughter and inched their horses closer to Elizabeth and Annie. The children huddled behind or beside their mothers, whimpering. Elizabeth chanced a quick glance at her children. Nora looked ready to dig a hole and crawl into it there was so much fear in her eyes. Silent tears streamed down Vera's cheeks, her usually vocal daughter silenced by fear, and Joseph and Sally's faces were both hidden in the folds of their older sisters' dresses.

"We're no threat to you. We're just trying to reach my kin." Elizabeth was getting that feeling again. "Let us pass."

"Let us pass," the soldier mimicked. "You're mighty uppity for one who's barefooted and walking the road in rags."

Elizabeth's sensibility snapped. "Listen you ignorant buffoon. We're barefoot and in rags because *your* General Ewing made it so! We've been walking for over a week in the heat, scrounging for what little food or water we can find since everything we owned was taken or destroyed by *your* soldiers, and you dare to accost us because we're leaving town like we were ordered, carrying a pot of water to keep us from perishing of thirst! Three women and fifteen frightened children!" she screamed. She'd overstepped again, just like she had the night she shot Walker, but it wasn't to be helped. One woman could only take so much!

As though rehearsed, Robert started to whimper, then went into a full-blown squall, drawing everyone's attention. He squirmed and screamed in Rebecca's arms, his hands and legs flailing. He was still pasty white and a little feverish, but after taking in some water, part of a biscuit, and gnawing on a piece of jerky last night until it softened enough for him to break off and swallow pieces of it with the few teeth he had, he'd regained some of his energy—and his lungs—and was letting everyone know he was very unhappy again.

Elizabeth's side of the carrier got heavier by the moment. She slipped the branch off her shoulder, waited for Annie to do the same then set the pot on the ground, letting the branch drop down beside it. Regaining her composure, over Robert's cries, she said, "Please, we just want to leave town. We don't want any trouble. We're of no threat to you or your men."

Behind Elizabeth, Rebecca fought with her unruly son. Robert howled and thrashed in her arms until she stalked forward. "Is this child such a threat that you would keep us from where we're going? Are you men so callous you would take life-saving water from the mouths of babes!" she waved her hand to encompass all the children, huddled together and crying. Rebecca's eyes were wild, her lips pinched, and Robert squalled louder.

"Enough!" The shout came from a rider coming up behind the others. "Leave these folks alone."

"Aw sarge, we were just funnin'," the first soldier said to the horseman who came alongside on a stocky bay horse.

"Well, you're finished. Move on and leave these folks be."

"But they're Rebs," he almost whined.

"They're women and children! Have we stooped so low that women and children are now our enemies?"

"Well, sir."

"Enough! You will accost these people no further. Is that understood?"

"Yes sir," was repeated four times before the men wheeled their horses around and rode back into town.

"I apologize for my men, ladies." The sergeant touched the brim of his hat. "I'm afraid this has been a long posting and they're bored."

Elizabeth's heart was slowing down, but Robert was still

screaming. Rebecca tried to console him, but he was having none of it.

"He needs milk," Rebecca explained. "He hasn't had any milk in days. He's just a baby and he needs milk."

The sergeant got down off his horse and stepped to Rebecca. "May I?" he reached for Robert.

Fear stretched across Rebecca's face. "I'll make him be quiet. Please don't take him from me. I'll make him stop." She crushed Robert to her chest and turned away.

"I mean him no harm, ma'am. I'd just like to hold him."

He had a smile on his face and appeared genuine, but Elizabeth didn't trust Yankees, not a one. She stepped beside Rebecca. "Why do you want to hold him?" Elizabeth was still calming down from her anger and couldn't help asking the question.

He pursed his lips. "Because I have a son at home in Ohio born eight months ago that I've never seen. I imagine he's about the same age as this little guy and I'd like to see how it feels to hold a boy his size in my arms."

"That's all? You're not going to hurt him or take him away to make him be quiet?" Rebecca managed.

The sergeant shook his head and smiled. "No ma'am, I have no intention of hurting this boy. In fact, I'd like to help." He went to his horse, lifted the cover of his saddle bag, and pulled out a can of condensed milk. He stepped to Elizabeth and extended it toward her. "Give this to the child."

Elizabeth stared at the can then looked up at the soldier. Unshed tears glistened in his eyes and he swallowed hard. "It's standard issue for our troops. I'll get more, but wish I had more to give you right now. Please, give it to the child. He needs it more than I do."

Elizabeth was still leery. She plain didn't trust Yankees. *Why should this one be different?*

"Why are you being kind to us?" Elizabeth couldn't help ask. "We're rebels. The enemy."

He shook his head and snorted in derision. "I see no enemy here, only women and children trying to survive a terrible situation." He took his hat off and ran his fingers through his thick, black hair before sliding it back into place. "I can't imagine my wife going through what you folks are living through. I pray every day that never happens, but if it did, I hope someone would help her with a kind word and a can of milk. Please, take it." He forced the can into Elizabeth's hands then turned and reached for Robert. "May I?"

Reluctant, Rebecca handed her son over to the soldier. Wide-eyed, the boy quieted when the man took him into his arms and settled him on his big hip. He rocked the child, cooed to him and tickled him. He touched Robert's fingers and toes and ran his fingers over his cheeks and face. Robert, in turn, pulled on the young sergeant's beard, making him smile more.

"He's so light. I thought he'd be heavier." The sergeant hefted him in the air and Robert giggled.

"He weighs more when he's well fed." There was a rough edge to Rebecca's voice. "He usually has chubby cheeks and a round belly, but those are long gone. Hunger does that to a child."

"Then I pray the milk helps." He kissed Robert on the top of the head and the boy squealed with laughter when the sergeant's beard tickled his face.

He handed Robert back to Rebecca and turned to mount his horse when Elizabeth remembered the milk and stopped him.

"Sir, I hate to ask for more after the kindness you've already shown us, but we have no way of opening the milk." She hefted the can in her hand and frowned. "I...acquired a can yesterday, but we don't have an opener and all the milk was lost in the effort to open it. Do you, perhaps, have one to give us?"

He shook his head. "I don't have an opener, but will open it for you." He pulled the knife from his belt and reached for the can.

Elizabeth handed it to him and he forced the tip through the top of the can.

Relief flooded through Elizabeth. Rebecca stepped to the sergeant, grabbed his hand and pumped it up and down, jostling Robert in the process, making him giggle again. "How may I thank you, sir? I do not doubt you've saved my child's life."

The man cleared his throat. "Just make sure you don't lose any of that milk and that the babe gets every drop." He grinned.

"Yes, sir," Rebecca said, tears brimming. "He'll get every bit."

Elizabeth tore a piece of material from her shabby dress and shoved it in the hole in the can to make sure none of the milk was lost before they were able to give it to Robert.

Minutes later, with a sad smile and longing in his eyes, the sergeant took his leave. They continued on with water, milk, food, and a new optimism that, perhaps, simple kindness wasn't dead yet—at least not completely.

THE JOURNEY
Day 10 - Evening

As it had been every other day, the heat was relentless by the time the sun was full up, the tedium as suffocating as the heat. Dust hung in the air like a smothering cloud, the muffled sniffling and grumbling of the children constant—but Robert was blessedly quiet. A short distance outside town they'd found a spot to rest, pulled the rag out of the can, mixed the milk with water to make it last longer, and Robert sucked it down like dry roots in a rainstorm.

After a blessedly uneventful day with fewer and fewer refugees traveling the road with them, they rested in a wooded area Elizabeth, James and the children had stopped at many times on their trips to Aunt Pearl's. Her heart felt like a stone as she recalled their picnics there and the children playing in the wide creek. *How she longed for her husband, her oldest son, and her home! How she missed her life as it had been prior to this horrific war!*

Realizing her sorrowful thoughts would make her melancholy she pushed them from her mind and tried to think only good ones. Not only had the day begun well, it would end well, too. They'd gone farther than Elizabeth hoped, they'd found a good place to camp, and there was water in the creek!

"How are we going to get down there?" Annie stood beside Elizabeth at the top of the bank looking down at the creek that appeared to be at least eight feet below normal. Along the high banks on both sides, long, protruding roots weaved in and out of the dirt walls like snakes. Rocks, branches, and leaves were strewn along the lower banks and on the bottom in big piles, but there was water—if they could get down to it.

On the road ahead of them a bridge crossed the creek, normally high and wide enough to merit such a convenience. Elizabeth recalled passing over it in the spring after the winter thaw, the creek so full it raced and swirled only a foot or two below the bridge, far different than it looked today.

"Elizabeth, are you listening?"

"Yes, yes. I was thinking about James and the children and our picnicking here on our way to and from Aunt Pearl's."

She looked up stream and pointed. "There's a clearing over there with shade."

"What are we waiting for?" Annie asked.

Rebecca stepped beside them, a drooling, happy Robert on her hip. "What are we doing?"

"We should be able to camp up there." Elizabeth pointed up stream again. "Since there's water in the creek, maybe there's fish, too. There used to be lots of bullhead. James and I used to fish while the children caught frogs. Maybe we can catch enough of both for supper," Elizabeth said, hopeful.

"That would be wonderful. The children can make a game of it. Whoever catches the most frogs will get...what? What will they get?" A hopeful smile outlined Rebecca's face.

"How about an extra portion?" Elizabeth suggested.

Rebecca and Annie nodded their heads.

"Right now, that's enough incentive for *me* to get down in the water and hunt frogs!" Annie said with a laugh.

"Then what are we waiting for? Let's set up camp and get about our business. There's fish and frogs to catch and supper to be made!" Elizabeth shouted.

The clearing was as Elizabeth remembered, although the trees were bare and offered little shade, but with night coming, it mattered little. As the creek level had receded, a well-worn slope was created in the bank where previous visitors drove their stock to the water, making for easy access. And they were blissfully alone, other travelers having thinned considerably after they left Clinton.

They drank till they thought they'd pop, bathed, washed the clothes they could take off then put the clean, wet ones back on and washed the clothes that were still dirty. When that was done Elizabeth and Annie looked for willow branches, the straightest and pointiest they could find, to spear fish. Shooing the children downstream onto the shallow rock riffle, they waited patiently as one then two then more fat bullheads swam into view. With a steady hand and sure eye, they speared six before the sun went down. While Annie and Elizabeth fished, Rebecca built a fire with a spit to cook the fish. Downstream the children hunted frogs, skewering four or five of them on one pointed stick before sliding them off into the pot filled with water set to boil in the hot coals. There were fat fish and frogs legs for supper, the skin and bones the only thing left when everyone had eaten their fill—especially Joshua who won the contest by catching the most frogs at six, and was rewarded with a second then third helping of fish *and* frog. Even Robert gummed and swallowed tender pieces of fish until he was so full he pushed what was offered away.

That night, lying on the hard ground with food in her belly, her thirst slaked, her hair and body clean for the first time in days, Elizabeth tried to sleep, but it eluded her as the day's events ran over and over through her mind. The day had started as a surprise, with a man whom she considered her enemy giving them life-saving milk for Robert, and had ended with a good place to camp, water *and* food.

Yesterday she hadn't been sure Robert would survive the trip. Today, there was no question he would, just like everyone else. She'd never have believed their saving grace would come in the form of Yankees, wouldn't have *wanted* to believe it after everything they'd done to her and her family. But she had to, and, for the first time since being forced from her home, Elizabeth's faith in humanity was restored—at least temporarily. One Yankee soldier and one grumpy shopkeeper had helped her remember *all* men weren't bad—no matter which side of the war they were on.

THE JOURNEY
Day 11 - Morning

Their excitement mounted. They were so close. Elizabeth could almost taste Aunt Pearl's homemade biscuits and feel Uncle Rupert's crushing welcome hug. Of course, that was *if* her aunt and uncle were still there, still alive, *and* had the ingredients to make homemade biscuits—or anything else for that matter.

They'd turned off the main road toward Osceola, leaving their few remaining fellow travelers heading south for Springfield. It was quiet *and* disconcerting after all the dust, ruckus and constant flow of other refugees around them. Now the only dust and noise was theirs echoing through the bare trees along the road.

Elizabeth trudged forward, she and Annie lugging one full pot of water between them, just in case the creeks and streams ahead of them were dry. They still had at least ten miles to go, and ten miles without water was a long way in this heat. Although they would pass two more good-sized creeks Elizabeth could remember before reaching their destination, there was no guarantee there'd be water in them.

"How much farther, Mama?" Vera whined, grabbing her mother's free hand to make her stop. "My feet hurt so bad I can't take another step! You said we were close. When are we going to be there?"

The carrier shifted painfully on Elizabeth's shoulder and she wanted to throttle her second daughter. Vera had whined and complained all morning after Elizabeth made the mistake of telling her how close they were. "Just one more, long day and they'd be there" she'd said. But excitement soon turned to complaining because they weren't there quickly enough or they were hungry already or too tired to keep going.

"Vera, we've had this conversation all morning and it's time you stop. We'll get there when we get there. I'm tired of your whining. Everyone is tired of your whining."

"But Mama."

"Enough! Does everyone hear me?" Elizabeth jerked the carrier off her shoulder and turned around so she could see everybody. "There will be no more whining or asking when we'll get there. Big Otter Creek is up ahead. We'll rest there, maybe even stop for the afternoon."

"But then we won't get to Aunt Pearl's today like you said. And we're all hungry again, Mama. And what if the creek doesn't have water in it? Or fish? What will we eat and drink?" Vera was voicing Elizabeth's concerns aloud, but in a most annoying tone.

"If there's water and fish in the creek, we'll have food and water. If not, we won't, it's as simple as that." She set the carrier down, went to her knee and put her hands on Vera's arms." We've all been hungry and thirsty on this trip. We're tired and our feet hurt, but we're almost there, Vera. We can't give up now, we're too close. So please be quiet and keep walking without further whining. You're upsetting everyone else with your constant complaining." Elizabeth's voice was stern and brooked no argument.

Vera's lower lip trembled, but she said no more and fell into step with the others when they started again. Slowly, they made their way toward Big Otter Creek, only a few miles from their destination.

Rounding a bend on the rough road, Elizabeth jerked to a halt. The water pot swayed back and forth, almost yanking the carrier off hers and Annie's shoulders. Annie looked at her askance, until she realized why Elizabeth had stopped.

Riders were camped along Big Otter Creek. *Who were they?* swirled in Elizabeth's mind like a dust storm. The children, spotting the riders, stopped their grumblings and jerked to a halt, silent in an instant.

A tall, lanky, dark-haired man stood up from where he sat on a big rock and started toward them. His hand rested on the butt of a gun at his hip.

Elizabeth's knees were suddenly weak. *They were almost there! What more indignities might they be forced to endure before getting where they wanted to go?* The man walked toward them. Four others stood up from where they'd been lounging, hands at the ready on their guns, but stayed where they were. Elizabeth saw no uniforms, no insignias of any kind. *Who were they?* she wondered again as the tall man stepped in front of her.

He eyed Elizabeth and the others, taking in their disheveled appearances, their bare feet and sun-blistered skin. Robert was squirming, but quiet, having finished the last of his milk a little while ago.

"Where're y'all from?" The man cocked his head in curiosity. His hand was still on his pistol and Elizabeth noticed a second gun on his other hip.

Elizabeth swallowed. *Were they Kansas Redlegs? Jayhawkers? Bushwhackers? Or merely travelers trying to reach their kin as she and her family were doing?*

"We're from Cass County," she managed her throat gone dry.

The man grimaced in acknowledgment and nodded. "Turned out by the Order?"

"Yes sir," she said, uncertain how to address him.

He shook his head. "Ma'am, I ain't no sir and we ain't in the army, so you needn't address us as such. We're just travelers, like y'all."

"Yes si...Yes Mister...?"

"Call me Peter. No need for formalities amongst friends."

Friends? Were they friends? Elizabeth wondered.

"Will y'all join us? We're resting up a while before we get back in the saddle. There's water in the creek and we happened upon some beef this morning."

He had a twinkle in his eyes, and Elizabeth was certain the animal had most likely been *happened upon* from a local farmer without their consent. *Hopefully, not from Aunt Pearl*, she thought absently.

"There's plenty to share," he added.

The thought of a beef steak made Elizabeth's mouth water and she saw Annie, Rebecca and the children were salivating at the thought, too.

Nora stepped up beside her. "Mama? How can we know he's telling the truth? We're all hungry, but should we trust them? We're close enough to Aunt Pearl's. We can make it. We should keep going," she whispered.

Elizabeth heard the panic in Nora's voice and knew her

daughter was remembering Randall and all the men that had accosted them throughout their trip. The tall man must have seen the fear in Nora's eyes. Before Elizabeth could reassure her daughter, he stepped closer.

"We don't aim to hurt you miss. We won't hurt none of y'all. That's a promise. You needn't worry on that account." He smiled wide, revealing a mouth full of yellowed teeth.

Elizabeth looked at Rebecca, standing beside her and then at Annie, across from her. "Well?" Her heart was in her throat.

Elizabeth saw the hunger in both their eyes, the hunger in the eyes of the children who understood what was being offered—except Nora. In her eyes she saw only fear. They'd eaten well last night and again this morning, but they were all hungry after the day's long walk and looking for their next meal. It appeared the prospect of a beef steak was too much to refuse— for any of them.

"We need to stop, if for nothing else than to get more water," Rebecca said. "This is almost gone." She pointed at the pot then looked over at the man awaiting their answer. "And if they're willing to share, I say let them. The meat will spoil if *someone* doesn't eat it," she added with a sparkle in her eyes.

"That's the spirit," the man shouted and grinned. "Come on now, put aside your fright and git on over there. Let me take that." He grabbed the pot and carrier and lugged it with him.

Elizabeth sucked in a deep breath and gathered her children around her. Annie and Rebecca did the same and followed the man. Entering camp they were greeted by the four others.

"Welcome," a short, man with more gray beard than hair said with a big grin and bowing at the waist. "Pull ye up a piece a ground, git comfortable, an' let me cook ye up some o' that beef."

Unable to think of what to say, Elizabeth only smiled and nodded. With her children close beside her and the other children clustered around their mothers, they stood silent and waited. The man's smile seemed to go ahead of him. He was almost toothless and the few teeth he did have were black and broken, but it didn't deter him from being cheerful.

"I'm Rufus," he nodded and grinned then waved a hand at a young man who looked to be almost six foot tall with sandy-colored hair and barely the shadow of a beard. Two gun belts crossed his chest, each with two guns holstered in it and a pistol on each hip. He was very young from what Elizabeth could see. "That there is Buck, the baby of our little family."

The young man shifted, touched the brim of his hat and inclined his head, but offered no smile.

"Buck's been ridin' with us since he was fifteen. His ma give him to us after his daddy was kilt a few months afore an' she couldn't feed him an' his four sisters no more. Seemed to her it was the only thing she could do, give him to us to watch after. She know'd he'd, at the least, have food in his belly ridin' with us. He's a few months shy of eighteen, as good a shot as any man an' better with a horse than anybody I ever seen." The man almost glowed with fatherly pride.

He swung his arm toward another man, big, black and muscular. "That's Nathan. Got the steadiest hand I ever seen. Can shave a man so close he don't even know he's been shaved. An' cut yore hair! If'n he takes the shears to ye the line is straight as a milled board." He leaned over and added, "If'n one o' them young 'uns wants his hair cut, he'll be happy to do it fer 'em, won't ye Nathan?" Rufus called out.

Nathan smiled, his teeth in stark contrast against his dark face. "Yas'm."

"You've met Peter, our leader so to speak. Knows this country better'n anybody. He grow'd up in Osceola. Lived there all his life—till them Jayhawkers burned it to the ground." Rufus pointed out the last man. "That there is Willie."

The old man with long, white, flowing hair, grinned and inclined his head. "Ladies. Childern." He smiled a wide, toothless grin.

Elizabeth nodded in response, but was uneasy. On the surface these men appeared friendly, but why were they together, where were they going, and why? She almost asked, but changed her mind. The less she knew the better.

"Come on folks, git comfortable." Rufus herded the Miers, Barrows, Annie and her girls to the center of camp where he spread some blankets for them to sit down on. The children stood looking down in uncertainty. It had been so long since they'd had the luxury of even a blanket to keep them off the hard ground they were afraid to step on them.

"Go on, children, it's all right," Rufus prodded.

Slowly, mothers and children stepped onto the blankets and sat down. Elizabeth noticed Buck sat upright when he spotted Nora. He studied her a moment then stood up and smoothed his hair, a smile on his lips that hadn't been there before. He strode over to where Nora, Helen, Clara, and Edna sat side by side on the edge of the blanket.

"Hello, ladies, I'm Buck," he said to everyone, but his eyes settled on Nora. Helen, Clara, and Edna giggled like the schoolgirls they were, being sparked by a beau. Nora looked away and grabbed Elizabeth's arm.

"Hello, Buck. We're the Miers," Elizabeth said. "They're the Barrows, and that's Annie and her girls." She pointed out who went with whom.

"And who is this pretty young lady?" He pointed at Nora, who scooted closer to her mother.

"This is my daughter, Nora, who is very shy. She's had a long, trying trip and is not feeling very sociable right now."

The boyish face turned hard and red. His lips tightened, his nose flared, and his bright blue eyes pinched and flashed with unconcealed anger. Fear ripped through Elizabeth. *Was this young man going to cause trouble because Nora had rebuffed him?*

She tried to smooth his ruffled pride. "Please understand, Buck, Nora doesn't mean to be rude, but it's been a grueling trip and she's normally very shy around other people."

With a quiet whimper, Nora scooted closer still to her mother and Elizabeth saw more anger jump into the young man's eyes.

Buck took a deep breath and raised his chin. His lips trembled when he asked, "Did a...did a Yankee do somethin' to her?"

In the quietly asked question amidst such simmering anger, Elizabeth understood his ire was *not* because he'd been rebuffed, but in the possibility someone may have hurt Nora.

Elizabeth swallowed and barely nodded.

"Damn those Yankees!" Buck exploded. "Damn them!" He looked up, red-faced. "I apologize for my harsh language and rude behavior, ladies." He stood, as though wanting to say more before he turned and stalked off into the woods.

Nora looked up with tear-filled eyes, her lower lip trembling. "He wasn't angry with me, Mama. He wasn't angry with *me*, at all."

"Nah, that Buck come from a hard place." Rufus plopped down in the dirt in front of Elizabeth and Nora. "I tole ye his ma give him to us, but that ain't the whole of it. Seems his older sister was, ah, soiled by a Redleg in one of the raids on their farm. She was so aggrieved, she, well," he looked at Elizabeth then over at Nora, her eyes wide and waiting, "well, it didn't turn out so good."

"What happened?" Nora's eyes darted to where Buck was stomping through the woods, mumbling angrily.

"Said his sister couldn't bear the shame and she—she kilt herself," Rufus stammered.

Nora took in a sharp breath and laid her hand across her chest. She looked back at Buck, yanking bushes out of the ground, tossing them aside then stomping on them. She watched him a few moments then got to her feet.

"Where are you going?" Elizabeth grabbed her daughter's hand.

"I want to help him."

"What do you mean, you want to help him? How can you help him? He has to figure things out the same way you're figuring out what happened to you," Elizabeth whispered.

"But I feel like I can help him. I *want* to help him." Nora looked over at the angry young man again. "Maybe he can help me, too." Nora's hand slipped away and, with a lump in her throat, Elizabeth watched her daughter walk toward the woods.

"Don't worry 'bout her, ma'am. Buck's a good boy."

Elizabeth ignored Rufus and watched Nora, her daughter's hands clasped in front of her, her steps sure and steady, until she stopped at the edge of the woods. Buck quit ranting when he noticed her, immediately doffed his hat, lowered his head, and walked toward her. Although Elizabeth couldn't hear what was said, there was nothing threatening in his actions, but there *was* something unspoken between them, something only the two of them shared.

"I tole you, ma'am, he's a good boy."

Elizabeth swallowed and watched with uncertainty as the two talked at the edge of the trees until Buck stepped out and stood in front of Nora. Elizabeth held her breath, afraid for her little girl, yet knowing it was something she had to let her do. Buck rolled his hat between his fingers and when Nora turned her face to the side, Elizabeth saw something she hadn't seen since before Randall accosted her daughter. Nora was smiling! Slowly Elizabeth relaxed.

Elizabeth watched her daughter and Buck for almost a half hour before she decided there was nothing she could do about Nora and Buck's interest in each other, short of tying her daughter up and standing guard to keep the young man away. She left Nora in Buck's care and went to see if she could be of any help in preparing their food.

"Can I help, Rufus?" Elizabeth stood beside the portly man who was bending over the fire fussing with six steaks sizzling in three huge frying pans.

"Nah. These are doin' jest fine," he said. "I'll let you know when they's done and you can split 'em up as you see fit amongst yoreselves."

"Thank you, Rufus. We're thankful for your kindness."

Rufus looked up, a big grin on his face. "Ma'am, y'all and others like ye is why we do what we do, so what's happenin' to you and yours don't happen agin. You enjoy these steaks oncet they's done and know we're happy to help ye."

With that simple statement, Elizabeth realized these were more than just five men riding together. How much more, she didn't know for certain and didn't want to know. The thought of what they might be should have scared her as the memory of bushwhackers in her home flashed into her mind. Although the men who'd called themselves "outriders" had sympathized with her and her family, they'd still taken what they wanted and left them with precious little. *Did these men intend the same?*

Uncomfortable now, she wandered around camp, waiting for the steaks to finish. Nora and Buck continued to talk at the edge of the woods and the other children had spread out and were chattering easily with the other men. Elizabeth noticed Joshua, Benjamin and Andrew clustered around Nathan, Rebecca close behind them with Robert on her hip.

"Y'all wants that scraggly hair cut!" Nathan shouted with a grin.

Wide-eyed the boys nodded as Rebecca looked on, her face frozen with uncertainty.

"Don't you never mind, ma'am. I ain't gonna hurt yore boys. Come on now, which one o' y'all is first?"

"I 'spect that's me since I'm the oldest." Joshua puffed out his chest, stepped forward and sat down in front of the big man. Nathan slid a long knife out of its sheath and Elizabeth held her breath. It was all she could do to keep from running to Joshua and snatching him away—and it appeared Rebecca was of the same mind. Her face was white as she watched the big knife slide through her son's hair, leaving it as straight as a ruled line. Slowly, hunk after hunk was cut away until he stood up, his hair neat and tidy above his shoulders, the boy strutting like a rooster.

"Me next!" Benjamin shouted, taking Joshua's place as soon as it was vacated.

The late afternoon was spent in quiet camaraderie. The children flocked to the men, giggling and transfixed by the stories the riders told them, while the men reveled in the attention the children gave them in return. Nora, Helen, Clara, and Edna wandered camp with Buck, the girls acting coy while he told them how to train a horse from the moment it left its mama's womb until you put your foot in the stirrup and sat down in the saddle—regardless every one of them already knew how, but acted like he was imparting the wisdom of the ages. The little children stayed close to their mothers, who conversed with Peter, Willie, and Rufus.

"Used to be a cook on a big spread outside Osceola," Rufus confided after the steaks were eaten. "Had twenty hands I fed three meals a day. Not a man ever went away unhappy or unsatisfied with what they got," he said with pride. "Then them Jayhawkers come through and burned us out. Took ever bit o' stock them folks had, set fire to the buildings, and killed the owner and hands that tried to fight 'em off. Only me an' ole Willie was left when the shootin' was done. They'd have killed us sure if they'd found us, but we hid oncet we know'd there was no beatin' 'em back." He went quiet a minute with a faraway look in his eyes before adding, "Don't know what happened to the missus. She run off an' hid—I hope. Don't even want to think 'bout what mighta happened if they took her." He shook his head as though to dispel that ugly thought. "Never seen her agin after that day." He slapped Willie on the back. "We lit out o' there just as quick as we could and come on Peter out in the woods, hidin' from them Jayhawkers who went through Osceola. He was a smithy in town afore everythin' in town went up in flames. We been together ever since."

Anger popped into the man's eyes, but disappeared quickly. Rufus slapped his hands on his knees and smiled. "Then we met Nathan. He come out o' the woods like a wild bear with a big ole knife in his hand, ready to kill the first man he saw. He had no love for Yankees an' since he didn't know if we was blue bellies or not, he was ready to relieve us of our lives until we convinced him otherwise," Rufus said with a gleam in his eyes. "You gots to understand, Nathan was a slave at a spread outside Osceola that was raided by Jayhawkers, too. They did the same they done to my place an' Osceola, but, well," he ran the back of his hand across his lips, "they took liberties with the owner's wife *and* the female slaves." He turned aside and said in a low voice, "Nathan's wife was one o' them. When they left she run screamin' into the woods. Nathan looked for her for days, but it was no use. She was gone. Nah, Nathan ain't got no love for Yankees, no way no how. Oncet we convinced him what we was about he joined up with us right off. An' Buck, well, you know 'bout him."

Elizabeth listened intently as Rufus spoke about the men they were camped with. These were rough men, men who once had lives and families before the Yankees came and changed it all. Just like her and Rebecca and Annie. Regardless of her uncertainty, she felt a strange kinship with them, borne of the desperation they all felt and the need to survive. Perhaps she should have been afraid, very afraid. She was sure they could gut a man in a heartbeat or shoot him down faster than she could blink—but she *wasn't* afraid. *Was she a fool? Maybe.* Instead of being afraid she felt safe.

THE JOURNEY
Day 11 – Evening

"Where y'all headed?" Rufus asked Elizabeth from where they sat across from each other around the fire later that night after they'd all enjoyed another fine steak meal.

"We're going to my aunt and uncle's farm a few miles north of the Osage River. The Ingram place. Maybe you passed it on your way here? There's a white washed, two-story house with a wide porch that wraps around it on three sides. And a big log barn behind it, two corrals, a buggy shed and some other outbuildings. Did you see it?" she asked, hopeful for any information he might have about her family.

Rufus cocked his head and frowned. "We ain't passed nothin' like that ma'am." He looked over at Peter. "You recall passin' the Ingram place, Peter?" Rufus asked.

Peter rolled his lips, glanced at Rufus then shook his head. "I knew Mr. an' Mrs. Ingram. Fine folks as I recall. Used to come into my shop on occasion, but I ain't seen 'em since Lane came through an' don't recall passin' their spread."

"Are you sure?" Elizabeth didn't like the way Peter said he *knew* her family and was suddenly uncertain whether either of them were being truthful. *Why would they lie?* she asked herself. *To protect her from knowing her family was dead and the farm gone, everything destroyed by raiders long ago? Or had these men stolen the very cow they were eating right now from her kin and they were trying to cover their guilt?* Her mind was running in circles of uncertainty when Rufus snapped her back to the conversation.

"Ma'am, I don't recall passin' a spread like that. I'd tell ye if I did," Rufus said.

Peter agreed. "We didn't go by the Ingram place, ma'am."

"Would you tell me if you had?" Suddenly leery and afraid of what they'd said and sorry she'd asked, Elizabeth got up and walked away. She went to the edge of camp and checked on Nora and Buck, sitting side-by-side on a log talking quietly. Circling back, she made sure Rebecca, Annie and the other children were all right, their exhaustion long since having dragged them to sleep on the blankets in the middle of camp. The only others awake were the men sitting around the fire. From a short distance away, Elizabeth studied their faces in the firelight. In another life one had been a cook, a smithy, a ranch hand, a slave, and a mere boy. *What were they now, made so by a war that turned men into murderers? Where were they going and what did they intend to do when they got there? And why were they being so nice?* ran through her mind over and over again.

Piqued with curiosity, before she could stop herself Elizabeth stepped back to the fire and blurted, "So where are you men headed?"

Four heads snapped up. They looked at her then at Peter, but no one spoke.

Elizabeth felt like the ground was opening up under her and she berated herself as a fool to ask such a stupid question. "Forgive me, it's not my affair. I shouldn't have asked."

"It don't matter, Peter," Rufus said. "Tell her."

Peter shrugged and said in quiet explanation, "Me an' the boys was headed south to winter, but got word to go to Kansas, instead. We're to meet up with...with some friends."

Peter had just confirmed what Elizabeth suspected. *These men were bushwhackers! On their way to meet more men. To do what? Had she opened Pandora's Box with her curiosity?*

"You're good folks," Peter began again, "put out of your homes by Ewing's Order," he added matter-of-factly. "You and your children are refugees, set into the heat and elements without food or water, forced to do whatever you have to do to survive." His voice grew hard. "Y'all have been strong enough to survive, but many aren't." He frowned and shook his head, his face hard. "It's shameful, ma'am, shameful." He stopped in thought a moment before he continued. "Them blue bellies burned my home and my business to the ground. They made honest, hard-workin', innocent folks refugees, just like y'all, when they destroyed the town and everything in and around it. And they killed people I called friends—and family."

Elizabeth remembered the nine men murdered by Lane and his men in Osceola and wondered if they'd been friends or relations of Peter's.

"We got debts to pay, ma'am," Peter finished, his voice low and calm. The others nodded silent agreement from around the fire.

Elizabeth swallowed. She couldn't speak. Fear wrapped around her heart like talons. *What had they done, staying with these men! Regardless how kind they seemed—these men were bushwhackers! Probably riding to join up with Quantrill or Bloody Bill Anderson somewhere! Union troops could fall upon them any time. They could wind up in the middle of a gun battle! The children!* Elizabeth almost shouted.

"Don't worry, ma'am. We haven't seen any blue bellies in weeks," Peter said as though reading her mind.

"And I hope not to see any soon. I've had enough Yankees to last a lifetime."

He pursed his lips. "If we was to run into Yanks and it come to a fight, we'd protect you and yours like you was our own kin. That's a promise."

Despite her uncertainty, Elizabeth believed him, and when she finally bedded down that night, ringed by bushwhackers, she prayed they wouldn't have to find out if he spoke the truth—or not.

THE JOURNEY
Day 12
The Reckoning

After what she'd learned from Peter, Elizabeth doubted everything she'd felt good about earlier that day and couldn't stop her mind from spinning with the possibilities of what could happen. *Had Rufus and Peter lied about seeing Aunt Pearl and Uncle Rupert's place? Had they stolen that cow there? Was her family dead—killed by Jayhawkers—or these men? They had no uniforms, nothing to mark them for who they were. They were heavily armed—like bushwhackers. Who were they meeting in Kansas, and for what?* Her head spun with so many questions she felt sick most of the long, sleepless night.

Elizabeth rose irritable and anxious as soon as she saw the first tinges of sunrise. She wanted to be away from here. They were only a few miles from their destination. *It was time to go. Now!*

"Wake up everybody it's time to be on our way." She shook Nora and Vera, who had fallen asleep face to face, as though in the middle of a sentence. Joseph and Sally stirred at Elizabeth's rising, but rolled over and went back to sleep. Rebecca sat up and wiped her eyes before shaking her children awake. Annie opened her eyes and looked up at the sky from where she lay on her back, one girl curled inside each of her arms.

"Why so soon, Mama?" Nora wiped sleep away. She smoothed her hair and dress and scanned camp, looking for Buck, Elizabeth presumed on a sigh.

"It's time to go." Elizabeth's response was curt. She wanted to be on their way, away from these men, and away from Buck, who had enjoyed Nora's full attention last night. *He was a bushwhacker! It didn't matter what Rufus or any of the others said about him—they were* all *bushwhackers! Bushwhacker's killed people and destroyed property, just like they had when they visited our home!* she wanted to scream to remind everyone.

"But Mama...." Nora's head was cocked to argue.

"It's time to go, that's all there is to it. We're only a few miles from Aunt Pearl's and it's time to get there."

"But I...."

"Nora, do not press me. It's time to go. Get Sally and Joseph around so we can be on our way."

Nora's eyes glistened and she was about to say something else when Elizabeth turned and saw the five men standing together at the edge of camp in heated discussion. Her skin pricked and her mind went into another whirl of doubts and questions.

"Come on," she prodded Rebecca who was looking up at her with wide eyes.

"What's wrong with you, Elizabeth? We're in no danger here."

"Aren't we? As much as they don't seem like it, they're bushwhackers, Rebecca. Bushwhackers, like the men who invaded our homes and took food from our children's mouths, more than once."

"But these men *gave* us food."

Elizabeth drew in a deep breath to calm down. Her fears were getting the better of her. They were almost to the end of their journey and she would *not* let anything, or anyone, stand in their way.

She looked back at the men, walking toward camp now, and fear tore up Elizabeth's spine. She swallowed and steeled herself for what was about to happen.

Peter tipped his hat and smiled. Rufus nodded and grinned, and Nathan and Willie did the same.

Buck turned to Nora then back to everyone else. "Mornin' y'all." His voice was deep and steady.

Elizabeth noticed the sparkle in his eyes when he looked at Nora and how she responded in kind. *What is happening? This can't happen! I don't care how young this boy is or how 'good' he is. He rides with bushwhackers! He is a bushwhacker!*

Peter stepped in front of Elizabeth and her breath caught. "Ma'am, we been talkin'."

Fear rushed through Elizabeth for the second time in so many minutes. "Yes? What do we have to do with anything you men might be discussing?" She tried to swallow, but her mouth had gone dry.

"I have to tell ye, the boy won't be swayed."

"Swayed? What do you mean, 'swayed?" *Did young Buck intend to steal Nora away?* Elizabeth felt like the earth was swaying under *her.*

"Buck made a decision and none of us boys could change his mind. Thinkin' on it, though, we believe it's the right thing to do and we stand by him."

Elizabeth couldn't breathe. *Buck was going to try and take Nora! He might try, but he'd have to go through her first!* She straightened her back. "I won't allow it!" she cried, her heart pounding.

"Ma'am?" Peter cocked his head in confusion.

"I won't allow it," she said again, glancing at Buck.

Peter sucked in a deep breath and a knowing smile crossed his lips. "Ma'am, you don't understand."

"Enlighten me then. Please." Elizabeth's knees felt like apple butter.

"Buck intends to ride with y'all to your kinfolk's," Peter said with a grin.

Elizabeth blinked, trying to grasp what the tall man said. "He wants to *ride* with us?" she said dumbly.

"Yes, ma'am. He wants to escort y'all to your kin's place."

"That's it? *That's* what you all were arguing about?"

"Yes, ma'am. Young Buck decided he was goin' with ye and he wouldn't be swayed in his thinkin'. He's been with us a long time. We been responsible for him an' lettin' him go off on his own ain't easy for us, especially Rufus. But we seen the wisdom of it—after he convinced us."

Buck stepped forward, hat in hand. "Even though we ain't seen no Yanks for a while, I want to ride with y'all just in case."

"But we're only a few miles away. We can make it without an escort." Elizabeth knew the reason Buck wanted to come along was because of Nora.

"Yes, Ma'am, I know that, and I think y'all are very brave for what you've done." Buck glanced at Nora before he continued. "A lot can happen in a couple miles. It's best you have someone along with a gun who knows how to use it."

Elizabeth *almost* let him know she was *quite* adept at handling a gun and had proven it more than once, but decided it wasn't relevant to their discussion—especially since she didn't *have* a gun.

Buck stood tall. "Ma'am, you won't be changin' my mind. I've decided to ride with y'all and that's what I'm gonna do. I'll light out as soon as I get you there safe, if I'm of a mind." He glanced at Nora again whose eyes sparkled in the morning sunlight. *Or was it the sunlight?*

Elizabeth took a deep breath and forced herself to relax. She'd worked herself into a ball of fear when these men had their best interests at heart. She shook her head and looked at Peter. "I...I thought...."

"No need to explain, ma'am. We are what we are and you *should* be leery, and watchful of anybody you come upon, which is why Buck *should* ride with you." He turned to the boy, standing beside Nora, their arms barely touching, but touching nonetheless. "He'll know where to find us after he delivers you to your kin—if he wants to."

Elizabeth looked at Nora and saw something in her daughter's eyes she hadn't seen in a very long time—hope.

She was staring at her daughter, uncertain what to do next, when Peter touched her elbow. "Ma'am?" He extended his arm away from camp.

Elizabeth followed him until he stopped outside camp. "I know you got concerns about the boy, ma'am. Like we told you last night, he's a good boy. He's had a rough time and the four of us would like him to have a chance at a real life. Not a life of fightin' and thievin'. And the best chance he's got, other than takin' a bullet with us, is with y'all."

Elizabeth could barely think. Buck wanted to go with them because of Nora. Fifteen year-old Nora—*who was no longer a child,* she reminded herself, *despite how much she wanted her to be.*

"It's obvious to anybody who has eyes the boy is smitten with your girl, and it appears his feelings are returned. Give him a chance, ma'am." Peter stared down at Elizabeth with hopeful eyes before he turned and strode away without giving her a chance to protest.

Elizabeth was as unsure about what she felt right now as the day they left their home. *This strange man was asking her to give the boy a chance with her daughter's life! The boy was a bushwhacker! But he wouldn't be a bushwhacker anymore if he went with them and never went back. Could she allow him that chance? A chance for a new life? With Nora?*

Elizabeth walked around outside camp, lost in thought for several minutes, before going back. Nora was the first to reach her.

"Mama?"

Elizabeth ran the palm of her hand over Nora's cheek, flushed red on a face full of hope. "My sweet Nora." Elizabeth's eyes filled with tears and she blinked them away. "You've seen so much brutality and hatefulness in your short life. You've lost your father, your home, your childhood, maybe even your dreams." *Until now, perhaps.* She glanced over at Buck, standing a few feet away, hat in hand, his back straight, his feet braced as though to show he wouldn't be swayed. "After all you've been through, can you trust him? *Do* you trust him Nora?" she asked, looking back into her daughter's anxious face.

Nora turned to Buck and when she turned back a huge smile lit her lips. "I do, Mama. I do trust him. We talked last night about everything. About his family, things he's done and why he did them, and what he wants. He's hard outside, but I know there's a good man inside. He just needs someone to pull him out. I can do it. I can find the good man inside. Give him a chance, Mama. Give *me* a chance. Please."

Elizabeth swallowed her tears yet again and squeezed Nora's cheek before her hand dropped away. "I guess young Buck here will be escorting us to Aunt Pearl's."

"Thank you, Mama. Thank you!" Nora ran to Buck. The smile he flashed Elizabeth eased her mind she'd done the right thing. Perhaps there was a good man inside young Buck and, it seemed, Nora would be the one to find him.

They left camp after breakfast with four small children holding tight to one another on the back of Buck's chestnut horse. Benjamin sat at the front holding the saddle horn with Andrew, Joseph and Sally wrapped around each other behind him. Not even Vera grumbled when they left camp with Buck leading the horse and the way, Nora walking beside him. The other girls and Joshua hovered close by as he regaled them with stories about places he'd been and people he'd met, without giving away who he and the other men were or the things they'd done. In the children's eyes Buck was a great adventurer with exciting stories to tell.

Throughout the day Nora never left Buck's side and it was obvious he didn't want her to. Although it was like any other day they'd spent on the road, they started out without complaint about the dust or heat. They didn't whine about being thirsty or that their feet hurt.

Their good humor didn't last long, though. By mid-morning the children were grumbling, anxious to be where they were going, thirsty and tired again. Even the adults were tense and anxious for the journey to end. The sun was almost straight up noon when they rounded a bend in the road and Elizabeth came to a dead stop. The farm was just over the rise on their right!

Rebecca stepped up beside her. "Are you all right, Elizabeth?"

"It's over this hill," she whispered so only Rebecca could hear her. "Or is it?" She turned to her friend. "Have we made this trip for nothing? Is my family here or burned out by Lane and his men long ago?" Elizabeth swallowed, terrified to find out. *What if no one was here? What would they do? Where would they go? How would they survive more of what they'd already lived through the past two weeks?*

Rebecca and Elizabeth stood staring up the hill, both women lost in her own fear of what they would find on the other side while everyone waited behind them.

"We'll never know if we don't go up," Rebecca finally said.

Annie came up beside Elizabeth and Rebecca. "What's the matter?"

"Nothing's the matter, except that the farm should be over that hill, *if* there's still a farm." Elizabeth pointed, took a deep breath and turned onto the small wagon path that led up the rocky hill. Dead, brittle grass stabbed at her bare, blistered feet, and she stumbled on the sharp rocks in the unused tracks of the road. *Was she stumbling because she was so tired and her feet hurt so badly, or because she was terrified to finally find what was over that crest?* They followed the wagon path up the hill. Scraggly bushes lined one side and a dried up creek bed bordered the other. The children sniffled and grumbled behind her, not realizing how close they were to their destination.

Buck came up beside Elizabeth leading his horse, the animal's hooves clacking on the rocks. "It's over this hill, ain't it?"

Elizabeth nodded, but looked straight ahead. "I'm so afraid of what we'll find, I can't go any farther." She swallowed hard and fought the fear clawing up her back, wondering again if this trip was for nothing.

"We'll go see."

Elizabeth swung around to face Buck, taking in Nora's hand clutched in his, the horse's reins in his other, and the children still on the animal's back. Elizabeth reached up and took Sally down, each of them helping the other children down until all four were on solid ground.

"Go," was all Elizabeth could manage.

The couple led the horse past Elizabeth and mounted, Nora behind Buck, holding him tight around the waist. They rode over the hill and out-of-sight. Elizabeth waited, her heart pounding, her breath short and labored. She heard nothing from the other side. Nobody rode back to tell her everything was still standing — or that it was gone.

Unable to wait a moment longer, she ran up the slope and came to an abrupt stop. Buck and Nora sat on the horse just inside where the pasture fence *used* to stand, staring below.

Squinting through the bright sunlight, Elizabeth glanced past Nora and Buck to the trees surrounding the property, most of them bare from the never-ending drought. The offshoot of the creek that ran the length of the farm's western border was dry, its banks crumbling into itself. Corrals stood empty, the pasture without cattle or horses, the crops dead and brown.

Her heart pounding with dread and fear, Elizabeth turned to where the house should stand. Shading her eyes against the harsh sun—she almost went to her knees.

"It's there!" she cried to Rebecca, having come up

beside her with a drooling Robert on her hip. "And look!" Elizabeth jabbed her finger. "There's Aunt Pearl." Her aunt was sitting on the porch, mending, reminding Elizabeth of the day James and Steven had ridden in to tell Elizabeth the war was on. The day their lives changed forever. She searched for her uncle around the house and spotted him hammering on the half-charred barn. "There's Uncle Rupert! They're here! They're both here!"

Although she wanted to run, Elizabeth felt as though her legs were mired to the knees in mud. She couldn't move. Her mind spun and her heart hurt with her memories of James and Steven. She missed her husband so much she felt it physically, as well as deep in her soul. She wondered if her son was still alive. *Would they ever see the land or place they'd called home again?* All the hardships they'd faced—and survived with dignity and no regrets—raced through her head. She turned and smiled at Rebecca, who had suffered equally on their journey. Rebecca smiled back. Tears streamed down her face. Annie had come up over the hill and plopped down on the ground behind her, laughing and crying at the same time, Eleanor and Caroline wrapped in her arms laughing and crying with her. The other children gathered around Elizabeth and Rebecca and stared below.

Elizabeth glanced again at Nora and Buck sitting erect on Buck's horse, staring at the house, their bodies a shimmering, dark silhouette against the sunlight, as though frozen in time. In Nora and Buck, the children, Rebecca, Annie, and Aunt Pearl and Uncle Rupert, Elizabeth realized her hope for the future was here. Her hope that this war would soon end, hope their lives would someday return to normal, and hope that love would guide the way. It was all right here in the people around her.

She was suddenly flinging up her skirts, unable to get to her wedding ring and the locket James had given her fast enough, the material billowing out around her as she tore at the sewn pocket that kept them from her. Finally, the ring and locket rested in the palm of her hand and everything they represented—her husband, her oldest son, her children, and all they'd lost—exploded like colorful portraits inside her brain. She kissed the ring and slid it onto her finger, tied the locket around her neck, and laid her ringed hand over it, comforted by the feel of the cool stone and the steady beat of her heart beneath it. Warmth, not from the sun, surrounded her and she felt her husband's presence.

Elizabeth looked up and saw only a beautiful, clear, blue sky, not the blistering sun that had hindered them for weeks, and felt hope for a new beginning.

"Thank you," she whispered.

Smiling, Elizabeth glanced down at Sally on her left, Joseph on her right, and Vera beside her brother. "Shall we?" Despite the pain she knew it would bring, she took a deep breath, grabbed Sally and Joseph's hands in hers—and ran down the hill toward the beckoning future, the others running and laughing behind her.

THE END

AFTERWORD

Initially, this author intended to follow the Jackson and Elizabeth McFerrin family on their journey from the onset of the Civil War through the issuance of General Order No. 11—what many locals call the "Infamous Order." However, as time progressed my characters asserted themselves and *my* Elizabeth took on a life of her own—begging to be released from the restrictive chains of fact. Her fictional character, Elizabeth Miers was born and this novel is the result.

The real-life Elizabeth McFerrin, a Christian woman, and her family were survivors of the Infamous Order. They were one family among thousands of displaced men, women and children, forced to leave their homes in the wake of Union General Thomas Ewing's General Order No. 11 who tried desperately to save themselves, their families, and what was left of their lives in the midst of the war tearing this nation apart.

Following the murder of Elizabeth's husband and after General Order No. 11 was issued, it is purported Elizabeth left her children, most likely with the slaves they held, and on an old horse went to relatives in St. Clair County. There she obtained a rickety wagon and two oxen, made the return trip north against the flow of refugees heading south, collected her children and what belongings they could carry then turned with the tide of the displaced and went back to St. Clair County. She returned to Cass County after the war to find her home and everything she'd worked for burned to the ground, but was also reunited with her oldest son, Steven.

Elizabeth McFerrin and Jackson Benton McFerrin are buried together at Reid Cemetery in Cass County. His headstone reads: Jackson Benton McFerrin, Murdered February 7, 1863 by Kansas Redlegs.

According to *Austin, Missouri: Where I Call Home*, by Debbie Stevens Morgan, the original "Bean Eatin' Festival" began in the 1880's when Union soldiers gathered with their wives and children to reminisce about the war, cook coffee and beans over campfires, and pitch tents for the night. Men who fought for the Confederacy, many of whom were neighbors, friends, and relations, were not invited to the gathering.

Today, every year on the last Saturday of September the Bean Eatin' Festival is still held. It is a fund-raising event to keep up the Austin Cemetery, a "silent city" housing those who, according to Debbie Stevens Morgan, "saw the killing of their husbands, sons, their fathers, and neighbors...men who were forced to kill or be killed" during that turbulent time in our history. Despite time, weather, and economics, the Bean Eatin' carries on, where old friends gather and new ones are made enjoying a meal of beans, cornbread and dessert, while reminiscing about today's world, and Austin's little known, yet rich history and the horrors that visited this small community during the Civil War.

Bushwhackers Rufus, Peter, Buck, Nathan and Willie are fictional characters headed into Kansas, presumably to join Quantrill and his raiders. At Baxter Springs, Kansas, near Fort Blair on the afternoon of October 6, 1863, Quantrill and his men attacked Union Major General James G. Blunt's command. Eighty-two of Blunt's men were killed in what has become known as the "Massacre at Baxter Springs."

306

TERMS USED: People and Events

Brown, Robert A. – One of Harrisonville's largest land and slave owners. A Constitutional Unionist, his property was raided many times by both sides for forage and food. The home still stands today.

Bushwhackers – The term applied to southern sympathizers who organized into units which fought against Union troops. "A rebel Jayhawker, or a rebel who bands with others for the purpose of preying upon the lives and property of Union citizens" (as described by Connelley, William, Page 412, and cited in *Caught Between Three Fires*, Rafiner, p. 642)

Cass County Home Guards – "A local militia unit which supported the Union. The Cass County Home Guards were organized in June 1861 and served until February 1862 when they were disbanded at Harrisonville. (*Caught Between Three Fires*, Rafiner, p. 647)

Constitutional Unionist – Members of an 1860 political party that "recognized no political principle other than the Constitution of the country, the union of the states, and the enforcement of the laws..." (*The Library of Congress, Civil War, Desk Reference*, as cited in *Caught Between Three Fires*, Rafiner, p. 647)

Jayhawker – "A Unionist who professes to rob, burn out and murder only rebels in arms against the government." (*Caught Between Three Fires*, Rafiner, p. 647) The term most generally referred to Kansans raiding over the Missouri Border.

Kansas/Nebraska Act – "The United States Congress enacted the Kansas-Nebraska Act in May 1854. The act stipulated that the citizens residing in the Kansas and Nebraska Territories would determine by vote whether the territories would enter the Union as slave or slave-free states. The act triggered violence along the Missouri-Kansas border (*Caught Between Three Fires*, Rafiner, p. 648) in what became known as *The Border War* in the years prior to the Civil War.

Missouri State Guard – "Was aligned against Federal involvement in Missouri more than it was Pro-South. However, after Brigadier General Lyons attacked the Missouri State Guard camp at St. Louis, the Guard aligned with the Confederates. (*Caught Between Three Fires*, Rafiner, p. 648)

Missouri State Militia – Were Federal units, supplied, trained, and organized by the Federal Government. (*Caught Between Three Fires*, Rafiner, p. 648)

Redlegs –Pro-Union, an independent organization formed to protect Kansas citizens from Missouri guerillas raiding across the border. It is also described as: "an efficient body of scouts organized by General Ewing and General Blunt for desperate service along the border," who came to be "regarded as more purely indiscriminate thief and murderer than the Jayhawker or Bushwhacker." (Connelley, William, Page 412, as cited in *Caught Between Three Fires*, Rafiner, p. 650)

THE BATTLES and Other Significant Occurrences
In the order they Occurred

The Border War (Missouri/Kansas Border) – 1854 – 1860. Following the enactment of the Kansas/Nebraska Act in May of 1854, factions from both sides crossed the Kansas/Missouri border to bring Kansas and Nebraska into the country as a free or slave state. Blood was shed in the efforts to "sway" citizens to the "proper" way of thinking. Kansans raided Missourians set on bringing Kansas into the Union as a slave state, and Missourians crossed into Kansas and voted (illegally) to spread slavery into Kansas. Men were murdered for their beliefs, many in front of a weeping family begging for their lives. Raiding on both sides of the border became commonplace, retribution and revenge spurring many men to murder.

The firing on Fort Sumter – On April 12, 1861, the beginning of the American Civil War when Confederate Forts Moultrie and Johnson fired upon Union Fort Sumter located in Charleston Harbor in South Carolina. The siege and bombardment continued two days before Union Major Robert Anderson, his food and ammunition depleted and the walls of the fort crumbling around him, surrendered to Confederate General P.G.T. Beauregard.

Declaration of War at Harrisonville (Missouri) – On April 26, 1861 at a town meeting in the Cass County, County Seat at Harrisonville, a Declaration of Civil War was made, causing a huge split between Secessionists and Unionists in the county. Most men spoke for the Confederacy and secession that night, but only one man, Andrew Newgent, spoke for the preservation of the Union. Later he was chased from the courthouse and followed, the men with murder on their minds. After that night he hid in the brush throughout Cass County and helped recruit for Federal forces.

The Battle of Carthage (Missouri) – Fought on July 5, 1861, was a continuation of southern victories in the early part of the war.

The (first) Battle at Manassas (as referred to by Confederates) or Bull Run (as referred to by the Union) (Virginia) – This first battle of the war was enjoined on Sunday,

July 21, 1861, and was met by both sides with eager anticipation. The Union forces were routed in a disorganized advance that had them fleeing back to Washington. However, as disorganized as their Union counterparts, the southern forces allowed the Federals to return to Washington without pursuit. The battle left the Confederacy overconfident they would win the war and the Federals more determined than ever to break them and bring them back into the Union fold.

The first Battle of Morristown (Missouri) – Was fought the same day the First Battle of Manassas/Bull Run was fought in Virginia on July 21, 1861. Here Jennison's Jayhawkers skirmished with local rebels. Two locals were killed and the following day a wagon filled with looted dry goods, clothing and other supplies was driven from town by Jennison's men.

Harrisonville (Missouri) - July 26, 1861, Union forces attacked Harrisonville. Most of the businesses were destroyed, the town taken over and utilized as a Union stronghold. The pendulum had swung from the Cass County Seat being pro-southern to becoming a Union fort.

The Battle of Wilson's Creek (outside Springfield, Missouri) – Occurred on August 10, 1861, where Union General Nathaniel Lyon was killed. By late afternoon, the Union forces were completely disorganized and, without their leader, left the field in defeat.

The (first) Battle at Lexington (Missouri) – This battle was fought September 13-20, 1861. General Sterling Price won a victory for the Confederacy by laying siege to the town, keeping Union soldiers from accessing the river and water, and eventually winning the fight by using rolled up, soaked hemp bales as cover against Union fire. Union Colonel Mulligan surrendered to the larger Confederate force after nine days with little water under a torturous sun.

The (second) Battle of Morristown (Missouri) – (The fictional) James Miers fought at this battle on September 17, 1861. After Jennison's earlier visit on July 21st, Morristown became a Confederate recruiting station and a month later Colonel Erwin's Missouri 10th Cavalry was camped there. Alerted to the advancement of Jim Lane's Kansas troops a battle ensued. The town was overrun by the Kansas troops, burned to the ground, and five defenders, after digging their own graves, were executed. (*Caught Between Three Fires*, Rafiner, p. 87) Morristown no longer exists.

The Burning of Dayton (Missouri) – Occurred at daybreak on the first day of January in the new year of 1862. On New Year's Eve, 1861, upon being informed of southern recruiting in Dayton, Lt. Colonel Daniel R. Anthony and his men raced 23 miles from Camp Johnson at Morristown where they were camped, to Dayton. Upon reaching Dayton, they found only women and children. Those women and children were herded out into the cold, their homes put to the torch, and left with nothing to survive the bitter Missouri cold. Three Dayton men were executed as a result, none of whom were in the army. Only one structure survived the flames, that of the (supposed) Unionist who alerted Anthony to the recruiting in Dayton. That house still stands today.

Disbanding of the (Union) Home Guards – On February 28, 1862, the Home Guards were disbanded. Many Union men re-enlisted with the Missouri State Militia.

The Battle at Independence (Missouri) – Fought on August 11, 1862, just prior to the Battle of Lone Jack. Here William Clarke Quantrill and his men met Union forces and came away victorious. However, after that victory, the countryside was swarmed by Union troops looking for Quantrill and his men. In their ensuing brutality they swayed many an undeclared man to the southern cause in the search that did not find Quantrill.

The Battle at Lone Jack (Missouri) – Fought on August 16, 1862, many of the combatants were relatives and neighbors who fought from opposite sides of the war. The blood of many family members from both sides flowed through the main street before this battle was over. Samuel McFerrin fought here.

Quantrill's Raid on Lawrence (Kansas) – On August 21, 1863, William Clarke Quantrill and his 450 raiders attacked the sleeping town of Lawrence, Kansas. For four hours they murdered and looted, killing between 150 and 200 men and boys, only a small number of which were associated with the Union army. Homes were burned to the ground, businesses destroyed and looted, men got drunk and murdered indiscriminately. This was the catalyst that caused Union General Ewing to put General Order No. 11 into effect.

The Massacre at Baxter Springs (Kansas) – This is the (insinuated) rendezvous point the five bushwhackers were heading toward when Elizabeth and her party met them outside Osceola in late September 1863. On October 6, 1863 Quantrill and his men surprised Federal troops led by Major General James G. Blunt outside Baxter Springs, which resulted in a Federal defeat and the death of 82 Union soldiers.

Resources Consulted

Caught Between Three Fires: Cass County, Mo., Chaos & Order No. 11, 1860 – 1865, by Tom A. Rafiner, 2010, Xlibris Corporation.

Historical Times Illustrated Encyclopedia of the Civil War, Patricia L. Faust, Editor, *Harper Perennial*, a Division of *Harper Collins Publishers*

CWSAC Battle Summaries, The American Battlefield Protection Program (ABPP), HPS, Heritage Preservation Services; www.nps.gov/hps/abpp/battles/mo002

The Burning of Dayton Missouri, 1 January 1862, Jackie Polsgrove Roberts, 2006 by Two Trails Publishing, Independence, Missouri

(Note: James Benton McFerrin's death is recorded in the cemetery records of Reid Cemetery as February 7, 1863. His headstone reads: ―Murdered by Kansas Redlegs‖)

Civil War on the Western Border, 1854-1865, Jay Monaghan, 1955 by Little, Barrow

Sacking of Osceola, Wikipedia @ http://en.wikipedia.org/wiki/Sacking of Osceola

Cinders and Silence, A Chronicle of Missouri's Burnt District 1854-1870, by Tom A. Rafiner, by Burnt District Press

Reminiscences of the Women of Missouri During the Sixties (Reprint of the original 1913 edition), Two Trails indexed edition 2006 (p. 153)

Austin, Missouri: Where I Call Home, by Debbie Stevens Morgan, Burnt District Press, 2013.

Massacre at Baxter Springs-NYTimes. Com – The Opinion Pages, Disunion October 7, 2013, 2:41 pm – *Massacre at Baxter Springs* by Nicole Etcheson. http://opinionator.blogs.nytimes.com/2013/10/07/massacre-at-baxter-sp rings/

The Author

About the Author...

Diane "D.L." Rogers grew up in New Jersey with a natural love of horses and cowboys, spending many delightful hours playing Cowboys and Indians—the Barbie doll (mostly) ignored. Coming from a family mixed with both northern and southern heritage, she found her love of history, and most especially, the Civil War. She and her cousin called themselves *"Yebels,"* being of "mixed" blood, each one having one parent from the North and one from the South.

As a kid Diane loved to read. She read every Nancy Drew and horse book she could get her hands on. That love of reading led her to her writing endeavors of today.

At the present time, Diane lives south of Kansas City, Missouri, with her husband, four horses, and a multitude of cats. She has two wonderful children, Eric and Kristen, and five grandchildren. Diane loves to hear from her readers. Feel free to do so at: www.dlrogers2@peoplepc.com.